"A little Lynsay Sands mixed with
—ParaNormalRoman

PRAISE FOR

LAST VAMPIRE STANDING

"*Last Vampire Standing* is a mystical novel that had this reader holding her sides from laughing so hard."   —*Romance Junkies*

"Seeing the world and all its wackiness through this spunky heroine's
eyes makes the adventure just plain fun. Don't miss out!"
—*Romantic Times*, 4½ stars

"Nancy Haddock is an amazing author who has the talent to mix
mystery [and] paranormal and twist it all up with a dollop of comedy."
—*Night Owl Romance*, Top Pick

"Witty humor will keep you glued to the pages of this delightful vampire romance."   —*Fresh Fiction*

"The second humorous Vampire Princess urban fantasy is an enjoy-
able, lighthearted thriller filled with tension somewhat abated by the
amusing observations of modern life by the heroine . . . Nancy Haddock provides a jocular tale."   —*Genre Go Round Reviews*

"A wonderful second part to this great new vampire series . . . With a
lovely leading lady, a well-written plot, and quirky characters, this has
all the ingredients of a great paranormal urban fantasy book."
—ParaNormalRomance.org

PRAISE FOR

LA VIDA VAMPIRE

"After reading Nancy Haddock's debut, I want to
pire. A quirky and fun read."

continued . . .

"Nancy Haddock had me hooked from page one with *La Vida Vampire*. The wonderfully charming heroine, sexy-as-sin hero, and fabulously engaging mystery kept me turning pages into the wee hours of the morning!"   —Julie Kenner

"A sultry setting, a clever mystery, and strong, sparkling characters . . . Nancy Haddock delivers everything it takes to make a fan out of me!"   —Jane Graves

"*La Vida Vampire* is fun, fun, fun! Nancy Haddock's fresh and sassy new voice enlivens a well-known genre, and her heroine is one of the most entertaining in years. Readers will enjoy the snappy dialogue, the irreverent tone, the fabulous setting, and the fascinating world. Wonderful!"   —Kathleen Givens

"I loved *La Vida Vampire*! Nancy Haddock has written a delightful blend of mystery and humor with a touch of romance . . . Haddock has moved to the top of my must-read list."   —Lorraine Heath

"I loved it. Distinctive, amusing characters and a brilliant mystery make this one exciting ride. Vampires, ghosts, and shape-shifters all wrapped up in one fun, sexy story. I can't wait for more! This is one vampire chick I'd love to hang out with."   —Candace Havens

"Bright, charming, imaginative, romantic, sexy, and suspenseful."   —Joyce McLaughlin

"One bite of this sassy story and you will be hooked!"   —*Romance Junkies*

"Funny, witty, and absolutely intriguing . . . A great debut!"   —*Fresh Fiction*

"This funny, clever novel is sure to hook readers and leave them wanting more."   —*Romance Reviews Today*

Titles by Nancy Haddock

ALWAYS THE VAMPIRE

NANCY HADDOCK

BERKLEY BOOKS, NEW YORK

THE BERKLEY PUBLISHING GROUP
Published by the Penguin Group
Penguin Group (USA) Inc.
375 Hudson Street, New York, New York 10014, USA
Penguin Group (Canada), 90 Eglinton Avenue East, Suite 700, Toronto, Ontario M4P 2Y3, Canada
(a division of Pearson Penguin Canada Inc.)
Penguin Books Ltd., 80 Strand, London WC2R 0RL, England
Penguin Group Ireland, 25 St. Stephen's Green, Dublin 2, Ireland (a division of Penguin Books Ltd.)
Penguin Group (Australia), 250 Camberwell Road, Camberwell, Victoria 3124, Australia
(a division of Pearson Australia Group Pty. Ltd.)
Penguin Books India Pvt. Ltd., 11 Community Centre, Panchsheel Park, New Delhi—110 017, India
Penguin Group (NZ), 67 Apollo Drive, Rosedale, Auckland 0632, New Zealand
(a division of Pearson New Zealand Ltd.)
Penguin Books (South Africa) (Pty.) Ltd., 24 Sturdee Avenue, Rosebank, Johannesburg 2196,
South Africa

Penguin Books Ltd., Registered Offices: 80 Strand, London WC2R 0RL, England

This book is an original publication of The Berkley Publishing Group.

Copyright © 2011 by Nancy Haddock.
Cover design by Diana Kolsky.
Cover illustration by Aleta Rafton.
Text design by Kristin del Rosario.

PRINTING HISTORY
Berkley trade paperback edition / May 2011

Library of Congress Cataloging-in-Publication Data

Haddock, Nancy.
    Always the vampire / Nancy Haddock.
       p. cm.
    ISBN 978-0-425-24088-5
    1. Vampires—Fiction. 2. Bridesmaids—Fiction. 3. Shapeshifting—Fiction. I. Title.
    PS3608.A275A79 2011
    813'.6—dc22

                                                    2010042083

PRINTED IN THE UNITED STATES OF AMERICA

10 9 8 7 6 5 4 3 2 1

This is for my extended family.
You know who you are,
and I hope you know
how very dear you are to me!

ACKNOWLEDGMENTS

First, a belated but sincere shout-out to wonderful author and friend Sandy Blair, who came up with the title for my second book, *Last Vampire Standing*. Apologies again for the omission last time, Sandy!

Thanks to my critique group and manuscript readers Lynne Smith (Lynn Michaels), Julie Benson, Sherry Winstead, and Thomas "Tommy" Kerper. They make my work better and my life brighter.

Leis Pederson is my editor and a special kind of star in my galaxy, and Roberta Brown is an agent extraordinaire and dear friend. I'm blessed to know and work with them both!

A mega thank-you to all the kind folks who assisted me with research. They include members of the City of St. Augustine government staff, the park rangers of the Castillo de San Marcos, and the officers of the St. Johns County Sheriff's Department, the St. Augustine Police Department, and the St. Augustine Beach Police Department. Everyone answered my questions with professionalism and humor. Any errors and/or embellishments are mine.

I must include Elizabeth Topp and Nicole Ritsi of the Nisiotes Dance Troupe in my gratitude. In the midst of the annual Greek festival, they took the time to patiently answer my dance questions, and later demonstrated the fire dance. Awesome, ladies!

I deeply appreciate my pals at Starbucks (Store 8484) for the caffeine and caring, and my friends at Barnes & Noble (Store 2796) for helping me ferret out books for fun and research. And to the ladies of Second Read Books, you have my heart for all you do and for all you are.

Never last or least, my abiding gratitude goes to my friends and fans for their encouragement and support. Thank you for sharing your Light!

ONE

~

Maid of honor.

That phrase may strike stark fear into the hearts of some women, but I'm not one of them.

Okay, that's partly because I'm a vampire. Not a scary one, mind you, but caterers and florists hop to when I'm around.

Of course, it helps that the bride is my mentor and friend, and is usually cool under fire. As an interior designer and home-restoration specialist, Maggie O'Halloran has calmed dozens of fractious clients, from the picky to the pushy to the outright psycho. With that kind of experience, I can't see her going bridezilla on me, no matter what the provocation.

Last, I have a secret weapon. I'm locked and loaded with a ginormous binder filled with lists, notes, and phone numbers. Not to mention printouts of every maid of honor scrap of information I could find on the Internet and pages torn from bride magazines.

Yep, I'm Francesca Melisenda Alejandra Marinelli, the Oldest City's only vampire, now doing my first and likely last tour of duty as a maid of honor. As Maggie's retired Army dad said, my mission was to make Maggie's Victorian-themed wedding perfect.

The only element of the wedding weekend that veered from the Victorian theme was the rehearsal dinner. Maggie refused to have one. Instead, she and Neil and those of the bridal party who wanted to join them would attend the first night of the annual Greek festival. Why the one-eighty on the Victorian theme? Because her first date with Neil had been at the festival. She was too sentimental to change her mind; no matter that Neil, her dad, and even I had tried to talk her out of it.

But, hey, I *had* talked her out of bustles for the bridesmaid dresses, hadn't I? Winning that skirmish was good enough for me.

With less than three weeks until the wedding day, I collected my trusty maid of honor binder to head out the door for a meeting with Maggie. The dining room in her restored Victorian home served as Wedding Central, and we were sorting yet another pile of invitation RSVPs.

Good thing I was leaving, because the perimeter alarm—the one Sam of Sam's Security Systems was supposed to be fixing—suddenly blared to life yet again. With my vampire hyper-hearing, the darn thing shrieked in my skull, rattled my teeth, and threatened to deafen me.

A streak of white tore past my feet on a beeline for the laundry room. Snowball—Saber's cat—taking cover in the dirty-clothes basket.

Me? I tore out the front door, slammed it on the worst of the noise, and tapped a sneakered foot on the cobblestone patio.

"Saber," I yelled to my ex-slayer sweetheart, who was "supervising" Sam's fix-it job.

Instead of Saber answering, Neil Benson popped his head around the corner of my carriage-house-cum-cottage.

"What?" Neil bellowed back.

"Turn. That. Volume. Down."

"Shut. The. Door."

"It *is* shut."

Neil, Maggie's fiancé and my surfing buddy, trotted past my Polynesian-style bar with its tiki carvings, moved me aside, and eyed my door.

"Hunh. That is loud."

"You think? Didn't Saber tell Sam to fix the volume?"

"Sam did kill the outside alarm."

"I noticed that. Otherwise Mr. Lister would be out here with a shotgun."

Hugh Lister was our over-the-jasmine-hedge next-door neighbor. He didn't seem to like us in general, but when the outdoor siren had whooped, Lister had charged through the hedge, swearing the September afternoon blue.

My system wasn't even supposed to *have* an outside siren.

"So where are Sam and Saber now?"

Neil shrugged. "Sam adjusted the volume inside our place, then he and Saber made a run to the hardware store."

"Wait. Your place?" I whipped my head to glance across the lawn where Maggie's home fronted the property. "Why are you running the alarm to the big house?"

"Remember the sniper? Shooting at you from the oak tree out front? Waking up the neighborhood?"

I recalled too well being shot at while Jo-Jo the Jester gave me a flying lesson in the shadows of our shared yard.

"Point taken. Is the noise window-shattering loud at your place, too?"

"No, but we don't have to wake the dead."

I narrowed my eyes. "I'm underdead, Neil, and I'm going to do something evil to you one of these days."

"Right, Fresca," he said with a cuff on my arm.

Yes, Neil calls me Fresca. Having a soft-drink nickname is

better than being called Cesspool, which is what Neil used to call me. At least Fresca rhymes with Cesca, short for my real name. My usually darling Deke Saber has another name for me. Which reminded me . . .

"Neil, will you please, please, please tell Saber to disconnect the siren when he gets back? And leave it off until Sam's ready to do a final test."

"Will do. Oh, and remember that when your alarm is set, so is ours. Having it on in the daytime is no problem. We're gone most of the time anyway, but turn that thing off if you'll be coming and going late at night."

"You got it."

He gestured at the binder in my arms. "You off to help Maggie with the wedding mail?"

"And to go over plans for the bachelorette weekend. Do you have the valet parking under control? And the music? You remembered a Victorian wedding should feature classical music, right?"

"Stop nagging. I've got it covered. Oh, but I think Maggie's having second thoughts about those poofy things for the bridesmaid dresses."

"Poofy things?" I gulped. "The bustles?"

He smirked as he trotted away.

Hell's freaking wedding bells.

Sure I owed Maggie more than I could ever repay. If not for Maggie buying and restoring the house she and Neil now shared, I'd still be buried in the long-forgotten half basement underneath this very property. Maggie had unearthed me, taken me under her wing, and was now including me in the biggest day of her life.

But if her big day included big bustles on the bridesmaid gowns? No, I'd just have to change her mind again.

I sped across the lawn to Maggie's back door, calling to her as I passed through the mudroom and into the kitchen.

"I'm in here," Maggie yelled back. "Walk softly, or you'll topple my piles."

She looked up as I entered, and we shared a grin. We'd both dressed for the September heat, me wearing aqua shorts and a tank top with my hair in a frizzy ponytail, Maggie wearing green shorts and a white T-shirt. With the humidity high enough to drain a body faster than a starving vamp, thank goodness for arctic-level air-conditioning.

Maggie's grin turned rueful as she gestured at the dining table littered with stacks of replies, lists, and the bulging wedding-planner binder that matched mine. The few cards resting in the cardboard Regrets box didn't cover the bottom of it. The piles in the Accepts box were ten inches high, and more haphazard stacks of unopened envelopes rested at Maggie's fingertips.

I carefully pulled out the chair on her right to prevent a paper slide.

"You think I can cram ten more tables and a hundred more chairs in the backyard?" she asked on a sigh.

"You have that many yeses for the reception? What happened to only half of the people you invited accepting?"

She snorted. "Obviously I underestimated."

"Maggie, you're an interior design guru, and Neil's a state anthropologist. With all the contacts between you, I'm not surprised at the responses. Don't worry; we'll deal," I added, patting her hand. "The rental guy is holding double of everything for us, and we'll order more food when we meet with the caterer again tomorrow."

Maggie turned her hand to grip mine. "What if we don't have enough food? What do I do then?"

"First, you'll have plenty of food. The caterer swears people eat less when the service is buffet style."

"And if she's wrong?"

"Then I'll put out the call to the Jag Queens and my bridge group. Daphne Dupree is doing your cakes anyway, and the rest of the gang will be happy to help with some last-minute hors d'oeuvres. Now, come on," I said, extracting my hand. "Let's open the new batch of RSVPs and get them recorded. Maybe they'll all be regrets."

Maggie rolled her eyes, but we set to work. She read names while I checked them off the master list. The acceptances were accompanied by quiet groans, the regrets with little whoops, and the pile dwindled. Neil walked by, headed to the kitchen, and shook his head as Maggie slit open another envelope and chuckled.

"You won't believe this, but Jo-Jo's coming." She waved the small rectangle at me. "And he's offered to entertain."

"Damn it to hell," Neil swore, frozen at the kitchen threshold. "Tell me you did not invite that lame vampire comic."

Jo-Jo had taken refuge with me in early August, escaping his Master in Atlanta so he could dive into showbiz. No matter that his jokes had been beyond bad to begin with, he'd quickly put a decent act together and caught the attention of a vacationing talent agent. The rest was history in the making.

"Jo-Jo's earning a mint in Vegas and doing a movie, Neil," Maggie said on a laugh, "so he can't be that lame. Not anymore."

"But you won't let him do his act at the reception, right? If he juggles, I'm giving DennyK orders to stake him."

"Your best man won't need a stake. Jo-Jo will just be attending."

"And on the upside, he won't be munching at the buffet," I added.

"Long as he doesn't munch on a guest," Neil muttered.

The fridge opened and closed, bottles clinked—beer bottles most likely—then we heard the back door slam. If Neil had grabbed beers, I hoped that meant Saber and Sam were back on the job.

"Poor Neil," Maggie said, laughing as she pushed back from the table. "I don't know if he's nervous or just impatient to have the wedding over with."

"And at nineteen days and counting, you don't have a teeny touch of nerves?" I teased, following her into the kitchen.

"Only about the reception." She pulled a gallon of sweet tea from the fridge. "Southern women are bred to feed the masses, but I've never hosted that many parties."

"The housewarming party came off with food left over."

"Yes, but we had fewer tables, fewer guests, and I wasn't wearing a wedding gown. What if I knock over a whole table of food with my bustle?"

I hid a smile, grabbed two ruby-colored glasses from the cabinet, and set them on the counter. "All the more reason for your two bridesmaids *not* to have bustles, but don't worry. I'll tell the caterers to make extra-wide aisles, and you'll be fine. The wedding will come off without a hitch."

"Mmm." She plunked ice cubes in the glasses and poured the tea, then turned serious. "Speaking of hitches, how is Saber? Still grouchy?"

I plopped into a kitchen chair. "He's moody, edgy, and positively grim. And he's hovered 24-7 since he got home Friday. It's driving me insane."

"You can't get him to tell you what's wrong?"

"No. He's paranoid about my safety, but he won't say why."

"He's always been concerned for your safety."

"True," I conceded as I stared at the crackling ice cubes in my tea.

Saber had insisted I have the security of the president and the pope combined—well, except for Secret Service agents and Swiss Guards. Even my cottage windows are UV reflective and impact resistant. Saber had wanted bulletproof windows, too, but those didn't come with UV protection.

As for the perimeter alarm, in theory it was brilliant. Since my home sat near the back corner of the yard, weight-sensitive and supposedly weatherproof disks were buried in a series of halo-like rings around the sides and front of the cottage. Smaller creatures could scamper through the yard, but a weight of fifty pounds or more on a disk triggered the siren inside my house and at the monitored security offices. I'd dive into a hidey-hole through the escape hatch in my bedroom walk-in closet and wait for the all clear via a phone system in the safe room. And when I expected company or was out late, I simply disarmed the system. Good plan, imperfect execution. At least it had been the first time around.

Of course, now that Sam was "fixing" the system, the darn siren went off at the drop of an acorn. If he didn't get the bugs worked out, I'd be ripping the alarm box off the wall.

"Hey," Maggie said, bringing me back to the moment. "Maybe Saber knows something about your stalker, and that's what's bugging him."

"I doubt it. I haven't seen Victor Gorman in weeks. No, I think this has something to do with the sixteen days Saber was gone."

"On the assignment to shut down vampire nests for the Vampire Protection Agency?"

"Yes, but he phoned me every day, and never mentioned any major problems."

Of course, not all the vamps wanted to abandon the nest system, or even transition from nests to corporate entities. Gotta love capitalism, but apparently some vampires were more resistant to change. Maybe Saber hadn't mentioned big problems because he didn't want me to worry.

"Whatever it is that's eating him, wring it out of him soon, will you?" Maggie rose and patted my shoulder. "He spooked the caterer when he did his bodyguard thing on Saturday."

"It wasn't me and my terrifying vampire gaze?"

She snorted just as footsteps stomped in the mudroom. We turned to find Neil all smiles, Saber scowling.

Maggie was so right. I needed to find out what was bugging my man.

But even with that forbidding expression on his face, my stomach did the dipsy-do it always does when I see Deke Saber. Drool gathered in my mouth, too, because Saber looked extra yummy with his bright white polo shirt and brown cargo shorts showing off his bronze tan. Hubba!

My body might automatically respond every time I looked at Saber, but I gave him my stern face instead of my sunny smile. "Is the volume adjusted now?"

"Down to a dull roar, and the outside siren is permanently cut."

"Saber here threatened to feed Sam to a hungry vampire if the system failed again, so I think we're good." Neil sidled up to Maggie and put an arm around her waist. "You have anything to hail the conquering heroes?"

Maggie wiggled closer. "You've had a beer. What more do you want?"

Neil gave her an exaggerated leer, and Saber cleared his throat.

"Come on, Cesca. We have an appointment to keep."

"We do?" I frowned at him. "But Maggie and I haven't finished with the mail yet. Or talked about the girl's weekend."

"I'll manage the mail," Maggie jumped in, "and I know you have everything under control for this weekend. You go ahead."

Go manage your man, her narrowed-eyed look plainly said.

In seconds flat, Neil shoved my binder into my arms, and Saber all but dragged me out the back door and across the yard.

"Since when do we have an appointment?"

"Since yesterday."

"And when were you planning to tell me about it?"

"When I got around to it," Saber said without so much as a glance at me.

I ground my teeth but held my tongue until we were in my cozy living room. That's when I dropped the wedding binder on my computer desk with a *whap* and turned to eye Saber closely. Signs of strain bracketed his beautiful mouth, and lines I hadn't noticed now furrowed his forehead.

I took his hand and tugged him to the plush coffee-colored leather sofa.

"Come talk to me."

Saber pulled away. "We don't have time, Cesca. You need to change clothes, and I need to make a call."

Fists on my hips, I stared into his cobalt blue eyes. "Not until you tell me why you've been as snappy as a starving gator in a feeding frenzy."

"I haven't been that bad."

"Trust me, you have. For five long days, and that's not like you." I threw myself onto the couch cushions. "I'm not moving until you spill."

He paced away from me, raking his fingers through his military-short black hair. When his shoulders slumped on a soul-deep sigh, I knew I had him.

"I told you about closing the vampire nests," he said, his voice low and rumbling. "I told you I ran into a few problems. The last two head vampires left in my territory were already so infected by the Void, I couldn't interrogate them, and I couldn't arrest them."

"You had to execute them?"

"Yeah, Rico in South Beach, and Martinique in Tampa."

I shuddered because I knew how far gone Rico had been with the infection. I'd seen him through the memories of another vampire, one who now lived in Daytona Beach and ran a club there. Ray, aka Ramon, had been in the South Beach nest and had witnessed Rico being slowly devoured by an oily fog blob that oozed ankle high in Rico's throne room. It drained Rico, not of his blood, but of his life force. Ray called the formless mass *la oscuridad*. The darkness that was, in fact, the Void.

That no one seemed to know what the Void was, much less how to stop it, made its threat all the more ominous.

"The thing is," Saber said as he continued pacing, "it wasn't just the heads of nests I saw affected. The infection has spread from the big nests to the small groups and even to vampires who've lived solo for years. They're all showing symptoms from fatigue to paranoia to violent outbursts."

"How about Ray and his gang? Did you go through Daytona to see him?"

"Yeah. They're drinking more bottled blood but are lower on energy." His hands fisted at his sides. "Cesca, I thought you were sick, too."

"Saber, I'm fine. The same as always."

He scowled. "Then why were there more Starbloods bottles in the recycling bin than usual when I got home last week?"

"Because I got a nasty-tasting six-pack and dumped them all." Nasty being relative since I hold my nose when I slug down my daily chilled bottle of artificial blood.

"The blood was bad?"

"Nope, the caramel-macchiato flavor was off. I called the company, gave them the lot number, and found out it was a recalled batch. If that's the reason you've been so grouchy and overprotective—"

I stopped cold. Oh, no. Oh, God, no. Pictures flashed in my mind's eye, visions I hadn't invited but couldn't shove away.

Saber visiting sick vampires. Saber executing Rico in the throne room. Saber wading away after the kill, his feet dragging through that oily Void muck roiling over Rico's tiled floor.

Saber had been exposed to the Void for weeks, but he wasn't an ordinary human who might be immune to it. As a boy, he'd been forced to ingest both vampire and werewolf blood. Now he was less than a preternatural but far more than a mere mortal.

He also had symptoms of the sickness. Irritability in spades, plus he'd been falling asleep by midnight instead of his usual two in the morning. Come to think of it, our lovemaking had slacked off.

Conclusion? Saber was infected or feared he was, and he couldn't bring himself to tell me.

Every muscle trembled as I pulled myself to my feet, skirted the coffee table, and walked into his arms.

"Deke," I whispered, using the name I reserved for our most intimate moments. "Don't worry. If you're infected, we'll fix it. We'll find the Void, kill it, and cure you. I swear. I'll do whatever it takes."

Maybe he knew I was talking a good game. Maybe he knew I wasn't as confident as I made myself sound. Maybe that's why he hesitated before he hugged me tighter.

"You'll do whatever it takes?"

"Absolutely," I said, leaning away to cup his cheek in my palm.

He gave me a slow smile.

"Good. Then let's go see Triton."

Triton? Oh, pelican poop.

TWO

I stiffened, and Saber wisely let me go. He also backed up a prudent step.

"Just why do we need to see Triton?"

"Honey, I know you have issues with him."

"Issues, Dr. Phil? You know darn well I want to wring Triton's neck."

Or drop-kick him in the ocean where he could shape-shift into his dolphin self and stay that way.

Just over a month ago, Triton had used me—and a mysterious amulet—to kill two vampires at a comedy club. Saber had termed it banishing, not murder, and in fairness, I'd made some peace with that incident. Both vampires had been consumed by the vile Void and were pathologically crazy to boot. Besides, it was a case of them or me, not to mention who else they may have harmed if they'd lived. Still, Triton had no right to put me in that position, especially since I hadn't seen him in the flesh in over two hundred years before that night.

No, I didn't count the ten seconds in March when I'd spotted him on the dunes. And, yes, we had quite a history, not all of it happy.

Saber's warm hands settled on my shoulders.

"Cesca, you've avoided Triton since he moved back here and opened his antique store."

"That's because I promised you we'd see him together."

"Then let's do it. The VPA hasn't got a clue how to track and eliminate the Void. Triton and Cosmil just might."

I bit my lip. On the one hand Cosmil had already yammered about Triton and me combining our powers to fight the Void. Not something I wanted to do since I'm a pacifist by nature, never mind that I had no clue which powers Cosmil meant us to combine. True, I'd faced down the French Bride killer in March and the two wacko vampires just last month. The point was that I hadn't had a choice either time.

And I didn't now. Not with Saber's life at stake.

"You're sure that Candy and Jim Crushman don't have any leads?" Candy headed the Atlanta VPA office, and her husband worked as a mercenary executioner overseas.

"Not a damn one. The Void has to be a physical entity, human enough to set up bank accounts with a photo ID, social security number, and other documentation."

"Unless it's working through a human slave."

"It could be working through a whole network of humans, enslaved or not. We need to follow every lead, and right now we have exactly two. Triton has the amulet and the knowledge to use it."

"And Cosmil is our friendly neighborhood wizard."

"He has to know more than we do, and he and Triton are tight. We get to one, we get to the other."

I thought about his logic for a second then nodded.

"All right. I'll go change and do something with my hair, but remember we need to be back by eight thirty so I can change again for the ghost tour."

"No problem."

I turned toward the bedroom then spun back. "One more thing. Next time you want to spring this kind of surprise on me, don't."

He held up his hand, his gaze solemn. "Promise."

I marched to the bedroom hoping Saber would live long enough to keep his vow. But as I wrestled to flatiron the worst of the curls and waves and frizzies from my hair, and debated what to wear, I struggled with a deep, persistent fear.

If I fully embraced my vamp powers, what kind of monster might I become?

Ocean Enchantments, Triton's new store.

I'd seen the two-story, 1950s structure every time I'd come to the island to surf. Built slightly catty-corner to Anastasia Boulevard in the shadow of the lighthouse, the cinder-block building housing Triton's store had been stark white with blue trim around the front door and the many oversized windows. Now it sported palm-frond green paint with deep gray green trim that should have been soothing. And the mermaid-shaped sign in bright, iridescent colors that swung from the store's covered entrance? That should've been cheery. Instead it creaked as if the salt air had already corroded the metal rings.

Since I didn't feel all that enchanted, soothed, or cheery at the moment, I took the creepy creaking as an omen. A very bad omen, I decided when a gust of wind made the sign screech again.

But, hey, I'd faced down killers. In comparison to that, this meeting would be a snap.

I smoothed my semi-tamed, claw-clipped hair back with a

trembling hand. From his stance beside me on the sidewalk, Saber put an arm around my waist and drew me to his side.

"In case he has customers in there, remember he goes by Trey now."

"Right." Trey Delphinus. Once the light of my life, now a pain in my backside.

"Ready?"

I squared my shoulders, straightened my new Walmart power red blouse over my dark blue jeans, and put one sandaled foot in front of the other. The same way I'd get through this meeting. One step at a time.

The bell over the ornately carved door tinkled when Saber shoved it open, but the sound faded as I was embraced by the soothing shades of beach sand, ocean blue, and polished wood. On my right, L-shaped antique glass display cases offered coins and jewelry, fans and snuffboxes, and much more. To the right and straight ahead, rough-hewn tables displayed vignettes of everything from weaponry to housewares. Art-gallery lighting picked up the rich hues and textures where the natural light from the large picture windows didn't reach.

The effect was stunning but not terribly surprising. Triton had been finding treasure in shipwrecks and dragging it back from the deep since 1795 when he was sixteen and had begun shape-shifting into dolphin form. He'd given me a few trinkets, but even then he'd dreamed of building a business selling his finds.

He'd also since become a dive master and had worked shipwreck recovery here and there. I knew that from the research Saber and I had done, and it was a smart move on Triton's part. Fewer questions about how he'd accumulated so many artifacts, fewer questions about the provenance of his treasures. Oh, Triton had diversified his business interests over the years, but it made sense that authentic sea treasures were his first love.

A faint chime drew my attention to the back wall where part of a small-ship's bow jutted into the room. The two tones of satiny wood shone like milk and dark chocolate, and the furniture nearby was staged to resemble the interior of a captain's quarters—much like my father's quarters had been on his favorite ship.

Then I saw Triton, rising from a barrel chair.

"Cesca, Saber," he said as he strode toward us. "Good to see you."

The men shook hands, all cordial and normal.

I stood very still, braced for an emotional riptide.

One that didn't come. No churning of angst or anger. No wave of lost-love regret. Only a ripple of nostalgic tenderness fluttered in my chest. As I stared, the image of Triton the youth in his homespun work clothes overlaid that of Triton the man in his charcoal suit and white shirt.

He'd always been model handsome in face and physique, but he'd grown a man's body. Taller than I remembered, Triton's swimmer's shoulders were wider, his chest deeper. His rugged features, so like his adoptive Greek father's, had lost their sharpest angles. I knew him to be a year older than I, but only a few fine lines around his cocoa brown eyes and perhaps a hint of silver in his tobacco brown hair aged him. Of course, the suit matured him, too, but as boy and man, the guy was a timeless hunk and a half.

Funny. I'd known Triton since we were toddlers. We'd shared a telepathic connection and more adventures than I could count, and he'd been my first crush. Even when he made his "let's be friends" feelings clear, I'd still loved him. All that time, and I'd never pictured Triton in a suit and tie.

"I had a meeting today, Cesca."

My gaze shot up from his tie to his cocoa brown eyes.

"What?"

"That's why I'm wearing a suit today."

"You read my thoughts?"

He gave me the cocky grin I remembered from our youth. "We've still got the mojo."

"What you have is the ego," I zinged back, a hand on one hip.

"Same old Cesca," he said with a wide grin. "The girl who'd take on any bully or BSer in town. My dear *tyranoulitsa*."

I froze, my throat suddenly clamped around a sob. One word, echoing across the centuries, triggered emotions merely seeing him hadn't.

A kaleidoscope of images flashed in my mind's eye. Triton and me together, inseparable friends, occasional pranksters, clandestine adventurers.

Heart thudding, it took me three tries to gulp away the choking lump and draw a slow breath to speak.

"I-I'd forgotten that."

Triton quirked a smile. "What?"

"That you used to call me little tyrant."

The smile widened. "You used to box my ears for it, too, when you could catch me."

His teasing eased the tightness in my chest.

"I caught you often then and I'm faster now, so don't mess with me."

"You two always got along this well, huh?"

I pivoted to Saber to find him grinning. An honest, full-out grin. An expression I hadn't seen in weeks.

"Yeah," Triton drawled. "I'd say this is typical."

Saber laughed then, and the irritations I'd harbored with Triton fell away. It was worth any price if Saber stayed alive and healthy to laugh with me for a very long time to come.

"Now that old home week is out of the way," Triton said, "come on back where we can be comfortable."

Saber and I followed him to the ship's bow setup where a cozy settee stretched along the wall. Saber settled next to me, while Triton took the creaky chair at the high point of our little conversation triangle.

"When I called," Saber said, "I told you I needed help identifying the Void. Any luck getting in touch with Cosmil?"

"Afraid not. I haven't seen him in over a week, and he isn't answering his cell phone. I haven't seen Pandora, either."

Pandora, another magical shape-shifter, changed from a panther to a giant house cat. She also communicated with me telepathically, and apparently did the same with Cosmil and Triton. I didn't know why Pandora had suddenly appeared last spring, but she'd helped me out of more than one jam.

Saber leaned forward, his elbows braced on his knees. "I'll lay this on the line, Triton. I need to find and shut down the Void, and I need to do it fast. Do you or Cosmil know what this thing is?"

"I can't speak for Cos, but no. I don't know what the Void is."

"You were hiding from it in August," I said. "You must've known something then."

"Not the way you're thinking." He sighed and loosened his tie. "I came home in March to look over this building and hire contractors."

"And you left your gold dolphin charm on the beach for me to find," I said.

"Yeah. I knew you'd seen me, but I didn't want to impose on you and Saber just then. I went back to California to pack up the business and finished moving here in early July. Right after a diving trip to the Bahamas. A week later, Cos found me."

"Here in the store?" Saber asked.

"Actually, he came to my apartment upstairs. He told me he'd been keeping track of me."

"Why?" I asked. "And for how long?"

Triton grimaced and rubbed the back of his neck. "This is where it gets weird. He said he was responsible for me being a shifter.

Something about a mermaid, a dolphin, and a spell gone wrong. Sounds like a bad 'walked into a bar' joke, doesn't it?"

It did, but I didn't say so.

"I take it," Saber said, "that Cosmil told you to hide out."

"Yeah. I made arrangements to delay the store opening, and he stashed me at his place in the country between here and Hastings."

"What about the amulet?" Saber pressed. "Did the one you used at the comedy club come from Cosmil?"

Triton shook his head. "I got it from a kahuna in Hawaii. A shaman. That was last November when I went out there to dive."

"Did the man know about the amulet's power?" Saber asked.

"The kahuna was a woman, and hell, she was ancient enough to have powered the thing herself. She said it was for protection, but she didn't mention from what. I took the amulet to be polite."

"Don't tell me you didn't know how it worked, Triton," I scolded. "You didn't seem the least bit surprised when it went all supernova and made the vamps go poof."

"I wasn't surprised. I was damn impressed. Cos gave me the chant that activates the magick and made me repeat it until it was as rote as reciting the alphabet. But, I only knew what *should* happen. I didn't take the thing out for a test-drive. I swear to you both. Everything I know about the amulet, about the Void for that matter, I know directly from Cos."

"Then we need to track down Cosmil and get answers," Saber said.

Triton narrowed his eyes. "Any reason for the urgency?"

I took Saber's hand and squeezed. "It seems that Saber is infected."

Triton cut his gaze to Saber. "But Cos said the Void feeds on magical beings, not humans."

"I'm somewhere in between," Saber countered with a tight smile.

"Saber's been in direct contact with super-sick vampires for weeks, Triton. You have to help us. Please."

Triton gave a jerky nod. "I'll call Cos again."

But before he could reach for the cell phone on his desk, little bursts of hell broke loose.

Vibrations shimmied through the room, rattling the artifacts in their display cases. The floor beneath us heaved, and Triton's creaky barrel chair lurched sideways.

Just as the three of us shot to our feet, the air in front of me shimmered like a heat wave rising from summer-baked pavement. The shimmer solidified into the human form of Cosmil, but he looked nothing like I remembered. Not the Santa in a sapphire wizard cape, not his scruffy carriage driver guise.

Instead, he looked like he'd been on the bad end of a back-alley brawl, inky dirt streaking and rips rending his white duck pants and tunic.

And then there was the blood.

So much smeared blood.

In another instant, Cosmil collapsed.

THREE

Triton and Saber leaped to grab Cosmil by the arms before he smacked face-first into the tiled floor.

I fought nausea. Not from the sight of blood, but from the smell. Coppery tinged with the taint of tar, like newly laid asphalt.

"Tell me what happened," Saber said, kicking into cop mode.

"Attacked," Cosmil gasped. "Void in the Veil."

"The Veil," Triton supplied, "is what he calls the passageway between dimensions. Think wormhole with scenery."

The injured wizard inhaled a raspy breath. "Get me home. Pandora at risk."

My chest ached with fear as his eyes fluttered closed. It hurt to see the quiet, confident wizard as an old, beaten man, but to lose him and Pandora, too? The panther shifter might be a cryptic critter, but she'd pawed her way into my heart. We had to save them. Both of them.

"We can take him out the back," Triton was saying to Saber.

"Done. I'll drive, you follow."

"I can drive him," Triton argued.

"Yeah, but I've got lights and sirens."

Saber fished his keys out of his jeans and tossed them to me. "Pull the car around, Cesca."

I sprinted through the store and outside, beeped the locks, and climbed into Saber's black SUV. In no more than a minute, I'd cut across an empty lot, dodged five old oak trees along the way, and angled the car behind Triton's store at the rear entrance. With the passenger-side door toward the building and Saber's tinted windows providing extra cover, a causal observer would see nothing amiss.

Like the bloodied man Saber and Triton half carried between them.

"Lay the passenger seat back," Saber commanded. "As far as it will go."

I reclined the seat then scooted out of the way to watch the guys load Cosmil in the car. Saber buckled him in and slammed the door.

"Okay," he said, grabbing my hand. "Triton gave me directions, but keep your phone on in case I need to check them."

"I will."

He gave me a peck on the cheek and sprinted around to the driver's door.

"We're right behind you," Triton called as Saber got in the car.

I watched Saber peel out, then Triton nudged me. "Move, Cesca. Help me lock up."

We sped back inside, down a hall, and through to the shop proper. I followed Triton's instruction to flip the dead bolt on the main door, and he set the security alarm mounted near his desk. His movements were quick and efficient, just the way I remembered from watching him cast fishing nets centuries ago, but I caught the fine tremor of tension in his hands and the worry in his eyes.

When we exited in the back, Triton bounded up the wooden exterior stairway I assumed led to his apartment. I trailed after him but waited on the small, east-facing deck filled with potted plants while he ducked inside. Seconds later, he emerged with a gray duffel bag.

"Just a few more things to get," he said as he locked up.

He strode to a monster-sized wood fern in a glazed yellow pot at the left corner of the deck and thrust his hand in the middle of it, ignoring the tiny sparks that fizzled on the fronds.

"Catch."

Good thing for vampire reflexes, because he tossed a missile at me. When I looked at the object in my stinging hand, I saw the amulet. Immediately, the hexagon-shaped crystal, shot with silver and gold lines and framed in copper, pulsed in my palm, warm and steady as a heartbeat.

"Tell me you don't leave this out in the open where anyone could take it."

"The fern hides it," he said as he crossed to the same fern in a matching pot in the right corner of the deck. "Plus Cos has warded the whole place against theft."

"Then why the alarm system for the shop?"

"Keeps the insurance company happy." He stuck his hand in the second fern, again to accompanying sparks. "Heads up."

He underhanded another disk, but I snagged it easily.

"What's this? A fake?"

"Nope, they work together. They're mates. Let's ride."

I was tempted to brain him with both amulets as he trotted past me, but refrained. Good thing because he opened the garage door I hadn't noticed to reveal a honking-huge silver F-250 truck that made my darling SSR look like a Tonka toy. It was also, I saw, a stick shift, which I couldn't drive.

I buckled up, opened the glove box, and stashed the amulets under the owner's manual.

"You don't want to hold those?"

I crossed my eyes at him. "Which way to Cosmil's place?"

"South down A1A to the 206 bridge, then west toward Hastings."

I chewed my lip as Triton steered out of the neighborhood and took a screeching left onto Anastasia Boulevard. Yes, I was nervous, but not because of his driving. Because we were alone for the first time in centuries, and I didn't know what to say.

We'd snuck out of our homes as children and teens, always to have adventures. Most often we'd borrow a rowboat, take it to the island, and end up swimming and racing on the beach. Unless it was the dark of the moon when Triton shifted. In that case, I'd stand watch until he was fully a dolphin and in deep enough water to swim away. Guess we were too predictable, though. That's how one particular vampire and his henchmen knew where to capture me.

I met Triton alone only a few more times after that. Once to beg him to get my family out of town, another time to beg him to leave, too. Without the leverage of loved ones who could be tortured, even Turned, King Normand had less power over me.

I knew when Triton had left St. Augustine. He told me telepathically, and we'd stayed in touch on and off for fifty years. Not that I could tell time once Normand had punished me by sealing me in his own coffin. Triton kept me apprised of the passing years and of his travels through our mind connection. And then, suddenly, he was silent.

"I like your hair." His mellow voice seemed to boom in the truck cab "The blouse, too. You look good in red."

I touched the cap sleeve of my blouse then the clip holding my partial updo. "Thanks."

Had he been reading my memories and thoughts a moment ago? If so, he wasn't taunting me. Yet.

"Am I getting the silent treatment?"

"Uh, no. After all this time, I don't know what to say."

"You? You always have something to say."

I punched him in the arm, but his teasing unwound another twist of tension in my chest. "Do you think Cosmil will be okay? I mean, should we have taken him to the hospital or at least to a doctor?"

"Hell, no. Doctors ask questions. We just have to hope Cos isn't too badly hurt, or we're all screwed."

"All?"

"I'm in the early stages of infection, too, Cesca."

"Oh, Triton, I'm sorry." My pulse faltered, and I touched his shoulder in sympathy. "Did the Void get to you before you went into hiding?"

"I don't know when it got to me. Remember a few weeks back when I told you telepathically that the Void was affecting all magicals?"

"Yes, but you didn't say you were ill."

"I didn't know I was then, and I sure as hell don't know how I got infected. Not even Cosmil knows if the disease is passed by direct contact, is airborne, or is magically delivered in some combination."

Was he thinner than he'd been five weeks ago? Were his cheekbones more prominent? What did I know? I'd seen him for maybe ten whole minutes at the comedy club, and I'm not all that observant when I'm busy banishing crazed vampires.

"What are your symptoms?" I asked as we flew past the island branch of the library and Ace Hardware.

"Itchiness under my skin, restlessness. I'm not sleeping well."

"You used to feel the same way near the new moon. That's in six days."

"This is different. More severe." He paused. "You aren't sick at all?"

"Not a bit, and I'm not looking that gift mule in the mouth."

"But you inhaled enough black energy from those vampires at the comedy club to choke a whale. That alone should have infected you."

"I learned to ground it out and rebalance."

Triton shot me a surprised glance. "From Cos?"

"From Saber."

Triton's hands tightened on the gearshift, but we sailed through the light where A1A intersects with Beach A1A.

"You love Saber."

Triton spoke softly, a statement, not a question.

"I do."

"Guess I blew my chance, huh?"

I snorted. "Your 'just friends' speech was loud and clear, Triton."

"I meant my second chance. I moved back here for several reasons, one of them being you."

My heart stuttered to a dead stop then pounded one painful beat. Was I hearing right? Triton had wanted a second chance with me?

"I heard on the national news," he continued, "that you'd been unearthed, but I couldn't get away from California for a while."

"I'd been out of the box for seven months before I saw you at the beach," I said carefully.

"I left my dolphin charm so you'd know I planned to see you again."

"And then you disappeared for another five months."

"I was a little tied up moving my business and dodging the big bad Void."

"Too busy to call?"

He braked at the Dondanville stoplight and turned to hold my gaze.

"Would a call have made a difference?"

Would it?

I'd once dreamed of waking to those twinkling brown eyes each morning. I'd dreamed of the twinkle turning to passion. I'd dreamed of a life of joy with my best friend.

The spring before I turned sixteen, Triton told me flat out that we'd never be a couple and shattered my dreams. I'd accepted his reasons, mainly that I was sister to him, not a lover. But years later, when I'd been trapped in that coffin, I'd hoped that Triton would be the one to find and release me. That just maybe, after decades apart, he'd see me differently.

Now?

A horn blared behind us, and Triton hit the gas.

I hit a reality check. So, okay, if Triton had come back sooner, come back anytime before I met Saber, maybe it would have made a difference. Triton was my first love, and seeing him stirred memories. But nostalgia faded. My feelings for Triton might be pond deep, but what I felt for Saber was ocean vast.

"Never mind, Cesca. I can see you're in love. Besides," he added, throwing me a grin that seemed only a little forced, "I'm still looking for a female I can shift with."

I made my tone as light as his. "Is that why you came back? You never found that special woman in California?"

"Or anywhere else. The kahuna woman in Hawaii told me I needed to return to the ocean of my birth to find my fin mate."

"Cosmil confirmed you were born in the Atlantic?"

"More or less."

"Huh. If you're the son of a mermaid and a dolphin, why do you have a human form?"

He shrugged. "I didn't ask. I figured it was a side effect of his goofed spell and left it at that."

"Probably a good plan."

We rode in quiet until he took the right turn on the 206 bridge.

"By the way, that display in my store? It looks like the captain's quarters on your dad's best ship because I designed it that way. Your father was a good man. Good to me, too."

"I know he was."

My father had thought so well of Triton that he'd left him with a responsibility most men would've turned down flat. Unbeknownst to me, Papa had bought one hundred acres on Anastasia Island in 1798, when I was eighteen. Maybe he meant to give it to me when I married or reached my majority, but even after I'd been Turned, my father kept the land. Then, before he and the family left St. Augustine, he put it in a trust and named Triton as trustee. I guess he hoped I'd break free of the vampires and would have a safe place away from town to settle. He couldn't have known Triton would have such a long life span. Heck, I'd never considered that Triton would be nigh on immortal, and I don't think he had, either.

I'd learned about the land and Triton's part in the trust by accident when I helped Saber house hunt. The real estate agent had shown us a beach house on the last three lots left in trust and let the secret out.

"About the land, Cesca," Triton said. "I didn't mean for you to get ambushed with that tidbit."

"Tidbit? Those are oceanfront lots worth a small fortune."

"Yeah, well, with hurricanes and all, oceanfront property wasn't worth much until the last four or five decades. And before you ask, no, you don't owe me for taxes. That's why I sold off parcels."

"All right, then thank you for taking care of my father's legacy."

"You're welcome."

"And Triton?"

"What?"

"As long as I can speak my mind, don't be reading it."

He flashed a grin. "Make that a ditto, and we have a deal."

He offered his hand to shake on it, and his palm warmed mine for a long moment before I let go.

"Deal," I said.

Only then did I realize I hadn't read his thoughts at all. Not a single one.

We caught up to Saber, idling on the side of the road at 206 and the far side of Interstate 95. He waved for Triton to take the lead, with a shouted, "Hurry."

Tense minutes later, Triton slowed, turned on the left turn blinker, and steered onto a barely there dirt track carved between pines and scrub oaks and vines. The trail twisted first this direction, then that one, and the truck rocked from side to side as we crept along the rutted ground like a sloop tossed in high seas. I held tight to the grab bar and fretted about how the jostling would affect Cosmil's injuries.

"Cos hides this entrance completely when he wants to. The times he's been expecting me out here, he's smoothed the road and took out most of the turns. Magically, of course."

"Then I suppose he's not conscious enough yet to do the smoothing. Not a good sign."

"No, but we're close now. If Pandora's safe, maybe she can tell us how to doctor Cos."

Triton hung another right, and like going from darkness to daylight, we rolled onto a smooth gravel drive. To my right, towering pines and ancient live oaks formed a perfect circle, sheltering a ramshackle cabin on the circle's perimeter. Uneven steps led to a rickety porch running the full width of the shanty, and the roof looked ready to collapse under the weight of tree debris.

The place didn't look habitable, much less sterile enough to house an injured man.

You will see, I heard in my head.

Pandora's voice, not Triton's. Thank God she was safe.

A single knot of tension unraveled in my stiff shoulders as I climbed from the truck and saw Pandora in her panther form emerge from the far side of the circle. Tail twitching, she eyed Saber and Triton as they eased Cosmil out of the car. The wizard wasn't steady on his feet, but he was upright.

Pandora paced to Cosmil's side, sniffed, and sneezed.

"Yes, my friend. I reek, but we are safe for the moment. Go."

The hefty panther whirled toward me. *Come, Princess Vampire*, she said, then loped to the shack.

She was her usual brusque self, but I psychically reached for any lurking remnant of the evil Void. Just in case. Since I came up with nada, and since Saber and Triton had Cosmil in hand, I hurried after Pandora. Fortunately, the shanty's steps and porch felt sturdier under my sandals than they looked. I twisted the rusty doorknob and braced myself for primitive.

What I saw inside was modern. And huge compared to the footprint of the house. My interior design senses were overwhelmed as I glanced at the open-concept space.

The living area reflected more comfort than style, but the upholstered sofa and chairs had a timeless quality. The kitchen was separated from the living room by a stainless steel topped island big enough to be a boat. Beyond that, another mile of stainless counters, appliances, and a double sink made the kitchen look more like a laboratory. The open wooden cabinets and a wall of stainless steel shelves held everything from plates to pickles, along with home-canning jars that could contain eye of newt and tail of dog for all I knew.

A fine illusion, is it not? Pandora boasted.

"The inside or outside?" I countered.

She snorted as footsteps clumped on the porch.

Go. Turn on the shower.

I followed her to a fair-sized master suite. Not magazine layout quality, but I spotted a queen bed and ornate armoire before ducking into the slate-tiled bathroom. A tankless water heater was mounted outside the curtain-free spa shower with built-in bench seat. Wow.

I found plush white towels in the linen closet and set them on the sink countertop. Every texture and temperature sure felt real, and I wondered if Cosmil simply conjured what he wanted. Talk about a cool way to redecorate.

The man himself entered on Triton's arm, seeming firmer on his feet.

"Thank you, Francesca, Triton," he said. "I will join you all shortly."

Dismissed, I scooted out behind Triton to find Saber poking around in the kitchen cabinets.

"Saber, stop snooping," I whispered. "It's not polite."

"I'm looking for the first aid kit." He opened a deep drawer near the double stainless sink. "Got it."

Triton sank into an armchair, and Saber set the kit on the coffee table before he settled on the sofa. I glanced at my watch and paced. Yes, I had another two hours before my ghost tour started, but I prided myself on being organized and early, whether for work or for turning in my online-design-class projects.

I was also pacing off my terror. I mean, come on. If the Void could get to a wizard as old and powerful as I suspected Cosmil to be, what chance did Saber, Triton, and I have? With amulets for ammo no less. We needed rocket launchers. And a division of Marines.

Sooner than I expected, Cosmil appeared in the bedroom doorway dressed in black pants and a deep purple tunic, his feet bare. His hand rested on Pandora's noble head, and he looked a sight better in spite of the jagged gash slanting across his forehead.

He made his way across the room and sank into a chair. Saber snapped open the first aid box and ripped open the packaged surgical gloves before he assembled the sterile pads and gauze on the coffee table. Cosmil pointed to a small clear jar filled with mint green goo.

"Dab that on the cut, if you will."

"Is it a magical potion?" I had to ask.

"Nothing so exotic, my dear. Over the counter antibacterial cream mixed with a few herbs and a small healing spell." Cosmil winced as Saber used a cotton swab to apply the cream. "I do wish the local herb store had a wider selection, but we shall make do until I can safely travel the Veil again."

"Tell us what happened," Saber said, dressing the wound with efficient, gentle movements.

"I had word that a visitor was to arrive. A member of the Council of Ancients." Cosmil cut his gaze to meet mine. "A vampire of your King Normand's European line named Legrand."

"Normand was not my king, Cosmil."

"Nevertheless, Legrand wanted to check you out, I believe you would say."

"Why?" Triton asked.

"And why now?" I added.

Cosmil leaned back in the chair and sighed. "He knew of your rescue from the coffin, but you were beneath his notice until you and Triton vanquished the vampires last month."

"How did he find out about that?" Saber asked as he peeled off his gloves.

Cosmil leveled his gaze on Saber. "I must report to the Council just as you do to the VPA, although I may have edited some details of the event. I withheld the extent to which you are able to drain energy, Francesca. At any rate, Legrand's stated intention was to test Francesca's powers and to help groom her to battle the Void."

"Why? Are vampires in other countries infected, too?" I asked.

"I must presume so, although Legrand did not speak openly of victims nor did he share details of the vampire community in general. Indeed, all of the Council of Ancients members are somewhat secretive about their communities."

"I get the impression," I said, "that you didn't believe his story about training me."

"I'm afraid Legrand was not known for altruism."

Saber finished gathering the used first aid items and wrapped them in a paper towel. "That's twice you used the past tense," he said. "What happened?"

"When Legrand was hours past due, I went into the Veil to search. I found a body, too blackened and withered to identify."

My stomach turned at the image, and I shuddered so hard, I rattled my teeth.

"That matches the way the vampires in VPA custody are dying." Saber confirmed. "When the life force is drained, the tissue darkens and shrivels like a raisin."

Cosmil nodded. "Legrand's legendary ruby ring was on the body's finger. When I bent to retrieve it, I was attacked by a force that slashed and attempted to smother me."

"Then you're infected now, too," I said.

He shrugged. "I am well enough, and I will conduct a full purge-healing later. Thankfully, my escape spell worked, because the close encounter gave me information about the Void."

"So you have a clue what we're dealing with?" Saber asked.

"I do. I believe the Void is a thought form, though an atypical one."

"You lost me, Cos," Triton complained.

"In the mundane world," he began, like a professor on a lecture roll, "our thoughts are merely thoughts. On the metaphysical plane, our thoughts have life and reality. They are powerful vibrations that can be consciously directed, but they can also be manifested unconsciously."

"Sorry, still lost. Give me examples."

"Thinking positive thoughts about getting a good job can yield a good job. Prayer circles sending health thoughts can assist in healing. And, relating to Francesca's field, places believed to be haunted can become haunted due to the group mind phenomenon."

"What does this have to do with the Void?" Saber asked.

"Most thought forms are nonphysical, but the Void is not. It is a magical construct, likely created in a ritual that focused willpower, visualization, and life force energy. It appears in and acts in the physical world as directed by its creator."

"You make it sound like a movie zombie," Triton said.

"Except our zombie is a black blobby fog," I mumbled.

"A zombie is a fitting comparison. To have this blob directed to do harm is bad, but it can get worse."

"How much worse?" Saber pressed.

"It can become an independent entity. Go off the creator's leash, as it were, and wreak its own havoc."

"Shit."

"Indeed, Saber, but there is good news of a sort."

"Cosmil, don't make us pry it out of you," I warned.

He heaved a breath as if bracing to tell us the bad news. "Being in direct contact with the energy gave me a clue to its origin. I suspect the Void is being directed by a wizard named Starrack."

"And who the heck is that?" I asked.

Cosmil's blue gray eyes locked on my face.

"Starrack is my brother."

FOUR

"Your brother?" I echoed.

You could've knocked me over with a gull feather. I glanced at Triton's stunned expression then at Saber's grim one.

"Sadly, yes. We have been estranged for several centuries, and in fact, I thought him dead."

"But why would he create a monster like the Void? What would he gain?"

"Money. Power. It might even be a whim. Starrack was an extraordinarily talented wizard. More talented than I. However, he lacked the level of discipline and the morals to be great. One could never be certain of his motives."

"Then let's deal in facts," Saber said. "Do you know where Starrack is now? Know how to track him?"

"I would like nothing better than to say yes, but I do not know where he is, and I cannot track him at this time."

"Why not?" Triton demanded. "Just cast a spell."

"Loath as I am to admit a weakness, tracking spells are not my specialty. I might have been able to follow the Void back to Starrack through the Veil, but that is no longer an option. The Veil is temporarily closed."

"Because it's a crime scene?" Saber asked.

"Yes, there is a team investigating, but they are also searching for the body I found. It has gone missing, you see."

I rubbed my forehead. "We don't see, Cosmil. Explain."

"Whereas the main portals are more or less static, the Veil is not. One does not step through a doorway to instantly arrive at one's destination for the series of pathways in the Veil are in flux. The Veil may fold in on itself, directing and redirecting a traveler, especially when one is traversing long distances. Or when there is a disturbance within the Veil's energy."

"A disturbance such as a murder," Saber said flatly.

"Are you sure this Legrand guy was dead, Cos? Maybe it was an illusion. Maybe he took off when you were being attacked."

"Had I not touched the body and were it not for the ruby ring, I might agree with you, Triton. However, the ring was not merely Legrand's affectation, it was his talisman. The stone is obscenely large, mounted in an ornate fifteenth-century gold setting, and was reputedly stolen from the true French royal line. It was one of a kind."

"No, it wasn't," I said slowly, my psychic sense and my memory kicking in. I'd seen the same ring or an incredible facsimile of it. "Normand had one that fits that description. Don't you remember, Triton?"

"Hell, no. I never got close enough to him to notice his jewelry. What do you remember?"

"That he had a honkin'-huge ruby ring, although . . ."

I lost track of what I was saying as I flashed into the past. The villagers and soldiers had come just at dawn to set fire to Normand's stronghold and to slaughter Normand and every member of his nest, including the humans held captive. I'd waited underground for the mob to discover me, but they hadn't. They'd been high on their victory, and the governor had come then to order that each body be stripped of its riches. The adornments and anything the soldiers gathered from the ashes of the house were claimed for Spain.

"Although what, Cesca?" Triton asked.

I shrugged. "The governor took possession of the loot from the bodies, so I suppose Normand's ring is long gone."

"Be that as it may," Cosmil said, "Legrand would not have removed his ring. Not for any reason. When the body is located and forensic tests are conducted, I feel certain it will be Legrand."

"Meantime, we have Starrack and the Void on the loose," Saber said. "What can you tell us about him? Is he older? Younger? Do you look like brothers? Does he have known associates or hangouts?"

"Starrack is the younger by thirty-two years, and yes, there is a strong family resemblance. But, as I say, it was centuries ago when I last saw him. I know little of his more recent movements."

More recent being how long? I might be over two hundred myself, but I thought in years more than centuries. And Cosmil was thirty-two years older than Starrack? Geez, how old did wizards live to be anyway? And how the hell long were they fertile? Talk about a late-in-life baby.

"I do have positive news, however," Cosmil said to Saber. "After my cleanse, I phoned another Council member who will help us. Ancelia is a sorceress who had dealings with Starrack for decades."

"When will you hear from her?" I asked.

"As soon as she has made her airline reservation."

"The sorceress can't conjure a plane ticket?"

Triton swore, either at me for being flippant or at the situation in general.

"Cos, we need answers, not another musketeer."

"A Council of Ancients member has been murdered, Triton. We need every resource."

"And this woman can't pop in sooner because the Veil is closed," Saber said flatly.

"Precisely. Ancelia—Lia— must arrive the mundane way. If she cannot locate Starrack on her own, we will work on a location spell together."

"Great. Then you two can work your magick to bring him down," I said.

"Not quite, Francesca. I told you weeks ago that you and Triton needed to train with me, to combine your powers to defeat the Void. Saber will join you as well, and Lia will assist me with the training." He paused to give each of us a long, level stare. "We must be ready to act when we have the opportunity."

I gritted my teeth. "Cosmil, I'm not saying no, but you have the whole Council of Ancients at your disposal. Why can't your COA put a stop to Starrack and the Void?"

"There are too many factions, my dear. Besides vampires, wizards, and sorceresses, the thirteen Council members represent the various faerie realms, the merfolk, and the werecreatures. We even have a dragon member."

Saber stiffened. "You have werewolves in Europe?"

"And in other countries. Werewolves are extinct only in the states, you see, because the drug introduced here to kill them was not widely used overseas. The population is controlled, they live in seclusion, and they are not allowed to immigrate."

"I'll have to let the VPA know about this," Saber said.

"Do as you think best. And now," Cosmil said, as he pushed to his feet, "I have kept you long enough. Saber mentioned that Francesca has a late ghost tour, and I must rest."

"Will you be okay alone?" I asked.

"He won't be alone," Triton piped up. "I'll stay with him tonight."

Saber and I exchanged a glance, waiting for Cosmil to object. He didn't so much as furrow his brow.

"I'll come by tomorrow," Saber offered, "while Cesca's sacked out and Triton's working. Maybe you'll have news from Lia."

The three men turned to me, but I threw up my hands.

"Hey, I have work tonight, and bridge club tomorrow night. I can't cancel this late."

"So your activities are more important than training with us?" Triton demanded. "It's only all our lives on the line."

"Don't start with me, Triton. I can cancel some things, but not my maid of honor duties. Maggie's wedding is two weeks and five days away. I can't and won't let her down. This Starrack jerk and the Void will have to take a number, and you can kiss my surfboard if you don't like it."

Cosmil laughed then, a deep, rich sound that washed through the room like a warm wave. "My dear, Lia will love you. Pandora, see them out. And Triton, retrieve your duffel and the amulets from your truck."

Pandora took the lead, padding by my side while Saber fell back to have a word with Triton.

Where is the kitten?

I did a double take at her unexpected question. "You mean Snowball? Probably still hiding in the laundry room."

I'd found the pure white kitten in the parking garage at Saber's old condo in Daytona Beach, before he bought Neil's place in St. Augustine. Snowball liked me well enough, but she adored and had adopted Saber. When Saber moved in with me five days ago, Snowball came along.

There will be times to keep her close by.

"Okay, why?"

She will sense the unseen and alert you to presences.

"You told me something like that before, but I think Snowball's more into lizards and beetles."

Pandora rolled her eyes.

We arrived at Saber's SUV, and I leaned a hip against the door. "Okay, I give. Are there any particular times Snowball should be with me?"

Heed her behavior. That will forewarn you.

Well, didn't that sound nice and ominous? I have manners in spades, but the last two hours had frayed my nerves, and Pandora's queen of cryptic act wasn't scoring points with me.

She pinned me with reproachful amber eyes. Great. Pandora had read my mind, and now I was being scolded by a feline big enough to eat my face. I had to learn to guard my thoughts.

Yes, you do. Pandora smirked, I swear, then she chuffed and trotted back to the cabin.

I climbed into the SUV, suddenly very tired and completely overwhelmed.

Much as I love interior design, I adore leading ghost tours.

While catching up to the twenty-first century, I had discovered an aptitude for history, studied hard, and passed the required licensing test to give tours. It helped in my job hunt that Maggie had contacts in the city's tourist industry, but I'd earned my place at Old Coast Ghost Tours and took pride in my work as a ghost walk guide.

One of my guide friends calls me a ghost magnet, and I admit to an affinity with Oldest City's ghosts. A few spirits aren't Casper friendly, but the playful ones are always ready to *oooh* and awe the crowds.

I'd even begun flying to work occasionally, but only when I had the late tour at nine thirty, after dark when I wouldn't spook anyone. And, okay, it wasn't real vampire flying as much as it was puddle hopping. I'd take to the air long enough to clear a few houses at a time, using landmarks such as the numerous church spires and steeples and domes to track my location. Sooner or later, though, I had to look down to spot my landing, and the vertigo was murder. Heights are not my friend.

Since I didn't need more stress tonight, I'd drive. That lifted my spirits, and my mood brightened even more when I stepped into my new silvery Cinderella dress. It didn't have frou-frou trims and tucks, or a huge skirt to get in the way, but it was magical anyway. Shirley Thomas, costume genius for the Flagler College theater department, had created new tour-guide togs for me when my old ones had been shot up. I'd also hired Shirley to design and make Maggie's Victorian wedding gown, and Shirley had later surprised me with this fairy tale inspired creation.

I felt like a Disney character as I drove my beloved aqua SSR downtown. Not that bluebirds and bunnies cavorted around my skirts. Not a single industrious dwarf fell into step with me as I hustled to the waterwheel near the Mill Top Tavern where I met my tour groups. Still, I felt happier than I had all day, more so when I caught sight of the waiting tourists.

Along with half-a-dozen couples and a smattering of teens, I spotted Millie Hayward and two of her Jag Queens friends chatting with three dapper older men.

"Millie," I greeted as she enfolded me in a Shalimar-scented hug. "You and the Jag Queens looked great on TV this weekend!"

"You saw the Jacksonville game, then?" Grace Warner beamed. "I thought we looked pretty sharp myself, but my TiVo didn't record."

"Mine did," Kay Sims chimed in. "We're having a watch party tomorrow night, if you want to come, Cesca."

I grinned, imagining the clothing and hair critique that would ensue. "I'd love to, but that's my bridge night."

"Maybelle Banks is back from her cruise?" Millie asked.

I nodded. "She showed us her pictures of Greece last week."

I didn't know how Millie and Maybelle had met, but Maybelle is sixty-something, wields a dry, sharp wit, and dabbles in astrology. She and Millie must make a pair.

So did Millie and—what was her swain's name? I'd seen him once a few weeks ago but not met him.

When he cleared his throat, Millie took the hint and introduced the gentlemen.

"Cesca, this is Dan Kelley."

"Nice to meet you, Miss Cesca." Dan's full head of white hair and a tan I pegged as golf course golden made his eyes a startling shade of green.

"And these gentlemen"—Millie gestured toward two more athletic types—"are Hal Lipkin and Joel Granger."

We murmured greetings while Millie continued, "The guys couldn't get tickets to the Jaguar game, so we're treating them to the ghost tour tonight."

"Then I'll do my best to be extra entertaining," I vowed.

Dan took Millie's hand, Hal smiled at Grace, and Joel lightly touched Kay's back. Ah, mature romance!

Though at my age, I should talk about mature. Even Saber isn't quite the young stud I'd assumed he was when I met him.

As I turned away to take ticket stubs, I noticed another elderly couple staring in a size-me-up way. Wearing colorful, tourist-casual slacks, shirts, and walking shoes, they looked older than Millie, perhaps in their eighties. I worried for a moment about them traversing the uneven pavement along our route, but the man nimbly dodged a teenaged boy who nearly backed into him. Okay, the man seemed surprisingly spry. Still, I'd keep an eye out. Subtle bursts of vampire speed had helped me keep more than one tourist from taking a tumble.

I paused to speak with Carol and Nancy when I took their tickets, two special ladies who'd become known around town simply as "the sisters." They'd only been in St. Augustine a few years, but were enthusiastic community volunteers and hard-core Pittsburgh Steelers fans. Good thing they weren't wearing Steelers gear or Millie and the Jag Queen ladies might've done some trash talking.

Grinning at that image, I went to the tour substation, a wooden structure with a cabinet behind padlocked doors. I keyed the lock open, stashed the tickets stubs in a manila envelope, and grabbed my battery-operated lantern. The lantern doesn't provide much light, but it's a beacon of sorts for people to follow and part of the ghostly ambiance. The cabinet relocked, I waved my tour group closer.

"Good evening, and welcome to Old Coast Ghost Walk. I'm Cesca Marinelli, your guide. St. Augustine is regarded as one of the most haunted cities in America, and tonight we'll visit the ghosts as I tell you what we know of their history.

"Feel free to take photos and ask questions when you like, but please watch out for uneven ground as we tour."

We started by greeting Elizabeth, the redheaded teen ghost at the City Gates, then crossed the street to the Huguenot Cemetery. The group gobbled up the stories of Judge John B. Stickney and Erastus Nye, and of the Bridal Ghost when we reached the Tolomato Cemetery. We spotted orbs in both locations, too. I suspected the orbs in the Huguenot Cemetery were caused by the reflections of headlight beams, but who was I to spoil the fun?

After leading my tourist troupe through most of the square mile of the historic district, almost an hour and a half had passed, but no one seemed tired.

"Our last stop," I said as I paused before a house on a downtown side street, "is Fay's House. Now Fay might be our crankiest ghost, but she's also one of my favorites."

I relayed what I knew of Fay's life and death, and saw a hand shoot up.

"You have a question?" I asked the young man.

"Isn't this where the French Bride killer shoot-out and capture went down?"

"Yeah," another man said. "And you caught the guy, right? You're the vampire Nancy Drew."

I blushed at the reference, especially since I fervently hoped my Drew days were over, but answered the question.

"It's true I was here, but the police made the arrest."

"Have you worked any more cases since then?" the first guy asked.

The case of the vanishing vampires at the comedy club hadn't made the news. Saber had arranged a quiet cover-up, with the public blessedly none the wiser. I wasn't about to change that, so I waved off the question.

"The papers exaggerated. I'm more interested in mystery reading than mystery solving any day."

"You're being far too modest," Millie put in. "Our guide is also a whiz at interior decorating."

Which Millie knew because she'd seen my place during the house-warming in August. I smiled and thanked Millie, and caught the strange old couple suddenly beaming at me like I'd created a cure for cancer. Talk about easily impressed.

I led my group back to our starting place near the waterwheel, ran through my closing spiel, and turned to put my lantern away as the group dispersed.

Except for Millie who edged closer on a Shalimar cloud.

"Cesca, dear, do you have a minute?"

"Of course," I said as she darted a gaze over her shoulder.

The rest of her party stood ten feet away chatting easily, so why did Millie look frightened?

When she didn't speak up, I moved deeper into the shadow of a towering pink bougainvillea.

"What's wrong, Millie?"

She stepped closer. "Did Maybelle Banks say anything special to you at bridge club last week?'

"Not that I remember. Why?"

Millie bit her lip, and now I was thoroughly mystified.

"It's silly, really, but she said she'd do my astrology chart to see how compatible I am with Dan."

"And she forgot to do it?"

"Oh, no, she did it, and it turned out quite wonderfully. The thing is, I asked her to do your chart as an anniversary gift from me."

I blinked. I'd celebrated my first anniversary out of the coffin on August thirteenth, but Millie hadn't given me an astrology chart.

Millie straightened and gave me a rueful smile. "I'm making too much of it, I'm sure. Astrology is fun, but it's not a science, right?"

"Millie, what is it you're trying so hard not to tell me?"

"It-it's just that Maybelle said she did your chart three times and had very odd results," Millie said in a rush. "That's why I got you a different gift."

"Odd results how?"

Millie gnawed on her lip again, looked over her shoulder again, and finally spit it out.

"My dear, you disappeared entirely from your own chart."

By the time I soothed Millie, promised to be careful, and sent her off with Dan and the rest of her party, it was nearly eleven thirty. I set off for the Cordova parking lot where I'd parked, taking the Orange Street route. The walk took me past the oldest drugstore, the Love Tree, and the Tolomato Cemetery, but I paid no attention to the hovering ghosts. Instead I thought about how I could rearrange my schedule once Cosmil's friend Lia hit town.

Thursday Maggie and I had a meeting with the florist and a cake tasting. Friday we were leaving to meet Maggie's friends in Fernandina Beach for the bachelorette weekend. Amelia Island was less than two hours north if the traffic was with us, and was convenient for her Florida and southern Georgia friends. The weekend was a must do, no room for negotiation.

If Lia arrived before Sunday, Triton and Saber would just have to start training without me. I'd allow nothing, no one, no how to stand between me and—

"Aaarrrggh!"

I squealed at the man suddenly looming in my path. He smelled like jalapenos and cheap cigars. My very own stalker, Victor Gorman.

"Surprised you, huh?"

I hadn't seen him since he'd tried to kill me. Or was it when we caught him breaking into a hotel room? Didn't matter. Between his bad breath and his gravely voice, ripe with malicious overtones, my last nerve threatened to snap.

"Gorman, what now?"

"What were those two vampires doin' on your tour?"

I blinked. "What two vampires?"

"The old, wrinkled couple."

Did he mean the ones who'd stared at me?

"Gorman, those people had to be eighty."

"So? I saw 'em fly off."

I reached for patience. "You actually saw them levitate and zoom away into the night?"

"They were there on the sidewalk, then they weren't. Old people don't move that fast."

"And vamps don't just disappear. They also don't Turn senior citizens."

He narrowed his eerie light blue eyes. "Why not?"

"Because there's nothing to gain. No power, no prestige, no money."

"That's it. Money. Vampires could steal old codgers blind."

"Vamps could enthrall them to do that."

He frowned, and I could almost see the wheels *thunk* in his brain. How Gorman got into the Covenant, I'd never understand. Originally a search-and-destroy-vampires group, the Covenant had now scaled back to watch and report to the VPA. At least the St. Augustine branch had, and two of the Covenant members I'd met were relatively pleasant. The most pleasant thing about Gorman was that, tonight at least, he didn't also reek of garlic.

I moved to step around him, but he blocked me.

"I'm warnin' you, don't bring no more of your kind into town."

That did it. The slow fizzle of my temper flared.

"Gorman, listen up. Knock off the threats and corny lines. You don't impress me, and you don't scare me. I'm sorry if some vampire did you or your family wrong, but it wasn't me, and I'm tired of taking the crap for it."

This time I stormed past him, only to stop when I heard him say, "You're wrong, bitch. You started it all."

When I spun to challenge him, he'd melted into the shadows.

FIVE

~

I thought about Gorman's comment for about five minutes on the way home then dismissed it. For one thing, he had shadowed me, threatened me, and generally annoyed me for months. Even his attempt to kill me with a well-aimed shot from a crossbow had angered more than frightened me. His antics were old news.

For another thing, I had bigger concerns, which came into sharp relief when I opened my cottage door. Snowball, the four-pound rescue cat, flew across the floor headed straight for me with Pandora in her twenty-pound house cat form smack on Snowball's tail. Snowball dove under my full skirts and a beat later thudded into the wall behind me. Pandora braked at my feet, morphed to her panther size in time-lapse-photography style, and calmly lifted and licked a dinner-plate-sized paw.

Then I saw Saber from the corner of my eye. He sat at my laptop housed in the computer cabinet tucked into an alcove in my living room. A few keystrokes later, he swiveled to face me.

I huffed a breath and dropped my car keys on the entry table. "What's going on?"

"Pandora brought a message from Triton."

I stared. "You're talking to the animals now?"

Pandora sat on her haunches and gave me a "you're a moron" gaze. Snowball, now at Pandora's side, mirrored the pose as if mimicking an adored older sibling.

"The note was in her collar," Saber clarified as he swung back to the computer screen.

I'd never seen Pandora wear a collar, and she wasn't sporting one now, but I let that pass.

"So what was the message?"

"Cosmil is better, but no word on when Lia will arrive."

"Why didn't Triton just call?"

"Maybe because he didn't want Cosmil to overhear him on the phone." He punched a key and swiveled back to me. "I asked him to get the names of the other Council of Ancients members."

"Ah, you're searching for anyone suspicious."

"Yeah, but I'm getting less than nothing."

"No handy-dandy COA website, huh?"

Saber and Pandora snorted in unison, and Snowball sneezed.

I ignored all three of them. "Do you know anything about astrology?"

"Why?"

"Oh, I saw Millie tonight," I said, waving away the question and my concern. "She brought it up. I talked to Gorman, too."

"You what?" Saber pushed out of the desk chair. "Did he have a weapon? That order of protection against him is still in force. We can lock him up for a damn-long time if you report the contact."

I held up a hand. "No weapons and I don't want to file a complaint. Gorman is imagining a vampire invasion again. He thinks he saw a couple of eighty-year-olds fly."

"You're kidding."

"Could I make that up?"

"I can't decide if Gorman is an idiot, a paranoid idiot, or an idiot on some seriously disturbing drugs." He pulled me into his arms and nuzzled my neck. "Did I mention I like this dress on you?"

"I believe you said you'd like it better off me."

His cobalt eyes darkened, and his sexy smile smoldered me to my toes.

"I do."

The moment hung suspended until Pandora chuffed.

Time for me to go.

"Downsize so you won't freak the neighbors," I warned as I opened the door.

She did and slipped out. Derived of her playmate, Snowball twitched her tail and headed for the kitchen.

I batted my eyelashes and sashayed into Saber's embrace.

"Now where were we?"

Within the space of a long, deep sigh, he stripped me of my Cinderella dress and carried us to our own fantasyland.

The afterglow of our loving should have been beacon bright, but I found myself crying softly.

Saber must've felt my tears on his chest, because he turned me over and wiped my damp cheek with his thumb.

"Hey, was I that bad?"

"No, that good. Like you were before your trip."

"So these are tears of sexual ecstasy?"

I gave him a watery chuckle, but my voice caught as I whispered, "Deke, I can't lose you."

"You won't," he said, nestling me to his side. "We're going to beat this. We have a prime suspect now, and that's more than we had this afternoon."

"What if we can't find and destroy Starrack? Or get to him before the Void cuts loose to do its own thing?"

"I contacted Jim Crushman in Atlanta. Crusher will put out the word through the merc network, and they'll contact their informants."

I pulled back enough to blink at him. "Mercenaries have informants?"

"Human and supernatural. Gnomes mostly, but I can't mention a particular group. Triton's note said Cosmil is making inquiries through his contacts, too." He hugged me close. "If all else fails, we have to hope Lia can track Starrack."

"Or the Void."

"Or both." He kissed my forehead. "Now remind me what you have scheduled with Maggie so I can help you work around your old-maid duties."

"Old maid?" I echoed with a playful punch to his ribs.

"You are a whopping 228 years of age."

"Don't make me hurt you."

"Tell me."

"We have the caterer, the florist, and the cake-tasting meetings tomorrow and Thursday, then the bachelorette get away to Fernandina Beach is Friday evening to Sunday afternoon. And isn't Neil's bachelor party Saturday night?"

"Mmm," he murmured, and kissed my temple.

A lingering kiss that migrated to my cheek.

I cleared my throat. "Then I have the bridal shower here next Saturday."

"Uh-huh," he breathed in my ear.

"And the couples shower and barbeque is Sunday at your hou-howza."

His next kiss landed in a place that robbed me of speech, robbed me of coherent thought, and rewarded me with joy.

* * *

An hour later, Saber slept. I lingered beside him for a while, basking in a sated stupor. Our joining might have been better than normal, but I'd keep diligent watch for signs of the illness. And pray I never saw them. I would not want to live with the horror of that sight.

Snowball jumped on the bed and curled herself around Saber's head, which was my cue to get up, toss on a nightshirt, and get to work.

After hanging my costume in the closet, I made a beeline to the living room to work at my laptop. First I read over the list of Council of Ancients members Saber had left on the desk. Hmmm. No wonder he hadn't found these folks. With names like Gandolph the Seer and Grover the Elf, the only sites that came up in my own search were for *The Lord of the Rings* and fantasy pages.

Next, just because I felt like it, I used Saber's VPA pass codes to access the private areas of the VPA site. There was zip info on the COA period and not much on the Void, other than a warning that vampires were falling ill and what their symptoms might include. Guess Saber wasn't fibbing about the VPA being clueless about tracking the Void. Heck, maybe the COA truly didn't know about the Void or about Starrack being rogue, either, unless Cosmil had alerted them.

With those searches done, Millie's concern about Maybelle's reading of my astrology chart nagged at me. True, Maybelle was a dabbler, not an expert, but the woman knew her stuff. If she mentioned something amiss to Millie, it wasn't an idle comment.

I'd see Maybelle tomorrow night at bridge club, but whether I'd have the privacy to ask her about my chart was iffy. Instead of stewing, I opted to be proactive. I plugged "astrology charts" into Google and turned up over two million results. Not helpful. I typed in "astrology charts disappearing from yours" and got over a hundred thousand listings. I refined the search to "disappearing from your own astrology chart" and got just over twenty-three thousand results, but they all dealt with habits and addictions not disappearing on their own. Duh.

I eyed the sites in the right column and spotted two astrologers who advertised free answers to short questions. What the heck. I shot each of them a note. Never hurts to see what one can get gratis.

Not that I'm a miser, mind you. I'm merely cautious with my money. The treasure that had been secreted in the false bottom of my coffin—or rather the French vampire King Normand's coffin— wouldn't last without good management. I'd shared some of the loot with Maggie and Neil, sold a few pieces for capital, and invested. I also had my earnings from tour guiding, but I had expenses just like everyone else.

And, okay, I could shop my checkbook into the grave if I wasn't careful. Yep, I'm a part day-walking, all night-stalking vampire, and my favorite prey is a bargain at Walmart. However, I'd learned the hard way that, if you find a goody you want in a St. Augustine shop, you'd best buy it on the spot. It will be gone when you go back, and it won't be restocked.

I'd also learned that St. Augustine businesses appear to operate in a different dimension. If you get what you want three weeks late, you got it a month early. That's why I put those extra tables and chairs on reserve with the rental company from the get-go.

Which reminded me, I had a list of wedding chores to make. Call rental company. Order more centerpieces from florist. Talk with Daphne about making the wedding cake bigger or ordering a second groom's cake.

By the time I tucked the list in my binder, my backlog of interior design homework didn't just beckon for attention, it bellowed. I buckled down and spent the next six hours finishing the projects due, plus the next weeks' worth as well.

Snowball grumbled when I finally crawled into bed. Saber decidedly did not. Yep, the Saber I knew and loved was back.

* * *

Wednesday bridge club is a mixed bag of nuts, as Shelly Jergason likes to say. She's the one who invited me to the group after we met at the historical society and I mentioned I was learning bridge online. No big stretch since bridge evolved from whist, but it was a boon to be accepted into the group. The two-table club includes youthful seniors, Maybelle and Shelly, and middle-aged movers and shakers, real estate agent Jenna Jones and perennial chairwoman Nadine Houseman. Our youngest members are artist Kathy Baker and elementary school teacher Missy Cox.

And, of course, our pastry chef for Maggie's wedding, Daphne Dupree. We didn't talk wedding shop at bridge club, though. Jenna held a grudge that she hadn't been hired to sell Maggie's condo.

The dress code is casual, so I wore black cargo pants and a white scoop neck T-shirt. We met at Kathy's home in the Shores, socializing and admiring her new paintings from six thirty to seven then playing cards from seven until nine on the dot. About halfway into the evening, Maybelle and I both happened to be dummies and in the kitchen alone. I hesitated only a moment before I took the plunge.

"Millie told me you did an astrology chart for me last month."

"Yes, for the anniversary of your coming out. I'd never run one quite so interesting." She turned away to pour herself a cup of decaf coffee and motioned me closer. "I admit that the results surprised me enough that I consulted a more experienced astrologer I trust."

"Millie said I disappeared from my own chart, but I don't think that's possible, is it?"

"Not in the way you're thinking, but there is a rather major transit coming up for you."

"Which means what?"

Maybelle leaned a hip against the granite countertop. "A transit is a transition. A crossroad, if you will. It's a time when life challenges may change you so much that you're nearly unrecognizable as the person you are now."

The Void. Starrack. Maid of honor. Gee, pick a challenge. A shiver snaked up my spine.

Maybelle patted my arm. "It's not necessarily a bad thing, Cesca. Certainly, it's no death knell. No more so than when the death card turns up in a tarot card reading."

Death card? That wasn't comforting.

"Maybelle, give it to me straight. Should I be concerned about this transit or not?"

She looked away and bit her lip, reflexive actions of a millisecond that took a dozen years off my afterlife.

"Transits can be tough, and this one could be a bear. You'll have hard choices to make, and you should be careful in the next few weeks."

That spine shiver became a full-body shudder. "But the transit will only affect me, right?"

The straw I grasped for dissolved when Maybelle grimaced.

"To be blunt, Cesca, I advise you to guard yourself and everyone around you. I may only be a dabbler, but my sense is that you're in danger."

Flipping pink flamingos. Like my life wasn't complicated enough?

With that grand slam of cheery news, it was no wonder the next hour of bridge passed in a blur. Only Jenna bitched at me for making a bad play, but it was a good thing I'd be calling to cancel out of bridge for a few weeks. That would distance me from some of the people I cared about. I didn't have specific plans to see Millie and the Jag Queens, so maybe they'd be out of the line of transit fire.

As for Maggie and Neil, I'd just have to do my best to keep them safe.

Then again, I doubted Starrack or the Void would be gunning for humans. Something to ask Cosmil next time I saw him.

I considered then rejected discussing Maybelle's revelations with

Saber. What could he say to reassure me? Nada. When the time came, I'd do my damnedest to protect everyone I loved.

Meantime, I detoured to Barnes and Noble en route home. The Kathys, Beth, and Brad were off for the night, but Jane helped me find an astrology-for-morons book, and I joked with Kristina as she checked me out.

I pulled onto the parking pad Maggie had included in the renovation plans. It wasn't precisely a period-correct restoration touch, but Maggie's property spanned two lots. She'd given up some side yard square footage to build a two-car garage and the additional parking space for me, melding the architecture so the small addition looked as if it had always been there.

As I trotted across the front yard toward the side gate, my vampire hearing picked up voices. Not Maggie and Neil, or even the neighbors. No, it wasn't yet ten o'clock, but most of the neighborhood already slept in the steamy, starry night.

What I heard were the voices of Grant and Jason of *Ghost Hunter* fame, coming from my cottage. Saber and I loved the show, but he had the volume awfully high, vampire hearing notwithstanding.

The lights were off in the front of the house, too. Only that weird television light flickered in the window. The side window toward the back of the house was softly lit, as if by a bedside lamp. Maybe Saber had something planned for me. Like sharing my made-for-two jetted bathtub. Surrounded by candlelight. Yep, that sounded like heaven.

With anticipation singing and parts of me zinging, I hurried to the door and turned the knob.

Only to have the door jerk open under my hand.

I half stumbled, half flew across the threshold, right into a forearm that clamped around my throat.

SIX

~

Shock and fear paralyzed me for a split second before self-preservation surged. The defense training Saber had drilled into me kicked in, and I went for a countermove that should have thrown a normal attacker through the wall.

Instead, the thing ramped up the crushing force at my neck and wrapped an iron band around my rib cage.

The television blared on as my attacker squeezed my body like a blacksmith's bellows. Fear bled into panic. I gripped and pulled on the arm crushing my larynx. Squirmed and kicked backward, hoping to hit a tender body part, but connected with a coquinalike wall of mass.

Had this thing killed Saber? Was it Starrack? The Void in a new form? If I were to have a prayer of saving Saber or anyone else, I had to save myself.

Then I remembered my secret weapon. Pulling auras.

Fighting to stay conscious, I narrowed my focus to sucking energy. Not taking delicate sips to sustain my life force as when I was buried in the coffin. I imaged thrusting my hand into the mass imprisoning me and pulling its life force inside out.

My attacker didn't drop like a stone, but the pressure at my neck slackened. When it did, I shouted a raw and raspy karate *kiai* and sank my teeth into the meaty arm. My attacker only grunted, but the wavering image of Saber and another figure appeared, backlit in the bedroom doorway.

"*Por los dioses*, Tower. Stop. Let her go."

Ray's voice, I realized as more oxygen flowed to my brain, and he advanced close enough for me to dimly see him. Saber reached for the small of his back where he kept his .40-caliber Glock in his waistband. The safety clicked off.

"Stop, Tower," Ray repeated. "It is the Princess. Francesca."

Tower, the pro-basketball-tall vampire from the former Daytona Beach nest, relaxed his grip another fraction but didn't let go.

"Princess Vampire?" Tower's voice rumbled in my ear, and his rancid breath turned my stomach.

"It's me," I croaked. "Let go. Please."

"No," he growled. "You won't trick me."

"It is no trick," Ray said, stepping closer. "The Princess and Saber will kill the thing that is making us sick, but you must release her."

"Tower," Saber said as he moved to the right and raised his weapon. "Let her go, or I will put a silver bullet in the center of your forehead."

The clock in my head ticked tense seconds. Tower still held me, but I felt his indecision. It helped that I continued to siphon his energy and that his hold had relaxed a little more. I took the chance of revealing my dark vampire secret.

"Saber, don't shoot Tower," I rasped. "You know the smell of blood makes me sick, and I don't want two messes to clean up."

The shock value worked.

Tower's arm fell away from my neck, and Ray jerked me out of reach. Saber caught me, his weapon still trained.

The huge vampire tilted his head at me. "You don't savor the aroma of rich, fresh blood, Princess?"

I straightened, stepped from Saber's loose embrace. "I don't, Tower. The stench of blood makes me gag."

"Truly?"

"Sorry to blow my image, but 'fraid so."

Tower looked over my head toward the bedroom door, contemplating the weirdness of my weak stomach—or the weekend's Florida Gators game, for all I knew or cared.

Ray put himself between his vampire and me. "Are you well, Princess?"

I nodded, bent to snag the remote, and silenced the TV.

"Now that I can hear myself think, what the blazes is going on? And why are the lights off in here?"

I turned to switch on a lamp but stopped at the tone of Ray's voice.

"Do not, Princess, I beg you."

I glanced at Saber's shadowed face. He nodded. "Leave it, Cesca."

"Okay, but tell me what's going on."

"It is *la oscuridad*," Ray answered. "The darkness is draining my people."

"Saber told me the Void had been sapping your energy."

"But it has grown worse. Far worse." He raked a hand through hair I knew to be thick and black. "It is disfiguring us now."

My stomach roiled and breath caught in my abused throat. Ray looked and sounded enough like Antonio Banderas to fire a million fantasies. Then there were the other vampires in the former Daytona nest, now all joint owners in Club Hot Blooded. Cheerleader-pert Suzy, and tall, severe Zena. Middle-aged-looking Coach, and the married couple, Miranda and Charles. If they were each shriveling to shells, their features growing gaunt and discolored—

I broke off the thought with a shudder.

"I came to tell Saber," Ray said, "that I am temporarily closing the club and dispersing my vampires. Tower insisted on guarding me tonight, but I did not expect him to attack you. It is part of the illness, Princess. *Un efecto secundario.*"

"A side effect. I understand, Ray. I'm not angry with Tower, but where are you all going?"

He shrugged. "Underground. Saber may explain further if he wishes, but we must go. "

Ray turned toward Tower and jerked his head toward the door, but paused to face us again.

"This evil will not stop feeding on us. It is voracious, and humans will be next on the menu. I beg you, Princess. *Vaya con la luz* and triumph."

Go with the light? Brilliant idea. Too bad our merry little band of Void hunters had only a bare glimmer in the dark to go on.

The door clicked softly, but the snick of Saber's Glock as he put the safety on seemed to echo. So did the sigh he exhaled.

I turned to find him carefully placing his weapon on the coffee table.

"Cesca, I'm sorry. I should have listened more closely. I should have heard you come in."

Without a word, I walked into his arms. The first kiss was a light brush of our lips. The second kiss deepened, a playful dueling of lips and teeth and tongues until Saber hauled me closer. I felt his desperation then and held him tight, reassuring him through touch.

I'm here. I'm fine. I love you.

Saber broke the kiss and buried his face in my hair, his breathing as labored as if he'd run a marathon.

"God, when I saw that Tower had you. He could have ripped your head off in a second, and I—"

"Deke, stop. It's over. I admit I had a fright, but my defenses kicked in. I could've pulled Tower's aura harder if I'd had to."

He released me enough to give me a level stare. "You don't hold back when you're in danger. Ever. Especially not now when we're going up against Starrack and the Void. Understood?"

"Got it."

"Good. Now lie on the sofa while I get the first aid kit."

"Let me see your neck again," Saber said half an hour later as he leaned over me.

From my reclining position, propped up by cushy throw pillows on the sofa, I removed the ice gel pack he'd insisted I use and let him inspect the damage. Or lack thereof. My tussle with Tower had left bruises, but they had bloomed and faded ten minutes into the cold-pack treatment. Still, it was sweet of Saber to coddle me. It gave him something to do besides continuing to rail at himself for failing to hear me come home.

The living room lamps blazed bright, but he squinted at my neck for any lingering discoloration.

"Saber, you're acting like a vampire searching for the choicest place to bite me. It's creepy."

He quirked a grin, but it didn't reach his eyes. "I think you need another bottle of Starbloods. Just to be sure you're healing internally."

"Gag, no. One a day is enough. What I need," I said as I levered upright, "is to know what Ray said."

Saber sat beside me and gathered me in his arms.

"You don't want to know how he looked?"

I tilted my head to see his expression. "How bad?"

"His skin is two shades darker and lined like a road map. The younger vampires are in worse shape."

Bile rose at the image. God, what would I do if Saber's gorgeous Latino skin began to blacken and shrivel? I resolutely push the thought away.

"You think he and the others will survive?"

Saber scooted deeper into the cushions and dropped his head against the sofa back. "I don't know, Cesca. Even if they do, the effects of the life force drain may not be reversible."

I snuggled closer, my head on his chest. "Are he and his crew going underground figuratively or literally?"

"Literally. Ray's heard on the undead grapevine that the illness slows in vampires who live in basements, so he's going one better. He's moving the crew deep into caverns."

"In Florida?"

"West of Tallahassee."

"Huh. Hope he has mega cases of bottled blood to take."

"He has enough, but he's also taking the blood bunnies."

I pushed upright and stared at Saber's somber expression. Blood bunnies were groupies and donators, and the three I knew of were romantically involved with some of Ray's vampires. But surely he wasn't forcing them to go.

"He's not," Saber said.

"Not what?"

"Not forcing the blood bunnies."

"You're reading my mind?"

"Your face. They volunteered to go, and I approved the plan."

"Simple as that? Don't those women have jobs and families?"

"Families not so much, from what I know. I assume they've taken leave or vacation time from jobs." He shrugged. "They may be young, but they're legal adults, Cesca."

"True." The blood bunny I'd had a fondness for, the lisping Cici, had cut her ties with the Daytona Beach vampires even before Ray took over. She'd moved to St. Augustine, was attending a local college, and worked at Walmart.

"Look at the upside. The bunnies can make grocery and Starbloods runs, thus protecting the public."

"The bunnies can also notify the VPA of any deaths."

"True," he said. "And best of all, their vampire lovers won't go through the illness alone."

Neither will you, I silently vowed, and cupped his cheek in my palm. "Saber, you're such a romantic."

He waggled his dark brows and pulled me close again. "Any fantasies I can fulfill while the night is still young? A candlelit bath, perhaps?"

I levered away and gave him my best intense stare. "Are you sure you don't read my mind?"

"Only as much as you read mine."

With that and an enigmatic grin, he rose and strolled into the bedroom. The faucets roared with water a moment later, so I locked the door, reset the alarm, and joined Saber. With candlelight flickering on the glass tiled walls of my art deco bathroom, the swirl of warm, scented water in the jetted tub, and my man both relaxing me into a rag and stimulating me to passion, I never did puzzle out if he was reading my mind or not.

I found Saber's note on the turquoise 1950s retro kitchen table the next afternoon. He wrote that he'd gone to Cosmil's and would see me after my ghost tour for some more quality time before I took off for the bachelorette weekend in Fernandina Beach. He'd also programmed Triton's and Cosmil's cell numbers into my phone. What a guy.

If you're wondering why a design student has an art deco bathroom, a retro kitchen, a surfer-chic bedroom, and a British-colonial living room, it's because I'd gone period mad when I decorated. However, since most of the period flavor was in the accessories, the décor could be easily changed if and when I ever moved out of the cottage and into a place truly my own.

I didn't think about Saber and I moving in together. At least I hadn't until this past week when he'd camped out with me. After coming home to an empty house during those weeks he was on the road, I admitted that having him to myself every night was tempting.

Did I have wedding fever?

I pondered that as I dressed in black shorts and a lime green T-shirt, and with my hair in a ponytail, my feet in black sandals, I headed out to meet Maggie at Daphne Dupree's store, Beach Bake. The shop was located on the island near Dondanville Road, so I avoided the downtown route in favor of taking US 1 to the 312 bridge, then heading south on A1A. The same direction we'd taken to Cosmil's place on Tuesday.

Maggie wore business casual and gave me a broad grin as I exited my SSR. "Things really are back to normal with you and Saber, huh?"

"How can you tell?"

"You're glowing."

"Only pregnant women and people exposed to way too much radiation glow, Maggie."

"And women getting great sex."

"Okay, if women glow, what do men do?"

"If they know what's good for them, they keep doing their women right."

I shook my head. "Good thing you're getting married."

"Isn't it?" she countered brightly. "Plus it's the perfect excuse to gorge myself with chocolate."

Once inside, we didn't limit ourselves to chocolate. Lemon, coconut, strawberry, and banana cakes made an appearance at the tasting table. I stuck to savoring nibbles. Maggie groaned in ecstasy over whole slices. Small slices, true, but I don't know where she put all that cake.

Daphne was clearly delighted that every sample met with our approval, and beamed over our final order that included a second chocolate groom's cake and a banana coconut sheet cake with coconut icing. Daphne talked Maggie out of a lemon cake but promised three-dozen lemon tarts on the house and agreed to add another layer to the traditional wedding cake to be decorated in a Victorian motif.

I faithfully recorded the order in my maid of honor binder, while Maggie insisted on paying Daphne in full. I wasn't surprised since she'd done the same with the caterer on Wednesday. The florist and rental company had three-quarter payments down, with the balance to be paid before the ceremony.

Maggie was nothing if not efficient.

We chatted outside for a few minutes after the tasting. I started to tell her that I'd seen Triton and made peace with my memories. Maggie knew all about my early years and even knew Triton was a shifter. But Maggie had an appointment with the photographer, so I let it go.

I'd turned my cell off during the taste test but had no messages from Saber when I checked at a stoplight. I had the early ghost-tour shift tonight, a special one with a book club from Palm Coast. I wore my emerald empire-waist gown, one fashioned to evoke the English Regency period, and decided to take the group on a slightly longer tour.

We visited Elizabeth at the City Gates, the characters at the Huguenot and Tolomato cemeteries, dropped by Fay's House, then headed to the bay front and Casa de la Paz.

"There are several versions of this story," I told my tourists when we stood across the avenue from the house, "but here is the one I like best. In the early 1900s, a young woman I'll call Philla came to St. Augustine to recuperate from an illness. Here she met a young man who had also come to town for his health. Let's say he's James. Well,

Philla and James resided here, in the same boardinghouse, where they eventually fell in love and planned to marry.

"The day before they were to leave, James insisted on going fishing against Philla's wishes. A storm blew up and James drowned. Heartsick, Philla's health worsened until she finally died in the boardinghouse, alone and in mourning for James. Now she wanders the halls or waits on the staircase, valise in hand, asking if it's time to leave."

"Is she the bride spirit at the Tolomato cemetery?" a lady asked.

"No, that's a different ghost. Philla isn't seen outside Casa de la Paz as far as I know."

"Then who's that standing on the porch?" another woman asked.

We all turned to stare, and sure enough, a woman in a period traveling outfit, complete with a hat and valise, stood on the wide porch. She seemed to gaze toward the Matanzas Bay inlet, then looked directly at my group before she turned toward the house and vanished.

My group and I exchanged wide glances, and I admit to having chills and a tear in my eye. I love it when our ghosts surprise me and give my tourists an experience to remember.

I bid my group farewell at the waterwheel, stowed my lantern, and headed to the office to check out and remind Candice I would be out of town over the weekend. I also mentioned needing time off the next few weeks.

"The wedding?" she asked.

I merely smiled.

She nodded sagely. "That maid of honor gig is a killer."

I laughed and waved and stepped out of the office onto St. George Street not looking where I was going. I ran full force into Saber.

"Thank God I found you," he said in a rush, his hands on my shoulders to steady us both. "We need to get to Cosmil's."

My gut tensed. "Has he been hurt again?"

"Not yet. The Council of Ancients headquarters has been attacked, and Cosmil is frantic that we're next on the hit list."

SEVEN

~

"Fill me in on the attack," I said once we were speeding south on US 1 toward 206 and the turn off to Cosmil's place.

Not that my first reaction had been so sedate. No, my mouth had gone dry, I'd gripped Saber's hands, and I'd scanned the sidewalk for magical assassins. Hell, I'd even looked skyward as if expecting an air strike by Oz's flying monkeys. I'd been that spooked by Saber's blunt announcement. At this rate, I'd be the only vampire on the planet with chronic high blood pressure.

Calmer now, I listened as Saber answered me without taking his eyes off the road.

"You know the Council is in an uproar over Legrand's murder and the body disappearing. Well, the members closed the local portals, but what they didn't do—or didn't do well enough—was put protection around the compound."

"The compound is a physical place?"

"Yeah, in Chambery in the French Alps. The members stay there while they hold meetings, and an administrative and support staff of both supernaturals and mortals live there permanently. According to Cosmil, the compound was hit by the magical equivalent of a terrorist bomb."

"Oh, God." My heart clenched, and dread churned in my stomach. "Was anyone hurt? Lia?"

"Lia's all right, but three humans are dead, and a fairy and werewolf are in critical condition."

"Those poor souls. This is the work of Starrack and the Void, I take it."

"Cosmil thinks so. Lia is staying over the weekend to help secure the place and unite the Council as much as she can. She'll fly Air France to New York City on Monday and take a charter to the St. Augustine airport."

The new moon was Monday. Or was it Sunday? Whenever, Triton shifted at the dark of the moon and usually needed a day to recuperate afterward. Or had in the old days.

"Triton will be shifting about then, so you and I will pick up Lia."

I startled. "Reading my expression again?"

In the glare of a streetlight, I caught Saber's grin. "No, Triton is the one who called about the attack. He mentioned shifting."

"Ah. So what does Cosmil expect to accomplish in this mini council meeting with us?"

"Circling the wagons? Casting protection spells? Triton didn't say, but whatever it is, it's fine by me. I'm not taking any chances, especially with you leaving town."

The dark of the moon might be only a few days away, but the area all around Cosmil's shack was washed in an unearthly, dusky glow.

Which made it easy to see Triton where he stood sentry on Cosmil's shabby porch. He was barefoot, had his arms folded, and wore cutoffs, a dark T-shirt, and a scowl. A lock of hair feathered over his forehead in the light night breeze, but it didn't make him look less ticked.

I lifted the hem of my gown to avoid getting grass stains and opened my mouth to greet Triton. He riled me before I was halfway across the yard.

"You are not leaving for the weekend."

"Hide and watch me, bub," I tossed back.

"It's too dangerous."

"I'm a big, bad vampire, Triton. I'll live."

"Maybe, but what about Maggie and the other women?"

"I'm already the designated driver. I'll take care of them."

"You're a pig-headed pain in the ass."

"Only when you're wrong."

"Children!" Cosmil's voice lashed from the far side of his shack.

I whirled to see the wizard wearing a royal blue robe over another outfit of white pants and a tunic. He must buy his duds in bulk.

"Ah, silence," he said as he strode to meet me. "Now I may concentrate. Francesca, has Saber told you why you are here?"

"He said there was an attack on the COA and you're concerned we're the next target."

"Protection spells are in order, yes, but you must also learn to use the amulet. In however rudimentary a manner."

I stiffened, but not in revulsion or fear, not of the amulet itself anyway. I remembered the warm pulse of the amulet, how simply *right* it had felt in my hand. Problem was, I knew what the amulet could do, so it was like a loaded gun. One I didn't want to aim, never mind fire.

"The amulet is a defensive tool as well as an offensive one, Francesca. It can hurt, but it can also heal. I would not put it in your hands if I thought you were not ready."

I wasn't surprised he'd read my thoughts. Annoyed, yes, but then it seemed every man in my life read me.

And, okay, I might've huffed a bit as I asked, "What if I learn just enough to be dangerous?"

"That shall not happen. The amulet responds to intent, you see." He eyed me. "Or perhaps you do not, but you will. Now, come, all of you. Francesca and Saber, remove your shoes. We have a ceremony to conduct and spells to spin."

"You need a ceremony to cast spells?"

"The ceremony is to bind our energies more tightly to one another."

I thought I was already pretty darned bonded, except maybe to Cosmil, but I didn't object. Saber took my hand as we trailed after Cosmil. Triton walked at my other side, and Pandora emerged from the tree line to our right. When we reached the center of the perfect circle of trees, Cosmil stopped beside a carved wooden box placed in the short, springy grass.

"Triton, you stand in the east," Cosmil directed. "Pandora, the south. Francesca, Saber, take the west and north."

We moved into the cardinal positions, me in the west, automatically adjusting our places to be equally distant from Cosmil in the center. Seven feet, I heard in my head and in my own voice. As if I'd been here, done this—or something like this—before.

Cosmil nodded his approval and bent over the box. He passed both hands over the lid—one clockwise, one counter—and mumbled a few words under his breath. A tingle of magick ran along my arms, and I jumped a little when I heard the lock on the box click. Then he opened the lid and lifted a rounded object wrapped in silver-shimmer fabric. Energy prickled across the back of my neck and trickled down my spine as he mumbled again and peeled away the cloth to reveal an honest-to-wizard crystal ball.

Or was it crystal? I sharpened my vampire vision and looked closer. Reflections danced over the sphere's surface, like a glass gazing ball in a garden. Whatever the material, my breath caught when

Cosmil let the fabric flutter into the open box, cupped the sphere in both hands, and raised it over his head.

"Powers of the East," Cosmil intoned, his voice suddenly a booming bass in surround sound as he faced Triton. "Illuminate the future and our path in it as you illuminate each day. Let us learn from our experiences and be continually renewed."

A shaft of white light shone over Triton for one long second. Then Cosmil turned to Pandora.

"Powers of the South, aid us in our growth and strength so that we may clear our paths of obstructions and face the challenges before us."

In the ball, I saw Pandora's reflection, but she stood in a meadow of tall grass and wildflowers. Had she teleported? Been beamed away? Or was she still sitting on her haunches on my right? I didn't have time to sort the images because Cosmil captured my gaze.

"Powers of the West, knowledge and growth thrive in the womb of introspection, of the waking and sleeping dreamtime. Let our visions birth pure intention and decisive action."

Pictures bloomed in my mind, snapshots in a vortex, swirling too fast to identify but vibrating with sound and color and emotion. I tried to slow the slide show, only to feel a cocoon enfold me. Was I still standing? Curled in a cradling cloud? Didn't matter.

I thought I heard Saber shout, but Cosmil's voice boomed over it. "Powers of the North, you wear the mantle of age and experience. Bring us the wisdom to guide our actions for the highest good."

In my muzzy vision, Saber's hair looked snowy white for a millisecond.

Now Cosmil chanted. Not in a language I knew to speak or read or truly comprehend, but some ancient part of me recognized its cadence. A waterspout of blues and greens and whites lazily rose around Cosmil with each note of the ancestor's song. I listened and drifted, seeing Cosmil and Pandora, Saber and Triton through a baffle. Seeing the sphere levitate from the wizard's hands to hover tree-top high. Seeing sunshiny rays of light play over our circle. Through it all, I stayed suspended in my cocoon, content to appreciate and wait.

Full awareness slammed into me when someone shook my shoulder. I blinked up at Saber's face.

Up? Why the hell was I flat on the ground?

I jackknifed into a sitting position so fast that I nearly bumped heads with Saber. Good thing his not-quite-humanness gave him great reflexes.

"Steady," Cosmil said from where he hunkered at my feet. "You channeled your direction more than I had imagined possible."

"You think?" I snarked. "I'm on my butt in the grass, Cosmil."

"Yes, indeed, you are. I have apologized to Saber for the scare. Had I foreseen this, I would have warned you both."

Saber shot Cosmil an irritated glance. "Somehow your apology rings hollow."

"Perhaps because I cannot regret the outcome." The wizard speared me with his gaze. "You are indeed ready to make the amulet your own, Francesca. Come. Pandora and Triton are preparing phase two."

Cosmil sprang to his feet and strode toward the shack, all but rubbing his hands in glee.

Saber watched Cosmil go with narrowed eyes.

"Why are you ticked at him?"

"Because when Cosmil invoked the West," he said, giving me a hand up, "you swayed and sank into the grass in a fetal position. Scared the shit out of me, but the old bastard froze me in place until after the ceremony." He cupped my face with his hands. "You sure you're not hurt?"

"Not an ache. Did I fall hard?"

"You didn't fall. You floated."

"And that freaked hunky you?"

"No, honey. The ground softened and absorbed your body. You were three-fourths buried. *That* freaked hunky me."

An icy fist seized my gut. Buried? I'd been buried again? Damn it. Why did I have to pull the West power straw? Being beamed by sunlight, basking in a meadow, hell, even turning temporarily gray were all happier choices. Being buried in anything except up to my neck in Saber's hot tub? That shook me to my little fanged core.

No more ceremonies for me, I decided as Saber and I entered Cosmil's shanty. And I'd tell him so after I cleaned up.

I didn't acknowledge Cosmil or Pandora or Triton, but marched straight to the bathroom to check my hair and Regency dress. Prepared to see twigs, soil, sand, at least grass stains, I found nary a smudge. Good for me, and better for Cosmil since I'd have slapped him with dry cleaning and hair-appointment bills. Heck, with an entire spa treatment.

Back in the living area, I found Cosmil alone in the room, standing at the far end of the boat-sized stainless countertop he'd littered with books and bottles and bells. No broomstick in sight, but a massive staff leaned against the fridge, and he tapped a crystal-tipped wand against his cheek.

"Where are Pandora and the guys? I thought our amulet training was next on the agenda."

"Working with the amulet is on your agenda, not theirs. The others are outside awaiting my instructions. Come," he said with a beckoning wave. "See what I have for you."

I followed the sweep of his arm to the coffee table. The amulets weren't there, but six silver necklaces in white gift boxes were arranged in a neat row. The silver pendant on each chain featured a mermaid poised atop a treasure chest.

Just like the ones Triton carried in his shop. Just like the one he'd given me as a talisman last month so Pandora could keep track of me, except mine had been pewter. And the chain hadn't been silver, because silver and vampires generally don't mix. Just being too near too much of the metal used to make my nose itch and the back of my throat raw.

Then I'd drained a crazed vampire into submission and absorbed one of his gifts in the process. An immunity to silver. Or perhaps I should say a tolerance for it. I didn't have allergy symptoms now and could wear the metal for hours at a stretch without being burned or having my energy depleted. Wearing silver near the beach in the salty sea air extended my tolerance time even more. I'd learned that when I'd gone on a four-hour jaunt to the Lowe's in Palatka wearing silver earrings and come home with red bumps on my lobes. The St. Johns River just didn't have enough salt content to allay the allergic reaction.

"Triton donated these for you to give the bachelorette party women," Cosmil explained as I approach to inspect the pieces.

I shook my head. "Maggie's already bought other gifts. Besides, there are nine of us counting Maggie and me."

"Yes, well, Saber and Triton are each using one for the moment, and I believe you will find a slight problem with the delivery when you go to retrieve the ordered gifts tomorrow. Not to worry," he continued, his hand upraised to stop the tirade I had opened my mouth to launch. "The proper items will arrive next week. Meantime, these will aid you in keeping the women safe for the weekend."

I gave him the laser look I'd learned from my mother. "They better not give off shocks like my pewter one did."

"No, no. Nor will they buzz, light, or otherwise cause an annoyance. They will instead attune to each wearer and transmit a warning to you should anyone be in natural or supernatural danger."

"So I'll have the receiver?"

"Yes."

"And it won't zap me, either?"

"Not if I have made the proper adjustments."

"You've already powered these things up?"

"Oh, yes." His eyes twinkled with amusement. "We had an exceptional circle ceremony, you know."

"One we will never have again," I said as I held his blue gray gaze. "I was buried more than two hundred years, Cosmil. I will not repeat that experience."

The humor faded under a somber, somehow regretful look. He took a breath, as if to speak, then pulled what had to be the ninth necklace from his wizard cloak.

"Here," he said, unfastening the claw latch. "Try your pendant."

I lifted the hair from my neck and tensed for a shock, but the chain settled cool and comfy around my neck. The silver pendant was much lighter than the pewter one, too, so I had no fear of conking myself in the nose when I leaned over.

"How is it?" Cosmil asked.

"No jolt, no burn."

"Good. Now for the test runs."

He crossed to the front door and flipped off the light switch. I blinked once so my vampire sight would adjust, and two distinct tones emanated from the pendant, vibrating against my chest and ringing in my ears. A vision swiftly followed, a picture of Pandora in a tree, haunches bunched to pounce with deadly intent. Saber and Triton stood in her line of attack, seemingly oblivious.

I yelped just as Pandora leaped and sailed far past the guys.

"Describe what you heard and saw, Francesca?"

I did and he nodded. "Excellent. We will conduct the second trial."

He flipped the lights back on, and I squinted against the brightness as another vision hit. This time, the same two tones resonated through me, and I saw a flash of Saber with Triton in a chokehold. Triton was hamming up the act. I chuckled.

"You know Saber's not quite human," I told Cosmil. "Is his fake assault a fair test?"

"A mugging is a natural sort of crime."

"So are animal attacks like Pandora simulated."

"Not quite, my dear. Pandora used magick to make Triton and Saber blind and deaf to her."

"You're kidding. She can do that?"

Of course, I can. I heard Pandora in my head before something swatted the side of my gown.

I strangled out, "Aaarrgghh," as I spun to see panther-sized Pandora parked at my feet.

She gave me that superior expression that only felines can flaunt.

I crossed my eyes at her then rubbed my temple. "Great. Now I'm getting a headache."

"You have used and absorbed a great deal of psychic energy tonight," Cosmil said with a pat on my shoulder. "Intense magical energy as well. Lia will teach you to shield better."

Peachy.

"Yes, it is. Now, let us commence a short session with the amulet."

He crossed to the kitchen island, moved aside a massive tome, and plucked the amulet from the counter.

"Catch."

He underhanded the disk, and since the guys strolled inside just then, my vampire reflexes faltered. I fumbled the damn amulet.

Fortunately, it landed on the sofa.

I glared at Cosmil. "What is with you and Triton throwing this at me like a baseball? What if it goes off?"

"Francesca, the medallion is not a loaded gun with a hair trigger. It is a highly unusual rutilated quartz with titanium oxide inclusions showing both gold and silver."

"Then it's too valuable to be tossing around, now isn't it?"

I snatched the hexagon-shaped disk off the cushion, ready to make another point, but lost it in a gentle waft of energy.

The size and thickness of a jelly-jar lid, the amulet immediately sent pulses into my right palm, and I curled my fingers around the copper framing the crystal as my heartbeat fell into the rhythm of the disk. Beats of time later, the copper frame rimming the amulet grew warm. A caress on each contact point of my hand.

I sensed recognition. Homecoming.

A rightness that unfurled in my heart.

I opened my hand, letting the medallion rest in my palm, and sucked in a shocked breath. The ancient-looking symbols etched into the amulet's rim were now stamped into my skin, a reverse imprint that flowed along the inside length of my fingers, along the sides and heel of my hand. I recognized part of a musical note and the Greek letter *mu*. Nothing else. More, the impressions appeared to glow from within my olive skin rather than riding on the surface.

Well, crap. What now?

Cosmil cleared his throat. "The true value of the amulet is not in the beholder, Francesca. It is in the holder. You."

I met his gaze. "Does the weirdness ever stop around you, Cosmil?"

He returned his patient, wise smile. "Tell me what you experienced."

I did, glancing at Saber and Triton where they sat in armchairs opposite my stance by the sofa. When I finished, Cosmil nodded.

"The contact has further opened your fourth chakra," Cosmil said when I finished. "You are bonded with the medallion."

"Like super-duper glue?"

"More like contact cement," Triton chimed in. He sat with an ankle propped on his knee, unconsciously jiggling his foot. "The same thing happened to me with the Atlantean amulet."

Saber gave him a sharp glance. "Atlantean?"

"It's the mate to Cesca's Lemuria medallion. The one the Hawaiian shaman gave me. I found the Atlantean amulet during my dive trip to Bimini in June."

"Lemuria, or Mu, was the sister civilization to Atlantis," Cosmil explained. "It was before my time, but it is said that because Mu perished first, the Atlantean's lost their divine feminine balance and thus self-destructed."

"I know the mythology," Saber said to Cosmil, then addressed Triton. "What I don't believe is that you just happened to stumble across a second disk."

"I didn't stumble. I swam across it. I was led to the amulet by a mermaid."

"For pity's sake, Triton," I snarled, "I don't care if Disney characters sang you under the sea to the medallion. Your hands don't have a single one of these inkless tattoos on them. Why not?"

"Because I'm not holding my piece."

I inclined my head toward Cosmil in silent question.

"Place the medallion on the table, Francesca."

I did, and the imprints faded.

"Now hold the amulet again," Triton said.

This time I scooped the disk into my left hand. The marks glowed on my right hand but looked more like faded scars than fresh ones. I rolled the amulet from palm to palm, absorbing its angles and textures. The symbols waxed with the amulet in my right hand, waned with it in the left.

Okay, I could live with this. Now to ask the question of the hour. The one I didn't really want to ask.

"What are the magick words that make this work?"

"Beg your pardon?"

"Triton murmured a string of words when he slapped it on the vampire's chest, Cosmil. Like an activation code or something."

"I see."

"Good. So how do I turn this on?"

Triton snorted. "You could talk dirty to it."

I didn't think I'd heard right, but Triton's smarmy smirk tripped my temper. Without conscious thought, I closed my hand over the etched copper and smooth crystal.

"You are so dead," I snapped.

A pop, a flash of heat, and blinding beams of light suddenly shot from every facet of the hexagon.

Triton flew backward out of his chair in an arc and thudded into Cosmil's front door.

EIGHT

※

I eyed Triton's crumpled body and the wisp of smoke curling from the charred circle on his shirtfront. Oops was not gonna cover this.

Saber shot me a sardonic glance as he rose to go to Triton's aid.

Cosmil chuckled, and I whirled on him.

"You told me the amulet wasn't a loaded gun."

"I also told you the medallion responded to intent." The wizard's eyes twinkled. "Triton agreed to, I believe the expression is, piss you off."

"With the amulet in my hand?" I dropped the still-warm crystal on the sofa. "Cosmil, I could've killed Triton."

"No, for no matter your words, you had no true intent of murder, manslaughter, or maiming."

"I wouldn't be too sure about the maiming," I muttered.

Cosmil shook his head. "Francesca, it was our way of testing your ability with the medallion. Triton's crude remark elicited your reaction, and the medallion focused your disgust."

"In other words, I got ticked and I went after him."

"Precisely. Of course, lashing out is not the way to defeat Starrack and the Void."

"Duh," was on the tip of my tongue, but I got distracted seeing movement from the corner of my eye. Triton was on his feet. Wavering but upright, with a hand on Saber's shoulder.

"You okay?"

I started toward him, but his sour expression and "stop right there" gesture halted me.

"Next time," he bit out, "Saber gets to bait you."

"Like hell," Saber shot back. Wise man, my honey.

Triton ignored us both. "Cos, are you still determined to let Cesca take the amulet with her?"

"I am."

"Then you'd better show her some finer points of using that thing before she blasts some bitchy bridesmaid this weekend."

"Maggie doesn't have any bitchy bridesmaids."

"No? Look in a mirror."

"Get off my case, cretin."

"Children, cease," Cosmil barked. He took two long steps to the sofa, picked up the amulet, and slammed it into my hand. "Francesca, close your eyes and imagine a bubble of peace encasing you. Do it now."

The picture that popped to mind was a shower of white light, not a bubble. A narrow waterfall, comfortably warm like the amulet in my hand.

"Good. Now expand the image to include me."

The waterfall widened to splash over and around Cosmil.

"Enfold Saber in the peace with us."

I did, and my heartbeat slowed to match the steady, measured pulse of the disk.

"Extend the protection to Triton, then see it grow until the peace blankets my property."

All right, I admit I had to push for Triton. Once I saw him within the shower, the image exploded. A Niagara Falls of light bathed my vision, brighter sparkles winking like silver and gold glitter.

"Open your eyes, Francesca."

I obeyed, swaying a little as the room came into focus.

"That, my dear, is how the medallion works. There are words for the banishing ritual, yes, but you will not need them this weekend."

I gave him a long, steady stare.

"You're sure about the no banishing bit? Wizard's honor?"

"As long as you keep yourself out of trouble."

I woke at two the next afternoon, an hour earlier than usual, but a quick shower got me fully revved. Saber had left a note on the bathroom deco mirror saying he'd been called to Jacksonville on VPA business but that it was nothing to worry about.

Good thing, since I was focused on breaking the case of the missing necklaces news to Maggie.

Her cell rang to the max before she picked up.

"Cesca, the Victorian tussie-mussie charm necklaces I ordered for the girls haven't come in yet," she wailed. "The store is checking but—"

"No sweat, Maggie," I interrupted. "I had a feeling we might need a backup plan, so I got just the thing from Triton."

"So you have seen him again."

"Just as friends."

"Let me guess what he gave you. That mermaid-on-the-treasure-chest charm like the one you used to wear?"

Okay, so maybe Maggie is a little psychic, too. "How did you know?"

"I saw them in his shop. Did you get just the charms or necklaces, too?"

"Silver charms on silver necklaces." I pictured Cosmil waving a hand to erase Triton and Saber's energies from the two charms they'd worn, and the wizard promised they would attune to their new owners. "Really, I think they'll be fine, Maggie."

"They'll be perfect. Fernandina Beach might be a Victorian-era town, but the mermaids will suit our beach-getaway theme. Hold on."

I did, and heard Maggie and Neil murmur, then smoochy sounds.

"Okay, I'm back. Neil insists we drive his SUV for the weekend so we'll have room to ferry the bachelorette-party ladies to dinner and shopping. Will you still be ready to go by three?"

"With time to spare. And, Maggie, I'll get on the missing necklace order Monday. You'll have them for the wedding, I promise." Even if Cosmil had to magically deliver them to me.

"Have I told you lately that you're a fabulous maid of honor, Cesca?"

"You just did," I said on a smile. "I'll be over soon."

I finished getting ready in record time. I held my nose and downed my daily six ounces of Starbloods, then stowed two more bottles for the trip in a blue zippered cooler lined with ice packs. The hotel had fridges in every room, so I was set on the meal front.

After brushing my teeth, I did the makeup and hair thing, and added last minute supplies to my little hot pink, wheeled suitcase. Snowball protested being shooed off the closed luggage lid, but better white cat fur on the luggage than on my clothing.

I snapped the mermaid receiver around my neck and would give Maggie her necklace before we left. Not that we needed to wear them for the drive, but we might as well. I didn't think I'd need the amulet on my person, either, but it fit nicely in a pocket of the khaki cargo shorts I'd paired with a seahorse-print tank top. Maybe I could use the disk's magick to zoom our way through Friday afternoon Jacksonville traffic. Couldn't hurt, and if that was a sign the amulet's power was already corrupting me, I would deal with it.

* * *

We left for Fernandina Beach on Amelia Island at a quarter of three, and maybe the amulet did clear a path in traffic because we arrived at our beachfront hotel at four. My room had an odd layout with the queen bed right inside the door, but that meant I'd be shaded from the morning light. The heavy drapes would protect me from the sun, too. No need to wear my industrial-strength sunscreen to bed.

As part of the special package deal I'd negotiated, the hotel had prepared refreshments of cheese, crackers, fruit, and assorted cold drinks set up in the lobby. Which came in as a handy way to break the ice as each wave of our party checked in.

Not that all seven ladies were bridesmaids. Sherry, who had known Maggie since childhood, would be Maggie's only other attendant. The others had been invited because they were good friends. Susan, Evelyn, and Carole were college buds of Maggie's, and Rhianna and Tiffany were longtime interior design associates. Fireball Jessica was Neil's younger sister. Her husband John, a college buddy of Neil's, would serve as his groomsman, but Jessica had declined being in the official wedding party because she was expecting twins.

"No way am I paying for a preggers bridesmaid dress," she'd said. "I'll be the cake attendant so I'll have something to hide behind in the photos."

The ladies snacked and sipped and chatted like they'd known each other—and even me—for years. Yes, I was a tiny bit surprised each woman so readily accepted a vampire in their midst, but my expectations for a successful weekend soared. Especially when, to a woman, they loved and immediately donned their mermaid charms.

Would've been darned difficult to insist that seven independent women wear trackers. But hearing distinct tones for each lady bolstered my confidence that I could keep everyone safe, and tucking the amulet in the pocket of the aqua capris of my dinner outfit didn't hurt, either.

With Jessica driving her SUV and me driving Neil's, the party headed to the Florida House Inn in high spirits.

Whereas old St. Augustine reflects its Spanish colonial heritage, downtown Fernandina Beach is dotted with Victorian buildings. We passed book and clothing stores, gift and antique shops, restaurants, and even a club housed in the old buildings en route to the side street where the Florida House took up most of the block. Laughter rang in our private room that overlooked the back garden, and the restaurant surpassed its reputation for fabulous food.

At eight thirty, after the wine had flowed during dinner, the wild wedding women insisted we go clubbing. Yep, the ladies had shucked the shackles of their real lives and slapped on their party-girl hats.

We walked the two blocks to the Painted Lady Saloon. The building had started life as a bank built in the Victorian style, but the interior was now sleekly modern. Large and small cocktail tables ringed a sunken dance floor with a little karaoke stage. Music throbbed, the bass so intense that it altered my heartbeat. Was the noise bad for Jessica's babies on board? I had no idea, but she led the charge to move three tables together.

The first round of drinks featured a concoction the waitress called the Blushing Bride. Jessica and I didn't partake, and I never did hear exactly what was in the frothy frozen libation, but the festive mood ramped into overdrive.

Until two male vampires approached the table.

Two square-jawed, buff males, late twenties to mid-thirties in human years. I didn't get a fix on how long they'd been vampires, but it hadn't been long as the vampire flies. How did I guess they weren't ancient vamps? Their dark slacks were classic, but the tropical-print shirts screamed 1980s. They looked like extras from *Magnum, P.I.*

Broad in the shoulders, narrow in the hips, their bearing military, they strode ever closer. Eyes friendly, but the tip of their fangs flashing in their smiles.

I think Rhianna and Tiffany drooled at the sight of those white fangs. I went on high alert.

"Evening, ladies," the slightly shorter, surfer-blond vamp shouted over the music. "I hope we're not intruding."

"Not if you ask us to dance," Carole crooned.

"I don't think that's a good idea." Call me overprotective, but I scooted back my chair in case I needed to move fast.

Rhianna waved an elegant hand. "Don't be a drag. It's a great idea."

"Uh, Rhianna, these guys are vampires."

"I know." She grinned. "Vampires are almost as good as gays on the dance floor."

"Better," Tiffany added with a secret smile.

The taller, black-haired vamp bowed toward Tiffany but speared me with his gaze.

"Aren't you the Princess Vampire?"

"Who wants to know?" I countered, waiting for the amulet in my pocket to somehow signal danger—maybe to become burning hot and vibrate like it had at the comedy club last month—but it did zip. If not for the lump in my capris, I wouldn't have known I had the medallion on me.

"My name is Ken, and this is David. We were in the Atlanta nest, and rumor has it you had something to do with the nest breaking up."

Every muscle tensed as I braced for a brawl. "And if I did?"

"Then we want to buy you a drink."

I blinked. "You do? You're not angry?"

"Hell, no, Princess. Begging your pardon, ma'am."

"It's Cesca."

"This is the first time we've been out of Atlanta in decades. The first time we've had a vacation since we were Turned, and we're making the most of it."

Blond David nodded. "That's right. We're free, ma'am. We owe you."

"Good," Jessica said. "Then you can buy a round of Blushing Brides."

"Someone's getting married?" David ventured.

"Not you, Princess," Ken said, eyes rounding.

"Not me, and it's Cesca."

"This is Maggie's bachelorette party," Sherry sang, saluting Maggie with her empty glass. "She needs to dance."

"We all need to dance," Rhianna decreed. "So, Ken, David. Can you handle nine girls who want to have fun?"

David winked. "Come on, bridal party, let's boogie."

The vampires danced, flirted, even sang a half an hour of karaoke with Susan, Evelyn, and Carole. They never crossed the line, and believe me, I watched for the smallest sign of a predatory glint in their eyes. I also used the amulet in my pocket to project a shower of protection over every employee and patron in the club, but I suspected the ladies' mermaid charms would have stayed silent anyway.

Seemed these vacationing vampires just wanted to have fun, too.

Which was the second thing to strike me as odd about them, and the itchy feeling wouldn't subside.

True, except for Jo-Jo the Jester, my experience with other vampires was limited. I hadn't spent much time with those I'd lived with in King Normand's court, but they couldn't have spelled fun with a dictionary and a tutor. As for my Daytona Beach vampire acquaintances, they tended to be a quieter, surlier bunch than Ken and David were proving to be.

These guys were gentlemen. Polite, charming, solicitous gentlemen. They even ordered water and encouraged the ladies to hydrate each time they returned to the table—especially after we'd all done a line dance to what seemed like an extra-long version of the Sister Sledge "We Are Family" song.

Yes, I said we *all*. The ladies got me to lighten up and take to the floor with them. To continue refusing would've looked snobbish or suspicious, so I unbent. I even danced solo with Ken to a song from *Dirty Dancing*. And, okay, I rather did have the time of my life. Ken had those movie dance moves down.

We left the club before midnight, Ken and David insisting they walk us to our cars. That put me on alert again, but they behaved. They thanked us for the evening, mentioned perhaps meeting the next night to dance, but didn't push. Just waved us off as we wheeled out of the parking lot.

When I'd personally insured that every last sleepy lady was locked in her room, it was time to call Saber and ask the question burning in my gut.

Why the hell hadn't Ken and David shown a single sign of Void infection?

NINE

〜

"Can you run a check on two vampires for me?"

I snuggled against the queen-bed headboard and braced for Saber to explode. He surprised me by merely sucking in a breath.

"Trouble?"

"No, and I don't think there will be."

He expelled a gusty sigh. "Names?"

"Ken and David, formerly of the Atlanta nest. No last names, if they use them, and I don't know what they do for jobs. Ken said they were vacationing."

Keys clicked madly in the background, and I knew Saber was checking the VPA website's restricted section. Silence stretched on the other end of the phone then more keystrokes. I pulled a pillow onto my lap and played with the lace-edged pillowcase. Waiting.

"Here we go. David Marks, Turned in 1988, and Ken Crandall in 1989. They did register to go on vacation with the Atlanta office. Both are former U.S. Marine Corps officers."

That explained their military bearing and the '80s vibe.

"Anything else on them?"

"No problems reported with either of them. David is a web developer. Ken is a dance instructor."

"Dance instructor?" I said on a chuckle.

"Why is that funny?"

"Because we just spent several hours in a club with both of them."

"We?"

"The entire bachelorette party, but keep that to yourself. Neil doesn't need to know."

"What happens in Fernandina Beach stays there?"

"And what happens at Neil's bachelor party stays there, too."

"Fair enough. Did these vampires recognize you?"

"They did, and they thanked me for having a hand in closing the nests."

I heard Saber drum his fingers. "If this was a positive encounter, what's bothering you about it?"

I took a breath. "Didn't you tell me that every last vampire you visited on your nest-closing trip showed signs of Void infection?"

"Are you saying these vamps didn't?"

"Not even close, Saber, and they're baby vamps. Triton told me not even Cosmil knows if the disease is spread by magical or mundane means, or both, but—"

"But," Saber interrupted, "from the way Ray and his crew are suffering, Ken and David would look like petrified raisins if they were ill."

"Exactly, especially since Vlad was severely infected when the VPA picked him up in August." I paused. "Unless David and Ken have some sort of immunity like I seem to have. Or unless Starrack is targeting Florida vamps. Is that likely?"

"I don't know. It's been over a week since I talked with Candy Crushman in the Atlanta office."

"There's no list of sick vampires on the private section of the website?"

"Just the regular tracking records." He paused, and I pictured him raking a hand through his hair. "I'll call Candy. See if she's keeping an account of infected vamps."

"Okay, but don't have her order Ken and David back to Atlanta. The guys have a right to finish their vacation."

"Not if they could get violent at any time."

"Saber, *I* have the potential to get violent at any time. Doesn't mean I will, and I think we should give these vampires the benefit of the doubt."

"All right, but I don't want you to question them. I mean it, Cesca. I didn't mention this before, but Candy told me back in August that Vlad had a disproportionate number of former military men in his nest."

"He was building an army. Like Normand tried to do with Spanish and British soldiers."

"Vampires who'd take orders without question. The vamps who carried out the sacrifice attack on Candy and Crusher were ex-military."

"Saber, I swear. If we see Ken and David again, I won't interrogate them." Though maybe I'd have a little just-among-vampires chat with them.

"Meantime, you're taking precautions, right?"

"I'm patrolling the ladies' rooms every hour through the night."

"Won't the mermaid charms alert you to danger?"

"Theoretically, yes, but I don't know if they have to be worn to send signals. I didn't get the chance to ask Cosmil about that detail."

"Be careful, honey."

"I will. I'll have the trusty amulet with me."

"Good. And, Cesca." He pitched his voice deeper, into the sexy range than made me go soft and liquid.

"Yes, Deke?"

"We'll have our own dance when you get home."

Rapid knocks jolted me out of a dream about being in Saber's arms.

"Hey, Cesca, it's two thirty," Maggie called from the hallway. "You want to get up now?"

I untangled myself from the sheets, crawled to the foot of the bed, and opened the door.

"Whoa, you weren't kidding about the odd layout," she said as she squeezed inside. "This is tight."

"How is everyone today?" I asked on a yawn. "Hangovers?"

"Not a one. We had brunch, went shopping, and now we're hitting the beach. I thought my right hand might want to join us."

"Let me shower and slather on my super sunscreen."

"Fine. We'll set up near that little snack shop." She turned to edge back out the door. "Oh, and Cesca, the girls might want to go dancing again tonight. Will that be a problem?"

I scraped the hair out of my face. "Why would it be?"

"Because I saw you keeping an eagle eye on Ken and David last night."

"I was just being cautious."

"You're certain?"

"Maggie, the vampires aren't a problem. The danger is one of the girls letting it slip to Neil that you and Jessica—"

"Danced with vampires and enjoyed it. And with her carrying twins. Damn. I didn't mention our partners to Neil when I called home last night. Did you tell Saber?"

"Yes, but I swore him to secrecy."

"Good. Except for you, Neil doesn't trust vamps. No point in upsetting him." She bit her lip, her expression pleadingly hopeful. "How about this? You enthrall the girls and wipe that part of their collective memories."

"How about you go be with your friends and I'll think about it."

I hustled Maggie out, shaking my head. Me enthrall and wipe memories? That was like asking a slasher to do brain surgery.

A few hours of beach time were followed by a few hours of rest, and then we met in the hotel lobby to hit a seafood restaurant that had been highly recommended. The conversation flowed easily, more lazily than it had on Friday. I chalked up the calmer energy to spending the afternoon in the sun. Whatever the cause, I figured we'd have a quiet night. Perhaps talking in Maggie's suite.

I figured wrong, and at nine o'clock we were back at the Painted Lady. Ken and David were there before us and immediately whisked most of the party to the dance floor. If either vampire had heard from Candy Crushman, neither gave any indication.

Or they didn't until the ladies decided to call it a night, and David and Ken again escorted us to our SUVs. While the women loaded themselves into the cars, the males politely pulled me aside.

"Princess," Ken said, his tone even, his expression serious. He seemed to choose his words carefully. "We understand you checked up on us, and we understand why."

I fingered my silver necklace and tried not to gulp.

"Candy talked with you?"

David nodded. "Scuttlebutt has it you know what made our former master ill and that you're on a mission to stop it from killing the rest of us."

I searched their faces. "Are either of you sick?"

"We're healthy. We just aim to thank you."

I shook my head. "Guys, I'm only one of a number of people try-ing to stop the infection."

"Still, ma'am, we appreciate it. You need anything, you call."

I had to smile. "Call in the Marines?"

"*Ooh-rah*," David said.

Ken nodded and handed me a business card. "Semper Fi, ma'am."

Ken and David's cell numbers were neatly printed on the back.

Thanks to a special late checkout time, I got to sleep until three Sun-day afternoon. Maggie wasn't in a tearing hurry to get home, so with the amulet tucked safely in the back pocket of my jean shorts, we hit a dozen garage sales en route and rolled into her driveway shortly after six.

When I offered to help her tackle any wedding RSVPs that had come in, she waved me away. Maybe because Neil had stepped onto the wide wrap-around porch. Talk about a pheromone spike.

"We've heard from most people," she said. "Let's put it off a day or two."

I laughed. "Fine. Have fun with your hunk of burnin' love."

"You, too," she said with a wink.

But Saber wasn't in the cottage.

I propped my little pink bag against the kitchen door frame, but my cell rang before I could pluck the note I spied off the fridge.

"Hey, Princesca," Saber murmured. "I missed you."

"So why aren't you here to show me how much?" I murmured back as I sank into a retro kitchen chair. Ouch. The amulet bit into my butt as it hadn't in the plush seats of Neil's car, and I dug it out of my pocket.

"Because Cosmil asked if Lia could stay at my place. She'll be landing about four tomorrow afternoon."

"Ah, and you're cleaning the house." Which shouldn't take long,

I mused as I spun the amulet on the kitchen table. He kept a neater house than I did—and he hadn't been living at his place for over a week. "I'm surprised Cosmil isn't going for safety in numbers. He could always conjure up a bedroom and bath addition to the shanty."

"I'd love to see that, but Cosmil seems to think Lia will want her privacy."

"Or maybe Pandora has a jealous streak and doesn't want another female shacking up with her wizard."

"Lame joke, Cesca."

"Long weekend, Saber. Are you about finished cleaning?"

"Yeah, but I found a problem with the hot tub. I want to fix it now, so I'll be here awhile."

"Want me to come over and help?"

"Thanks, but no. I need to run out to Cosmil's when I finish, so I'll pick up something to eat before I come back to your place."

"Get more food and litter for Snowball, too."

"Got it."

"By the way, what's Lia going to do for transportation? Will we be shuttling her around?"

"Not a clue, honey. I figure Cosmil has something up his sleeve."

"So long as it's not my SSR."

Saber disconnected on a chuckle.

I snapped my cell closed, set it on the table, and sighed. I would have loved to take a nap, but once I'm up, I'm up for eighteen hours. Okay, with occasional exceptions. Most of those involving Saber. Maybe this would be one of those good lovin' nights when he'd leave me boneless *and* sleepy.

Meantime, might as well be productive. I left the amulet on the table, grabbed my luggage, and unloaded the dirty clothes right into the washer. With the machine filling, I headed to the bedroom with the near-empty suitcase but stopped short in the doorway.

Snowball, her back arched, her tail fluffed to three times its normal volume, stood statue still at the closed closet doors. She didn't so much as flick an ear at my entrance. What the heck?

Then I heard an echo of Pandora's warning. *She will sense the unseen and alert you to presences.*

Oh, damn.

A thump drew my attention back to Snowball, who emitted a low, unholy growl. She swiped one paw then the other at the bottom of the door.

In a horror movie, the idiot heroine would march to the door and ease it open. This was no movie, and I was sure no heroine. But Snowball had cornered something, and I needed to know what. Pronto.

I opened my senses. Stared at the white wood door. Imagined it slowly, ever so slowly, becoming opaque glass. It did, and a shadow appeared.

Snowball went bonkers, launching herself at the shadow. Hissing and spitting and yowling as if she were in a cat fight to the death.

I blocked the noise and opened more. I visualized the opaque glass growing window clear. Willed the shadow to be identifiable.

I knew it wouldn't be Starrack or the Void. I also knew that was no living being behind the door. It felt too old. Too dead. Too fragile and frightened.

Of a kitten.

The vision sharpened with an audible snap, and I gasped to see a tiny woman wearing an eighteenth-century court dress. The tiny human woman who had been King Normand's mistreated mistress and main meal deal—and my personal maid. The tiny woman who had helped bind me in that cursed coffin and hours later had been slaughtered by the townspeople.

She'd been the closest thing I'd had to a friend in King Normand's court.

"Isabella?" I said on a wave of relief.

She gave me a hesitant nod.

"What are you doing here?"

She pointed at the still-crazed Snowball.

"You're frightened of the cat?" Well, of course she was. Isabella had jumped at her own shadow in the old days, and not without reason.

"I'll take care of her. Snow," I crooned, crossing to the kitten. "It's okay. Calm down now. This is a friend."

Snowball flicked an ear at my approach but stayed hunched by the door. When I spoke singsong assurances to her, gently petted her, she only growled louder. I glanced at Isabella. Was Snowball telling me the ghost was an enemy in a friend's guise? My psychic senses said no. So maybe the cat just didn't like spirits in her territory. Whatever her issue, mine was to talk to Isabella.

I scooped Snow up, only to have her squirm and dig her hind claws into my ribs. Before she could scratch her way up my chest or twist out of my grasp, I shut her in the bathroom.

When I turned back, I half expected Isabella to be out of the closet. She wasn't, and the door still looked like glass. Did I need to let her out?

Not without a further question.

"Isabella, are you alone?"

Her brown eyes narrowed as she seemed to look past the door and into the distant yard. "I am alone for now."

"Do you want to come out?"

She shook her head and shrank away.

"Okay, but why are you here?"

"There is little time, but I have come to warn you," she whispered.

Oh, great. Another warning. Like I didn't have enough on my plate. Still, I nodded.

"Go on."

"Something is awakening the king and his court. Something evil. Something with a darker soul than even Marco."

My breath hitched. Finding a darker soul than Marco's would be a trick. He was the psychopath who'd courted me when he was human. When I rejected him, he voluntarily joined the vampires, rose to become Normand's right-hand vamp, and then captured me so I could be Turned. Marco had counted on pairing up with me, but Normand wasn't a vampire to be manipulated. He'd nixed Marco's plan.

Did Isabella know Marco was dead?

Didn't matter. The evil she spoke of had to be Starrack and the Void, but awakening the ghosts of vampires?

"What does the evil want with the king and his cronies?"

Isabella's nearly solid shoulders lifted in a shrug. "The evil creates chaos. Fear. Vampires excel at both. This is all I know."

"All right, but I've never felt their spirits on this property. Or yours, either, Isabella. Not even when I was still buried under the ruins."

"After the massacre and fire, the vampires were dismembered and their pieces scattered. We humans, our remains were thrown into the river."

"I'm sorry you were treated with disrespect."

"It was not your fault, Francesca." Isabella said, stepping closer to the door, her voice gaining strength. "You might have known the villagers were coming, but telling Normand would not have made a difference."

I flushed with old guilt. "How did you guess I knew about the plot?"

"I saw the weight of knowledge in your eyes, my friend, but we were ready to die. We were at peace away from the monsters, even those of us who did not immediately cross over. The vampires, I do not know what happened to their wretched souls, if they possessed souls at all."

"So you're saying this evil is calling Normand and his crew back from wherever they went?"

Isabella nodded.

"Are they coming to this property?"

"Oh, no. This ground has been reconsecrated. They cannot come here."

I gaped at her. "A parish priest blessed the land?"

"No, the holy man. The one with the great panther at his side."

I inhaled so hard the room spun. Cosmil had been on Maggie's property? When? And why hadn't he released me from the coffin? He had to have known I was buried right under his twitchy wizard nose.

"Francesca, you are woolgathering when I must leave."

I blinked at the ghost's fast-fading form.

"Sorry, Isabella. Thank you for the warning." I paused, caught by the sad smile she flashed. "Um, do you want out of the closet now?"

"I have used much energy, so yes, if you would be so kind."

Three steps brought me to the closet. When I twisted the knob, a wisp of white streamed into the bedroom, just like a Hollywood special effect. Isabella's essence floated to the living room, leisurely enough that I could follow, then when I opened the front door, Isabella's thin trail of white shot toward her burial place. The Matanzas River.

The River of Slaughter.

Dark clouds had gathered. I'm not sure when that happened. After Isabella's shade left, I wasn't aware of much at all—except the questions chasing through my brain.

Then a crack of thunder rattled the cottage, echoing as it rolled out to sea. I shook off my mental fog to find myself propped on the sofa, Snowball curled sleeping on my lap.

It figured the cat would nap while I worried, but what freaked me was that I didn't recall letting her out of the bathroom. Talk about being zoned out.

I needed to tell Saber about Isabella's revelations. I needed to confront Cosmil about leaving me buried in that stinking coffin.

I needed to know what the hell time it was.

Snowball barely twitched as I eased her from my lap and rose to check the digital clock on the kitchen stove. Eight forty. Damn, I'd spent more than two hours lost in thought. That wasn't like me.

In fact, it wasn't like me to be so lethargic that I'd wanted a nap, either.

A rash of goose bumps climbed up my arms.

Was the Void beginning to infect me?

No. No, no, no. Think positive, I commanded my brain. *You're perfectly hale and hearty. Your vitality meter is off the charts. You're the Energizer Bunny with fangs. Now move it.*

I scooped up the cell phone, flipped it open as I marched to the laundry room, and punched Saber's number. One ring, and I moved my clothes to the dryer. Two rings, and I added softener sheet. Three rings. I let the machine lid slam shut and paced into the living room.

Saber answered on the fifth ring.

"Cesca," he shouted. "You'll have to talk loud. We have a hell of a storm going on out here."

"Are you at Cosmil's?" I yelled loudly enough to hurt my own ears. Clearly, this was not the time to tell him about Isabella.

"Yeah, and downed trees are blocking my SUV."

"Are you all right? Do you need me to come get you?"

"We're fine, and I don't need a ride, but I do need a favor." He paused a beat. "You still there?"

"I hear you."

"Listen, Triton was supposed to be here hours ago. I can't reach him on the phone, and Cosmil is worried."

"He's probably just resting before he shifts tonight. Or there may be broken limbs blocking his streets."

"Is it storming there?"

I peered out the window. "Not now. It's moved off shore."

"You're likely right about Triton resting, but will you go check on him anyway? Give Cosmil some peace of mind?"

I'd rather give the wizard a piece of *my* mind, but in the spirit of staying positive, I agreed.

"I'll call you when I get to his place." No response. "Saber?" I hollered.

The line was dead.

Peachy.

Not feeling quite the urgency Cosmil did, I took the time to re-wrap my ponytail and then changed from my shorts outfit and san-dals into a pair of cutoffs, a Florida Gators T-shirt, and sneakers. No socks. Maybe I'd head to the beach myself. Meditate on health af-firmations while I listen to the ocean. Heck, maybe I'd stick around until sunrise and surf. I kept an extra bathing suit in my truck. If the storm still sat off shore, the waves might be worth catching.

I grabbed a beach towel, stuck my phone in my pocket with my driver's license, and then wrestled my board out of the laundry room. The amulet still on the kitchen table winked in the light, so I snagged it, too. I locked the cottage but didn't set the alarms. I remembered Neil's warning about arming them if Saber and I would be coming and going half the night.

It was tricky to load my board in the SSR with any stealth, but I managed. Within ten minutes of talking with Saber, I cruised out of my neighborhood and down San Marcos, past the bay front and over the Bridge of Lions. I sang along to my favorite CD because it revved me and because, really, who can be stressed or scared when the Beach Boys are blasting through the speakers? I even had the bushy-bushy hairdo the lyrics touted. Brown, not blond, but still.

Triton's place was soon in my sights. Faint light shone from the shop, but his apartment upstairs was dark. Great. He'd either run late getting to Cosmil's, or he'd already left for the beach to shift. Back in the days that I'd gone with him, he'd insisted on being near the ocean between nine and midnight, no matter what the true astronomical time of the new moon.

It was just nine now.

Of course, Triton might be sleeping, in which case I'd bang on his door and chew him out.

I drove past his store and turned on the road that took me by the lighthouse. A few turns on backstreets would take me to the one that ran behind his property. I'd park in the drive, knock on the door, maybe peek in a window. Then I'd call Saber back with a clear conscience.

I maneuvered around two lights-flashing cop cars at the end of Triton's block and crept on down the narrow road littered with storm debris. A few sizeable limbs were down, but only twigs and leaves covered Triton's driveway. Nothing to scratch up my SSR.

As I exited the truck, the wind rose, caught my ponytail, and lashed strands across my face. Interesting. The air crackled with a different energy here than at home, and the scent of rain was heavier. Old storm going or new one coming? I looked up to search the sky, and a fat drop of water plopped dead center on my forehead.

I swiped it away and stomped up the stairs to Triton's door. More twigs and leaves carpeted the deck, and what looked like muddy footprints clumped around the apartment's entrance.

I sidestepped the mud and briskly knocked.

And the door flew open under my knuckles.

Nothing reached to jerk me inside, but my every muscle clenched in dread as soon as I smelled the stench of blood.

TEN

"Triton?" I whispered.

No answer.

"Triton?" I spoke louder to push the fear from my voice.

It didn't work, but I gingerly crossed the threshold anyway. Between the streetlight filtering in the room from behind me and my trusty vampire vision, I took in the destruction.

Lamps broken. Couch cushions askew. Books and knickknacks scattered helter-skelter on the carpeted floor. Beyond that, a kitchen area that was similarly trashed. Guilt that I hadn't hurried more threatened to flood me, but it didn't look like five minutes would've made a difference. I didn't have time for regrets anyway. I had to find Triton.

Then I spotted two legs sticking out from behind an armchair.

Crap and triple crap.

In a blink, I stared at Triton where he lay sprawled face up, one shoulder against the wall as if he'd slid down it. Blood oozed from a gash on his forehead and from his nose, and his lower lip looked

split in the corner. Dark stains smeared his light-colored shirt and
shorts, and one of his sneakers was untied.

"Triton," I said as I shook his shoulder.

His eyelids fluttered open. "Cesca?"

"Who else? What the hell happened?"

"Bounced myself off the walls."

"With help from what army? Here, let me help you up."

I held out my hand. He grasped my forearm instead, grunting and
gasping until I had him on his feet.

"Can't go to the hospital, Cesca," he panted as I tugged his arm
over my shoulder to help him to the armchair. "Have to shift soon."

"Duh. Where's your first aid kit?"

"Heal when I shift. Don't need first aid."

"Yes, you damn well do," I snapped, and released his weight.

He fell into the chair with a tortured, "Ugh, you had to drop me?
Might have internal injuries."

"I'll drop-kick you around the block if you don't listen. You can't
drive in this condition. You can't be seen outside bleeding like you
are, or some Good Samaritan may call the police. Two cop cars are
down the street right now."

"Heard the sirens. So did my workout buddies."

"That's what made them leave?"

He gave me a weak nod.

I didn't ask if they might come back. "What did they want?"

"The amulets. Told them all I had were some nice doubloon medallions. In the shop. They started ripping up my stuff."

"And then pounded on you?"

"Pounding came first. Said the boss got what he wanted."

"These were humans?"

"Two crazy, mean mortals."

"How would a mortal know about the amulets, and why would
one care about having them?"

"Think these guys worked for Starrack."

"Did they stink like the Void?"

"Maybe. Don't remember. Busy dodging fists." He paused, panted for breath. "What time is it?"

"A little after nine."

"Got to get to the beach. My skin is itching with the change."

"Then stop stalling and tell me where to find your freakin' first aid kit."

"Bathroom," he said, jerking a thumb over his shoulder.

As I hurried to the doorway, it crossed my mind that the amulet might aid in healing Triton. Then I dismissed the thought. I didn't know how to use the darn thing for such a delicate operation.

In the short hall, I instinctively turned left. Yep, there was a decent-sized bath in the same chaotic shape as the rest of the place. The first aid kit, however, was in plain sight on the floor. I snagged it then grabbed a few towels that had been dumped in the bathtub. After soaking a face towel in hot water, I hustled back to Triton. What I didn't do was turn on the lights. If Triton's attackers were hanging around to have another go at him, no point in making us better targets.

"Here, hold the box while I wash your cuts."

"Careful," he whined, but he seemed to be breathing easier. "You were never much of a nurse."

"You didn't complain the last time I cleaned you up," I said as I dabbed the blood from his temple with the sopping face towel.

"I was drunk then."

"That was the next to last time. Now be quiet while I dab your lip."

He complied, and I worked in silence for a few minutes, grateful that he had the wind and wits to speak in full sentences. His wounds had stopped bleeding, and a lot of mouth breathing helped me keep my gag reflex under control. When I'd sponged away all the blood, I patted his face dry with the second towel.

"Okay, hand me the antibiotic cream."

"You get it," he said, thrusting the box in my belly. "My eyes hurt."

"Baby," I teased to ease my own tension. A spot between my shoulder blades itched, as if someone had me in their sights.

"So when *was* the last time you nursed me?"

"When Sophia Pappas nailed you in the back of the head with a water pail," I replied, twisting off the tube cap and then smearing antibiotic cream on his forehead.

"Oh, yeah. She was a pretty little thing," he added with a half smile.

I snorted and dotted cream on his lip. "She was the most vicious girl in the Spanish Quarter, Triton."

"She was jealous of you."

"Right."

"She was. So were most of the girls our age. You had freedoms they didn't have." He wheezed a chuckle. "They thought you had me, too."

That shot a little pang in my heart, but I shook it off and re-capped the tube. "I suggest you downsize that ego so you can walk out of here."

"No problem."

Slower than grass grows, he levered himself out of the armchair, then wove to the left, and pitched into my arms.

So much for walking under his own power.

I slung his arm around my shoulders. "Put your weight on me."

He did, but even with vampire strength, my knees almost buckled from the unexpected awkwardness of holding him semi-upright. Gee, getting him down the stairs was gonna be fun.

I half dragged him to the deck accompanied by his soft groans. Damn, maybe he did have internal injuries. Would shifting heal those, too?

"Lock the door, Cesca," he muttered.

"Where's the key?"

"Was on the kitchen counter."

I looked back through the doorway, then at Triton's white face and clenched teeth. He was barely vertical, barely conscious, but propping him up was the best plan I had at the moment.

"Lean against the deck rail, okay? Brace yourself with your arms. I'll get the key and be right back."

When he nodded, I got him into position and tore back inside to look for the house keys. They weren't immediately visible, so I began lifting things. Cereal box, power bars, hamburger-casserole package. Stinky sponge, sticky dishtowel. Ick, gross. I searched a few seconds longer, then plunged my hands into a mound of cereal squares and white flakes that smelled like potatoes.

Pay dirt. I found the keys. Two of them on a dolphin ring.

I dashed back to the deck and dangled the set for Triton to see. "These the right ones?"

"Uh, yeah, but we have company."

He inclined his head toward the driveway where an elderly couple stood. The same couple who'd taken my ghost tour. The ones Gorman thought were—

"Can we be of assistance?" the man called up.

"No. No, thank you. My friend is just, um, sick."

The woman, dressed tonight in stylish slacks and a sweater set, shook her head.

"No need to tell tales to us, dear. We heard the ruckus in this young man's apartment and phoned the police."

I frowned. "Then why are they down the street?"

"Because we told the officers we mistook the address," the man said. He pulled up his trousers and puffed out his polo-shirt-clad chest. "Since there was a rather raucous altercation in progress down there, they believed us."

"Now be honest, Clarence," the woman inserted with a pat on the old man's arm. "It helped that we're seniors." She looked up at me. "People expect seniors to get confused, you know."

"So true, Imelda," Clarence agreed.

I concurred. I'd turned 228 my last birthday, and I was sure confused at the moment.

"Here now, let us assist you in getting this young man to the car," Clarence said as he trotted up the steps. "Mother, you open the car door."

He moved so fast, he was three stairs short of the deck before I moved to block Triton.

"Sir, thank you, but I can help my friend."

"Nonsense, Princess. I was a fireman. I know how to carry a person without hurting my back."

"Princess?" I echoed.

"You're the vampire tour guide. Cesca. Francesca, Princess Vampire."

"Yes, but—"

"My dear girl, Melda and I are vampires as well. I promise you, I will neither drop this strapping young man nor harm him in any way."

"You're vampires."

I turned to Triton, who shrugged.

"You didn't know? Oh, but of course you did," Clarence chirped and turned to Triton. "Right, then. Up you go."

Clarence levered Triton onto one shoulder and secured his hold on Triton's leg and arm. When Clarence straightened, he levitated just above the stair treads and flew down them instead of walking.

"This way is less jostling, don't you think?" the old man said over his shoulder.

I nodded absently, wondering why Saber didn't know about these two vamps. Or was he keeping that information from me? And how had I pegged them as human? Damn good questions, but for the moment I lingered long enough to lock Triton's door and sped to catch up as Clarence gently lowered Triton onto the SSR's passenger seat.

Melda patted my arm. "There now, not to worry. Your friend will be fine as soon as he shifts."

I blinked at the wrinkled face. "Shifts, ma'am?"

"Oh, we won't mention it to a soul," she assured me.

"But how do you know he shifts?"

"Because we're vampires, of course. We sense it."

I had *such* a headache coming on.

The car door closed, and Clarence laid a light hand on Imelda's shoulder.

I shook off my latest shock. "Thank you, both of you."

Melda waved a hand. "It's nothing, dear. Drive carefully."

They stepped around me and walked off down the street. I knew I should let it go, but I couldn't.

"Wait, Mr. and Mrs.—"

"Clarke," Melda supplied.

I nodded. "Forgive me, but have you been vampires long?"

Clarence grinned. "You're wondering why we're old, is it?"

"Father, don't tease her," Melda scolded. "The short version, dear, is that a young punk vampire caught us returning to our retirement village and Turned us. That was fifteen years ago. We were eighty-five then."

"But why would he Turn you instead of draining you?"

"He wanted us to serve as his grandparents," Clarence said. "Forever."

"But my dear husband," Melda said with pride, "finally grew strong enough to kill the little criminal. We went to the Vampire Protection people, and they've been kind enough to relocate us."

"Relocated you to where?"

"Why here, of course. We're renting in this neighborhood until we can find the perfect house for our special project."

Special project? Why didn't that sound like a good thing?

"That's right," Clarence said with a wide grin. "We're opening a bed and breakfast exclusively for vampires."

Ai-yi-yi. Could the day get any more bizarre?

Minutes later, Clarence and Melda disappeared, and I sat at the steering wheel rubbing my temples.

"The Clarke's knew, Triton. That you were in trouble, but also that you'd be shifting tonight. They called the cops to save you then waved them off to the house down the block so you wouldn't be detained giving a statement."

"Instead I'm detained listening to you rant. Can we go now?"

"You don't get it. They sensed your nature, but I didn't sense theirs."

"I do get it. You're worried your otherness radar is busted."

"Or I never had it. At this rate, I won't recognize the Void if it smacks me in the face."

"Sure you will. It looks like a rolling oil spill, now drive."

"I have to call Saber."

Triton growled.

"En route," I added, as I started the SSR. "Which beach do you shift on?"

"Try the pier," he said, meaning the St. Augustine Beach fishing pier.

The police cars were gone when I cruised past the corner. Triton didn't notice because he was slumped against the car door, eyes closed. At least his color was better.

I punched up Saber on the cell when I hit A1A.

"You find Triton?" he said with no preliminaries. At least he wasn't shouting this time.

"I did, and he's with me now, but we have a complication. He was attacked and beaten in his apartment by two men looking for the amulets."

"Shit. Humans or supers? Were they working on their own?"

"Triton is sure they're humans. They mentioned a boss but not a name."

"Ten to one Starrack is behind this."

"We think so, too."

"How badly is Triton hurt?"

"Bad enough that I need to stick with him until he shifts and I can be sure he'll heal." I paused to take the short cutoff between A1A and 312. "Listen, I'm taking Triton to the pier beach, and I don't know how long I'll be, but I have a couple of other things to tell you about."

"Then I'll wait for you at home. You can fill me in, and we'll get Triton to look at mug shots in a few days."

"Will that do any good?"

"Can't hurt. If we can track down his assailants, maybe we can persuade them to tell us who hired them. If we get lucky, they'll not only finger Starrack but tell us where he is."

"Hold that thought. Is the storm over out there?"

"Yeah, we're moving tree limbs and picking up the debris. I might be another hour or so, but call me if you have any more trouble."

"We'll be fine."

We disconnected, and I put my cell on the dashboard as the pier parking lot came into view. Bad news was that there were twenty cars parked in the lot and all the closest slots to the beach were taken. Worse news was hearing a party in progress.

I poked Triton on the thigh. "Hey, we need to find a quieter spot."

He inched his head high enough to see out the windshield. "Damn it. I really need to get in the water, Cesca."

"You trust me to pick a beach?"

"Just make it quick."

* * *

Normally I'm not a big fan of allowing cars to drive on the beach. Tonight, it was a blessing.

I eased down the Dondanville beach access ramp and onto the sand. And, since the tide was in, I parked close enough to be steps away from the surf. Now to get Triton into it.

I shook his shoulder. "Hey, are you awake?"

"Getting there." He pushed against the armrest until he was more or less upright. "I smell the ocean."

"Let's find out if you can walk."

My sneakers slapped wet sand when I hopped out of the truck. Hmm. I'd parked even closer to the tide line than I'd thought, but no matter. I'd have better traction by the time I left.

Triton had opened the passenger door, but he moved like a broken puppet just attempting to swing his legs out.

"Damn, I'm stiff as a corpse, Cesca. I need more help than I thought."

"Then put your arm around my shoulders. I won't drop you."

He raised his head and gave me a long look. "What I meant is that I need help stripping."

"Strip—oh, yeah. I forgot."

Some vampires may not blush, but I do. And I did. Violently. Thankfully, it was too dark for Triton to see it.

"Can't you shift and just let your clothes rip?"

"Probably, but I always shift nude. Besides, I'll need these when I change back in about thirty hours." He shot me a weak but wicked grin. "Unless you want to drive me home in the raw."

"I have to pick you up, too? Geez, anything else you want me to do? No, don't answer that," I added when he opened his mouth. "Fine, unbutton your shirt while I get your shoes off."

I toed off my sneakers, then unlaced his and tossed both pairs onto the floorboard. He'd only managed to pull his T-shirt halfway up his chest, so I eased it off.

All the while repeating the mantra, *Be clinical. Be detached. It's only a chest.* A very ripped chest and an abdomen I could bounce coins on.

"Okay, undo your shorts."

"Thought you'd never ask," he teased.

Maybe the rat had seen me blush. Which I now willed myself not to do as I heard the slide of his zipper. Was that skin where boxers or briefs should be?

"I always go commando on shift nights. Don't you remember?"

I did now, and I gulped.

"Surely Saber does the same on occasion," he added.

I answered him by crossing my eyes. "Stand up, turn around, and brace yourself on the door."

"Yes, ma'am."

He followed orders, slowly and with teeth bared in pain. The shorts rode halfway down his hips, and I jerked them to his ankles, not letting my gaze linger on his tight butt for more than a second or three.

When I'd released each foot from the shorts, I tossed them on the car seat. With another reminder to be clinical, I took a discrete deep breath.

"You ready to get wet?" I asked.

The big louse chuckled, and I belatedly got the joke.

"Let me rephrase that, Triton. Are you going to behave, or are you dragging your sorry self to the surf alone?"

"I'll be good. Come on."

I ducked under the arm he held out and took his weight. Which wasn't as dead as it had been at the apartment, but we hadn't taken three steps into the water when he collapsed to his knees, taking me with him.

Both of us paused there on all fours, Triton panting and mooning the condos on the dunes, had anyone been looking. I tried not to get my shorts any wetter than they were.

"This isn't going to work," I said.

He glanced at me then turned his face to the surf. "Just get me in deep enough, and the water will support me."

"Triton, there are sandbars out here," I said sternly. "The waves are higher because of the storm. And if they don't knock you on your bare behind, the riptides may pull us both out. I'm not in the mood to be sucked out to sea in the dark."

"You have another idea?"

"I do. How close are you to changing?"

"Thirty minutes to an hour."

I reconsidered my solution for another minute. It might be risky, it might be downright crazy, but it was my port in this storm.

"Triton, have you ever surfed?"

He gave me a long look then nodded. "Cowabunga."

ELEVEN

I changed into my black, scooped-back maillot behind the open driver's side door. No chance of Triton peeping, and since I had killed the interior lights, no me mooning the condos.

Having dry clothes to wear on the drive home? Priceless.

As I slid my surfboard free of the truck, I peered over at Triton. He lay curled on his side, arms around his middle as if protecting himself. Damn, what would I do if he couldn't shift? Or only partly shifted? I shook away those negative thoughts, grabbed a chunk of wax, and swiped it over the board in a zigzag pattern. I didn't need the waxing for super traction, just to render the fiberglass less slippery.

With the leg leash strapped to my ankle, I hoisted my board and hurried back to Triton.

"Hey. Big, fat, Greek shifter."

He opened one eye. "I'm not fat."

"Tell that to your lip. Roll on your knees so I can help you up."

He did, groaning and moaning. I purposely put my vampire strength in gear, grasped his sandy arm, and got him to his feet.

"Come on. I need to get you in deep enough to put you on the board."

With my board under one arm and supporting Triton with the other, we shuffled into the surf. Ankle deep, then knee deep, then ankle deep again when we hit a sandbar. Finally, I had us in hip-deep water.

"Okay, time to get on the board," I shouted over the roar of the waves. "Can you help me paddle out?"

"I can try."

"Try hard. I'll take the front. You get on behind me. Scoot up enough that your head will be in the small of my back."

"My feet will stick off the end of the board."

"Then keep them together or they'll act like a rudder."

He nodded and I straddled the board. My legs were just long enough to dig my toes into sand shifting with the strong undertow, but it helped steady the board while he mounted close behind me.

"All right, let's go flat together."

I eased down on the board, felt Triton mimic my progress. The board swayed with the waves, but we didn't capsize. I began paddling hard and fast, focusing on slicing through the water, chesting up to breach each breaker. I ignored Triton's labored breath on my bare back. I ignored the feel of his chest pressing into my butt. I even ignored the tickle of a more intimate part of him brushing my calves.

It seemed to take hours to get to the line up, the place where surfers turned their boards to wait for a wave, but we made it without taking a spill.

"How are you holding up?" I hollered over my shoulder.

His guttural "Fine" rumbled up my spine.

"Ready to straddle?"

"Rest first."

"All right, but if you think you're ready to shift, slide off."

"I won't sink the board. Not like I almost did your father's boat."

I grinned at the memory. Triton had been late for our monthly new-moon rendezvous, and we'd rowed like Vikings on speed in our attempt to reach the beach before he shifted. We'd only made it to the inlet before he'd torn his clothes off and flopped over the side.

"My father would have killed me if we'd sunk that boat."

He chuckled, a gentle vibration that trickled all the way to my feet. "Your mother would've killed you if you'd shown up soaking wet again."

Or she would have had Triton's ring on my finger faster than she could filet a fish.

"Cesca, I'm going to slide off now."

I looked over my shoulder. "You're shifting?"

"No, but I'll feel better in the water."

"You'll burn too much energy treading the swells."

"I'll hold on to the board."

Still facedown, he eased away, pushing himself backward until his chest cleared my butt. One more push and he was off, hand-over-handing himself to mid board as I scooted back for better balance. When I levered up to straddle my board, Triton rested his hands by my knee.

"Better?" I asked.

"Yeah."

We floated with our own thoughts for a moment, but Triton's breathing sounded better every second he was cradled in the sea.

"I'm sorry, Cesca."

He'd barely breathed the words, yet I'd heard him clearly.

"What for?"

"Not protecting you from the vampires that night."

I shrugged. "What could you do? Fluke them to death?"

"If you hadn't been with me, you wouldn't have been captured."

I patted his head. "Marco would've kidnapped me anyway. It was just a matter of time."

Triton shrugged. "Maybe, but I've felt guilty about that night. And about the other time I failed to rescue you."

I stared at his upturned face. "What other time?"

"In 1820. Florida was still being transferred from Spain to the U.S., and the whole town was being surveyed. I came back to reclaim the land trust for you. And I came back to search for you. I couldn't find the vampire's house."

"The foundation was gone by then?"

He shook his head. "I don't know. I ran across a lot of rubble. Thought I was close a few times. None of the places I searched felt right."

I took a deep breath. Remembered Isabella's revelation that Cosmil had reconsecrated the ground. Had he really blessed it, or had he bespelled it?

"Why didn't you open our telepathic connection, Triton? Maybe I could have led you to me."

"I didn't want to get your hopes up and fail you again."

"Oh."

"The worst is that I got away. Made a life for myself. I'm sorry you didn't have the same chance."

I laid my hand on his shoulder. "I never blamed you, Triton. Not for the vampires or leaving town. I wanted you gone and safe."

"Then you accept my apolo—"

He broke off, his neck muscles contracting in a savage spasm. Hands flailing, he sank under the surface. The ocean around me churned violently, but I didn't fear a shark attack. I adjusted my seat on the board. Waited.

Minutes later, a beak bumped the nose of my board and water sprayed me from a blowhole. Triton in his dolphin form.

Shifting injured hurts like the devil.

"But you'll be okay?"

If you accept my apology.

"Done."

He swam near enough to rub against my leg under water. His way of saying thank-you, I guessed.

See you Tuesday morning. An hour before sunrise.

Or his way of reminding me of that extra favor, but I nodded. "I'll be here, and you'd better be ready for butt-kicking boot camp."

He slapped his beak on a swell, and a cascade of water smacked my face.

Tyranoulitsa.

"Cretin."

Wrong, I'm cetacean.

He laughed in joyful dolphin speak, then arched away.

All in all, I guessed it was good to have him home.

Saber welcomed me back to the cottage with a deep kiss and a long hug.

"I missed you," he murmured as he nuzzled my neck.

Darling man. He focused on me before he asked about Triton. I framed his head with my hands and kissed him again.

"I missed you, too." I released him and looked down at our feet so I wouldn't step on the ever-present cat. "Where's Snowball?"

"Passed out in her carrier in the kitchen," he said, turning to flip the deadbolt. "Any idea why she's hunkered in there?"

"She had a hissy fit over Isabella, a ghost she cornered this afternoon."

"I take it you know this ghost?"

"She was Normand's human mistress and my only friend, and she came to warn us that evil is stirring up vampire ghosts. Normand and company."

"Is Starrack behind this, too?"

"She didn't give me a name, but who else could it be? I'll tell you about her and other things, but I need to shower this salt water out of my hair first."

He eyed my loosely ponytailed hair with a mess of escaped wavy strands. "More trouble with Triton?"

"He was too weak to wade in deep enough to shift," I said, taking Saber's hand and leading him to the bedroom. "I floated him out on my surfboard."

He leaned against the doorjamb while I turned the shower faucet on hot and peeled off my T-shirt.

"Tell me about the attack."

I paused with my cutoffs half unzipped, the weight of the amulet pulling one side lower than the other. "Now? You don't want to join me in the shower?"

"Not tonight." He rubbed the back of his neck. "Truth is, I'm done in."

"As in Void tired?" I dropped my shorts, and the amulet in my pocket made a dull *thunk* on the bathmat covering the slate-tile floor.

He shrugged. "So what happened with Triton?"

I swallowed back my concern and my urge to fix Saber a can of chicken soup. Instead, I hollered the high points of discovering Triton through the shower door as I washed the salt water from my hair and body. Saber stopped my tale to ask if I'd smelled anything distinctive, and I relayed that I hadn't and Triton didn't remember a smell.

"I hope those jerks weren't carrying the Void infection," I added as I stepped out of the shower, and Saber handed me an oversized white bath towel. "I know we don't have a handle on how the illness spreads, but if it got into his blood stream through those cuts, that would be beyond bad."

"If Triton was severely injured, how'd you get him down those stairs?"

"I didn't. Two other vampires did, and why didn't you tell me they were being relocated here when I first mentioned them to you?"

He straightened, his shoulders tense. "What two vampires?"

"Oh, hell. You don't know."

"Cesca, tell me."

"The old couple Gorman thought could fly? Turns out they can. Clarence and Imelda Clarke are vampires. And they're planning to open a B&B. Want to take a guess who they'll be catering to?"

"Damn it."

He wheeled, heading for the living room. And my laptop, unless I missed my guess. I threw on undies and my long pink flamingo sleep shirt and followed, mopping at my hair with the towel as I went. Sure enough, Saber sat at my desk, the computer booting up.

"I'm sorry I dumped the Clarke info on you, Saber."

"It's okay, but you know I wouldn't keep that from you. The Jacksonville VPA office should notify me of every new vampire moving into Florida, especially when we're on alert."

I frowned. "Alert, why? Because so many vampires in the state are ill?"

"Exactly. My last printout listed 157 vampires. None were newcomers. Did the Clarkes say where they relocated from? Did they sound southern, northern?"

"A little British, a little southern, and very upper-crust."

He logged into the VPA website then into the restricted pages, fingers zipping over the keyboard. He typed in "Clarke" as I peered over his shoulder. Clarence and Imelda's photos and vitals filled the screen in living color. They hailed from Charleston, and the first lines recorded that the senior center where they'd lived had reported them missing fifteen years earlier. The rest of the data read pretty much as they'd told me. Except for the side note that both had worn dentures before their Turning. Afterward, they'd grown fangs. Now they wore specially designed dentures with spaces for the fangs to extend.

I learn some new, wacky thing every day.

"Jo-Jo would love that denture bit," I said, grinning.

"He still uses that joke in his act?"

I shrugged, and Saber shook his head as he clicked to the next page.

"All right, the Clarkes passed their physicals and are GPS implanted."

"Whoa. I never had a physical."

"It's a new policy." He shut down the computer as I perched on the coffee table. "With the nests closed, vampires are free to stay in the same city or move almost anywhere within the U.S., so long as the area isn't already loaded with vamps. But we're checking for symptoms of infection with questionnaires, physicals, and psychiatric profiles. By the way, your dancing buddies, David and Ken, passed their physicals, too. Candy confirmed it."

"Good to know. So these physicals will work like an early warning system to scout potential infectees?"

"And Rampants. Whether these precautionary measures will work, or work well, is yet to be seen."

Rampants were rogue vampires, those Saber was licensed to kill. A run-of-the-fang rogue is dangerous. An infected vampire is insanely dangerous.

"Will the Clarkes be allowed to open the B&B?"

"If they screen their clientele, I don't think we can stop them." He arched a brow. "The Clarkes do know that St. Augustine isn't exactly the nightlife capital of Florida, right?"

"They should, but that's their problem. Saber, why didn't I sense that the Clarkes were vampires during the tour?"

"Honey, you saw what you expected to see. Typical tourists."

"What about tonight? Shouldn't I have picked up a vampy vibe?"

"You might've if you hadn't been preoccupied with Triton. You'd already pegged them as elderly tourists, and they obviously don't project otherness."

"So you don't automatically know a supernatural when you see one? Would you have known I was a vampire if you'd first met me on the street?"

"Oh, yeah, I would've known." He waggled his brows. "You were too gorgeous to be anything but a vampire or a supermodel."

Cobalt blue eyes twinkled with that special look.

I smiled and shook my head. "And here I thought you were tired."

"Maybe I'm getting a second wind." He stood and held out his hand. "Besides, I believe I owe you a dance."

That's all it took for my body to go liquid with heat. I put my hand in his, and it was a very long time later before I thought about anything but Deke's hands and mouth and murmured endearments. I simply reveled in his maddeningly slow lovemaking, and returned every kiss and caress until we found that long, intense release.

As he slipped into sleep, I hugged him tightly and whispered.

"You'll be well again, my love."

I eased myself from Saber's arms a little after three. After donning my nightclothes, I semi folded the comforter we'd kicked off on the foot-of-the-bed bench, gathered a wide-toothed comb, my saltwater-damp clothes, and the amulet from the bathroom, then padded to the front door to check the alarms. I could've sworn they were off, but on the panel, the green lights blinked their armed mode. When had Saber reset them?

"He didn't. I did."

I spun toward the voice, clasping my armload against my chest, and screeching a soft but solid C above high C. Snowball echoed me as Cosmil emerged from the shadowed kitchen.

"Be calm. I mean no harm."

I wasn't sure if he was speaking to Snowball or me, but my stuttering heartbeat slowed as I took in Cosmil's hippie-grunge look of flip-flops, faded jeans, and a Grateful Dead T-shirt. His hair hung limp to his shoulders.

"What in the name of marsh gas are you doing here?" I whispered, shooing him back into the kitchen so Saber wouldn't be disturbed.

"I came to talk and to retrieve the amulet for safekeeping, but do not worry. I only just arrived."

I blushed in the dark. "Well, thanks for that, but how did you get in? I'm positive the door was locked."

"I did not use the door," he replied, calmly pulling out two chairs at my retro kitchen table. "I connected with your energy signature and transported myself on thought waves."

"Through the Veil?"

"My short-distance version of it. Please, come sit. I know you have a few bones to pick with me."

"Hah. I have a whole skeleton of them."

"Then let us begin."

I peered at his sincere expression. Oh, hell, fine. I looked a mess with my unruly hair down, still damp, and sticking out all over, but my pink nightshirt fell to me knees. I was perfectly decent, so there was no point in straining my vampire vision by remaining in the dark. I pushed the microwave's surface light that shone over the stove, then pried the amulet out of my cutoffs as I carried my clothes to the laundry room. Back in the kitchen, I plopped into the chrome and turquoise chair and slapped my comb on the table.

"Here," I said, passing the amulet to him.

He turned it in his hands. "You used it on the trip."

It wasn't a question, but I answered anyway. "Yes, to send a shot of protection when we were in a club."

"This is good, Francesca." He pulled a pouch from under his T-shirt and placed the amulet inside. Then he folded his hands on the table. "Will you give me an update on Triton?"

I did, and Cosmil concurred that Starrack might well have hired the thugs.

"What I don't get," I added, "is how Starrack knew about the amulets."

Cosmil sighed. "Regrettably, I mentioned the Mu amulet in my report to the Council. Starrack must have contact with one of the members. Perhaps a nymph," he mused, "though I do not know how he learned of the second disk."

"Why does he want them? Just because they have powers?"

"Because they can destroy darkness."

"Good thing Triton doesn't have them in his ferns anymore."

Cosmil gave me an almost smile then shifted in his chair. "Francesca, Triton has told you something of his heritage, has he not? That because a spell I cast went awry, he was born."

I nodded and picked up the comb to start working the tangles from my hair. It might be bone-picking time, but I needed something to do with my hands besides make fists.

"I can undo most errant magick, but not when conception results. To mitigate my mistake, I have watched over Triton since his birth. Pandora, too, though she was conceived in an entirely separate incident."

I shook the comb at him. "And in your watching, you've also interfered from time to time."

He inclined his head, conceding the point. "But only occasionally, when the need was great. A small spell influenced Triton to move home in a more timely manner."

"Another small spell kept my butt buried for more than two hundred years, didn't it?" I jerked the comb through a massive tangle.

"True, though you must see the entire picture." Cosmil clasped his hands on the table. "When you were lost to the vampires, I feared for Triton's sanity. You were his beloved friend, and he was wild with grief that he had failed you. He had heard tales of the atrocities the monsters committed before and after they Turned victims. If they Turned them at all."

I swallowed hard. Normand had declared me his heir, princess of his little fanged kingdom, and he'd sheltered me from many of the nest's activities. Still, I'd heard the screams. Smelled the blood. Seen the helpless, empty expression of human captives like Isabella. Each newly Turned soldier or villager had radiated malevolence, blamed me for their predicament.

They would have rather been dead. And more than once, so would I.

"I had fears that Marco would go after Triton," I admitted quietly.

"He did, my dear. Magick protected Triton, but it could not compel him to leave St. Augustine. It took your pleas to convince him to move away."

"And afterward, you left me alone in that dank, smelly coffin."

"Not quite alone, Francesca. Did you not feel another presence with you from time to time?"

"I felt Triton when we talked telepathically."

"Think back. Did you ever smell this scent?"

The kitchen bloomed with the aroma of fresh rosemary, like the potted plants Maggie and I had given friends for my first Christmas last year. I inhaled deeply, let my eyes flutter shut, and allowed memories to wash over me. That scent had permeated the coffin more than once, as if it had wafted in on a fresh breeze. It had calmed me, it had relaxed me, it had filled me with peace.

I opened my eyes. "That was you?"

"Yes, dear girl. Just as I had foreseen that you would walk in the day, I foresaw an era in which vampires would not need to feed on the living. I bespelled your resting place to keep you safe until the right rescuer could release you at the perfect time."

"That smacks of the sleeping beauty story."

He merely smiled. And, okay, I had to admit that Maggie totally fit the bill of right rescuer, as well as mentor and friend. And since I'd gagged at the smell of blood since the moment I was Turned, I would have had a darned-hard time feeding before Starbloods was perfected.

"Francesca, I would not have left you buried if it had not been the wisest choice for the long term."

I laid the comb on the table with a snap. "It was still a manipulative, sneaky thing to do. That doesn't foster warm fuzzies."

I rose and paced to the sink, then faced him again. "Listen, Cosmil, I know Triton thinks I'm not taking this whole Starrack and Void thing seriously, but I am. I would die to save Saber, and I just might take a bullet for Triton."

"And me?" he asked with a quirk of his lips.

I gave him a level stare. "You need to earn my trust."

He nodded. "Fair enough. What can I do?"

"No more manipulating. No more secrets. When we train, tell me what we're doing, why we're doing it, and inform me of possible side effects."

"I will do the same for Saber and Triton. Anything else?"

I hesitated, sorting my thoughts. Would he know about vampire ghosts? About boosting my supe-detecting radar? Maybe, but I had a more nagging question.

"What's the real reason you're relying on Saber and Triton and me to fight the Void? And don't," I said, shaking a finger at him, "give me that tripe about the COA squabbles. You must have other resources. Know people who know people. Heck, Saber could get you mercenaries who are already trained in combat with supernaturals."

His expression clouded. "Mercenaries work for the highest bidder."

"Then how about Marines? I met two vampires who'd be gung

ho to help us. You know what they say on *NCIS*: 'Once a Marine, always a Marine.'"

"You feel strongly about recruiting more help, don't you?"

"You bet your crystal ball. Even with training, sending us into this battle is like sending—" I groped for a comparison, and a movie Saber had watched popped to mind. "It's like sending the Three Stooges to take out a terrorist cell."

He sat back and regarded me for a long moment. "The life of most wizards is solitary, meetings with the Council notwithstanding. You have doubts about me, but there are only four individuals I trust implicitly. You and Saber and Triton are three of them. Lia is the fourth."

I sagged against the countertop. "Oh."

"Remember, too, that I witnessed you drain a vampire nearly dry. I saw you and Saber and Triton work together at the comedy club without the benefit of training. With training, you will be formidable."

"Those two nutso vampires weren't in the same league as Starrack and the Void."

"But Starrack and the Void can still be defeated. Lia and I will teach you and Saber and Triton to work in concert. We will prepare you as best we can."

"And fight this battle with us? Call in help?"

"Indeed. If it appears we need more troops for our battle, I will talk with Saber about these mercenaries."

I crossed to my seat. "You will? Promise?"

"I only promise to discuss it."

"That's a start." I placed my hand over his. "Thank you."

He cleared his throat. "Yes, well, in the meantime you must promise to cultivate more confidence in your own abilities and in the combined abilities you three can bring to bear. Truly, Francesca, your power is nothing to fear."

Before I could respond, he rose. "And now, I shall leave you to help Saber through his nightmares."

Nightmares?

I didn't get the chance to ask, "What nightmares?"

Cosmil disappeared in a puff of rosemary-scented smoke just as Saber shouted agonized gibberish from the bedroom.

TWELVE

I hit the gloom of the bedroom in time to see Saber arch his back and emit a prolonged, eerie cry that frightened me more than facing down the Void.

"Burns. Get out, get out!"

He thrashed in sweat-soaked sheets tangled at his hips and twisted around his legs. I flipped on the bedside light as he kicked and flailed his arms and knocked the lampshade askew.

"Saber, it's okay. I'm here."

He didn't acknowledge me, but his voice weakened when he shouted again. "Get out. Burns. Run."

I didn't know what he dreamed of, but seeing welts break out on his chest and upper arms heightened my terror. First red, the welts darkened to angry black. Was this the Void sickness or a physical reaction to the dream? Remembered injuries, perhaps? The smell of fear and scorched skin filled the room, and I swallowed back a gag.

"Saber, wake up!" I yelled the order.

Following my instincts, I threw my leg over his hips and captured his wrists, pinning his fevered body with my weight.

"Saber. Saber, it's Cesca. Wake up."

His upper body jerked, then he bucked his hips. I clamped my knees tighter and held on.

"Saber, wake up now. Please."

Suddenly, he stilled. His breath came in short gasps, but the welts began to fade to a deep brown that almost blended with his tan. Almost.

I leaned closer. "Deke? Darling, I'm here."

A harsh inhalation, and his eyelids snapped open. He blinked, struggled to place me.

"Cesca."

"Shhh. It's okay now." I brushed a kiss across his lips, releasing his wrists as I sat up. "You had a nightmare."

"Nightmare." He tested the word as if he'd never heard it.

"Do you remember the dream?"

"Don't want to talk about it now. I'm hot. Need a shower."

"Will you be all right while I turn on the water?"

His head lolled on the pillow, and I dashed to the shower stall. With lukewarm water running and a fresh towel on the countertop, I hurried back to help him out of bed.

His knees buckled once, just as I got him on his feet, and again crossing the bathroom threshold. He maintained a grim silence all the way.

"Want me to wash your back?"

He gave me a quick glance. "I can manage."

So much for my attempt at levity.

He gripped the slate-tiled shower frame with one hand, the shower door with the other. "I won't be long."

But he was. Long enough for me to put fresh linens on the bed—the ones with the funky surfboard print that matched my comforter.

Long enough for me to see him through the frosted shower door, his hands braced against the wall, his shoulders heaving.

Long enough for me to pace a rut in the bedroom's bamboo flooring.

Forget frightened. Forget worried. I was freaked.

Should I ask about the dream? Would he relive the horrors if I did? If he remembered the nightmare but kept it bottled up, would that be worse?

The shower cut off, and I leaped to hand him the towel as the shower door clicked open.

He took the towel like a robot, his movements stiff, jerky. He never looked at me, but I searched his body for remaining signs of those welts. They'd faded more, but I picked up light bruising here and there.

"Saber, it's all right."

"No, it's not." He toweled his hair then his body, and hung the bath sheet on a brushed-nickel rack.

Finally he met my gaze, his expression flat. Again, I did what my instincts demanded. I crossed the step that separated us and folded him in my arms.

"Talk to me, Deke."

A shudder shimmied through him, but he didn't return my embrace.

"I need a glass of juice."

He spoke as emotionlessly as he stood. I stepped back and nodded.

"You want it in the kitchen or served in bed?" I paused a beat. "I changed the sheets."

He glanced toward the bedroom, as if measuring how far he could walk.

"In bed." He swallowed. "And then we'll talk."

That simple concession had me zipping to the kitchen. Snowball meowed, and I took a second to open her carrier before I yanked the fridge open hard enough to rock it. Snowball took off for the bedroom, skidding around the corner on the hardwood. With a sixteen-ounce, napkin-wrapped glass filled with Florida OJ in hand, I followed her.

Saber had turned off the bedside lamp, but the Tiffany lamp in the bathroom cast a soft glow on the bed. He lay atop the sheets in the middle of my king bed, propped against the sand-colored padded headboard on two of my four king-sized pillows. He'd put a third pillow longway over his abdomen and lower chest, and that's where Snowball was ensconced, purring as Saber petted her fur in long strokes.

The hems of his boxer shorts were visible below the pillow. Had he donned them so he'd somehow be less vulnerable?

I could relate.

"Here you go," I said, keeping my voice neutral as I placed the crinkled napkin on the side table and handed him the glass.

"Thanks."

I moved to my side of the bed by the double window. I paused to adjust the fall of the blackout curtains then settled cross-legged at the end of the mattress. And, yes, I tucked my nightshirt around my knees. Now was not the time to flash my darling.

Not that he would've noticed. He stared into his orange juice for a full minute before he spoke.

"What did I say in my sleep?"

The question came out low and steady, but a nuance in his voice sliced my skin like a cat scratch.

"You mentioned burns. You said to get out and run."

He took a gulp of juice. Then another. I folded my hands. Waited.

"About twenty years ago, I tracked a vampire to a residence. He held a man, a woman, and two teenaged girls hostage, locked in the attic. It should have been easy to go in at first light, execute the vamp, and free the family."

He sipped then put the glass on the napkin. I waited.

"I broke into the house, but the vampire wasn't resting in the dark. He stood on the second-floor landing with a baseball in one hand. He said that I wouldn't catch him. That he was going out in a blaze of glory. Then he opened the door to the attic stairs, and tossed the ball. The house exploded."

A picture of Saber being blown into a wall flashed in my mind's eye, his shirt peppered with burning debris, welts forming on his chest and arms. My stomach roiled, and I clenched my hands so tightly, my knuckles cracked.

"The vampire died, but so did the family. I learned later that the vamp had been Special Forces in Vietnam. His expertise was disarming and arming booby traps."

I swallowed bile. "Saber, there was no way you could have known."

"No, but this time, the dream was different. The vampire was in the house, but you were outside the back door being consumed by the Void. I lost the innocent family, and I lost you, too."

"You're not losing me, you hear?"

I unfolded my legs and crawled to him. I needed to touch him whether he wanted it or not. Thankfully, he lifted his arm so I could snuggle into his side.

"We're not in this alone, Saber," I said as I laid my hand over his heart. "We have allies, plus we have the VPA and the COA to ferret information from. We will kick ass and take names. We'll come out of this alive and well."

"Oh, yeah?" He put his other arm around me. "What happened to my little vampire pacifist?"

I tilted my head to meet his gaze. "She wants her normal afterlife back, and she's mad enough to mow down anything in her way to get it."

He smiled, just a quirk of his sexy mouth. "I love a take-charge woman."

"Thank you." I stretched up to give him a smacking, noisy kiss. "Now, what time do we get Lia at the airport?"

"She lands at four eighteen."

"And it's ten minutes to the airport. I'll be up by three." I slanted him a mock-stern glower. "*If* I get my beauty sleep."

He brushed back my hair and sighed a kiss against my lips.

"Just let me hold you."

I left Saber only twice, and only long enough to snag Triton's clothes and my swimsuit from my car, and then to launder them with my cutoffs and tee and the sheets I'd stripped from the bed. Though I doubted that Saber would forget the incident any time soon, I didn't want him to see—or smell—the sheets in the basket and be reminded of the nightmare.

When dawn broke, and Saber's breathing had remained deep and even through the rest of the night, I allowed myself to relax and drift to sleep with Snowball curled between us.

At three on the dot Monday afternoon, I blinked awake. Saber was gone from the bed, of course, but I heard him in the kitchen. Whistling. Thank God. Maybe he didn't have the nightmare hangover I'd feared he would.

What to wear to meet a sorceress? Let's face it, I had a limited wardrobe in limited colors. Heck, before Maggie had chosen burgundy for the maid of honor dress, I'd seldom worn reds or pinks at all. Since then, I'd added more color variety, and sure, I owned a few dresses and a skirt or two. But shorts, capris, jeans, and various mix-and-match camis, blouses, and tees dominated my closet. And, eeks, I'd forgotten to take the sheets and Triton's clothes out of the dryer.

I washed my face, brushed my teeth, and made the bed before heading for the laundry room. Saber half turned from the sink he was scrubbing as I entered the kitchen.

"Hey, honey."

"Hey, yourself hot stuff. You feeling all right today?"

"I'm good. Oh, and I have your laundry on the steam cycle and a load of my clothes in the washer."

He smiled, and though it didn't quite chase all the shadows from his eyes, I let it ride.

I crossed to lay a big kiss on him. "Do you know what a keeper you are?"

"Glad you think so. I figure we'll be slammed with training this week, so I got some chores taken care of."

"Like what?"

"Look in the fridge."

I did and saw four six-packs of Starbloods chilling in addition to the three bottles I already had. Saber had also restocked milk, bread, and lunchmeat for himself. I bet there was a new box of his favorite cereal in the cabinet, too.

"I went to the car wash. The Vue is cleaned and vacuumed."

"You are a domestic god, my darling, and I am your slave."

"Then I've got you where I want you."

As I kissed him again, the dryer buzzed. I wore a huge smile of relief as I hung and folded my clothes, then put his in to dry. Saber showed no serious side effects from his nightmare or from sharing the truth behind his dream, and I was giddily grateful for those favors.

I heard his electric shaver going in the bathroom, so I slammed one of my caramel-macchiato flavored Starbloods then put away my clothes. I saved out the aqua capris, a white bra-top camisole, and an aqua shell embroidered with white dragonflies. White sandals would complete the outfit. Heck, I might go wild and carry the miniscule white purse Maggie had given me. Obviously, I paid zero attention to the no-white-after–Labor Day rule.

Just as obviously, I soon learned, Lia did.

As Saber and I peered out the regional airport waiting-area window, the French fashionista stepped off the chartered jet wearing a gold silk blouse, deep chocolate linen slacks, and black low-heeled pumps. Her auburn hair cut in a short, sassy style, Lia looked tanned, fit, and not a minute over forty as she rolled her monogrammed Louis Vuitton suitcase across the tarmac.

Wow. The sorceress business must pay better than Cosmil's wizard gig, but geez. I had to get this woman into St. Augustine casual.

Lia breezed into the waiting area like she'd been here a thousand times.

"Ah, here you are," she said, only a smidge of an accent lilting her speech. "Cesca and Saber, and aren't you the perfect couple!"

I exchanged a grin with Saber then offered my hand in greeting. "We're pleased to meet you, Lia. Did you have a good flight?"

"Not the mode of transportation I'm used to, but mortal innovations do have their uses."

She waved her hand and pulled a cell phone from the air.

Saber laughed. "Let me take your bag. My car is right outside. We'll have you settled in no time."

"*Merci*, most kind, but before I forget, I want to give you my cell number."

Saber and I whipped out our phones to add Lia to our contacts.

"And now, may I beg a favor?"

Saber held the terminal door open. "Yes?"

"On the way, might we stop for something called a MoonPie?"

* * *

We didn't find moon pies at the nearest grocery store, not the original, trademarked brand or a knockoff, either. But en route, Lia informed us that she had phoned Cosmil from New York to get a status report and to arrange a tentative schedule.

"Since one of our group is unavailable tonight," she said from the backseat where she'd insisted on sitting, "I suggested gathering only to dine tonight. I do not wish to drop from jet lag when there is so much to be accomplished. Cosmil and I, we will cast location spells to search for Starrack tomorrow and begin your training in the evening."

"Do you have a restaurant in mind?" Saber asked.

"Cosmil suggested Saltwater Cowboy's. Do you know it?"

We nodded.

"Good. One can never be sure of Cosmil's recommendations. The man needs to get out more."

Saber choked. I snickered. At least Lia wouldn't be a boring teacher.

"I take it Cosmil will need a ride, Lia?"

"Yes, and we also need current area maps for the location spell."

"Done. Cesca," he said, taking my hand and squeezing it with a firm, deliberate pressure, "I'll drop you both at the cottage so you can get your car."

I startled and looked at our entwined fingers, because I'd clearly heard Saber in my mind's ear ask, *Will you be okay alone with the drill sergeant?*

I squeezed back, projecting, *She has a sense of humor. I'll be fine.*

Aloud I said, "I'll take Lia to your house and get her settled. We'll meet you at—"

I glanced at the dashboard clock then twisted around to check with Lia. "Is six thirty good for you?"

She nodded, grinning as if she knew something I didn't.

I found out what that something was when I showed her my cottage.

Thank goodness Saber had cleaned. Lia pronounced the living room lovely and my funkier décor darling. She even charmed our resident feline.

"Do you and Saber live together?" she asked, cuddling Snowball against her chest and scratching the cat's ears.

"Not all the time, but he's been staying here more lately. Lia, you're going to be covered in cat hair."

"Not to worry. I must say you and Saber have a strong telepathy working. Untrained, but we will address that."

I cleared my throat. "Uh, you read our thoughts in the car?"

"Yes, and I'm not offended, but you need to learn to shield from others. I have added that to our schedule." She patted my arm then addressed the cat. "All right, sweet kitten, we must go."

Lia lowered a reluctant Snowball to the floor and then waved a hand down her blouse and slacks. Cat hair lifted from her clothes, swirled like an allergy sufferer's nightmare, and compressed into a ball that disappeared with a poof of white smoke.

"Now that trick would make you a fortune."

"It is a handy little travel spell," she agreed. "What time do you fetch your shifter friend?"

"Triton? I'll pick him up an hour before sunrise."

"Be sure you have the key to his apartment. After dinner, we will tidy up a bit for him. Don't worry, he won't mind," she added before I could object to taking a stranger into Triton's home. "He'll rest better with his home in order, and he'll need that energy for training."

The sorceress was a steamroller. What else could I do but agree?

Lia enjoyed the sites as I drove through town, and I was soon ushering her into Saber's home, a 1950s three-bedroom ranch house that he'd bought from Neil. Maggie had helped Neil renovate and re-decorate, and Saber hadn't changed much.

We stayed only long enough for Lia to pull a few things from her suitcase. Three cotton outfits, which she ironed with another wave of her hand, and a dozen semitransparent fabric bags in jewel colors. The bulging bags were closed with leather ties, and I detected the scent of rosemary and other herbs I couldn't name as she stowed them in a drawer.

Saber and Cosmil waited for us on the outdoor deck at Cow-boy's, but I didn't immediately recognize the wizard. He wore black slacks with a light blue shirt, and his hair was shorter than Saber's. Had to be an illusion, but Lia's green eyes sparkled as she beamed her approval.

"Talk about cleaning up well," I whispered to Saber as Lia and Cosmil clasped hands and exchanged kisses on each cheek.

"I think he was going for a mature Cary Grant–casual look."

"I think he nailed it."

At Saber's request, the hostess seated us at a table where we could watch the sunset. Cosmil and Lia ordered Minorcan clam chowder and the Florida Cracker Dinner, Saber opted for fried shrimp, and I stuck with my usual sweet tea, heavy on the ice.

By halfway through the meal, I expected us to be talking shop. I even introduced the subject of Starrack in hushed tones, but Cosmil stonewalled me. I put up with that nonsense until dessert.

"Cosmil, put a dome of silence over us if you have to, but I want some questions answered. Now."

"Unpleasant conversation is bad for the digestion," he hissed back.

"Then take a gas pill," I snapped and turned to Lia. "What's going on at your COA headquarters? Did your investigators find Legrand's body? How are the bomb survivors doing?"

"COA?" Lia glanced at Cosmil.

"Council of Ancients." He sighed. "Francesca is nothing if not to the point. Never mind persistent."

"Fine traits," Lia said. "The survivors will live, thank you for asking. And yes, parts of the body were located just before I left."

"Parts?" Saber echoed.

"When the Veil folded in on itself, it fractured the remains."

"Geez, people, if the Veil is that dangerous, why do you bother? It can't be for the bonus miles."

Lia gave me a Gallic shrug. "It's true that one must concentrate on one's destination while in the Veil, but it is pleasant, and it is simply our preferred mode of travel."

"Did your investigators," Saber asked, "find enough of Legrand's remains to run DNA?"

"They did. Vampires in Europe and other countries are not compelled to submit DNA samples as you do to the VPA, but those holding Council seats are required to do so."

"So you *will* have data to compare Legrand's tissue against?" Saber pressed.

"Hopefully, yes. He put up quite a fight when we began the program a few years ago, citing invasion of privacy."

Saber nodded. "The VPA ran into the same argument early on, but it's proven valuable."

"Yes, well, forensic tests on vampires are more complex due to layers of DNA from both the family of origin and the vampire's Maker. We send all preternatural remains to a private, discrete morgue with a special laboratory, so it will take time to get the results. Perhaps up to a month."

"You guys ought to consider having your own lab at the compound," I said. "You know, for emergencies like this."

"We are not in the habit of needing such a facility, Francesca," Cosmil admonished.

"And in this case, it would not have helped," Lia said. "A lab would have been placed near the medical clinic, and our clinic was damaged in the incident. Even without the injuries and fatalities, you can imagine the chaos that ensued. Factions suspected each other of the deed until I informed them we had a rogue wizard."

"Is the COA helping to look for Starrack?" I asked.

"I implored those holding seats to spread the word, but I cannot say that anyone is actively looking for him."

"Except the two of you," Saber said.

When Saber put it that baldly, hiring mercenaries and Marines for backup sounded better and better.

"One more question, Lia," I said. "Cosmil told us you'd dealt with Starrack before, and might be able to find him. Did you try a spell on your own?"

Lia's glance darted to Cosmil before she spoke, an odd energy zipping between them.

"My solo tracking spell failed," she admitted as she turned back to me. "However, I talked with a nymph before I left France. She hasn't seen Starrack in more than a year, but she gave me a focus to assist us in locating him. She also swore she'd ask her friends if they'd seen him recently. Nymphs are notorious gossips, so I should hear back from her soon."

"Gossipy nymphs are good," I said, "but what the heck is a focus?"

"It is a tool," Cosmil answered. "Hair or nail clippings are most often used for a location spell, or it could be an object the target has handled often."

"In this case," Lia added, "I have the wine goblet generally reserved for Starrack's use during nymph gatherings. It is customary to leave dregs in the cup, and the goblets are not cleansed until the next use."

Saber looked skeptical. "You think Starrack's DNA is still on the goblet?"

"Enough for magical purposes, yes," Lia said, "provided that the

goblet remained untouched by others. Given the nature of nymph
parties, well, we shall see."

On that note, our meal concluded, and Cosmil paid the check,
with cash money, no less. I idly wondered if he had a stash under his
mattress or had conjured the bills. No matter because I was certain
the bills were real. I couldn't see him stiffing the restaurant.

Outside, we agreed to meet at Cosmil's the following night at
seven, then Saber walked me to my car while Lia and Cosmil chatted
a few minutes more.

"I'll be home as soon as I drop Cosmil at the cabin," Saber said.

"You may beat me there. Lia wants us to go clean Triton's
apartment."

"Want my help?"

"Nah. Maybe Lia will use her sorceress powers and wave away
the mess. Although, I suppose you could pay a call on the Clarkes."

He glanced at the magical couple. "Might as well. I don't know
when I'll get to it once we start training."

"You got that right. I'll get Lia settled, give her your other spare
key, and be ready to get the scoop on Melda and Clarence. Oh, and
warn them about Gorman, would you? I forgot to mention him, and
you know he's obsessive when he has a vampire in his sights."

Lia didn't wave the apartment back to order, but we still finished
tidying, dusting, and vacuuming Triton's place in under an hour. I
made the effort to sniff for any smell that didn't belong, but the in-
truders had dumped tilapia and salmon in the sink, still half-wrapped
in foil. The defrosted, spoiled mess masked every scent but a slight
gasoline smell that I chalked up to the apartment being built partly
over the garage.

As we drove to Saber's house, Lia asked me about my maid of

honor schedule, and I promised to get her a list of both my wedding and ghost-tour commitments. Then, after showing her how to work the thermostat, I gave her the extra key and headed home.

Saber had the Cowboys-Eagles Monday Night Football game on the tube when I came in and collapsed on the sofa beside him.

He lurched away. "Did you clean Triton's place with fish oil?"

I crossed my eyes at him. "Lia stuck me with the gag-inducing mess in the kitchen while she took the bedroom and bath. She smells lemon fresh."

"She outmaneuvered you, huh?"

"I've known her five hours, and I'm worn out trying to keep up with her. The best thing about training will be coming home."

"You don't like Lia?"

"Actually, I do. It's just that she's just so busy, and always thinking and planning and *scheduling*."

He chuckled. "Honey, you're the same way. You're just not used to marching to someone else's drum."

"Maybe, but I'll be glad to get back to my quieter afterlife. Did you see the Clarkes?"

"They weren't at home. Before the game started, I fired an e-mail to Dave Corey asking for a copy of the Clarke's entire file."

Dave was the Jacksonville VPA agent who was also my handler, though he seldom bothered to keep tabs on me.

"Dave's a good guy," I defended.

"But he's not as on the ball as Candy in Atlanta. He should have notified me about the Clarkes as soon as he dispatched them here."

"True, but no one is as prompt as Candy."

Just then, Saber got sidetracked when the Cowboys threw a long pass. He shouted, and Snowball raced out of the kitchen. She paused, sniffed, then launched herself into my lap to lick my hands.

I let her rough tongue and soft purrs soothe me while the replay officials reviewed the catch, and the cameras showed the Dallas Cowboy Cheerleaders jiggle on the sidelines. Saber denies it, of course, but he's a bigger fan of the cheerleaders than the team.

Of course, I'm a bigger fan of the players, so it evens out.

The play stood. Touchdown. Snowball abandoned my lap for Saber's. I headed for the master-bath sink to scrub my hands with a concoction of sea salts, and pear and coconut essential oils I bought at the weekly Saturday morning farmers' market.

It did the trick. No fishy stench when Saber and I retired to celebrate the Cowboy's win. Go team.

The Internet listed sunrise as 7:14, but I arrived at the beach at five thirty with extra towels and Triton's clean clothes, just in case he shifted early. Rain had blown in from the ocean overnight, and I hoped the early walkers would stay indoors long enough for me to whisk Triton into the car. Or at least into a beach towel.

Since the rain didn't bother me, I sat on the hood of my SSR, keeping watch with vampire vision. At six, I saw Triton's head—his human head—break the ocean surface. He waved to signal he'd seen me, then faced back out to sea. I barely had time to wonder what he was waiting for when a dolphin shot straight up from the swells, not ten feet from Triton's right side.

The dolphin arched to dive back into the water, and thirty seconds later I saw a second human head above the waves. This one had shoulder-length hair that shone silver, even in the darkness. Before the figure swam to join Triton, even before they kissed, I knew.

Triton had a girlfriend.

THIRTEEN

〜

You might recall that my hair is a pain. It waves more than the royal family. It curls in random coils. It frizzes if the humidity hits 20 percent, and Florida humidity averages 60 percent.

So, if I gnashed my teeth as Triton wrapped the tall, gorgeous woman he'd introduced as Lynn Ann Heath in one of my beach towels, it wasn't with jealousy over Triton. It was pure envy over the woman's perfectly straight silver blond hair. Never mind her perfectly spaced, perfectly arched eyebrows that I'd swear had never seen tweezers.

With Lynn shivering in my one and only passenger seat, I cranked the heat up, flashed her a smile, and hopped out to confront Triton.

He met my gaze as he zipped his shorts.

"All the dolphins in all the seas of the world, and you have to find your mate now? Triton, this is the definition of poor timing."

"Jealous?"

"Envious, and only of her hair." I pushed him toward the end of the truck and spoke quietly. "Why did you bring her with you?"

"I tried to swim her home, but she lives in Daytona, and we were fishing up by Jax Beach when we felt the stirrings of the change. We barely made it this far, so get off my back."

"Fine, then you explain her to you-know-who when we show up for you-know-what tonight."

"Chill. I'll drive Lynn home after we shower, then come back home and sleep." He paused with his rain-wet T-shirt halfway over his head. "Damn. My apartment is wrecked."

"Not so much. Remember the visitor flying in from France? She and I cleaned it for you."

His head emerged from the neck hole. "You did?"

"Yeah, but I hope you have some powerful air freshener. The place may still smell fishy."

"Is that a crack?"

"No, idiot, it's a fact. The yahoos that, uh, visited you dumped your frozen fish along with a lot of other food."

"Oh, well, thanks for cleaning."

"You're welcome. What's with Lynn? She seems a little unsteady."

He shrugged. "I don't think she's been a shifter more than a few years."

"Just how many years past puberty is she? Is she of legal age?"

"I don't know yet. Is the interrogation over? Can we go now?"

"You'll have to ride with her on your lap."

"No problem."

And it wasn't, except that Lynn's teeth continued to chatter so much, it was difficult to make conversation. I gave up when she rested her head in the crook of Triton's neck and closed her eyes.

Okay, so maybe she'd heard my exchange with Triton. Maybe I'd alienated my best friend's new girl. I'd worry about that if she stuck around.

In my peripheral vision, I saw Triton tenderly brush a lock of hair from Lynn's cheek. Who was I kidding? She'd be sticking around.

But I could and would insist on investigating her. I'd put Saber, Cosmil, Lia—hell, even Pinkertons—on the case of discovering who Lynn Ann Heath really was. I believe in synchronicity, but really. After all Triton's years of searching for a mate, why had a human-dolphin shifter suddenly appeared on his sonar just as we prepared to fight Starrack and the Void?

If that wasn't hinky, I'd eat a flip-flop.

Saber ferried Lia out to Cosmil's on Tuesday evening so that I could do wedding errands. And, no, I hadn't told Saber about Lynn. I wanted Triton to drop that bomb to the entire group tonight, and *then* I'd voice my concerns.

I met with Maggie in Wedding Central at five bearing the delayed but delightful tussie-mussie charms she'd ordered. The jeweler's catalog photos hadn't lied about the delicate filigree.

"They're perfect." She teared up as she let an ultrafine silver chain spill through her fingers. "Oh, Cesca, the wedding is in twelve days. This is really happening, isn't it?"

"You're just eager for the honeymoon."

She gave me a watery grin. "That, too."

"Let's get these RSVPs recorded before Neil gets home."

We did that and reviewed the plans for both the bridal and couples showers coming up on Saturday and Sunday, but I still changed into black cotton drawstring shorts and a workout T-shirt, and made it to Cosmil's with ten minutes to spare.

Triton beat me to the shack, but I could tell he hadn't spilled the Lynn bean the moment I joined the confab gathered at the coffee table. The warning glance he sent me as I sat on the floor at Saber's feet said it all.

I won't tattle, I projected at Triton, *but you better fess up soon. Don't get your fangs in a bunch.*

I rolled my eyes then jumped when Cosmil slapped the coffee table. "Francesca, are you listening?"

Yikes, the reprimand reminded me of Mr. Genopoly, the first schoolmaster in St. Augustine. I hadn't lied then and didn't now.

"Actually, no, I wasn't. Sorry."

Saber squeezed my shoulder and winked when I looked up.

Cosmil puffed an exasperated breath and pulled on the sleeves of his wizard robe. Yes, he wore his uniform of white tunic and pants, but also sported a purple robe tonight. Lia was similarly dressed, but in what looked like light blue scrubs and a green sorceress robe.

"We will begin," Cosmil said pointedly, "by evaluating your individual skills. After that, we will teach you an energy exercise to deepen your collective connection. Francesca, you will go with Lia, and I will coach the men."

"We're not working with the amulets?" I asked.

"Not tonight," Lia said. "Come along."

"No." I folded my arms on the coffee table. "I'd like some answers first."

Behind me, Saber snorted. Across from me, Triton shifted in his seat.

Guilty conscience? I projected at him.

No.

Hah.

Lia looked from one to the other of us, genuine puzzlement on her face. "What answers do you seek?" she asked.

"For starters, did you find Starrack?."

"Only two faint traces of him, and we estimate those are five to seven days old. It is apparent that the goblet is contaminated with other DNA. But come. I will demonstrate."

Saber and I bolted in Lia's wake as she crossed to the island, with Triton and Cosmil bringing up the rear.

"As you see, we're using three maps. A detailed map of St. Augustine," she said, pointing, "an area map of nearby counties and cities, and a world map. Simply put, we sprinkled a luminescent powder over the maps, added scraping from the wine goblet, and pushed our intention to find the DNA owner into the spell. The glowing green points indicate hits."

I squinted at the city and area maps, each smudged with a single, barely-there glow. In contrast, bright dots on one section of the world map looked like an outbreak of green measles.

"I take it," Saber said, "you don't think Starrack is touring Western Europe."

"Just one or more nymphs or other guests who used Starrack's goblet. But look here and here." She waved a hand, and the two local maps slowly magnified. "We are certain Starrack has been in these locations."

"Daytona Beach," I murmured to Saber. "You think he was hanging out near Ray and the crew?"

"It's this King Street at US 1 hit that bothers me," Saber said. "That intersection is a just a few miles from your cottage."

"And not much farther," Triton piped up, "from my place."

"We don't yet know," Lia continued, "if our poor results are due to the diluted DNA, to time lapsing, or to the strong possibility Starrack is deliberately covering his tracks."

"Why would he be covering his tracks?" I asked. "Does he know we're looking for him?"

"If he has contacts on the Council, yes," Cosmil replied. "I mentioned in my report that the Void needs to be found and destroyed."

"Does Starrack know where you live, Cos?" Triton asked.

"And know Lia is here now, too?" I added.

"I do not know for certain, but we must presume he is aware on both counts."

"Which is why Cosmil and I began casting protection spells over each of you today. We will tweak the location spell later tonight, but you must understand that the magick doesn't give us real-time readings like a GPS tracker does. When Starrack is stationary for thirty minutes, the map flares to light his location and an alarm sounds."

"And then you call us," Saber said. "Day or night."

"But of course."

"What about other information on Starrack?" I asked. "His appearance, his personality."

Lia stiffened so subtly that, had I not been standing beside here, I wouldn't have noticed. I did catch the glance Cosmil gave her, though. One that spoke of shared history, shared secrets. Secrets that better not have squat to do with our search.

"When I knew Starrack, he fluctuated between being a free-spirited, charming rogue and an arrogant, devious SOB. He was more a wanderer than a man of home and hearth, and more a trickster than a fighter."

"We think he's behind the attack on Triton," Saber said, "but why would he want the amulets?"

"Because they can destroy the Void, I suppose," Lia replied. "He'd want to protect his creation. However, the amulets are also valuable artifacts, so perhaps he would sell them. Starrack was never easy to read, or to predict."

"What does he look like, Lia? Cosmil said there is a family resemblance, but I could see this guy on a ghost tour and not know him. Maybe he was even in Triton's store, casing the place."

"Starrack and Cosmil looked a good deal alike when they were younger, but Starrack's proclivity for spirits and general debauchery aged him rather severely in the last years I knew him."

"Hold on," Saber said. "Starrack drinks a lot?"

"He had that reputation."

"He's a boozer, yet he came up with the Void? Doesn't that strike anyone but me as odd?"

"Not necessarily," Triton put in. "Several men that history considers geniuses have been giant lushes or addicts. Poe, Hemingway, Fitzgerald."

"I wouldn't call Starrack a genius," Lia said, "but he has a high-enough tolerance for alcohol to make him quite functional."

"Functional enough to create and control the Void," Cosmil agreed.

"I'll take your word for it," Saber said. "What else can you tell us about his appearance? Does he use spells to change his looks?"

"If so, he made only minor changes. Much the way Cosmil does."

Triton crossed his legs, ankle on his knee. "Too bad you can't conjure up a photo so we can see him."

"Such an image would be an old one from my memory, but I was rather a dab hand at sketching once. Perhaps I can draw a portrait that will project an aged Starrack. Would that do?"

"It's better than operating blind like we are now," I said.

"Very well, I will work on a sketch. Now, we really must proceed with your evaluations."

Our tutors led the way, and Triton hustled after them. Saber helped me to my feet and gave me a hug. "Way to beard the lioness, honey."

"You helped."

He grinned. "Always."

"Cesca, Saber, now," Lia called.

We complied, Saber peeling off to join Triton and Cosmil, me following Lia to the far arc of the circle of trees.

"All right, Cesca, Cosmil tells me you are a master at draining life force energy, and that is excellent. But before I begin formally evaluating your other skills, a woman-to-woman talk is in order."

My hackles rose. "I've had the sex talk, Lia. I think I'll pass."

"No you will not. Sit."

Much as I wanted to rebel, I reluctantly dropped to the grass.

"Cosmil has sensed you fear your power, and I sense that fear stems from ignorance."

"Gee, thanks."

"Cesca, listen to me. When a woman claims her sexuality, when intimacy is her choice rather than being coerced or outright forced, she claims a great fullness of her feminine power. In most cases, this relates to her body's reproductive power. You being a vampire, that issue is moot, but the power is very real, and it is potent."

"I know. I'm much better at flirting now."

"Cesca." She gave me an exasperated look then narrowed her eyes. "Normand didn't allow a single male to touch you, correct?"

I squirmed. "He kept me fairly isolated."

"Of course he did. Normand did not want you to come into your full powers until he deemed it time. He might have lost command of his own court."

I snorted. "Not likely."

"Perhaps not, but that was his fear. Legrand, the vampire killed in the Veil, inherited many of his sire's powers and ultimately challenged Normand."

"So Normand lost and hightailed it to the New World?"

"He did not lose. He left Legrand at the mercy of his loyal followers and brought those who sided with Legrand to America."

"Huh." No wonder there had been such an odd vibe in the nest. I thought the other vamps had resented me because Normand had proclaimed me his daughter and princess of his realm. Seems they'd hated Normand long before that.

"So you understand now," Lia was saying. "Your powers—all of them—are natural and normal."

Sure, yeah, whatever, crossed my mind, but I wasn't rude enough to speak the words aloud. Lia might be right about the natural and normal part, but I didn't trust that embracing my powers wouldn't destroy my soul.

"Up with you now, so I may assess your skills. First, I want you to fly over the cabin and back to me."

"All right, but I have a little vertigo."

"Then don't look down."

Easy for her to say. Sure I'd flown higher and farther, but not by much and not with an audience grading my performance. Still, off I went. I completed the circle and subsequently flew to the main road, but I looked down on the return run and dizziness hit. I lost altitude, coming in low over the trees. Lia made a moue of disappointment.

"You'll need to work on distance flying," she said, and I psychically saw her make a check minus on her mental list.

Her brows arched in surprise. "You read my thought?"

I shrugged. "An image that clear is hard to miss."

"Only because you wanted a peek at your report card."

"Okay, I'm busted. I wanted to know your opinion, so I looked."

She gave a sharp nod. "Good, we can build on that. Now we'll test your other vampire skills."

For the next half an hour, Lia tested my vamp speed, sight, hearing, and sense of smell. I did wind sprints fast enough to make a running back weep with envy, spotted a bird's nest through twenty feet of overgrown woodland, and heard a raccoon foraging from seventy feet away.

I tracked the animal by her scent with Lia trotting at my heels. I swear the limbs seemed to move out of her way, because her robe didn't snag on a single twig. When the raccoon stopped, backing her hindquarters into a fallen pine tree near a stream, Lia soothed the agitated female coon with a word.

The next trial, though, was a stumper.

"All right," she said in hushed tones. "The creature is calm now. Your turn to enthrall her."

"Um, Lia, I don't think that works on animals," I whispered back.

"Of course it does. Did King Normand not teach you?"

"I must've skipped that class."

"How is your ability to enthrall humans?"

"It sucks. I laugh every time I try it."

She held my gaze. "You never saw enthrallment used for good, did you?"

I snorted softly. "In a nest of vampires? Not even close."

"Then I take it Normand only demonstrated the death gaze."

I gaped. "That's a real thing?"

"I fear so. Legrand excelled at it. He even used it on other vampires."

"Well, we can skip right over that trick."

"No, we cannot. The death gaze is an extreme version of enthrall-ment and is related to your ability to drain life force. You need to know how to enthrall in order to send energy as well as take it. Now, when I lift my calm spell from the little mother, I want you to will the raccoon to be easy again. Ready?"

"Wait, no. She's a mother?"

"Her kits are nearly six months old. Listen to them in the log."

I tuned in and heard the scratching of claws.

"Lia, I'm not messing with a mother. Find me another animal or move on to the next test."

"No, you need to prove to yourself that you won't injure the creature. Think becalming instead enthralling. Now squat on your haunches, look at her, and assure her she and the kits are safe."

I followed orders, and to my shock, I connected with the coon's confusion and fear. She paced at the opening of the den, the instinct to protect her family strong. I sent her gentle thoughts, mentally told her that she was a wonderful mother with beautiful children and that I meant no harm. As I crooned to her in my head, she ceased pacing, stood on her hind legs, and made eye contact. A moment later she shambled away to hunt.

I rose slowly, in awe.

"There, now you understand. You did not compel her to leave her den, you only helped her understand it was safe to go about her business. You must remember that distinction. Manipulation isn't necessarily destructive."

"Sit in a circle on the grass," Cosmil instructed a short time later. "Get close enough to comfortably hold hands. Left hand up, right hand down."

Surrounded by four white candles in tall jars, Saber, Triton, and I folded to the ground cross-legged then closed ranks until our knees almost touched. We clasped hands, Triton on my left, Saber on my right, and looked up at Cosmil for further direction.

"The point of this exercise is to connect by channeling energy. You will be tuning into each other, so to speak."

"This will help us fight the Void how?" I asked.

"If one of you is weakened, the others will quickly be able to transmit an energy boost."

"Once learned," Lia added from where she stood opposite Cosmil, "the technique will work even if you're separated. You'll also be able to locate each other through your energy, but you must practice until you can create a vortex."

"Correct." Cosmil turned to Saber. "You are neither shifter nor vampire, but you carry the mark of both. You are the balance between Triton and Francesca, so you will start the flow for the first session."

"What do I do?"

"Fill yourself with a thought or an emotion that brings you joy. Hold that energy until you feel its pressure. When you're ready, imagine turning on a water spigot. Let the energy flow through your right hand into Triton's left. Triton and Cesca, picture yourself as pipelines and let the energy pass through you and back to Saber."

Sounded easy enough. I relaxed my shoulders, closed my eyes, and wondered if I'd know the energy when I felt it.

Less than a minute later, I sensed the first trickle of the warmth I associate with Saber pass from Triton to me. I kept the pipe analogy in mind and felt the fingers of my right hand tingle as the energy moved back to Saber. Then, the tickles and tingles came faster, flowing up one arm, through my chest, and out of the opposite hand until I thought I might float away.

"Excellent," I heard Cosmil say. "Now do not break your handclasps. Saber, imagine slowly turning off the spigot and dial down your flow of energy the same way."

The tickles and tingles gradually stopped.

I opened my eyes when Triton freed his hands and wiped them on his jeans. Cosmil and Lia beamed their approval.

"Fine job, Saber. You have done this before?"

"I did similar exercises when I studied Eastern and Western disciplines to improve my skills as a slayer."

"Your studies serve you well." Cosmil pointed at me. "All right, Francesca, your turn."

I held hands with the guys, closed my eyes, and pictured surfing. Catching a wave, flying across its face, and being rocked by the sea when I paddled out again.

The smells and sounds and splashes of the ocean enveloped me so much, that I almost missed Cosmil's signal to ease up and stop.

Saber gave my hand a warm squeeze. "If that's what surfing is like, maybe I'll learn."

"You saw what I pictured?"

He nodded. "Did you see the image, too, Triton?"

"Yeah."

Even Cosmil blinked at the terse reply. "Is something amiss, Triton?"

"I'm fine. Just tired. Can we get on with this?"

I narrowed my eyes at him but only read a jigsaw puzzle jumble of pictures.

Until we all reclasped hands. In seconds, a rogue wave of ecstasy rolled through my body, and so did a slideshow. One featured Triton in his dolphin form meeting Lynn in hers. Others depicted the pair racing and chasing and leaping from the water. Then the image switched to a man and silver-haired woman wearing only towels, falling onto a bed. I didn't know if it was Triton's bedroom or Lynn's, but I wanted out of the vision before the towels came off.

I jerked my hand free of Triton's.

"Geez, you couldn't stop with the Flipper scene?" I snarled. "You had to go X-rated?"

"Francesca," Cosmil snapped, "why did you break the flow?"

I turned to Saber. "Did you see pictures this time, too?"

"Leaping dolphins, and a woman with light hair."

"It's blond." Triton pulled his knees to his chest, wrapped his arms around his legs. "Silver blond."

Cosmil's bushy gray eyebrows shot up, two gull wings of surprise. "It has happened, Triton? You have met a mate?"

We retired inside to the living area for Triton's revelation. Cosmil and Lia shared the sofa, Saber took an armchair, and I leaned a hip against the stainless steel counter sipping water.

Okay, my body language screamed that I was divorcing myself from the group, but I wanted to watch their reactions.

Triton started his tale with the men who assaulted him, answered a few questions, and agreed to have a look at mug shots. He didn't commit to a date, I noticed, but then Saber would have to contact Detective Bob March with the St. Johns County Sheriff's Office to arrange a viewing. Good thing we had an in with law enforcement.

Triton also mentioned that transfiguring while being injured had been difficult and that he'd been too weak to want to travel far. He'd headed to the fishing pier where he usually shifted, and that's when and where he echo-located Lynn. Since she was alone, they swam farther north to Vilano Beach where he began to feel stronger. Eventually they'd gone to Jax Beach.

The rest I knew, so I studied Cosmil's, Lia's, and Saber's expressions. Cosmil's "you finally got a girl" grin had faded, though he held a hopeful gleam in his eye. Lia seemed the most thoughtful, and the longer Saber listened, the more his cop face settled into place.

Triton finally dropped the key piece of information I'd been waiting to hear—that Lynn had been a shifter for only five years. Good to know I hadn't harbored a minor, but no way should shifting have made Lynn as shaky as she'd been. Not with five years worth of shifter experience.

Last, Triton revealed that Lynn shared a duplex with three college friends. The roommates believed Lynn to be Wiccan and assumed she conducted new-moon ceremonies when she went off alone each month. A perception that Lynn fostered, in part by working in a New Age shop.

When he finished his story—without the X-rated parts I'd seen in his mind—silence reigned until Lia turned to me.

"What impressions did you have of Lynn?"

"Not many. She was shivering on most of the drive back to Triton's. She didn't do much more than murmur hello and good-bye."

"You're a vampire," Triton put in. "You intimidated her."

"Perhaps," Lia agreed, "but there is more. Cesca, what's bothering you about the young woman?"

Triton sent me a glare, which I sent right back.

"You have to take this in the context of timing, but here it is." I held up a hand to tick off my points. "First, it doesn't quite fit that Triton and Lynn wouldn't have met before now."

"Why would we have met?" Triton muttered. "I don't know every dolphin in the sea."

I ignored him.

"Second, it's hinky that Lynn would be hanging out at the pier where Triton usually shifts."

Triton objected. "Plenty of dolphins hang there. So do sharks."

"Yes, but to avoid the party at that beach, I took you farther south. If you had shifted injured at the pier beach, you would have been more vulnerable to a shark or some other kind of attack."

Saber nodded. "True."

"Third, it's odd that Lynn is such a young shifter."

"Why?" Lia asked.

Saber answered. "Because unless you can tell me differently, there are no weredolphins. Never have been."

"Which means," I concluded, "that Lynn could be the product of a spell, and we know of only one wizard on the loose."

"Damn it, Cesca, Lynn is not Starrack's tool," Triton raged as he came off the sofa and stormed at me. "You're jealous and petty. You couldn't land me when we were younger, so you thought you could have me on the side and keep Saber, too."

"Honey, are you jealous of Lynn?" Saber asked.

I whipped my head toward him. "No, but I lust after her straight hair."

Triton sputtered. "You undressed me at the beach."

"You whined that you were too weak to do it yourself."

"You looked at my goods."

"So? I've seen you since we were kids. Nothing's changed."

Suddenly, Triton's skin darkened, and his brown eyes went pitch black. In slow motion, I saw his fist take aim at my face.

In the next instant, Saber yanked the back of Triton's shirt, pulling him away from me enough that his fist *whooshed* harmlessly through the air.

My heartbeat pounded in my throat as the five of us stood frozen. Then Triton wheezed, exhaling the smell of oil, and dropped to his knees in an unconscious heap.

FOURTEEN

My first instinct was to rush to my unconscious friend, even if he had intended to clock me.

Cosmil's voice whipped across the room.

"Do not touch him, Francesca. No one touch him."

"He's had a flare of the Void illness, hasn't he?" I asked softly, my gut clenching with new dread.

"I fear so," Cosmil confirmed as he strode to the far side of the stainless steel island and opened a drawer.

A pile of surgical gloves and masks hit the countertop, and Cosmil slammed the drawer shut before donning a pair of gloves. He tossed a second pair of gloves and a mask to Saber.

"Lia, please prepare a healing circle. Saber, if you would kindly help me examine Triton and then move him outside?"

I stepped aside as the men went into action. And, yes, I wondered at the precaution of gloves and masks. Cosmil hadn't insisted we wear masks after he had been attacked, although Saber had worn gloves to treat Cosmil's oozing head wound. I supposed taking any measures to slow the spread of infection was a good thing.

But, damn. Why would he be having a flare unless his attackers had reinfected him? Or Lynn had been the culprit. Other diseases spread through blood and other body fluids, and from the bit of love scene Triton had projected during our image-projecting exercise, it was a darn good bet he'd been intimate with Lynn.

Lia touched my arm.

"Come. Help me with the circle."

With a last glance at Cosmil checking the pulse in Triton's ankles, I trailed after Lia to a cabinet filled with candles of every color and a whole shelf of leather-tied pouches. Just like the ones Lia had brought with her, but my gut told me Cosmil had made these.

Lia piled nine jars containing candles in my arms, while she snagged pouches, crystals, and a handful of sage bound in rough twine.

"Hurry, now," she said and motioned me outside.

She walked straight to the center of Cosmil's circle of trees. I followed with glass jars clanking.

"Put the colored candles in the cardinal directions. You know which color goes where?"

Amazingly, I did. A quick vision showed me what to do.

"When you've done that, put the white candles in the non-cardinal directions, and set the black candle in the circle center."

While I distributed the jars around the perimeter, Lia laid a length of white cotton on the grass and arranged the healing aids she'd carried. As I started to place the black candle, Cosmil and Saber exited the shack carrying Triton. Saber had Triton's shoulders, Cosmil his feet. I hesitated.

"Give me the candle, Cesca, and leave the circle."

"You don't want my help to do the healing?"

She shook her head. "It's too soon. You and Saber need to practice, and I fear your energy in particular may agitate Triton."

"Understood, but, Lia, can you pinpoint what caused the flare?"

"Is the cause important?"

"It just bugs me that Saber and Triton are infected when I'm not."

Lia patted my shoulder. "We'll try to discover the underlying reason Triton has suddenly become so sick, but treating him quickly is more important. You must go now."

I hustled out of the circle as Saber stepped into it.

"You two may go home," Cosmil said when they'd laid Triton on the ground. "We will do better alone."

Saber nodded. "Lia, do you want my car keys, or do you know your way back to my house?"

She glanced at Triton's still form and shook her head. "I will be staying the night."

A vision flashed of Lia and Cosmil working on Triton, but it went blank before I saw the outcome. My heart hurt with sympathy for Triton. My head locked on one fact. Damn, a man down and the battle hadn't even begun.

I led the way home in my truck and Saber followed in his SUV, but when we arrived at the cottage at midnight, we were of one mind.

We needed to conduct a good old-fashioned investigation.

Saber had retrieved his own laptop when he'd picked up Lia for training. With a chair from the kitchen, he set up next to my workstation at the desk. Snowball shadowed him, but she must've sensed our urgency, because she didn't leap onto the keyboard tonight. She curled on an armchair.

We started with an online phone directory and found ten Heaths. No listings for Lynn Ann, Lynn, Ann, or L.A. No hits in the towns around Daytona, either, and we did searches from Flagler Beach to Ormond Beach to New Smyrna, and even Deland.

"Why couldn't she be easy to find?" I muttered.

"What would you have done? Driven down to confront her?"

"It crossed my mind."

"You really are a little tyrant."

I heaved a shoulder-slumping sigh. "Tonight I was worse. I should have been more tactful. Triton has waited over two centuries to find a mate, and I accused her of being an enemy spy."

"Honey, he had his own doubts, or he wouldn't have been defensive about Lynn to begin with. And if he'd been in his right mind, he would've blown you off. Instead, he went from annoyed to angry to black rage in minutes."

"Did you smell his breath as he collapsed?"

"It's from the infection. It may not be a universal sign, but about ninety percent of the vampires I met with had that rank breath. They were sucking down more breath mints than blood."

I reached for his hand. "Are you feeling okay?

Saber laced his fingers through mine and gave me a long look. "Triton made a lot of accusations. Were any of them true?"

"I admit to having a few what-if twinges that first day I saw him, but he was right all those years ago. We knew each other too well to marry. We'd have snipped each other to death inside a year."

"One more question. Did you ogle Triton?"

"More like glanced."

"And?"

"I might've admired some aspects of the view."

"You're a tease."

"Not about this." I framed his face with my hands. "You're my guy, Saber. Only you."

He leaned in for a kiss. "I'm available for ogling later."

"I'm counting on it."

One more kiss and we each turned back to our monitors.

Saber accessed law enforcement and background check websites to which he had access while I thought back to what little Triton had revealed about Lynn.

One, she'd been shifting about five years. Two, she lived with college friends. Three, she worked at a New Age shop. Not a wealth of information to go on, but three clues were better than none. Plus everyone over twelve seemed to be on a social network. Couldn't hurt to start with a general name search. Maybe I'd get lucky.

Sure enough, I found a few matches on people-search and business-directory sites. The name was spelled differently, but I clicked to the photos with fingers crossed. No hits.

Okay, if Lynn had begun shifting at the usual age of sixteen or so and had been shifting five years, that put her at between twenty and twenty-two years old. She and the roommates might still attend college, but I knew I wouldn't find a public roster of current students. However, if Lynn had graduated, maybe I had a shot at locating a list with her name on it.

That shot went wide. None of the universities, colleges, or vocational schools published the names of their graduates for public consumption.

Last chance. I found four New Age stores in the general area, clicked on each website in hopes of finding a photo with Lynn in it. Again, no luck, but I sent carefully worded e-mails to the contacts, asking if Lynn worked there.

Which reminded me that I'd also written to several astrologers days ago. I opened my e-mail program to check for responses and found only one. That for a tiny discount on an expensive full reading.

I sighed and stretched in my swivel chair.

"No luck?" Saber asked.

"Not unless one of the New Age stores answers an e-mail. You?"

He smirked. "Take a look."

I leaned sideways to see the two images on his screen. On the left,

Lynn's Florida driver's license appeared. On the right, there were two mug shots of her. She was younger, but there was no mistaking that sleek hair.

"She was arrested at eighteen in Orlando for drunk and disorderly conduct during a spring break time frame and again that summer in Volusia County on a minor possession charge. She completed probation and has kept a clean record since."

"Do you have a last known address?"

"It's the foster parents' address in Ormond Beach."

"Is there a chance she's still in touch with them?"

"I'll find out tomorrow. Did you remember to cancel out of bridge club?"

"I talked to Shelly Friday, but I'll check to be sure she has me covered." I grabbed a notepad and scribbled that reminder. "We also need to talk about the couples shower."

"The barbeque bash? It's at four Sunday, right? I've got the cooking covered. Hamburgers and chicken breasts."

"We'll get the slaw and beans from the store. Oh, and remember that the rental company is delivering the tents, tables, and chairs about one o'clock on Saturday afternoon."

"I'll be there."

"Uh, Saber, what are we going to do with Lia during the party?"

"I suppose we have to invite her or bring her here or ask if she'll hang out with Cosmil."

"I opt for door number three. Okay, when can we go food shopping?"

"Bring your master schedule up on the computer."

I did, and with a printed copy for each of us, we moved to the sofa to coordinate our schedules for the next few days. We could shop tomorrow afternoon if Saber wasn't paying a call on Lynn's foster parents. Thursday and Friday before my eight o'clock ghost tours were also open, so we penciled in each possibility.

The looming question was when we'd be training again. And if Triton would be with us. Should we call to check on him?

"No, we won't call. Cosmil will send Pandora with news."

"Did you read my expression or my mind?"

"Both." He plucked my pencil and paper from my hands, and put both our sets on the coffee table. "Want to read what I'm thinking?"

I peered at his forehead. "Hmmm. Is it bring beer and show up naked?"

"Not quite. No beer."

I ran my fingertips up his arm. "Lia did say we should practice that energy exchange."

"Then I say we should practice all night."

Our lovemaking may not have been Lia's idea of energy channeling, but it sure worked for us. Saber finally slipped into a peaceful slumber around three with no nightmares on the dreamscape horizon.

I got up to read my design-class lessons and do homework, but worrying over Triton took a big chunk of concentration. I hoped Cosmil's and Lia's healing would be successful, because I already had concerns that Triton wouldn't be a reliable team member. Not if he had no fuse on his temper. Worse, I fretted that being around him would aggravate Saber's infection. Not that the Void was an airborne virus, but then, could we take the chance it wasn't? Last, I prayed hard that Triton would heal because I did love him. In spite of the way we snipped at each other, I didn't want to find my old friend only to lose him again.

As dawn broke on Wednesday morning, I gave up on class work and crawled back under the sheets. Snowball's rumbling purr and Saber's soft snore were just the background noise to lull me to sleep.

I heard the phone later. Saber answered on the first ring, and I heard his voice but not the words. Only an emergency would get me out of bed at this hour, so when Saber didn't come to the bedroom, I drifted off again.

I startled awake from a dream of being on a flat rooftop. Saber had lain bleeding a dozen paces away, but I couldn't reach him. My black knee boots stuck fast to the roof, and I couldn't get them off my feet. I'd screamed and cried to no avail. Saber hadn't stirred, and no one came to help.

As the dream faded, my panicked breathing eased enough to wonder at the spate of bad dreams Saber and I were having. Did I chalk it all up to stress, or was something more at work? Saber's nightmare had been based in fact, and I'd never had many prophetic dreams. Maybe it was extreme stress.

One thing was sure, the dream had left my teeth feeling like they'd grown moss. I needed a toothbrush and a wake up shower.

In fifteen minutes, I had my hair in its standard ponytail, a smidge of makeup on, and was dressed in hot pink shorts, a pale pink bra-top camisole, and white sandals. I didn't see Snowball when I went to the kitchen for my daily slug of Starbloods, but I sure heard her yowl when the perimeter alarm blared a second later.

I jumped and spewed Starbloods in the kitchen sink, which splashed back onto my fresh clothes. Damn.

I quickly rinsed my mouth then whirled to go shut off the siren just as Saber stepped into the house carrying a lumpy plastic drug store bag. He quickly dealt with the blaring alarm then gave me a once over glance.

"You have Starbloods on your blouse."

"I have punctured eardrums, too." I pointed at the bag. "Did you go to the store without me?"

"No, Lynn's foster mother gave me greenhouse tomatoes."

"You saw Lynn's mom?" I nearly danced a jig. "What cover story did you give her? What did she say? Tell me all while I treat these stains."

I dashed to the laundry room to dab stain remover on my cami. Saber put the sack of tomatoes on the counter then joined me.

"I told her part of the truth. That I was an investigator tracking down Lynn for a distant relative. Mr. Tidwell is deceased, and Kate Tidwell isn't in the best of health, but she said they had cared for Lynn since she was four. They had no other children, and since Lynn responded so well to them, they were allowed to keep her. They even tried to adopt Lynn several times, but the proceedings were blocked. And not by the state."

"Isn't that unusual?"

"From what little I know about adoption, yeah. Anyway, Kate Tidwell said Lynn was a good girl who made good grades, and everything was fine until she was in her mid-teens. Then they caught her lying about spending the night with girlfriends and sneaking in early in the morning."

I capped the stain-buster stick. "Which is roughly when she would've started shifting."

"Right. Kate even said the incidents only happened about once a month. The telling point is that she has a good bit of background on Lynn. It doesn't match what you told me of Triton's history exactly, but it's close. Abandoned at about age three, taken by the state, placed with a first family, then with the Tidwells. Lynn's conception might have been from a magical source, but nothing I uncovered indicates that she's being manipulated."

"Plus it would be a ridiculously long-term plan to create a mate for Triton twenty years ago. Is Lynn still in touch with Kate?"

"At least once a week. Kate confirmed Lynn attends community college part time and lives with roommates in a duplex. They just moved in, so Kate didn't have Lynn's address or directions to the new place."

"No phone number, either?"

"A cell. I got the address through a contact and checked it out."

"No wonder you're looking so pleased with yourself. Was she home?"

He shook his head. "I struck out there. I can stake out her place, but I'd rather arrange a more casual meeting."

"Casual like running into her on the sidewalk or inviting her for coffee?"

"If we can persuade Triton, I was thinking a double date. Would it bother you to go out with them?"

I tried to imagine dining with the silent young woman I'd met and came up blank. "Not if she has more conversation than she did last time we met. Have you heard how Triton's doing?"

"Got a report from Cosmil this morning. He didn't give me details about whatever mojo he and Lia did last night, but said Triton was resting and healing, and would be until tomorrow. He and Lia are keeping watch over him, and training is suspended until tomorrow night after your ghost tour."

"Which means we should make our shopping run tonight before some new crisis crops up."

"I'm game. Oh, and Lia passed on another message."

"What?"

He crowded me against the washer. "That you and I are to keep practicing our energy exercises."

"Now I wonder," I said, looping my arms around his neck, "which kind of exercise she means."

We put off our shopping trip to Walmart until after we'd exercised. And rested in each other's arms. And exercised again. Hey, we were nothing if not willing students.

Besides, Walmart wasn't as crowded at night.

The theme for Maggie's Saturday afternoon bridal shower was Victorian High Tea. Okay, so it wouldn't exactly be the highest of teas, not with me hosting it at the cottage. For starters, I didn't have the floor space to seat all sixteen of us at tables. Instead, we'd sit on chairs, and I'd borrow extras from Maggie. Seating aside, I did have a few elegant touches planned.

Maggie was loaning me the double set of pink Depression glass grill plates, cups, and tumblers she'd inherited from her mother, and I'd bought pink cloth napkins woven with a white lace pattern to complement the dishes. I'd also purchased flatware in a Victorian pattern to use at the shower. True, the service for twelve was a reproduction in stainless steel, but it was lovely. Plus, I'd finagled six extra teaspoons and luncheon forks for the set. The flatware and napkins were my shower and wedding gifts to Maggie.

The florist was providing nosegays of miniature pink and white roses, and I'd ordered snack trays and teacakes from the caterer. The flowers and food would be delivered an hour before the party, and I'd serve two kinds of hot teas and have sweet and unsweetened cold tea on hand, too.

Now the couples shower on Sunday was to be way more casual. With twelve couples including Maggie, Neil, Saber, and me, there'd be seating in the den for those who wanted to watch football and seating under the tents for everyone else.

"Okay, we need plastic tablecloths and dinner napkins."

"I have napkins, Cesca."

"The big kind? Barbeque is messy."

We moved up and down the aisles loading up with chips, condiments, soft drinks, and anything else we thought we'd need. As we doubled back to get picnic-sized salt and pepper shakers, I heard voices I recognized.

Two of them I welcomed hearing. The other one, not so much.

I motioned to Saber to follow me.

"Young man, you've followed us around for days. What do you want?"

Clarence Clarke spoke as Saber and I rounded the corner of the soup aisle. He and Melda were dressed much as they'd been at Triton's. Senior chic.

Victor Gorman wore his usual redneck-ops outfit of black jeans, shirt, and sneakers, and sneered at Clarence.

"I'm waitin' to catch you, and by damn, I will."

"Catch us buying groceries?" Melda scoffed.

"We don't want your kind in town."

"Discriminating against retirees in Florida, Gorman?" I steered the cart straight for his knees but refrained from slamming it into him. "Mr. and Mrs. Clarke, how nice to see you. This is my friend, Deke Saber. Saber, I met the Clarkes on a ghost tour and again when they were out for a walk."

Clarence and Saber shook hands. Melda smiled and winked at me.

Gorman glared at each of us, finally landing his beady-eyed gaze on me.

"So, you do know these two."

"I just said I'd met them twice."

"I'm tellin' you, these are—" He stopped and looked around, then held curved index fingers to his mouth. "Vampires."

Clarence leaned close to Saber. "Is he quite all there?"

"This is Victor Gorman, sir. He's a member of the Covenant."

"Is that like the Lions Club?" Melda asked, oh-so-sweetly.

Saber about lost it, so I answered. "No, ma'am, the Covenant is a group that watches vampires."

Clarence scratched his head. "Watches them do what?"

Saber and I shrugged. Gorman ground his teeth.

"You're gonna give yourselves away sometime, and I'll be there."

"Well, if you're going to tag along," Melda said, "you may as well help. Get that box of onion soup off the top shelf."

"Oh, no, Mother. You know what onions do to my colon."

"True. Shall we stick with the chicken noodle? Mr. Gorman, get that jumbo can of soup, if you please."

Gorman strangled out a growl. "I ain't your lackey."

"Then I suggest you take yourself off, young man," Clarence said. "You're in our way."

The elderly vampire locked Gorman in a stare-down, and I felt as much as saw a small, careful burst of "go" in Clarence's eyes. Seconds later, when Gorman stomped off, I realized that Clarence had subtly enthralled Gorman to leave. Very cool and certainly not destructive. Point to Lia.

I smiled at Clarence and spoke softly. "I'm sorry I forgot to warn you about him, but that was masterful."

"Not to worry," Melda said with a pat on my arm. "We spotted him quickly and have led him all over town. I must give the man high marks for persistence, though."

"Just don't let down your guard," Saber warned. "He's made attempts on Cesca's life."

Clarence looked grave. "We shall be careful."

"Cesca tells me you're planning to open a bed-and-breakfast inn, Mr. Clarke. We may need to discuss that project."

"Of course," Clarence replied, "though we're having a difficult go of it, finding the right property at the right price. Much as we like this area, we're looking farther south and inland. But I'm keeping you from your shopping."

He broke off and pulled a card from his sports jacket pocket. "We often house hunt at night, but call and we'll be happy to receive you."

Saber nodded his thanks, and the Clarke's started down the aisle when I stopped them.

"If Gorman is following you everywhere, he'll talk to your real estate agent. Does she know your natures?"

Melda grinned. "We told her that we sleep late, have doctor appointments in the early afternoon, and nap after that."

"And she bought it?"

Melda chortled. "Of course, dear. We're old."

The couple toddled off, and I turned to Saber.

"I'm beginning to wish I aged."

"Why?"

"I have a feeling seniors get away with murder."

We got out of the store with our party goods, but without a major purchase like the blender I had my eye on for Maggie. That baby did everything but turn into a butler and serve smoothies on a silver platter, but I restrained myself. With only a toy added to the cart for Snowball, we were out of there.

Saber's huge refrigerator-freezer held all the food we bought with room left over. I did a little maintenance house cleaning while he checked on the hot tub to be sure his repair had taken. We wouldn't be using the tub for the party. We wouldn't have time since the gift opening was scheduled to coincide with the football game halftime. But, hey, I know better than to get between Saber and one of his projects.

The moon shone a silver sliver, the stars twinkled brightly, and the night was mellow. After arriving at my cottage at nine, Saber and Snowball played with her new toy while I checked my costumes for the next ghost tours to make sure they were clean.

At ten, we snuggled on the couch to watch the Cary Grant romantic comedy *Father Goose* on TV.

At 10:08 Saber's cell phone rang.

A quick look at the readout, and Saber answered and activated the speaker.

"Mrs. Tidwell? Are you all right?"

"No, Mr. Saber, I'm not. I know this is a huge imposition, but Lynn is insisting I call. I told her about your visit when I spoke with her this afternoon, and an hour ago she came home very ill and terribly distraught. She won't let me take her to the hospital. She only wants to see you. I'm at my wits' end."

Saber shot me a grim look, the same one I felt on my face.

"Mrs. Tidwell, Kate, what are Lynn's symptoms?"

"Chills, mood swings, anxiety. Her breath smells foul. Is there a history of this kind of thing in her biological family?"

"I'd have to check, but I think I can help."

"Oh, would you come tonight? I'm not just afraid for my daughter, Mr. Saber. I'm truly terrified."

FIFTEEN

I shucked my shorts for jeans, threw a tan T-shirt over my bra-top camisole, and shoved my feet into sneakers. With food and water in Snowball's bowls and the alarm shut off, Saber and I took off for Ormond Beach within five minutes of Kate Tidwell's call.

"This could be a trap," Saber had warned before we left.

"Nice try, but you know I'm coming along. If it will make you feel better, though, I'll call Cosmil from the road. Tell him what's up and have him peer into his crystal ball for signs of danger."

"And if *he* says it's a trap?"

"We go in stealth-mode, and I'll have your back."

"You watched too much *NCIS* while I was gone."

Cosmil's concern on the phone was palpable, but he saw nothing but danger to Lynn in his find-the-truth spell. Or whatever he called it. Maybe I'd be in training long enough to learn the lingo, maybe not.

We arrived at Kate Tidwell's home forty minutes later. The modest home boasted lovely landscaping with uplighting on the magnolia trees flanking each side of the center front door. I had a moment to wonder if we should have gloves and masks before Saber pressed the doorbell.

Mrs. Tidwell answered so fast, I was sure she'd been on the lookout for us. Or rather for Saber. She barely glanced at me.

"Thank God you're here," she exclaimed when she threw open the door. "Lynn's in her old bedroom."

Kate limped slightly as she led the way past a formal living room to a den, and then into a hallway. Short and pleasantly plump, she wore a green knit pants outfit and off-white house shoes on her swollen feet. Her dark hair had gray streaks at the temples that were likely growing grayer by the minute.

At the open bedroom door, we all paused. Lynn sat on the edge of her bed, head down, arms wrapped around her stomach. Her cutoff jeans and pastel purple T-shirt seemed too big for her thin body, and her silver blond hair hung limp at her shoulders as she fretfully rocked and twitched and moaned.

"Lynn, here's Mr. Saber. And—" She looked at me blankly.

"I'm Cesca, Mrs. Tidwell."

Lynn head snapped up, dull blue green eyes darting from Saber to me.

"Why did you come?"

My heart went out to her. "To help."

"You're a vampire. You hate me."

Behind me, Kate sucked in a breath. "I invited a vampire into my house?"

Saber jerked his head, projecting, *Get her out of here.*

"Mrs. Tidwell," I said mildly as I took her elbow, "that thing about inviting a vampire into you home is pure fiction. Let's go in the den while Saber talks with Lynn."

"You can't break in whenever you want?"

"I wouldn't dream of breaking in to anyone's home. Saber and I date, and since I was with him when you called, I came, too. He thought I could help."

"If you're here to help," Kate said as her knees gave out, and she sank into a reclining chair, "why does Lynn think you hate her?"

I spread my hands. "It's just a misunderstanding. Would you like some water, Mrs. Tidwell?"

She eyed me doubtfully then seemed to give up the fight. "Please. There are bottles in the refrigerator."

The kitchen was open to the den, and I suspected that Kate watched my every move as I retrieved a cold bottle from the fridge and a napkin from the bar countertop.

"I'm sorry I'm a poor hostess tonight," she said when I handed her the water. "What is your name again?"

"Cesca Marinelli, ma'am. I'm a ghost-tour guide in St. Augustine."

Kate's gaze narrowed, then she looked into space for a moment. "You worked with the police in the spring. You caught a killer."

"I only helped."

"And you say you date Mr. Saber?"

"Yes, ma'am. We met on that case."

She cracked open the bottle top and took three healthy swallows, then nearly choked when Lynn cried out.

"Cesca," Saber called. "Come here a minute."

Eyes flooding with renewed panic, Kate started to rise, too, but I held up my hand. "It might be better if you stay here, Mrs. Tidwell. I promise Lynn is safe with us."

The angst melted from Kate's face in seconds, and she nodded. "Go on."

I eased into the bedroom so as not to spook Lynn any further. Saber hunkered at her feet, crooning softly and reassuringly.

"Shhh. It's okay. We'll take care of you." He glanced at me over his shoulder then patted Lynn's knee. "I'll be right back."

Lynn fixed her gaze on the sea-colored striped bedspread, picked at it with stiff fingers. Saber motioned me farther down the hall.

"She has the rancid breath of Void infection, and she's in a lot of pain. We need Cosmil to see her."

"I'll call and tell him we're bringing in another patient."

"The key is getting her there. She's so traumatized with the illness, she's scared to go with us."

"Then what do we do?"

"Can you enthrall her? Make her feel safe enough to get her out of here?"

"I don't know. Lia tried to teach me, but—"

Lightbulbs suddenly flashed in my head with 3-D pictures. I'd becalmed a raccoon with Lia. I'd becalmed Kate Tidwell just minutes ago. I'd enthralled Kate without intending to, but I'd done it all the same.

Okay, calming two agitated mothers was vastly different than enthralling a half-crazed-with-pain shifter, but I could try.

I refocused on Saber. "If we can get her to look at me, we have a shot."

"Good girl. Let's go."

So that she wouldn't feel crowded, I moved Lynn's desk chair near the bed. Saber stood behind me.

"Lynn? I need to tell you some things, and I hope you'll listen. I don't hate you. I'm an old friend of Triton's, and I want to see him happy. He'll be devastated you're sick, so we need to make you well."

Lynn cautiously lifted her gaze. "Triton said you'd be jealous of me."

I tried not to grimace at the smell of her breath, but it reminded me all too vividly of Tower's breath when he'd attacked me last week. That alone scared me to my core.

"I'll let you in on something," I told her, smiling my most friendly, unthreatening smile. "Triton can be a big pain in the arse."

Her eyes widened.

"It's true that I love him, but only like a very bothersome brother. I'm glad he found you. In fact when you're better, we'll, um—" I did a mad mental search for inspiration. "Go on a double date. You and Triton, me and Saber."

Lynn suddenly clutched her stomach and moaned. "I feel like dying."

"I know, but Saber and I know a fabulous doctor. The guy is practically a magician at curing people."

"A regular doctor won't help me. I have something awful."

"What kind of doctor is this?"

I turned to find Kate framed in the doorway. She wasn't wringing her hands, but concern etched her forehead. "Lynn doesn't have insurance and isn't covered on mine."

"Dr. Cosby is an alternative medicine specialist," Saber answered without missing a beat.

Kate titled her head. "Like an acupuncturist?"

"And an herbalist. He's a personal friend who only takes referrals to his clinic, but he's willing to see Lynn right now."

I took Lynn's limp hand and fixed my gaze on her with a little push of will. "I promise you both. Lynn will be safe with Dr. Cosby."

A spark in the back of Lynn's eyes flickered, and I held my breath, hoping the tiny push had been enough.

"It's okay, Mom," Lynn said in a stronger, more determined tone. "I feel too sick to wait, and I can call you from the doctor's office."

"I'll keep you updated, too, Mrs. Tidwell," Saber added. "I'll phone as soon as we get Lynn to the clinic."

Kate chewed on her lip then nodded. "She is of age, so it's her decision. But, please, don't forget to call me. Either of you."

Saber used his emergency lights sans siren, and we made it to Cosmil's compound in warp-speed time. I'd phoned the wizard twice, once when we left Ormond to let him know he had a patient incoming, and again five minutes out so he'd smooth and straighten the road for us.

Cosmil and Lia hurried to the car, but I noticed Triton on the porch gripping a support pole. Since Cosmil barked questions at Saber about Lynn's symptoms, I approached Triton.

"She's going to be okay," I told him.

"She's infected with the Void?"

"We think so. She has foul-smelling breath, and that worries me."

"Triton, Francesca," Cosmil called.

I turned to see the wizard sweeping toward us. Behind him, Saber carried Lynn, but not to the shack. He headed toward the circle where Lia walked clockwise, lighting candles.

"Triton, I realize you are concerned, but I do not want you exposed again if Lynn is indeed Void infected. I do not have room here for two patients."

"So you're kicking me out? Cos, let me stay. Lynn will appreciate a familiar face when she comes around."

"No, I must be firm on this point and on my conditions. First, I want you to leave your pickup truck here. I may need to use it."

"You can drive?" I blurted the question without thinking.

Cosmil pulled himself taller. "Of course. You saw me once. Driving a tourist tram."

"Oh, yeah, I did."

"Back to my conditions. Triton, here is the second. I do not want you to be alone, so you and Saber will spend the night in his home. Francesca will watch over you. Then tomorrow, you will open your shop and go about your normal life."

Triton would've argued further, but Cosmil laid a hand on his arm.

"Attend me well. It is vital to be visible in your world. Starrack's alleged hirelings failed to get the amulets, and now he has failed to make you critically ill so you could be bent to his will. When he sees his failures, he may become frustrated."

"So, if he has to work harder to get at us," I said, "he might get reckless. Do something to expose his hiding place."

"Exactly, Francesca."

"But being visible will make me a target he can't miss next time," Triton argued.

Cosmil shook his head. "Though Lia and I have not located Starrack yet, we have cast protection spells, which we reinforce several times a day."

"Your spells didn't help Lynn," Triton shot back.

"Ah, but we did not know about Lynn," Cosmil countered. "Now we will extend protection to her as well."

Triton's shoulders slumped. "All right, Cos. I suppose your plan makes sense."

"'Course it does," I quipped. "It works on TV all the time."

Triton rolled his baby browns at me. He didn't add a crack, but the eye roll was an encouraging sign that he was getting back to his normal self.

"Cos, one question. Saber's been in physical contact with Lynn. If he's been reexposed, is it wise to put us together?"

"Precisely why I will scan him. Francesca, I shall check you now. Stand over here. Arms at your sides. Breathe normally."

I obeyed his instructions, breathing my normal ten times a minute. After one exhalation, Cosmil held his palms six inches from my body and moved them over me from head to fang to toe.

"Remarkable. You emit no signs of the illness whatsoever."

I silently sighed my relief then asked a question that had been nagging me. "Cosmil, why can't Saber and Triton ground out all the Void gunk like I did. After all, Saber's the one who taught me the trick."

"That puzzles me as well, Francesca. I can only surmise that when you drained the blackness from the vampires at the comedy club, you gained immunity against reinfection. The men did not absorb as much of the Void as you did, and may not have effectively shed it."

"So sucking the gunk acted like a mega flu shot?"

Cosmil merely nodded as Saber joined us. Cosmil began scanning my honey, palms hovering over Saber's chest longer than I wanted to see, but the wizard finally nodded his satisfaction.

"No change in your energy, Saber. Be off with you, then."

Triton's brooding gaze followed Cosmil to the circle.

"Hey," I said. "The sooner we leave, the better they'll focus."

He straightened his shoulders. "Right."

Once in the SUV, Saber kept his promise to call Mrs. Tidwell, and we were on the main road before I twisted in my seat to catch Triton's attention.

"Hey, I'm sorry. Last night when I voiced my concerns—"

"Suspicions."

"—about Lynn, I could've been less—"

"Bitchy?"

"Forceful," I corrected firmly. "I'm apologizing, moron. You could be a little more gracious."

"Nah, it's too easy to get a rise out of you."

I narrowed my eyes. "It's a good thing you're out of punching range."

He looked out the window and back again. "About that. Cosmil told me I nearly slugged you. I'm sorry I lost it."

"Now that you two are playing nice again, Triton, do you want to hear what we learned about Lynn?"

"Am I going to like the information?"

"Well, it doesn't look like Lynn is in cahoots with Starrack. That should cheer you up."

"Okay, what did you find out?"

"Saber found and talked with her foster mother," I said, then related Saber's ruse as an investigator for Lynn's distant relatives. "So, when Lynn showed up at Mrs. Tidwell's house sick tonight, her foster mom called Saber."

"Did Lynn say how she hooked up with me?"

"Not exactly," Saber said. "You have to understand that she was in a bad way when we got to the house. I talked with her alone for a few minutes and only got something about an online network with an entry stating there was a human-dolphin shifter in St. Augustine."

"What network?" Triton and I demanded in tandem as Saber braked at the US 1 intersection.

In the streetlights, I saw his hands tighten on the steering wheel. "That's what I intend to find out. The only other thing she said was that she first began to feel ill when she shifted back and that she felt progressively sicker."

"So if Starrack is using Lynn," Triton mused, "he's doing it indirectly."

"Right," Saber said. "In addition, Mrs. Tidwell has been Lynn's foster mother since she was four. Now that we know more about her, Cesca and I have a hard time believing that Starrack pulled off some spell twenty years ago just to use Lynn against you now."

"Us. Use Lynn against us."

Saber inclined his head. "The upshot is that, at worst, she appears to be Starrack's unwitting pawn, not an active weapon. He may just have wanted to distract you, and Lynn served as a diversion."

"Divide and conquer?" Triton asked.

"Why not? It's a time-honored tactic."

As Saber took the left turn on US 1, I twisted in my seat so I could see both him and Triton. "You know, guys, if Lynn is the innocent we think she is, we might need to stash her someplace safe. Just in case Starrack does have designs on her, or she has a relapse."

"I'll watch over her."

"Not gonna work, Triton," I said. "We've assumed Starrack sent those thugs, so he already knows where you live, and I'm in the freaking phone book."

"What about Cos's protection spells?"

"The spells are great, but if Starrack or his minions come to your door with a gun, I wouldn't count on magick. saving the day. Do you want Lynn smack in the line of fire?"

"Point taken. Okay, I agree she can't stay with us, but where can we put her?"

We halfheartedly debated safe house possibilities for the rest of the drive to Saber's house, but they were all academic until we got an update on Lynn's condition.

The guys went to bed at one o'clock. I spent the night flipping between TV Land and the movie channels, and checking on Saber and Triton. I didn't think Triton would make a break for Cosmil's to see Lynn because Saber's security system covered every door, window, nook, and cranny. Besides, from the way Triton sprawled all over the bed, he looked down for the count. I grinned as I quietly closed the guest-room door. If things worked out for him and Lynn, he'd have to learn to share the mattress.

Saber was conked for the night, too. I feared his nightmare might return, so I looked in on him more often after three, the real witching hour. His soft snore reassured me.

I itched to have my laptop so I could search for the networking site Lynn had mentioned to Saber, but that task would keep. With luck, Lynn would be well enough to give us the URL later in the day, even walk us through the site.

The guys were up at seven thirty. Saber fixed breakfast while Triton and I changed the guest-room sheets. Poor Lia. I don't know where she was sleeping, but she had to be missing her privacy. And clothing. Last night she'd worn the same light blue scrub-type outfit from our first training session. I made a mental note to call and ask her if she wanted fresh clothes.

After breakfast, Saber ran Triton up the road a mile or so to his shop then returned to take me home.

"You don't think Triton will bolt out to Cosmil's?"

"Not without his truck. Besides, he respects the wizard. He may not like waiting, but he'll stay away from the cabin until Cosmil gives the all clear. You have an early ghost tour tonight, right?"

"At eight. I guess we'll find out if training is on hold again."

Saber grinned at me. "In which case, I'm sure we can find something to entertain us."

"Like those energy exercises?"

"We did miss practice last night."

I laughed. "You're insatiable, you know that?"

He captured my hand. "Only with you."

Okay, I admit my heart was still pitter-patting when I let myself in the cottage and set the alarm for my daytime sleep. I missed Saber being there with me, and Snowball did, too. She meowed at the door even after I set out fresh food and water.

I fell into bed at nine, hugging a pillow instead of Saber's warm body.

Which might be why my dreams turned ugly.

The vision opened in Cosmil's perfect circle, except where there should have been trees, rough stone walls stretched to the sky. Triton and Lynn writhed on the grass, black mucus running from their noses like blood from a severed vein. Cosmil and Lia were there, too, coughing and vomiting the same inky goo that smelled like hot asphalt and swamp.

I woke up gagging and found Snowball draped over my neck and chest.

Damn, when did she get so heavy?

These spooky dreams were getting old fast, but I refused to dwell on them. Instead, I showered, downed a Starbloods, and called Saber's cell from my cordless house phone.

"Any report on Lynn?"

"She's stable. Cosmil believes she had a mild case of the Void illness, but one that hit her hard. He'll let Triton see her after he closes the store at five. Cosmil wants to resume our training, too."

"So you'll drive Triton to the compound and hang out there?"

"Yeah. Oh, and I used Triton's computer to look up that networking site. You have to register, and it looks more like a gaming thing to me, but the address is www.shiftermagic.net."

"Got it," I said as I jotted the URL on my note pad. "I need to check in with Maggie to be sure there are no wedding snafus, but I'll get on the computer before I leave for my tour."

"You'll come out here straight from town?"

"Probably. I should ask Lia if she wants some fresh clothes. If she does, I may drop by your place on the way, but I won't stop at home. I can change into jeans and a tee at Cosmil's."

"Good deal. See you about ten tonight."

We signed off, and I called Lia first. She asked for a cotton outfit I'd seen her do the magical ironing job on, and she asked me to bring her pouches.

I disconnected and immediately called Maggie's cell. She answered on the third ring.

"Are you with a client?"

"The one who can't pick a bathroom tile to save her snooty life."

"Tell her to go with neutral glass tiles. It's the rage."

"Says HGTV?"

"Just tell her it's the choice of celebrity designers."

Maggie laughed. "So, what's up?"

"I have a tour tonight and then another thing," I said as I opened my laptop and powered it on.

"You've had a lot of other things lately. I've noticed all the late comings and goings. Should I know specifics?"

"We've been hanging out with Triton a lot," I fudged, then hurried on. "But I called to be sure all things wedding are going smoothly at your end."

"They are. I'll be over to help with last-minute preparations for the bridal shower Saturday."

"Okay, but Saber and I have Sunday's party covered. You and Neil just need to show up, eat, and open gifts."

"And then write thank-you notes. Oh, here comes my client. I'll catch you later."

I put the phone unit on the desk, entered the Shifter Magic web address, and waited. The registration screen flashed up with hokey depictions of vampires and shifters and fairies in the outer frame. I signed in using my secondary e-mail address, and borrowed my mother's maiden name to set up enough of a profile to give me access.

A list of games appeared in a navigation bar at the top of the page. I clicked on shifters, and a long, five-column list popped up. Human-dolphin was in the first column, but so was human-butterfly.

Hmm. Did a butterfly shifter experience a cocoon stage first?

I entered the shifter "game," went through the tutorial, and finally got into the forum. Sure enough, supposed shifter sightings were reported from St. Augustine to the Barbary Coast by people with screen names like ahab930, adam12, and flipper21, but I couldn't tell if these were gaming comments or sightings people legitimately believed they'd seen.

I watched the clock so I'd have plenty of time to change, drive to town, park, and meet my tour on time. Meanwhile, I scrolled through scores of entries until I found one that referenced St. Augustine. Sent from magicman1463 three days before the full moon, the message read: *Single St. Aug dolphin seeking female.*

This lame line had sent Lynn in search of Triton? I guess women fell for worse. The "magicman" moniker could be Starrack's, but it seemed hit or miss that Lynn would have seen the post, much less acted on it.

I continued scrolling and searching, but never saw a message quite so pointed. I also never saw another message from magicman1463, though there were other magicman users with different numbers. Could Saber pull strings to get 1463's identity? If so, could he do it in a remotely helpful time frame?

That was the rub.

I decided to break out my female pirate outfit for the ghost tour. It wasn't precisely period perfect, but it wasn't a sexy Halloween getup, either.

Since I was dressed for it, I told my ghost tour group tales of St. Augustine's pirate raids. I told them that English corsair Sir Francis Drake attacked and burned the town in 1586. Then I spoke of the pirate Captain John Davis. In 1668, he and his men had plundered the town, killing sixty inhabitants, including a young girl whose ghost haunted Davis until he fled from St. Augustine half mad.

"You really didn't like this Davis dude, did you?"

The question came from one of the teen tourists. I acknowledged him with a smile.

"I wasn't around then, but you're right. Just thinking about him makes me angry. Davis strikes me as having been a particularly vicious bully."

"Well, if you're so antipirate, why the costume?" a teen girl with the same family asked.

This time I grinned. "Three words. Captain Jack Sparrow."

She laughed, and the group moved on.

We'd seen the haunts, I'd given my closing spiel, and the tourists had dispersed when two young transients approached me.

"Excuse me," the girl of about twenty said. "Aren't you the local vampire?"

Uh-oh. Good things didn't usually follow a question like that.

"Yes," I answered cautiously, an eye peeled for one or both of them to whip out a weapon.

The girl fidgeted. "I don't know how to put this."

"Let me," the young man said, bumping the girl aside. "We'll let you bite us for money."

My jaw dropped.

"Say what?"

"We'll donate blood if you pay us."

I gathered my wits. "You need to know two things. First, I don't bite people. Second, I don't have any cash on me."

Which was true. I'd left my emergency five dollars in the truck, but I did have my Visa in my pirate pants pocket.

The girl spoke up. "Wouldn't you make an exception? We're awfully hungry."

Something about her face tugged at my heart. And wallet.

"I won't bite you, but I will buy you a pizza."

"I thought you didn't have any cash," the young man said.

"I don't, but I know a guy who'll help you out." As soon as he swiped my credit card.

"You'd do that for us?" The girl's eyes glistened with hope.

"Sure, but we need to move it. The restaurant closes soon."

I began walking south on St. George. I sensed them weighing whether to follow me or not, but I soon heard their footsteps.

We arrived before closing, just in time to order one sixteen-inch pizza with the works, two bottled waters, two bottled colas, and two jumbo plastic cups of tea. The girl took hers sweet. Maybe that's why I hadn't been able to turn her away. She was a sweet tea soul sister.

Surprisingly, the young man thanked me with as much sincere

warmth as the girl did. They went off toward the bay front, juggling their dinner and drinks. I hotfooted it to my truck, calling Saber to leave the message I was running behind.

Time to pick up Lia's things at Saber's. Time to burn rubber to Cosmil's shanty.

Time to see if Lynn was the innocent our research indicated she just might be.

SIXTEEN

Saber waited on the porch as I climbed from my truck, my change of clothes slung over one arm, Lia's things in a plastic Publix bag.

"Hey, you okay?"

"You didn't get my message, did you?"

"Cosmil's protective wards here must be interfering with our service. That or reception is iffy out here. What happened to hold you up?"

"I bought a pizza and drinks for a homeless girl and her boyfriend."

He shook his head and hugged me. "Word will get around that you're a soft touch."

"Maybe," I said, holding him tightly, "but the girl got to me. She looked like I was her last hope for a meal. Speaking of girls, how is Lynn?"

"Sleeping. I called Mrs. Tidwell with an update. I told her Lynn had a severe reaction to something she ate, but that she'll be fine in a few days."

"Is Triton hovering over her?"

"He's in there watching her breathe." Saber gave me a kiss and a pat on the butt. "Better get a move on. Cosmil is getting testy."

I entered the shanty to see Cosmil and Lia on the sofa quietly talking. Triton stood at the bedroom door.

Lia glanced at me, then did a double take. Her brows rose in surprise, and her lips twitched. I held out the bag to forestall a comment.

"Here are your clothes and pouches, Lia."

"Thank you. Now scoot on into the bathroom and change. I'll be supervising the three of you tonight, and we have a great deal to do."

"Did you make that sketch of Starrack for us yet?"

"I've begun, but not completed it. Healing work has taken most of my time."

"So your location spells haven't panned out, either?"

"No, and we feel like old dogs following a muddled scent."

"We surmise," Cosmil added, "that Starrack is using a cloaking spell. He excelled at those, as I recall, and before you ask, Francesca, yes. We have added our own cloaking spells to the other protection we have cast on all of you."

I doubted the cloaking would help if Starrack already knew our physical addresses, as we suspected he did. But, hey, the more spells, the merrier.

"Cosmil," Saber said, "you told us you might have been able to track the Void to Starrack if the Veil hadn't been closed."

"I did."

"Then what about using Void residue in your spell? The Void may not have typical DNA, but it must've left some foreign material on Legrand's remains. Have the forensics lab rush a tissue sample to you."

A smile bloomed in Cosmil's eyes, and Lia beamed.

"Brilliant, Saber," she praised. "Cosmil will make the call while we train."

As I squeezed past Triton on the way to change clothes, he barely glanced at me. Man, he did have it bad. Pandora, though, in her hefty-house-cat form, lifted her head to meow a greeting from the foot of the bed.

When I was ready, my ponytail resecured, I stowed my costume in the truck and joined Lia, Saber, and Triton in the yard.

"We'll be running through several exercises tonight, then we'll work with the amulets. We'll start with telepathy, but you'll be send-ing information via pictures rather than words."

She handed each of us a magazine and tiny flashlights like I'd see at the dollar store.

"All right, pick any page and project it as a whole but with as many details as you can. Cesca will send first. Gentlemen, raise your hand when you first begin receiving an image, but don't speak what you see until I ask."

I opened the decorating magazine to a kitchen-remodel photo and mentally sent the image. Saber and Triton raised their hands almost simultaneously and accurately describe the photo. Saber took the next turn, and his image of a meadow with a background of snow-capped mountains came to me a few moments before it did to Triton.

"That's to be expected, Triton. Cesca is more bonded to the two of you, than you men are to each other. Proceed."

Triton's image of a shipwreck came, and I saw it first, but Saber mentally read the name of the ship in the photo legend.

"Very good." She clapped her hands, and the magazines and flashlights disappeared. "Now, you know that every living organism has an energy signature, down to each leaf of each tree. You recog-nize a rose by its shape, color, fragrance, yet every rose on a bush resonates with its own vibration.

"Saber, sight is your most enhanced preternatural sense. Smell is yours, Cesca, and Triton has the sharpest hearing and the gift of echolocation even in his human form."

I snapped my gaze to his face. "You do?"

"Cesca, attend me please. Using your unique talents and skills, your next task is to find Pandora."

"Do we spread out or stay together?" I asked.

"Follow your instincts."

Triton found Pandora first. He blasted sound high and low in every direction, and let me tell you, it was freaky hearing him make dolphin sounds with a human head. Yes, the clicks and whistles were different from those he made in dolphin form, but they did the job.

Pandora moved locations, of course. Saber spotted her on the high branch of an oak tree where she'd sat perfectly still. I tracked her scent to scrub brush.

"Excellent. We're moving right along," Lia said. "Next you will locate Pandora only by her energy signature."

It was easy for Triton to simply not use his echolocation, and for Saber to close his eyes. Lia made me stuff rolled gauze doused in rosemary oil up my nostrils. I felt like an utter dork.

The bad news, none of us found Pandora by her energy alone. The good news, the rosemary did wonders for my sinuses.

At midnight, when the guys and I were dragging, Lia lectured us on stamina. "You must stay awake, alert, and aware. Enemies strike the hardest when you let down your guard. Here."

She passed the Mu amulet to me, the Atlantean one to Triton. The symbols immediately shone in my skin.

"As you know, the amulets may be used to hurt or heal. Cosmil told me you all had a lesson in these properties before I arrived."

"Yeah, when Cesca blasted me across Cos's living room. Do I get to return the favor?"

"Triton," Lia said repressively.

He grinned, that schoolboy smile that used to spell mischief.

"There are two trees about ten yards beyond your cars. Both are diseased, but one has a chance of thriving while the other does not. You will locate the trees using your enhanced senses then use the amulets to heal the one tree and kill the other. Come."

She led the way to the general area and set us loose. Within minutes, we found the fifteen-foot oak that didn't have a squirrel's prayer of surviving. Saber saw the rot in the tree, I smelled it, and Triton's small burst of sonar confirmed the oak's core deterioration.

"Cesca, Triton, hold your amulets against the trunk. Saber, stand close enough to sense the energy. Focus your intent that the tree should pass over, and remember, Cesca, this is an act of mercy, not malice."

We moved into position, not on opposite sides of the tree, but with me on the left, Triton on the right, and Saber in the middle. We placed the amulets on the rough bark, and Saber held his hands above ours. Squeamish as I was to kill anything but spiders and roaches, I projected my intent that the tree should die. In seconds, pure white light rays burst from the amulets. They weren't as intensely bright as they had been in the comedy club. In fact, they seemed almost gentle as they pierced the tree, as if escorting its life to a leafy ever after rather than blasting it there.

Then the amulet suddenly sucked the rays back into itself.

"Back away now," Lia instructed.

We'd moved about eight feet when the tree imploded. Sawdust rained in the spot where the oak had stood.

Wow, would these babies wipe out invasive vines? We could retire as billionaires in months. No, megatrillionaires.

"Cesca, focus," Lia scolded. "Go locate the tree that can live."

I followed the guys, and we found a sad-looking palm sending the vibe that it was fighting for life. Again, we positioned ourselves roughly on either side of the trunk, placed the amulets on the bark, and sent healing intent. A lizard dashed over my fingers, scampering for safety and startling me so much that I started to jerk away. Saber grasped my wrist and held the amulet tight to the tree. This time when the rays shot from the amulets, they circled and climbed the trunk like Christmas lights. And the lights didn't all retract into the amulets. Instead, the rope beams continued to glow on the bark and slowly be absorbed into the palm.

I exchanged a glance with Saber and Triton.

"Super cool," I breathed.

"No shit."

"I felt it just holding your wrist, Cesca."

Lia chuckled. "Lovely job, all of you. Your last tasks of the night are these. Saber and Triton, you're doing twenty minutes of martial arts drills. Cesca, you practice distance flying and jump-flying. I'll return the amulets to Cosmil's care."

I started to ask her to define jump-flying, but I saw the image in her mind of me leaping into a fray or out of one. The only difference between jumping and jump-flying was that I'd stay airborne longer.

Okay, so I didn't make it through a whole twenty minutes in actual flight. Maybe I was a natural sprinter instead of a distance flyer. I did cruise higher over the tree line than before, and when an owl out hunting caught my eye, I followed it. The owl was faster, of course, but then I flew upright, feet toward the ground. That created wind resistance, right?

Cosmil emerged from the shanty and called a meeting just as the guys and I quit for the night. The wizard stood beside the cabin door, Lia and I took the chairs, and Saber and Triton sat with their backs propped against the pillars supporting the porch.

"First, the forensics lab will send a tissue sample. The Veil is still in flux and safe only for short trips, but the sample will arrive with all possible speed. In the meantime," he continued with a twinkle, "it occurred to me that we have clippings of both Triton's and Lynn's hair from the healing ceremony."

"Oh, well done," Lia exclaimed. "The Void's essence is so distinct, even a small bit of it may help overcome any cloaking spell Starrack is using."

"Just so," Cosmil agreed, a blush tinting his cheeks as the continued. "Next, Lynn is responding well, but she is weak. I believe she should stay another day."

Triton leaned forward. "Is she awake?"

"She is stirring, and you may see her when we are finished here, but we must consider her immediate future."

Saber turned to me. "We told Lia and Cosmil about our research on Lynn."

"Yes," Lia said, "and from our own reading of her, we agree she's probably not under Starrack's control."

"What'd you do?" I asked. "Mind-probe her while she was sleeping?"

Lia waved a hand. "But of course. A case of simple self-preservation. She was not sent to harm any of us or to steal the amulets. Odd as it may seem, her meeting Triton seems to have been pure synchronicity, not part of a malicious plot."

"More important," Cosmil said, "we discovered a birthmark on the bottom of Lynn's foot."

I blinked at that, and so did the guys.

"You would not have noticed it," Cosmil continued, "but Lia has heard of such a mark and has contacted the Council of Ancients for more information."

Triton huffed. "Aren't you going to tell us what you do know about the mark?"

"No," Lia said firmly. "However, if I am right, the birthmark will explain Lynn's origins."

"But for now, you think we can trust her," I said.

"I believe we may offer at least limited trust," Cosmil answered.

"Why limited?"

"Because now that she and Triton have met," Saber said, "Lynn could be on Starrack's radar."

Lia nodded. "Precisely, Saber."

He straightened. "We talked about putting her in a safe place last night," Saber said. "Can she hide out here with you and Lia?"

Cosmil grimaced. "No. We must remain focused on tracking Starrack and training you, and no one on the Council will shelter an unknown shifter. There is still too much suspicion among the factions."

"Damn." Triton looked from Saber to me. "Do you know any supernaturals who would take her in? What about that old vampire couple? Or are they infected, too?"

"The Clarkes have a clean bill of health for now," Saber said, "but they can't watch over her in the daytime."

Cosmil eyed Saber. "Have you considered your law enforcement contacts? Would one of them be willing to house Lynn for a short time?"

"If this were a threat from a human source, maybe, but most cops steer clear of preternatural matters. That's why they call me to consult."

I sighed. "It sounds like we have two big questions. One, if Starrack were to come after Lynn, where is the last place he'd look? Two, who is strong enough, fanatic enough, or foolhardy enough to protect her from a nonhuman threat?"

No one in the group answered. My little voice whispered an idea, but its solution was ludicrous. Laughable.

We'd have to be drop-dead desperate to even consider it.

Back at my cottage, Snowball was pathetically happy to see us. Or rather Saber. From me, she wanted food.

And, gads, how many days had it been since we changed her litter?

We took care of pet chores, then I showed Saber what I'd found on the networking site.

"Can we get an ID on magicman1463?"

"We'd need a warrant, and we don't have a tangible crime to ask for one."

"Could a hacker get to the user's profile?"

"I'll ask Bob March when I take Triton over during the lunch hour, but it's doubtful."

"So this website is a dead end unless Lynn can tell us anything else."

"About as dead as I am tonight. I haven't been this tired since—"

"Your nest-closing tour of Florida?"

"Hey," he said, pulling me into his arms. "We're going to beat this."

"How do you know?"

"Because you keep telling me, and once you've made up your mind, it's a done deal."

"Yeah, well, let's get you into the shower and then bed, big guy."

Since we're water conservation conscious, we showered together. Since I worried that he'd have nightmares, I watched over him through the night and worked on more design homework in on the side.

Fortunately, Saber spent a restful night and was up by eight thirty Friday morning. I sat with him while he breakfasted on cereal, a scrambled egg, and orange juice.

When he left at 9:05 to look in on Triton and help move some display tables in the shop, I set the perimeter alarm, brushed my teeth, and fell into bed at nine fifteen. Snowball purred from her place on Saber's pillow, and I drifted off hoping daymares didn't invade my sleep.

A deafening siren jerked me awake. My gaze darted to every corner of the darkened bedroom, looking for the source of the noise.

The digital clock read 12:10, but the alarm was never set for that time of day.

Then it hit me.

The perimeter alarm.

It seemed stupid to go to my hidey-hole, but I scrambled out of bed. That was the drill, and Saber would stake me himself if I didn't follow the plan.

I tripped into my walk-in closet, slapped shoe boxes out of the way, and shoved the hidey-hole door open. A forty-watt bulb in a white ceramic fixture lit the way as I stumbled down the two steps into the concrete bunker. Snowball shot inside, too, stampeding over my back. Heart pounding, blood pressure soaring, I shut the safe room door.

The phone tied directly into Sam's Security rang, and I grabbed the receiver off the wall mount.

"Yes."

"Ms. Marinelli, do you know what triggered your alarm?"

"No, I was sleeping."

"The police are en route. Sit tight and we'll call back."

My hidey-hole was more attractive and better ventilated than a dark, dank coffin, but being underground in a small space still made my stomach cramp with unpleasant memories. Plus, even sealed in the bunker, I heard the siren blare on.

I waited. Wondering how quickly the police would arrive. Attempting to calm Snowball. Picking at a frayed cuticle Snowball had scratched.

When the phone rang again, I dove for it.

"Ms. Marinelli, are you all right?"

"Yes."

"This is your all clear. The police are waiting for you at your door, and we're remotely shutting off the alarm now."

The house went silent, save for the faint knocking sound that got louder when I exited the safe room.

"Ms. Marinelli," a deep voice boomed as I came out of the closet. "St. Augustine police, ma'am. Open the door."

"Just a minute," I called back, frantically searching for a robe.

I settled for a long, terrycloth swimsuit cover-up and threw it on as I raced to the living room and flipped open the dead bolt.

Two officers stood on my cobblestone patio, both male, both buff, both wearing grim cop faces.

Across the way, my neighbor Hugh Lister stomped to the jasmine hedge separating our back yards. "Jesus H. Christ in boxers, Marinelli, can't you people be goddamn quiet?"

"Bless His holy name," his wife Selma said, standing at his side, wringing her hands. "Hugh, come have some sweet tea."

The younger officer covered a snicker with a cough. The older one eyed me sternly.

"Are you alone, ma'am?"

I nodded. "I was sleeping when the alarm went off."

The older officer looked at his little spiral pad. "You're a vampire, correct? That's why you're sleeping during the day?"

"Yes. Officer, what triggered that infernal siren?"

"This."

The men stepped aside, parting like a curtain, and there on the edge of my patio laid two bodies.

The very dead bodies of the homeless couple I'd met last night. Eyes wide open, expressions frozen in horror.

I clapped a hand over my mouth and sagged against the door casing.

"You gonna faint?" the older officer shouted through the roaring in my ears.

I swallowed bile but couldn't answer. Not because the poor

couple were covered in blood; there was no blood at all as far as I could see. It was the woman's open, empty eyes that tore at my soul. The terror in her death stare.

The older officer took my elbow and steered me inside to the sofa, and I sat in a daze while he went back to the porch. I heard him speak to his partner about securing the scene, and then he settled into an armchair across from me, the door left open. I didn't fear that Snowball would escape. She'd headed straight for her carrier before I ever opened the door, and she wouldn't venture out in all this commotion.

"Ma'am, I need to ask you some questions."

I blinked at his face then his name badge. P. Huntington. I gave him a stiff nod.

After confirming the basic information he had from Sam's Security, including my age and occupation, Huntington asked a few more basic questions before getting to the meat. Thankfully, the waves stopped crashing in my ears. Shock receded, burned away by low, slow anger.

"You know the victims?"

"Not by name." And that gave me a heart pang that nearly made me cry. I swallowed hard to block the tears.

"You want to explain that statement?"

"They were homeless people I met last night after I'd given a ghost tour."

"How were you associated with them?"

"I wasn't other than I bought them a pizza and some drinks."

"Alcohol?" Huntington asked sharply.

"Colas, tea, and water."

"Why did you buy them a pizza?"

I sighed. "Gross as this sounds, they offered to let me drink from them if I gave them money."

"Drink, as in blood? Feed from them?"

"I don't bite people, ever, but I could see that the girl was desperate. I told them I didn't have any cash, but I'd buy them a pizza and drinks. I paid with my credit card."

"Where'd you buy the food?"

"I'm blanking on the name, but it's the Italian restaurant on St. George Street between Hypolita and Treasury."

He scribbled on his pad then eyed me again. "When did you last see them alive?"

"Thursday night. They took their pizza and drinks to go, and walked toward the bay front."

"What did you do then?"

I knew not to mention too much, yet to tell as much of the truth as I could. "I went to meet the man I'm dating and another friend."

"What time did you come home?"

"About one thirty, I think."

"What did you do with these friends?"

"We exercised and talked."

"You exercise that late at night?"

"We have for the last few nights."

"Uh-huh."

The younger officer knocked on the door frame. "Supervisor is here, and so is the Florida Department of Law Enforcement crime scene unit and the investigator from the ME's office."

Huntington looked vaguely surprised. "Thanks, Blair."

"There is also," Officer Blair added, "a woman here who says she's Ms. Marinelli's landlady. Says she got a call from the security office."

I must've groaned, because both officers gave me a sharp look.

"That's Maggie. Maggie O'Halloran. She does own this property."

"Ask her to wait," Huntington said, and looked back at me. "All right, I need the names of your friends."

I opened my mouth to speak, but another deep voice from the door interrupted.

"Her friends are Deke Saber and Trey Delphinus."

My mouth dropped open far enough to catch dragonflies. "Detective Balch? You're on this case?"

Jim Balch worked for the City of St. Augustine PD. I'd met him during the French Bride murder when I'd been shot outside the condo where I'd first lived with Maggie. He'd been leery of me at first, but he'd attended the housewarming party Maggie and I had hosted in August.

Officer Huntington stood as Jim entered. "You want the rundown?"

Jim nodded, and Huntington read from his notes, condensing here and there while giving a perfectly accurate recap.

"Ms. Marinelli says the victims approached her after her ghost tour last night. They offered to let her bite them for money."

Jim raised one brow at me. "What did you do?"

"I bought them a pizza and cold drinks instead." Jim raised both brows, and I shrugged. "Hey, they were homeless and hungry."

"You're a soft touch."

"That's what Saber said."

Officer Blair knocked yet again, this time stepping inside to stand by Officer Huntington.

"The ME's people are ready to move the bodies," he reported. "You want to talk to the investigator before he leaves?"

"I've got what I need for now. Blair, Huntington, good job. I'll take over the interview from here, but please instruct Ms. O'Halloran to stay put about another thirty minutes. If she needs to speak with Ms. Marinelli right away, tell her to phone."

The officers gave me a last, suspicious glance, but I smiled and thanked them for their help.

Jim took the chair Huntington had vacated. "I give it thirty seconds tops before Miss Maggie calls."

"May I go get the house phone? It's in the kitchen."

He inclined his head, and I snagged the cordless unit from the kitchen.

"How worried is Maggie?" I asked as I tapped the phone in my palm.

"On a scale of one to ten, about fifty."

I cringed. "I'm hosting a bridal shower here tomorrow. Will I have to change the location?"

"Depends on what the techs find and the answers you give me."

The phone rang, and I punched the Talk and Speaker buttons, the latter so Jim could hear the conversation.

"Maggie, I'm fine," I said before she uttered a word.

"What the hell is going on?"

"I wish I knew. Listen, everything is still a go for the bridal shower, so don't worry. Detective Balch needs to talk with me right now, but I'll fill you in as soon as you're cleared to come over."

"Can you stay awake that long? How much sleep did you get?"

"About three hours, but I'll stay up as long as I need to."

I disconnected the call and set it on the coffee table. "Okay, what do you want to know, Detective?"

"Have you talked to Saber this morning? Has he called you?"

"I haven't talked with him since he left for Trey's apartment to help move display tables. Wait a minute. How did you know I was with Saber and Trey last night?"

"Because I just finished taking their preliminary statements."

My heart stuttered and so did my mouth. "S-statements? Is Saber okay?"

"Fine, but he and Trey discovered two other dumped bodies."

My knees wobbled, and I sank slowly onto the sofa.

"Where? When?"

"The Alligator Farm's secondary parking lot. Saber called in the bodies at nine forty. He and Trey aren't under arrest, but they voluntarily went to the station to file complete reports and wait on me."

I swallowed back my fear that the guys would be convenient suspects, but damn. Though the Alligator Farm was situated a little more than a block from Triton's place, neither of the parking lots were within casual view of his shop or apartment. How did the guys end up over there?

"Who are the victims?" I forced myself to ask.

"A couple of local thugs with a long arrest history."

Thugs? The men who'd beaten Triton were dead, too? But why?

"Trey wouldn't confirm it, but my gut says he recognized them. Your face says you know them, too."

"It's more that I may know of them."

"How? Tell me what the hell is going on."

I met his cop gaze and gave him the best answer I could.

"The supernatural shit is hitting the fan."

SEVENTEEN

~

"You want to be more specific?"

What could I say? That a crazed wizard had created a thought form that had infected and killed vampires. That the crazed wizard and his thought form were now killing humans? Hell, I wouldn't believe me.

I slumped against the cushions. "I would tell you if I could, but I'm baffled. I mean, why kill a couple of criminals and two homeless people who were little more than kids?"

"And why dump them on your doorstep?"

"Or dump those men so near to Triton's business."

"Triton?" Jim said sharply.

I waved a hand and thought fast. "Trey. I call him Triton to tease him."

Jim looked blank.

"You know. Son of Poseidon. Trey's heritage is Greek and he sells shipwreck treasures, so I call him Triton."

Jim stared past my shoulder for a moment, and in my head I felt him weighing what to say. "Saber believes the homicides are tied to an ongoing investigation he's conducting. Tell me straight up. Is this a preternatural crime?"

"I'm as sure as I can be that the killer isn't human, but I didn't see wounds on the bodies. How did they die, or can you not tell me?"

"The autopsy will determine the times and causes of death, but I spoke with the ME's investigator when I arrived. He worked the other scene, too, which is why he and the FDLE crime techs got here so fast. All the investigator can say with certainty is that each of the four victims also shows lividity patterns indicating they were moved after they were killed."

"That's it? There are no wounds?"

"Not even defensive ones. There was no blood in the parking lot or here. No tire tracks to isolate, no drag marks in the grass near the lot or in your yard, not a single footprint to chase down. If the FDLE crime techs have found one scrap of real potential evidence, I don't yet know about it. These bodies didn't just drop from the sky or magically appear."

"I wouldn't bank on that."

He paused and leaned forward, elbows on his knees. "Whatever supernatural shit is going down, you need to understand this. We have four bodies with no visible wounds, dumped in pairs within hours of each other. For all intents and purposes, we have a serial killer."

I inhaled sharply. "I hadn't thought of that."

"The department will want this guy caught and caught fast, because if the media get their teeth in it, the pressure will be intense. You know anything that can help me, then you need to open up."

I shook my head, at a loss for words that some supernatural ass ended four human lives just to, what? Make a point that he knew where we lived? Show us we were vulnerable? Keep us distracted?

Whatever the reason, I was damn mad now. For the first time in my life—or afterlife—I was out for blood.

No sooner had I finished that thought when a tingling coolness pooled at the base of my spine. I straightened my back as the cool stream flowed upward, spurting through the core of each vertebra, streaming past my shoulders and into my neck. Instinct urged me to stand, and when I did, the sensation flooded through me as if it had breached a dam. From the soles of my bare feet to my scalp, each cell of my body exploded with awareness. My body, my being, felt charged. Powerful.

Jim Balch slowly came to his feet. "Ms. Marinelli—"

"It's Cesca," I corrected, "and I promise you this. If I learn anything concrete that will help you solve these cases, I'll tell you."

He locked gazes with me. "You really will, won't you? You hate that this happened."

"I didn't know their names, Jim." My voice broke, and I had to swallow hard. "The girl was pathetically grateful for that pizza, and I never learned her name. I didn't ask."

He looked away, cleared his throat. "When the medical examiner finishes the autopsies, I'll let Saber know."

"Thank you. And if no one claims the bodies of the homeless couple, will you call me?"

"Yeah."

"Oh, and if you don't have to tell Saber you talked with me, please don't. He has enough on his mind without worrying about me."

Jim nodded, albeit reluctantly, but then he didn't truly consider Saber or Triton or me suspects.

We moved to the door, and as soon as I opened it, Hugh Lister hollered at us from his side of the jasmine hedge.

"Hey, Officer, come here and bring Marinelli. I got something to report."

Jim gave me a desperate glance. "Is that the compulsive cusser?"

"Mr. Lister, yes, but there's Maggie, too. And Selma Lister. She'll drag Hugh inside if he goes on too long."

Jim snorted, but since the crime-scene techs appeared to be finished with that portion of the yard, we crossed to the jasmine hedge.

Maggie's eyes narrowed on me, but she didn't have the chance to speak first. Hugh took the stage.

"I tried to tell the uniforms that the vampire here didn't kill those people. The bodies just appeared out of nowhere."

"I see," Jim said.

"No, you goddamn don't. I'm saying I've been out here in my backyard all morning pruning and raking. Her boyfriend left around nine, then everything was quiet until that son-of-a-bitching siren went off. I can hear it in this one's house." He hitched a thumb at Maggie. "That's when I saw the bodies, but not who put 'em there. I told Selma to call 911."

Selma nodded.

"Perhaps you had turned away while you worked, Mr. Lister. That would be natural."

Hugh snorted. "Son, it takes some muscle to move dead weight, pardon the expression. Takes time, too. I was pruning the jasmines right here in front of your face when the alarm went off. I would've heard or seen body movers, but I didn't."

I felt Jim's interest spark. "What time did you start working in the yard, Mr. Lister?"

"Eight, eight fifteen."

"Eight forty-five, dear," Selma corrected. "Before that you were getting your gloves and all your tools out of the garage."

"And the trash can and lawn bags," Hugh added.

Selma nodded her agreement and turned to Jim. "That's right. I brought Hugh some water, but he never came into the house until he banged in the back door yelling for me to call the police."

"I'm telling you, I would've seen it if those bodies were dumped there in a normal way. This wasn't normal."

"Are you willing to put that in a signed statement?"

Hugh's chest puffed a little. "Sure am. Marinelli here draws a hell of a lot of chaos, but she isn't a killer."

"I'll have an officer make an appointment for you. Thank you, Mr. Lister. Mrs. Lister."

As Jim strode away, Hugh squinted at me. "You might want to get some sleep, Marinelli. You look bad. Blotchy."

Which meant my skin was beginning to sunburn, but I didn't dash for a shady spot as I would have in the past. The cool tingle still streaming through my body dropped a degree. I'd heal.

"Come on, Cesca," Maggie said. "You need some aloe vera."

"Hold it," Hugh called before we'd taken a step. "Is the big wedding shindig still on for next weekend?"

"It's called a reception, dear," Selma said, her expression embarrassed.

"Whatever, it better not be canceled. We can't return your goddamn gift."

"Bless His holy name," Selma muttered as she turned toward her house.

"Who are you blessing?" Hugh demanded, trailing after her. "What did I say? Was the gift a secret?"

Maggie's wide-eyed gaze met mine. "Did they RSVP?"

"I don't think so. I don't remember panicking."

"Me, either, but I'm having a moment now."

Though the crime-scene techs were packing their gear, we were careful to take the same path back to my cottage that Balch and I had taken out of it. Once inside, Maggie forged ahead to the bathroom.

"Is your aloe in here?"

"I don't need it, Maggie. I'll heal fast."

"Tough. I need you to need it. Now sit on the toilet lid, and I'll do the applying while you do the talking. What's going on?"

"The short version is that there's a power-mad wizard on the loose," I said as she dabbed gel on my reddened cheeks. "He conjured up this thing we call the Void that's infecting and killing vampires with some kind of illness."

Maggie's hand froze. "Are you infected?"

"No, but most of the vamps in Florida are."

"What about the vampires we met in Fernandina?"

"They're healthy, and the illness isn't transmitted to humans as far as we can tell."

"So you and Saber have been coming and going at all hours because you're tracking the wizard?"

"Essentially, yes. We're working with Triton."

"Did the wizard kill those people who were dumped in the yard?"

"It looks that way. They were homeless, and I bought them a pizza last night. That's my only connection with them, so killing them doesn't make sense."

She put a swipe of aloe on the bridge of my nose and clicked the bottle closed. "Are Neil and I in danger? We can cancel the wedding and elope."

"Cancel when you're nine days out?" I said, dodging the danger issue. "Hell, no. Absolutely not."

I stood and took Maggie's hands. "You are not eloping. On October eleventh at six in the evening, you have cordially invited guests to the most perfect Victorian wedding and reception in history. The festivities will be held in your own home, and in your own backyard, as planned. Are we clear?"

"You're certain this mad wizard isn't after us?"

I sidestepped again and instead steered her toward the living room. "If he were after you, we'd have a sign by now, but I'll take more precautions. I know a sorceress who is going to spell you and

Neil, *and* this property, *and* the entire neighborhood with enough protection to deflect a bomb."

"Really?"

"I swear. I'll die before I let you or Neil be harmed."

"Well, don't go that far or I'm out my maid of honor." She patted my cheek in a motherly gesture. "Go on back to bed, Cesca. I'll be home the rest of the day, so I'll keep an eye out for trouble."

"No diva client today?"

"She canceled. Besides, I want to hunt for the Listers' RSVP."

We hugged, and Maggie opened the front door. Then at the threshold, she turned and titled her head at me.

"A sorceress?"

I smiled. "Yep."

"You do know the most interesting people."

I watched her cross the yard to her own back door, bracing for the mound of guilt that should heap on my head at any moment. Yes, I'd hated ducking her questions about potential danger, but, really, what did I know for certain about Starrack? Not very frickin' much, because why would he go after the homeless couple with Maggie and Neil at home and handy? Wouldn't they have been easier targets?

Sure they would have been, if Starrack was watching me. And he had to have been spying on me last night to connect me with the homeless couple. A realization that made my stomach clench so hard, I was glad I hadn't had my daily shot of Starbloods yet.

As little sleep as I'd had, I should've been a zombie. I wasn't. The odd, cooling energy that had infused me an hour ago still flowed like a river current, strong and steady. The sensation puzzled me, but I'd examine it later.

I couldn't talk to Saber right now, but I could take control of my next steps. Change out of the terry cover-up, place calls, and make lists.

Minutes later, wearing shorts and a bra-top cami, I grabbed a note pad and pen from my desk, the cordless phone from the coffee table, and marched into the kitchen. Snowball crept from her carrier and meowed at her empty bowl.

Okay, one detour to feed the cat. Then another when I smelled something funky in the laundry room. Snowball's doing? No. I sniffed the air and wrinkled my nose at the faint odor of eau de mildew. Damn. With Saber living here, it seemed I always had clothes and sheets and towels to wash. I must've run a load that never made it to the dryer. I opened the washer lid to confirm my suspicion. Geez, how many days had this load languished in laundry limbo? If I couldn't recall, it was too long.

Well, hell. A woman who couldn't do her laundry from start to finish couldn't kick butt. I would not be that woman.

I set the washer to run through another entire cycle, and set the egg timer so I wouldn't forget again.

My next order of business, phone Lia about increasing the protection spells, and hope the wards didn't block the call.

She answered on the second ring, and I launched into my questions.

"Have you talked with Saber or Triton today?"

"Cesca. You are awake."

"Lia, the guys. Have to talked to them?"

"Twice. We found a strong trace of Starrack this morning, and I called Saber with the location at nine thirty."

"The bodies at the Alligator Farm."

"Yes, Saber called back to confirm that, but how did you—" I felt Lia in my head, seeing my thoughts. "Oh, Cesca, I'm sorry."

"Your spell didn't show Starrack at my cottage?"

"Merde, no. I would have alerted Saber immediately."

I bit back a sigh and forged on. "Listen, Lia, I don't know what else you have in your magical arsenal but I need it. Can you lay a mondo protection spell on Maggie and Neil?"

"And on your neighbors and friends. I'll start right away, and Cosmil will help. We've already covered Lynn's foster mother and roommates. And all of us, of course."

"How is Lynn?"

"She could rest more, but she is well enough."

"Well enough to move her if we can find a safe place?"

"I believe so."

"Then I'll talk with the guys. Keep the locator spell running."

"Done. We must also continue training tonight."

"I'll be there after my ghost tour. And, Lia, we need that sketch of Starrack pronto."

"You'll have it."

I broke the connection and tapped my pen on the pad while I organized my thoughts. Jim Balch's questions had crystallized how lost we were when it came to Starrack. We didn't know what motivated him, where he was hiding, or what he might do next. So what facts did we have?

First, the Void was real. A thought form brought to a zombielike state of being, according to Cosmil. Whether the oily fog was the Void itself or its residue, it was terrifyingly tangible.

Second, Cosmil was 99 percent certain that Starrack had created the Void. Why he'd done it, what he was accomplishing, those details were blank.

Third, Starrack was spying on me—maybe on all of us—and he was nipping at our heels. Cosmil had been injured in the Veil. Triton had been assaulted at his apartment. Lynn had taken ill after she'd hooked up with Triton. And now four humans were dead for no good reason.

Bottom line, we were floundering like mullet on the beach. Time to find facts and formulate a plan.

In cop shows and mystery novels, the good guys investigate suspects by looking at phone, financial, and employment records. They look at family and known associates. They visit locations where suspects hang out. I doubted there was a wizard's bar and grill that Starrack haunted, and maybe he didn't leave a paper trail of bills or bank statements or income tax payments. But had anyone looked?

I jotted questions to ask Saber and Cosmil, and Lia, too. The COA had to keep records, however archaic they might be. Presuming that Starrack was behind the magical bomb that had hit their headquarters, it was in their best interest to help us, and perhaps Lia could use her clout. For that matter, we hadn't grilled Cosmil about Starrack's younger years when the brothers had been in touch, and we hadn't pinned Lia down about her dealings with the mad wizard. Any little tidbit of information, any old habit they remembered might lead to a real clue.

Next on my list was the question of where to stash Lynn. My little voice offered the same suggestion it had last night, so I turned it over in my head. There were gaps in the plan, hulking whale-sized holes, to be honest. Then again, nothing ventured. It just might work.

I rummaged in my closet to find a certain business card then snagged the phone book off my desk. The first call ended up being easy. The second? Let's just say I'd done some heavy hinting and abject begging to get a meeting. Closing the deal might be riskier than playing tag with a shark, but I was pretty sure I knew what buttons to push.

Selling the idea to Saber and Triton, and to Lynn herself, would be another hurdle, but one challenge at a time.

Saber came in the cottage door at two forty-five, just as I'd finished putting my laundry away. He didn't sneak in, but obviously made the effort to be quiet. So he wouldn't wake me, I supposed.

He nearly jumped out of his skin when he saw me at the bedroom door.

"Hey, you're up."

Don't you love it when men have a good grasp of the obvious?

"Yes, dear, I've been awake for a while, and I heard you had some excitement this morning."

Guilt flashed across his face, deepening worry lines I hadn't noticed yesterday.

"You know about the bodies dumped at the Alligator Farm?"

"In the parking lot. I do. Detective Jim Balch was here."

"To verify my alibi?"

"No, to interview me about the bodies dumped on my porch."

"What?" He had me in his arms in an instant. "Are you all right?"

I held him tightly, took comfort in his warmth, and breathed his unique Saber scent. And my heart broke all over again.

"They were barely more than teens, Saber, and they're dead."

"Who, honey?"

"The homeless couple I met last night."

"The ones you fed?"

I nodded against his chest. "I couldn't tell Jim their names, so I don't know if they'll be identified."

"I'm so sorry, Cesca. When did this happen?"

"The alarm went off about noon."

"Balch didn't say a word to me."

"I asked Jim not to tell you. He said you were at the station."

"Yeah, but Triton and I left at one thirty. I would've come right home if I'd known."

"Jim said the department will see the murders as the work of a serial killer."

"What did you say when he questioned you?"

"I confirmed what you told him. That the murders are connected to a case you're working, and that the killer is a supernatural being. I didn't say what kind. It was just too hard to explain."

We stood there, clinging to each other for long minutes. Saber sent waves of sympathy to me, and I sent them on to the spirits of the dead.

When Snowball interrupted our moment with a plaintive meow, I eased out of Saber's arms.

"Go get her a treat. We'll talk in the kitchen."

He shot me a wary glance but went for the treat box, then took a new catnip toy from the cabinet. I folded my hands over my note-pad and waited for him to sit.

"First, have you pumped Cosmil for information about Starrack?"

"Asked, yes. Pumped, no. Did their spell pick up Starrack here?"

"No, just at the Alligator Farm, but these murders have upped the stakes. It's one thing if Starrack used those criminals to attack Triton, then tied up the lose ends by killing them. It's plain patho-logical to kill those homeless people for no reason."

"You were with them, which means he was watching you."

"I've already tumbled to that, but I don't think he's constantly tailing us."

"Why not?"

"Partly a gut feeling, partly because shadowing all of us would be work. The man Lia and Cosmil have described is basically lazy. He could've learned I was on the tour schedule with a simple phone call and decided to check me out."

"And then decided to kill those kids?"

The rhetorical question made me shudder. "Do you think Cos-mil's compound is still secure?"

"I think if Starrack wanted to hit it and had the ability to break through the wards, he would."

"So he could attack us directly at any time."

"Except that Cosmil and Lia have protection spells on us."

"Still, we're putting out fires instead of making progress. I'm over it. We need to investigate Starrack in the mundane way. You found Lynn after all."

"Because she had a driver's license and had been arrested."

"Understood, but the COA must have records of some kind, even if they're on scrolls. And Cosmil is a blood relative, for heaven's sake. He has to remember some details about Starrack's likes, dislikes, habits. Interview him as you would a witness. Lia, too."

"I can do that."

"Good. Interview both of them together. Maybe they'll spark each other's memories. We can't have less to go on than we do now."

"Agreed. It's also critical to find a safe place for Lynn to stay until this is over. I considered asking Candy Crushman, but sending Lynn to Atlanta doesn't make good logistical sense."

"I have an idea that might work, and I've already put out feelers to the people who'd be involved in helping us."

"You put out feelers. On your own."

He wasn't wild about me taking the initiative. I caught that undercurrent in his measured tone, but that cool sensation spread through me and I stood my ground.

"Yes, I did."

"Want to enlighten me?"

Just as I opened my mouth, the doorbell rang three times in quick succession. Then the knocking started. Make that pounding.

"Hey, vampire, I know you're in there. Open up."

Great gull droppings. Victor Gorman was on my doorstep.

EIGHTEEN

"What the hell is Gorman doing here?"

Saber thrust his chair back so fast that it crashed to the floor. His fierce expression alarmed me, but the subtle darkening of his skin made my stomach churn with dread. Triton's skin hue had changed when the Void sickness had flared.

I did what my gut told me. I rose slowly, laid a hand on his chest, and imagined waves of calm, peaceful energy passing from me to him.

"Honey, it's okay. Gorman is part of my idea for protecting Lynn."

"You want to stick her with him? Are you insane?"

"Probably, but he's not a sure thing yet. Just follow my lead. Please."

Saber's anger downshifted a notch. I felt the difference as I brushed a kiss on his rigid jaw and left the kitchen. He stomped behind me to the living room, not happy but not murderous, either.

The bell rang again. I braced myself and opened the door to Gorman's perpetual jalapeno breath. In his signature black-ops-wannabe outfit, he glanced from me to Saber with a ferocious scowl.

"Is this a trap?"

His gravelly voice grated, but I put on a smile.

"Now how can it be a trap, Gorman? We set this meeting for tonight. After my ghost tour."

"Yeah, well, I figured that might be a trap, too."

I didn't roll my eyes, but boy, I wanted to. Maybe I *was* insane to try this plan with a blockhead like Gorman, but I couldn't turn him away now. Crazier ideas had worked, so I motioned him inside. He gave me a suspicious glare but edged past me into the living area.

"Won't you have a seat while I explain?"

He looked like he'd rather be attacked by a swarm of mutant sand fleas, but he lowered himself into the armchair closest to the door. Saber hesitated then threw himself into the matching chair, arms folded across his chest, scowl on his face. He might not help me, but maybe he wouldn't hinder me, either.

I settled on the sofa, madly reconstructing the points of persuasion I'd listed on my notepad.

"As I told you on the phone, we have a situation. A young woman is in mortal danger, and you're the only person who can keep her safe."

Gorman's ice blue eyes narrowed. "Danger from what?"

I leaned forward, as if eager to spill state secrets.

"From a rogue vampire. The nut job has already attacked her once."

"What's the perp's name?"

"Name?" My gaze ping-ponged around the room, seeking inspiration. Then I spotted my book in progress on the end table. "Hess. His name is Hess."

"Never heard of 'im. This chick ain't one of them blood bunnies, is she?"

"Oh, no, not even close. She's an innocent, but Hess is hounding her. He won't leave her alone."

"Son of a bitch wants to Turn her, huh?"

"Exactly. Saber is tracking him, but he's hard to catch."

Gorman's gaze swung to Saber's stony expression then back to me. "You sure this chick ain't jailbait? You ain't gonna trick me into committin' no crime."

Like he needed any help in that department. I bit my tongue and forged on. "She's of age, and you'd only need to protect her during the day."

"Wait. If this dude is a vampire, why ain't she safe in the day?"

"Minions." I blurted, but the lie seemed to take hold in his tiny mind. "The vampire has human minions, but I know they won't get past you."

"Damn straight they won't." Gorman's barrel chest puffed out. "I can take care of her day and night."

"Not at night. It may take Saber a week to find this vamp. You won't be effective if you don't sleep, so I've arranged for vampire guards at night. Two Marines who were Turned against their will. They work for the VPA."

"Shit in a bucket, you gotta be kiddin' me. I ain't lettin' any blood suckers in my house."

"They won't guard her at your place, Gorman. They'll pick her up when it's full dark and take her to another location, then bring her back before dawn. You just send her out the door, and they'll take care of the rest. You won't have to see or speak to them."

"But they'll know my name and where to frickin' find me."

"We'll give you a code name," I improvised. "Tell them it's just another safe house."

"I dunno."

I ground my teeth and reached for patience to continue the charade.

"Please, Gorman. You're our only hope to keep this girl safe. And did I mention we'll compensate you?"

Dollar signs instantly danced in his eyes.

"How much?"

"Fifteen a day," Saber said out of the blue.

I shot him a glance, struggling to keep a straight face at his sudden leap into the conversation.

"Gov'ment has to pay better'n that. Make it thirty."

"Twenty."

"Twenty-five, and money for her board. Girl's gotta eat, right?"

Saber raised a brow at me. "Is that agreeable to you, Cesca?"

"I'm sure we can get the VPA to approve the funds," I replied, then eyed Gorman. "Do we have a deal?"

"Not so fast," Gorman said, still eyeing Saber. "I'll need my weapons back. The ones you arranged to have confiscated."

Saber snorted. "The ones you've already replaced on the sly?"

Gorman reddened and would've blustered his way out of the accusation, but thought better of it. Instead, he said, "Then you hafta okay me usin' deadly force if it comes to that."

Saber gave him flat cop eyes. "Don't let it come to that."

"Gorman," I said quickly, "we'll speak to the sheriff's office if needed, but this is more an undercover operation than a shoot-out. Okay? Do you agree to the deal?"

"Yeah, I'm in. So, when do I meet this chick?"

"She's not a chick, Gorman, she's a young lady. You'll probably meet her tomorrow afternoon. She has to agree to the plan, but I'm sure she will when she knows you're the one who'll be protecting her."

"I do have a reputation."

"You sure do," I said as I stood.

Gorman popped out of his seat, too. Not to be a gentleman, but so that I didn't stand over him.

"Now you'll need to come up with a code name and a distress

word, too," I said as I walked to the door. "Not that I expect trouble, but you're a man who likes to be prepared, so I'm sure you know what to do."

Gorman left muttering under his breath. Fang Fighter Alpha? Geez, nothing like a comic book code name. Well, whatever made him happy. I had a more pressing problem. Placating Saber.

But when I turned, he wasn't on his feet ready to explode. He sat still in the chair, his mood belied only by his fingers digging two inches into the leather upholstery.

As I resumed my place on the sofa, I saw my darling visibly rein in his emotions. His skin color had lightened some, almost back to its Latino tan color, and I took that as a positive sign.

"How much of what you just told Gorman is bull? Are the Marines really landing?"

"I don't know yet if Ken and David are willing or able to come down here. I left each of them a message."

"And where do you propose to house them if they come?"

"At the beach house."

The house that sat in the middle of the last three lots of property my father had bought for me. The same property he'd entrusted to Triton's care before my family left town. The worn little cottage on the dunes we'd discovered when Saber was house hunting in July.

"That place is a dump, Cesca."

"Was a dump. I hired a plumber and an electrician while you were on your nest-closing trip, then did some power washing and painting. I scrubbed the place squeaky and even found a load of furniture at a garage sale. Cheap, because I hit the sale at the end of the day. The place isn't a five-star hotel, but it doesn't suck."

"It's a decades-old beach shack. With no protection from the sun."

"Did I mention the guys who installed storm shutters? I found blackout curtains at Walmart, too. Though they're off-white, not black."

He shot me a look of pure vexation. "You think that'll protect your fanged Marine buddies?"

"If not, they can always go to a hotel."

"And what will you do if Triton and the others balk at your plans, or Lynn refuses to cooperate?"

"I'll tell them to come up with a better idea." I paused and searched his face. "Is that what's bothering you? That I didn't discuss all this with you before I started things rolling?"

"Partly." He exhaled a breath that seemed to come from his bones. "It's been a demanding day, and it's not over."

"You're tired."

"Exhausted."

I slid off the sofa and grasped his hand as I knelt beside the chair. "Saber, I'm worried about you. Please let Cosmil and Lia do a healing on you tonight."

"I don't need it. We have too much training to do."

"Which won't mean squat if you're not at your fullest strength possible. Please. Just ask if a shot of healing would help."

He brooded for a full half a minute before he met my gaze. "I'll ask only if you make a promise to me."

"What is it?"

"If I'm mortally injured when we go up against Starrack and the Void, promise you'll Turn me."

I sat back, butt on my heels, mind spinning. "Turn you?"

"Swear it, Cesca."

"Saber, I can't."

He took my hands, pulled me up and then into his lap. "I've thought long and hard about this, honey. Even before I was infected. I want to be with you."

My emotions collided at such supersonic speed that I couldn't begin to name them. Only one stood out. Anguish.

I took his face in my hands. "I want to be with you, too. For as far into the future as I can imagine. But I can't Turn you, Saber. I don't know how."

"Then call Ray for instructions. Or ask the Marines. Even Jo-Jo."

"What if I do it wrong? Or your bit of werewolf blood interferes and it doesn't take?" I held his gaze, searching for any flicker of reaction to my questions. "Saber, what if you hate being a vampire once it's done?"

He threaded his fingers through my hair. "Princesca, if you can drink Starbloods, I can. I'd rather live without sunlight than without you."

He kissed me then. His lips teased, coaxed, and I opened to him even as that cool flowing stream of energy inside me heated.

"God, Cesca, don't you feel this power between us?"

He slanted his mouth over mine, his kiss demanding now. And then I felt it. For the first time, I felt not merely his heart frantically beating with desire, but his blood rushing through his veins. I sensed the vampire in him straining to possess, the wolf straining to mate. I sensed the totality of the man who loved me.

And when he kicked the coffee table out of the way and tumbled us to the floor, I tore at his clothes with as much single-minded purpose as he.

"It can be like this always," he whispered, skimming a hand down my side. "Promise me, Cesca."

"Deke," I whimpered when his tongue laved one nipple then the other.

My pulse pounded in my ears, and nerve endings thinned. With each caress, my fingertips found joy in the tension and texture of his skin.

"We. Belong. Together." He punctuated each word with a kiss then cupped my sex with his palm. "Promise me, Cesca."

I cried out, arching to his touch. "Deke, please."

Please don't push. Please don't make me choose now. Please just love me and let it be enough.

No.

"No," he said again, this time aloud.

I blinked away a sliver of mindless passion to find Deke poised over me, ready to join our bodies. The solemn expression in his cobalt eyes commanded me to see into him.

"Promise me, Cesca. Even if the Turning fails, I have to know you won't simply let me die."

"You will live, Deke," I said as I wrapped my legs around him. "I promise you will live."

We took Saber's SUV because he decided to go with me on my Friday night ghost tour. I think because he expected Ken and David to show up out of the blue. They didn't, but they did call me before the tour started. The vampire buddies were together, still on vacation, and—surprise!—in Orlando. That put them about two hours away by car, a bonus considering I'd figured on eight or more hours of travel. Ken offered to come to St. Augustine right away, but I told him to wait until the following night. We arranged to meet Saturday at ten in the South Beach Grill parking lot near A1A and Highway 206.

That is, if Lynn, Triton, and our magical mentors agreed with my plan. If not, I'd phone them to abort the mission.

Saber hovered during the ghost tour, on alert for any disturbance. I stayed alert to his health and to my twenty-five tourists, shepherding them along, answering questions, and generally doing my best to insure they got a bang of boos for their bucks.

We arrived at Cosmil's just after ten, me still in my green Regency costume, Saber in blue jeans and a white polo shirt. A similarly dressed Triton sat on the couch, his arm around Lynn. Cosmil and

Lia stood at the gleaming stainless steel island, both wearing those white scrublike uniforms, whipping up either a late dinner or magical potions. Judging by the spread of bowls piled with ingredients, the flasks filled with liquid, and the aroma of herbs, my money was on potions. I didn't see Pandora, but as soon as I thought of her, I sensed her outside in the tree line. Patrolling, I gathered.

"Wow, Lynn, you look fantastic," I said when she acknowledged me with a shy smile. Her silver blond hair shone in the soft light, her skin no longer looked sallow, and her blue green eyes sparkled. "I'm not sure Triton is good enough for you."

She laughed and plucked at the hem of her navy shorts, paired with a warm pastel pink scoop-neck T-shirt. "Triton ran me home to get fresh clothes, and we stopped by Mom Kate's to prove I'm okay."

"The phone calls home weren't cutting it," Triton added.

"How did you explain Triton to Kate?" Saber asked.

"They introduced him," Cosmil said, "as my intern and assistant. I sent a note along for Mrs. Tidwell explaining that Lynn had contracted a particularly nasty bacterial infection that would need several days more treatment."

"Nice work," I said, leaning a hip against an armchair.

"Yes, well, we have explained the potential danger to Lynn and bought time so that we may protect her, but now tell us, have there been further developments in the murder investigations?"

"No," Saber answered. He sank into the matching chair across from Lynn. "The autopsies may be done this weekend, but I doubt we'll hear from Detective Balch until Monday."

Cosmil nodded as he moved a pinch of red powder from a bowl to a flask. The liquid popped, and a very thin line of smoke rose. Lia leaned into the wizard to inhale the smoke and smiled her satisfaction.

I cleared my throat. "If that's more miracle cure you two are mixing up, Saber could use a shot of healing tonight."

"Why not heal him yourself?" Lia's eyes fixed on my face.

I blinked. "You mean with the am—"

"Way," Triton jumped in. "Wasn't that the stuff you bought on the Internet? I think you left that here, didn't you, Cesca?"

Never say I can't take a hint. "That's right. I don't have any at home."

Lia had watched impassively, and now waved her hand. "Never mind, then. We'll see to it. Right now, tell us your plan for protecting Lynn. We must get this settled."

"How do you know I have a plan?"

"You're mentally broadcasting bits of it. We really must work on shielding your thoughts."

"Damn, Cesca," Triton said, "tell us already."

"Okay." I stood straight, ready to sell the idea. "We want to hide Lynn but also have someone looking after her in case she gets sick again. When I thought of safe places and people, the first name to pop to mind was Victor Gorman."

I looked directly at Lynn. "I warn you, Gorman is not the most couth of men. In fact, he reeks of jalapenos and cigar smoke most of the time, but he is relentless. He's stalked me for months."

"He's a stalker?" Lynn asked nervously.

"Not in the typical sense, I promise. He's a vampire hater. A member of the anti-vamp group, the Covenant. Think a redneck Van Helsing."

"Why would your stalker agree to protect Lynn?" Triton demanded.

I gave her a conspiratorial grin. "Because I told Gorman a rogue vampire was obsessed with a gorgeous, innocent heroine."

"She also offered to pay him," Saber put in dryly. "I don't like the guy, but he'll bust his butt for the money."

"He won't harm her?" Triton pressed.

"No. He knows to do the job and nothing more."

"Plus," I said to Lynn, "you'll only be with Gorman during the day. I've made other arrangements for night guards. Two male vampires I met in Fernandina Beach."

Triton shot off the sofa and paced toward me. "Vampires? Are you using grits for brains? They're more infected by the Void than we are."

"These two aren't sick at all, so chill. Ken and David are former Marines who were trapped in the Atlanta nest. They're very grateful that the nest system has been dissolved, and want to do me a favor. They also happen to be on vacation in Orlando right now, so they can be here tomorrow night."

"Oh, yeah? Why can't they get here tonight? And where will they stay?"

"They'll keep Lynn at the beach house. Starrack may know about the property, but it's kind of off the radar so I have a gut feeling he doesn't. As for question two, David and Ken could have come to St. Augustine tonight, but I told them I'd need Lynn's approval. If she says no, David and Ken stay in Orlando, and I can nix Gorman, too."

"Well, I say no. No way in hell."

"You have another solution?" I shot back.

"Triton," Lynn said mildly.

"What?" he snapped.

She arched her perfect eyebrows. "I believe Cesca said I'm the one who has to approve."

"Lynn, you could be stuck with these strangers for days."

"Cosmil and Lia were strangers when I got here. I can manage."

Panic flashed in Triton's eyes. "Cos, what do you think?"

"I do not have an alternative idea, and I believe this is Lynn's decision."

Triton eyed Saber. "What about you?"

"I think it's been a while since you had a girlfriend. It's Lynn's call."

"Traitors," Triton muttered as he plopped into the second armchair.

I patted his shoulder as I took a seat next to Lynn. "Triton, I know it's an unorthodox solution, but please give it a chance."

His mulish expression didn't change, but he nodded. "All right. So how will you execute this plan?"

"First, if Lynn can stay one more night here, Saber will pick her up tomorrow afternoon while I'm hosting the bridal shower. Then we can both take her to meet Gorman."

"Where," Saber interjected, "I will put the fear of God, the VPA, and prison into him."

"Of course Lynn is welcome another night," Cosmil confirmed.

I turned to Lynn again. "And if you change your mind after you meet Gorman, just say so."

"Deal. Will I stay the rest of the afternoon with him?"

I shook my head. "I thought we'd go to dinner with Triton at South Beach Grill. Then all of us can meet David and Ken there in the parking lot afterward. That will give Triton and Saber some peace of mind."

"Won't being in public expose us to Starrack?" Triton asked.

"Not if Lia's and Cosmil's whiz-bang spells perform as advertized."

Lia nodded. "We've already reinforced the protection and cloaking spells on all of you, and we'll give Lynn a charm to wear around her neck. Like the mermaid charms Cosmil told me Triton carries in his store."

Triton looked unsure but didn't comment, so I turned back to Lynn.

"If you're good to go with Ken and David, I'll get you all settled at the beach for the night. The guys will drive you to Gorman's house every morning, see that you get inside safely, and pick you up after dark."

"I won't be able to see Triton?" Lynn asked.

"Not for a while. I'm convinced that Starrack knows where Triton and I live."

"And because of the murders," Saber added, "we believe he's keeping tabs on our movements to some extent or another."

"I know it's not ideal," I continued, "but the less you and Triton are together, the safer you'll be."

Cosmil nodded. "Francesca is correct. However, I have a proposition that will give you two some time together if Saber is amenable."

Saber nodded for Cosmil to continue.

"Triton, you may stay here alone with Lynn tonight. The wards are strong, and I will leave Pandora to stand guard. Lia and I will spend the night in Saber's home. While there, I will reinforce the wards on his property."

"Can you make those wards long lasting?" I asked. "At least until after the couples shower on Sunday?"

Saber gave me a look.

"What? Can't hurt, might help. And while you're at it, Cosmil, you and Lia can lay a major protection ward on Gorman and the vampires, and the neighborhoods where Lynn will be staying. And maybe Pandora can do her invisible-stealth thing and patrol the areas, too."

Cosmil chuckled, the first sign of humor I'd seen from him in days. "Ever practical, Francesca. Is there anything else we may do for you?"

"You can do a healing on Saber, and Lia can finish her sketch of Starrack."

"Ah, yes." Lia pivoted to the counter against the far kitchen wall and turned back with a sketchpad in hand. "It is not my best work, but it will serve."

She drew a thick sheet of paper from the pad and held it up for all of us to see. Her rendering favored Cosmil in the cheekbones and forehead, but Starrack's face was fuller and the eyes colder than Cosmil's. The hair was grayer, too. More salt than pepper like Cosmil's was.

"This is the guy you're after?" Lynn said.

Triton eyed her with apprehension. "Do you recognize him?"

"Not at all," she said, and I knew she spoke the truth.

"I haven't seen him, either," Triton said.

"At least he hasn't been under our noses," I said, then turned to Saber. "We'll need photocopies of this for Gorman, Ken, and David."

"I wouldn't share it with the authorities, though," Lia said.

"Lia is right," Cosmil said. "Starrack is too dangerous at this stage. I would not want officers hurt or worse attempting to apprehend him."

Saber shrugged. "I suppose law enforcement can stay in the dark for their own protection."

"Excellent," Cosmil said, then eyed me. "Time for you and Triton to train."

"What about healing Saber? Aren't you taking him outside to the circle?"

"No need. We shall do it right here." Cosmil pointed at floor on the other side of the island and a wooden stool with a white padded seat appeared. "Saber, sit there. Francesca, Triton, go."

We went, right after I changed out of my costume into workout shorts and a tee. First we tried a telepathy exercise, but that was a bust. Triton and I were far too tuned into Saber and Lynn, and not each other.

Within five minutes, Triton called a halt. "Since this isn't working, spar with me."

"I won't be much of a partner. Saber's only taught me a few moves."

"Then I'll attack and you react."

Without further warning, he swept my legs out from under me. I fell hard enough that it momentarily stunned me.

"Is that payback for my protect-Lynn plan?" I asked, flat on my back.

"Hell, yes. I don't like it that she'll be at the mercy of a redneck stalker and two vampires you barely know."

"Hey, those vampires can dance." I sat and held out a hand for him to help me up. As he grudging complied, I admitted, "It's not an ideal situation, but it beats having her all the way in Daytona if trouble comes knocking."

He lunged at me, and this time I jump-flew backward ten feet.

Triton smiled. "Good move. Now come at me."

I did, and he fell backward, taking my momentum but thrusting a foot in my belly to toss me over his head. I would've eaten dirt, but my flight instinct kicked in. I levitated upright, turned in midair, and landed on my feet, astounded and outright impressed with myself.

"You want to go again?" Triton asked, up and in a defensive stance.

"I'll quit while I'm ahead. Triton, have you fallen for Lynn all the way?"

He looked toward the shack we were fast approaching, his expression one of guarded longing. "I'm infatuated, and I'm fascinated that she's the only other dolphin shifter I've met."

"And?"

He raked a hand through his hair. "I'm frustrated. I feel like I got her into all this, yet I can't be with her. I can't be the one to protect her."

"But you trust her in your gut?"

"Yeah, I do."

"Then why didn't you want me to mention the amulets?"

"Cosmil said it's need-to-know. Lynn understands about the danger and where it's coming from, but we haven't told her about our major weapon."

"Makes sense. If the worst happens, she can't reveal what she doesn't know." I smiled up at him. "Is your age difference an issue?"

"It doesn't seem to be. I want her damned desperately."

"Then be patient. After all these years of waiting, a week or so isn't a deal breaker. Besides," I added, bumping his hip as we reached the porch steps, "Cosmil's giving you all night to impress her."

He flashed a grin. "I've already done that. This'll be an encore."

A moment later, when we walked though the cabin door, a bell pinged madly.

"What the hell is that?" Triton asked.

Saber turned from the stainless counter, excitement lighting his eyes.

"The tracing spell got a solid hit. Let's roll."

NINETEEN

꩜

I barely had a chance to see Lia and Cosmil bent over the maps spread on the island counter as Saber hustled us right back out the cabin door. Lynn wasn't in sight.

"Wait, Saber," I said as my feet hit the porch. "We need the am— weapons."

"Got 'em."

"What about communication?" I asked as we trotted across the yard. "We have a phone glitch out here."

"Cosmil is taking care of it."

"But we're not ready to fight."

He opened his passenger door and all but shoved me in as Triton climbed in the back. "Let's find the bastard first, then we'll see about being ready."

In seconds, the engine roared, and the SUV tore over the packed earth of Cosmil's straightened drive toward the state road.

"Where did they find Starrack?" Triton asked, leaning between the seats.

"The outskirts of Hastings."

I shook my head. "They can't be more specific?"

Saber handed me his cell. "Call and ask."

I did, and Lia not only answered, she stayed on the line as we flew past Hastings, then on toward Palatka. The tracking spell may not have been GPS accurate, but she managed to guide us to an abandoned, boarded-up house in a deserted area just off the highway. Saber rocked the SUV to a stop in what was left of a wide gravel-and-weed drive.

"Do you smell the Void?" Cosmil said over the speaker.

I cracked the window and cautiously sniffed.

"I smell something, but it's not all the Void. Guys, you see anything?"

"We need to investigate on foot, Cosmil," Saber said. He reached across me to pop the glove compartment and pull out the giant flashlight, then passed it back to Triton.

"Be careful. All of you. Francesca, drain the Void's energy if you find it. Do not hesitate. Let Saber and Triton handle Starrack. And check in as soon as you can."

"Got it."

We piled out of the car and fanned out around the derelict house, Saber with his Glock held in both hands and pointed down, Triton with the flashlight. The scent of the Void hung over the property like a musty shroud, and I reached to sense its essence the way Lia had tried to teach us to find Pandora. I didn't feel the Void inside or a presence that might be Starrack, but then I hadn't been able to find Pandora, either. When I sucked energy, I sucked more memory of the Void than the Void itself.

When Saber and Triton circled to the back of the house, I followed to find the exterior door hanging by a single hinge. Pungent odors emanated from the house itself, but the oily Void smell was stronger from the field behind us. Strong enough to make my nostrils itch.

"Guys," I whispered, tilting my head at the gap in the rotting fence. "The smell gets worse that way."

Saber hesitated, and I knew he wanted to search the building. I sent the thought, *Later*. He nodded, then led the way through the fence into the high weeds. Keeping two arm spans apart, the three of us walked slowly forward until we'd gone roughly two blocks. I stopped and raised a hand.

"What, Cesca?" Saber whispered.

"The smell is dissipating fast. Do you see or hear anything?"

Triton panned the light over the field in a complete circle, he and Saber peering into the shadows. Nothing moved, except the bugs attracted to the flashlight's beam.

"Want me to try echolocation?" Triton said softly.

"Can't hurt," Saber answered.

I braced myself, but Triton's clicks and whistles, even a shrill screaming sound, didn't do a thing but flush a bird from the scrub brush.

"Damn. Cesca, is the scent still fading?"

"Afraid so. Starrack must be dragging the Void around like an ugly puppy."

"You sense the wizard here now?"

"No, but if he parked the Void somewhere populated, it would smell like an oil slick. The neighbors would be screaming complaints."

"Good point. Let's go check out the house."

Oh, great, another stink hole. Bad as the Void smelled, the sour stench in the house made me wish I had a mask handy. Urine, vomit, booze, unwashed human, and who knew what else. The combination nearly drove me back as we eased inside onto a sticky, cracked linoleum floor. Triton played the flashlight around what had been a kitchen in a happier incarnation. We edged past a sink teetering on skeleton plumbing and through another doorway.

Watch your step, Saber said in my head, and Triton nodded, too.

Triton panned the bright beam steadily around the room, and I about jumped out of my skin when a raccoon waddled from the far corner. I sent a nudge of "Go" energy, and it took off through a hole in an interior wall just as we heard a distinct and very human moan from our right.

I stayed put while Saber and Triton checked the man curled in a fetal ball, his face mashed into floor. He seemed to be cradling one liquor bottle, laying on another, and more bottles and beer cans littered the floor around him. Saber toed one bottle out of the way as he bent to peer at the form.

"Is he injured?" I asked.

"Just passed out drunk. Cesca, get some gloves and bags for us, and my other flashlight. We'll check the rest of the house."

I knew what he meant. The crime-scene evidence supplies he kept in the back of the SUV. Where I'd also find a mask. I sprinted into the relatively fresh air, out to the car, and donned a mask before trotting back inside.

Saber took the second, smaller flashlight and two gloves.

"You're bagging the booze?" Triton said with a frown. "Why?"

"Most of this stuff is rotgut variety alcohol. Cheap wine, vodka, gin, malt liquor. But look."

Saber motioned to the debris, and I read several labels. Thunderbird. Mad Dog. 20/20. Then Saber eased another bottle from under the drunk man's bent legs.

"That's ouzo," Triton said. "And it's one of the more expensive brands."

"That's why I'm bagging the booze. Remember when Lia mentioned Starrack's drinking?"

"She didn't mention ouzo," I said.

"Yeah, but the ouzo is the anomaly in this mix. The booze that doesn't fit the pattern here. If Starrack was this guy's drinking buddy, maybe he left enough of his DNA on one of these bottles for Lia and Cosmil to refine their spell."

"I suppose," I said as I held out a bag for the ouzo bottle, then another for the 20/20. "But surely Starrack wouldn't be stupid enough to leave bottles for us to find."

"He might've if he left in a hurry," Triton said. "Or if he was buzzed enough not to notice this guy was laying on it."

"For now, it's a lead," Saber said, and bagged four more samples. "Let's get back to see if it means anything more."

"Wait, we're just leaving this guy here? Don't you want to question him later?"

Saber sighed. "Honey, I doubt he knows his own name half the time, and he'll just be passed out here or somewhere else tomorrow night."

"I-it's just so sad."

"Then I'll phone the cops. What to do with him will be their call."

When Saber opened the sacks to place the liquor bottles on Cosmil's island counter, the stale, sour smell overwhelmed the herbal scent of the cabin. Lynn coughed from her cross-legged perch on the sofa, and I fought a gag.

Lia paled as she gazed at the bottle of ouzo. "Merde, I should have remembered."

"So the ouzo means something to you?" Saber demanded.

She sat hard on the bar stool Cosmil had conjured earlier and gulped. "Starrack had a great weakness for ouzo. He loved all things Greek."

Lia looked past me, past all of us in the room. Her expression a little wistful, a lot rueful, she shook her head.

"It was a very long time ago. In my youth, I spent a great deal of time with Starrack."

I took a quick peek into her mind and my jaw dropped. "You mean you *dated* the psycho?"

"Far worse, I'm afraid. I married him."

You could've heard dragonfly wings beat in the profound silence.

"You were married," I said slowly, "to public enemy number one?"

"Handfasted, actually, but it amounts to the same thing."

"When was this? And why the *hell* are you just telling us?"

Cosmil moved protectively closer. "Lia's past with Starrack has nothing to do with the present, Francesca. I resent your implication that it does."

"Past and present are colliding, Cosmil, and I resent being kept in the dark. You told me you wouldn't withhold information."

"Please, both of you stop. It was not Cosmil's story to share, Cesca, and I have not shirked my duties to you, to any of you, because of my past association. But I'll give you the short version now."

She paused and glanced up at Cosmil. He gave her a subtle nod.

"I first met Cosmil and Starrack many years ago. We even trained together with the same master on and off. Starrack and I became involved. For twenty years, we lived all over Europe, but I finally had enough of his philandering and his self-centered ways. I left him, and I've not seen or heard from him since the beginning of the French Revolution in 1789 when I fled my country."

"You chose the wrong brother, didn't you?" I said softly.

"I did. I hope to correct that error now."

Cosmil smiled and pheromones flared. Gads, love certainly wafted in the shanty-house air. Triton and Lynn. Cosmil and Lia. No wonder Pandora hadn't been hanging around inside as much as I'd expected. But that didn't absolve Lia of withholding information.

"Lia, if you knew Starrack that well, you must know something more about him beyond his being a Grecophile and ouzo drinker."

"Think back," Saber said. "Did he have any habits we could use to track him? Fascinations or compulsions? Did he ever use an alias?"

"No aliases that I knew of. He was compulsive about his ouzo, although he wouldn't pay for a bottle if he didn't have to."

"You mean he'd steal the liquor?" Triton asked, he and Lynn joining us at the island.

"By bespelling shopkeepers, yes. Stealing ouzo and anything else he wanted was a game to him."

"That's good information," Saber said. "I'll contact the liquor stores in area. Show them the sketch and see if they're missing stock."

"Even if they have Starrack on security cameras, that won't tell us where he's staying." I turned to Lia. "What about the COA's records? Don't you keep a database of supernaturals and where they live? Please, we need to find him before he kills again."

Lia shook her head. "That's what doesn't fit. The murders. Starrack was a con man. He delighted in playing people, not in killing them."

"He must've diversified since then," Triton said darkly, "and not in a good way."

"I'll make a call to the Council records department," Lia promised, "but you must understand that it is early morning in France. On a Saturday at that. And research will take time."

"Time we don't have," Triton muttered.

Lynn cleared her throat. "Isn't the St. Augustine Greek Festival being held soon? If this Starrack guy is a Grecophile, maybe he'd show up there, and you could catch him."

Fear punched my stomach so hard and fast, I almost doubled over. "Oh, no. No, no, no. We can't confront Starrack at the festival."

"Why not?" Triton snapped. "It's a perfectly reasonable suggestion."

"But Maggie and Neil are taking the wedding party to the festival after the wedding rehearsal next Friday. If Starrack is there, they'll all be in danger."

"Then get her to change her plans."

"Triton, I've already tried. Neil took Maggie to the Greek festival on their first date, and she wants the last date before they marry to be at this one. It's a sentimental journey. She won't budge."

"That's so sweet," Lynn said.

"The festival may be our best chance of putting an end to Starrack," Triton insisted.

I wheeled to plead with Saber. "We can't put Maggie and Neil at risk."

"Just hold on, both of you. You're jumping to conclusions. First, we don't know that Starrack would bother to attend a local festival. Second, even if he were to attend, he has no way of knowing about the wedding party's plans."

I crossed my arms. "None that we know of."

"Third, Starrack has no reason to target Maggie or Neil. Hell, if he'd wanted to, he could've killed them instead of the homeless couple."

"That's true, but what if he's saving Maggie and Neil for a big finale killing spree?"

"Honey, it's us he really wants. We have the amulets. We're the finale." He squeezed my hand and turned to Lia. "Is it remotely possible that Starrack would go to the festival? Say to steal some ouzo?"

"Very. He'd enjoy the challenge of lifting a bottle from under the noses of so many people. He did so many times at village fairs."

"Then *if* he shows up, and *if* we can find him there," Saber said slowly, "we should be prepared to take him out."

"No," Cosmil barked. "I must agree with Francesca on this. Aside from her friends, there will be a large crowd, and Starrack has proven he cares nothing for innocents. In that climate, we cannot risk a confrontation."

"I understand your concern," Saber said, "but Cesca made two valid points to me today. One is that we don't know where Starrack is, or what's in his mind to do next. We've only been able to react."

"We have done our best with the location spells," Lia said defensively.

"I don't doubt that, but it's not enough. When I hunt Rampants, I don't wait for them to come to me. I find them, or I set a trap."

"Are you suggesting," Triton put in, "that we lure Starrack to us? How?"

"I don't know yet. Maybe we simply lure him from the Greek festival, if he shows up."

"That's still a big if," Triton said.

"It is, but here's the other point," Saber continued as he turned to me. "Cesca, when we left to chase down Starrack tonight, you said we weren't ready. You were right. We need to know what Starrack might do in a head-on fight. What weapons he'd use. What tricks he might throw at us. We need information and a plan so we have less chance at being blindsided."

Saber's cold logic didn't vaporize my fears, but he was right. Making plans meant taking action, taking control. I could do that. I took a calming breath and felt the pool of energy swirl in my spine.

"I do not," Cosmil said quietly, "recall seeing Starrack fight anyone, but Lia and I will put our heads together and see what we can remember."

Saber smiled. "Your insights will help, thank you. Cesca, are you on board?"

"All right, fine, I'll play what if. The festival is held at the events field, and there are only a few exits. Maybe we could set a trap for him away from the field."

"Was that a knee-jerk comment or do you have a trap in mind?"

"Knee jerk," I admitted, "but we should be able to figure some way to ambush Starrack or lure him into coming after us."

Saber nodded. "Where can we lure him that's far enough away from the festival patrons?"

"Not to mention the regular tourists and locals in town," Triton added. "What about the northern grounds of the fort? That part of the Castillo de San Marcos is more isolated."

"I don't know. Whether this goes down at the festival or not, the last thing we need is for witnesses to call the cops." Saber drummed his fingers on the island. "Cesca, you know the town better than any of us. What location is close to the events field and open enough for us to maneuver, but away from prying eyes?"

"The top level of the parking garage," I tossed off.

Immediately, the hair stood stiff on the back of my neck, and goose bumps plowed their way up my arms. The dream I'd had about being on a flat roof slammed through my memory. Saber unconscious, my feet stuck in tar muck. The settings weren't an exact match, but then when had I last been on the top level of the parking garage? The similarities between the dream roof and the real roof lot were too close to ignore.

"Honey, what did you see?"

I shook off my case of the willies. "I've had some weird dreams lately, and in one of them, I was on a flat roof, stuck in black goo. It could have been the roof-level parking lot."

"Then it's an option to check out. We'll take a look at Triton's suggestion, too. Maybe the north grounds of the fort are more shielded than I remember."

"Speaking of shielding," Lia said, "we shall work on that tomorrow. Cesca especially needs instruction and practice."

Saber put his arm around me. "She also needs rest. Let's pack up and call it a night."

Cosmil and Lia shooed us out of the cabin while they cleaned their potion mess and gathered spell paraphernalia. They'd keep the spell running and call if they got another good hit.

The guys walked away to talk while Lynn and I sat on the porch steps.

"Cesca, you and Triton really are just friends, aren't you?"

"When I don't want to whap him upside the head, yeah. I'm no competition, Lynn. I'm a one-man woman."

"I've felt like such a freak since I started shifting. I've been scared to let anyone get close."

"Triton felt the same way."

"Is he a one-woman man, or does he play the field?"

I grinned. "In his younger days, he was a bit of a player. Now? I don't think so, but he is a guy. Men can be too exasperating to be worth the trouble."

"Or wonderful enough to wait a lifetime for," Lia said from behind us.

I looked up at her then at Lynn.

"When she's right, she's right."

We arrived at Saber's house thirty minutes later, and he insisted on showing Cosmil how to operate the hide-a-bed in the couch. I could've told my darling not to bother, that Cosmil and Lia would be sharing a bed tonight. But why ruin his fun in showing off his home?

While they moved on to setting the thermostat, Lia motioned me into the guest room.

"You're different today," she said as she set an old-fashioned cloth satchel on the bed. "I noticed it when you called this afternoon, but it's more apparent in person. What happened?"

"Besides the bodies on my doorstep?"

"Don't be facetious. You know what I mean. You experienced a shift. You slept perhaps three hours, yet you emanate a well of energy." She searched my eyes. "You came into your power today, and I'd like to know how it happened so I can help you channel it."

I thought back to the moment when the cool sensation first pooled in my tailbone, and the feeling stirred.

"I was angry that Starrack murdered those homeless kids."

"And you wanted his blood."

"I still do."

"Good. The anger will fuel your determination. How do you perceive your power? Like the element of fire? Earth?"

"Water. Cool water. It flows from the base of my spine through my torso and into my arms and legs."

"Water? Well, of course. You're the sign of the Moon Child."

The men came into the hall, and she lowered her voice.

"I want you to practice shielding your thoughts. Imagine they are submerged in water. Only when you purposefully bring them to the surface can they be read."

"It's that simple?"

"It can be. Women are more likely to project because we're more emotionally open. It will take practice to balance shielding with the openness of your nature. But never mind that. You only need to hide your thoughts from Starrack. I'll prepare a special pouch for you to wear that will assist your focus."

So I had a water fountain of power? All right, how corrupting to my soul could that be?

"Lia, I know you've already cast protective spells on everybody and their dog, but if we have to go up against Starrack and the Void next Friday, will you and Cosmil cast extra protection on Maggie and Neil and the wedding party?"

"We're way ahead of you on that score, my dear."

"Here you are," Saber said from the threshold. "Lia, I've told Cosmil he can use my bathroom so you can have some privacy again."

"Thank you, Saber. Now you go along to Cesca's. You've had an eventful day, and tomorrow will be just as busy with the bridal shower and phoning the liquor stores and then getting Lynn settled."

Sheesh, getting the bum's rush out of your own home? Talk about cheek.

But Saber and I left, and drove extra slowly as we passed the Castillo de San Marcos and its expanse of grounds. Since the fort was truly a fortress and was a national park, the feds didn't spring for a lot of security lighting. They didn't even decorate for the Nights of Lights when the rest of the town was festooned for the Christmas holiday season.

"Too exposed," Saber declared. "Too many escape routes."

"And too much of a chance that Starrack could grab a hostage off the streets."

"Think the parking garage is open for a quick drive through?"

"It's open 24-7, but I'd rather explore it on foot and in the daytime when we're fresh."

"Works for me. I am beat."

He parked on the street, turned off the engine, and closed his eyes. "Cesca, when this is all over, let's take a vacation."

"Vacation?" I echoed as if I'd never heard the word. And I hadn't, not from Saber's lips. "Where?"

"A remote island? A cave?" He rolled his head toward me and opened his eyes. "I don't care, as long as we don't have to chase bad guys."

I leaned across the console and cupped his stubble-roughened cheek in my palm. "Let's go with the island. Bats give me the creeps."

"Says the vampire."

"Bad joke, Saber. Come on, let's get you inside before you fall asleep at the wheel."

Saber was out almost before he hit the sheets, and I wasn't far behind him. Oh, I stayed up long enough to feed and water Snowball, and set the alarms, but the well of energy Lia had perceived in me was plumb pumped dry.

Because I crashed a full five hours earlier than normal, I was up by eleven. I heard Saber in the kitchen, talking on the phone, so I quickly brushed my teeth, showered, and dressed. Not in my bridal shower sundress, but in jean shorts and a tan bra-top camisole.

"Yes, I understand." Saber scribbled on a legal pad as I entered. "I'll meet you at the store at noon."

He flipped his cell phone shut and caught me around the waist. "How'd you sleep?"

"Siren free. Who are you meeting at what store?"

"Palatka. None of the stores I've called so far stock more than a few bottles of ouzo at a time, but the clerks I spoke with confirmed that bottles are unaccounted for. They reported the discrepancy to their managers, who already pulled the security tapes. The Palatka store may have Starrack on film."

"That's great. Are you still making photocopies of Lia's sketch, or do I need to?"

"I'll make some in Palatka right before my meeting."

"Can you get back to your place before one this afternoon?"

"Don't fret. I'll be there when the party tents and tables are delivered. Then I'll take Cosmil and Lia back."

"Will you hang out at the cabin? Did you ever get that healing session?"

"I'm good. I may take Lynn with me to a couple more liquor stores. See if anyone else recognizes Starrack."

"I'm not sure that's safe."

"Our wizard and sorceress assure us it is, and they want us to go about our lives."

"Yeah, they do. Just be careful."

"No sweat. I have things to do at the house to get ready for the barbeque, so I'll take Lynn to my place until it's time to pick you up."

"You're brilliant."

I leaned in for a kiss, which he skillfully returned.

"Mmm. Good to know you feel so much better today."

"I do. Almost normal, whatever that is."

"From what I hear, overrated, but I miss it anyway."

He swatted my butt. "Go drink your Starbloods and get ready for the party. I'll pick you up about six to take Lynn to Gorman's."

Saber left, and I went into high gear. First I phoned Maggie to tell her I would pick up the dishes and cups early. Then I phoned the caterer and florist with instructions to deliver the food and flowers directly to the cottage anytime after one. No point in restricting them to that hour-before-the-party time now that I was up and at 'em.

Before I tackled the next job, I typed a note for Gorman, Ken, and David. In Gorman's, I listed my cell number and Saber's, and the approximate times of day he'd be responsible for Lynn. I know, over-kill. But with a slow top like Gorman, better to have everything in writing. In my note to the guys, I listed our cell numbers and the address of the daytime "safe house." I also wrote the directions to Gorman's via Google Maps and gave them the approximate times to drop Lynn off and pick her up. I'd tell them Gorman's code name when I knew it.

I made short work of cleaning the house, especially the living room, kitchen, and guest bath. Dust wasn't so much an issue as cat hair might be. I also emptied, disinfected, and refilled Snowball's box. I'd put her in her carrier in the laundry room during the party and close the door. She might get her revenge later, but *que sera*. I just hoped none of the guests had allergies.

As it happened, no one did, and the bridal shower tea came off perfectly. The women were gracious guests, showing no fear of me or of being in a vampire's space. They praised my décor as well as the food, drink, and the nosegays they took home as party favors.

They chatted and laughed, never once hinting that they knew of the murders.

In spite of the party gaiety, my stomach churned. Perhaps I should tell Maggie we needed to have a proper rehearsal dinner after all. Surely between the two of us, we could find a suitable place to hold a dinner even at this late date. Of course, I'd have to tell her why, and all I had were suppositions. Bottom line, Maggie was so radiantly happy, I just couldn't rain on her wedding parade.

The guests left at five thirty on the dot, and Neil must've been watching for the exodus because he was on the doorstep minutes later to help haul Maggie's gifts home. I'd planned to wash the dishes and utensils, and return them later, but Maggie insisted that we just rinse them. She'd take care of washing them at her house.

Of course, Maggie didn't say a word about the murder victims, but the surprise was that Neil didn't make a single crack. He had to know. Maggie wouldn't keep that to herself because she wouldn't want a neighbor to blindside Neil with questions. Hmm. Had Lia cast a forget spell on Maggie and Neil along with the protection spell?

Saber and Lynn arrived right at six. Snowball, free of her carrier, lapped up Saber's attention but snubbed Lynn. Typical. Lynn wore khaki pants and a striped khaki and turquoise boatneck blouse that made her eyes look brilliant. I thought about changing out of my emerald green sundress but didn't want to hold up the meeting with Gorman. Lynn was nervous enough after having waited all day for this moment.

Gorman answered his door wearing black jeans, a black tee, and a scowl. His expression went slack as soon as he laid his cold blue eyes on Lynn.

"God Al-freakin'-mighty."

"Lynn Heath, meet your daytime protector, Victor Gorman," I said.

"You said she wasn't no jailbait," he choked.

"She isn't," Saber said in his steely cop voice. "She's a job. One you'd better do damned well."

Gorman recalled himself and straightened. "Course I will. Ms. Heath, nice to meet ya."

"Thank you." Lynn offered a shy smile. "Shall I call you Mr. Gorman?"

"No! I don't want those damned vamps guardin' you at night knowin' my real name."

"Oh, okay. I could call you Vic for victory," Lynn said in such a sugar-sweet way, I thought Gorman would call her on it.

He didn't. He nodded. "Vic for victory. Yeah. That'll do."

"Are you going to keep us standing on the porch," I asked, "or show Lynn around?"

"She can come in, but you can't. I ain't takin' no chances invitin' you inside."

"You believe that tripe of vampire lore?"

"Better safe than sorry. Tell me how this is gonna work."

"The guys will drop Lynn off forty minutes or so before sunrise and watch to be sure she gets inside safely. At night, they'll pick her up as soon after sunset as they can get here, but the exact time will depend on traffic."

"I still say I can guard her at night, but I'll go along."

"Yes, you will," Saber said, "or we won't help you with that other matter."

"And remember that the vampire Hess has human minions," I added. "Call the police if you have any problems, then call Saber or me."

"I ain't an idiot."

I so wanted to debate that, but I waited in the car while Saber and Lynn went inside Gorman's house. Which was fine. The less time I spent with Gorman, the better, and Saber would give Vic a copy of the sketch.

They came out again in under five minutes, Lynn with a good-bye wave at Gorman, Saber with a look I couldn't decipher. He opened the back door for Lynn then slammed into the driver's seat.

"What's wrong?" I asked. "Does he have a cannon in every window?"

"No, but he has a shotgun in every room."

"Even the bathroom," Lynn piped up.

I twisted to see her face. "You're joking."

"I'm not. He asked if I knew how to shoot."

I bit my lip. "Are you going to be okay with him? We can still call this off."

"Oh, no, I wouldn't miss this experience for the world."

"Why not?"

"Because I'm studying psychology, and he's a trip. The perfect subject for a paper next semester."

"Tell Triton that, will you? Maybe it'll calm him."

"Oh, I will."

And she did, as soon as we arrived at South Beach Grill. While the two of them hung back, Lynn gabbing away to Triton, Saber and I went inside to request a table upstairs with an ocean view. Sure it would be sundown soon, but South Beach is right on the dunes, and the colors of the sunset reflected in the wet sand. Might as well enjoy it.

Saber ordered the famous pasta dish with chicken, and I sampled a few bites of his pasta with my sweet tea, heavy on the ice. Lynn and Triton split an enormous seafood platter, and now I noticed that Lynn wore a gold charm on a gold necklace. The mermaid seated on the treasure chest. I didn't know if Triton had chosen the gold version in deference to the vampires who'd be guarding Lynn or if he was just that wild about her. Whatever the case, I hoped Cosmil and Lia had spelled it to the max.

Dinner conversation flowed naturally, and we lingered at the table while Saber and Triton had coffee, and Lynn ate a mile-high dessert.

Straight silver blond hair *and* a high metabolism? Good thing I was a vampire, or I'd have been envious for two reasons.

The four of us took a short stroll on the dark beach to kill time before meeting Ken and David, me praying they wouldn't be delayed. Much as I was coming to like Lynn, I'd done about all the entertaining I could do for a day.

When we topped the beach access steps, I spotted the vampires on the south end of the parking lot, half sitting on the hood of a tan Ford Taurus sedan. Not an entire division of Marines, but they were the keys to phase two of my plan, and, boy, did they look the part. In uniforms of black slacks, medium blue shirts, and dark sneakers, they exuded the spit-and-polish spirit. They even came to attention as I approached with my party in tow.

"Hi, guys. Thank you for coming."

"We're at your service, Princess Cesca," surfer-blond David replied.

"It's just Cesca," I said automatically. "David Marks, Ken Crandall, meet Deke Saber and Triton Delphinus."

"Pleasure," each of the vampires said as they shook hands.

"And this is Lynn Heath. Your protectee."

"Ms. Heath, nice to meet you," tall, dark, and fanged Ken said.

"Ma'am," David acknowledged. "Would you like to ask us questions before you accept our protection? We can sit there in the arbor."

He pointed to the structure at the head of the beach access walk, and I watched Lynn, Saber, and Triton for their reactions.

Lynn's eyes sparkled at the males, but Triton and Saber were tougher sells.

"How long have you been vampires?" Triton asked.

"Since the 1980s," Ken replied.

"So before the VPA," Saber said.

I knew where Triton was going, and David apparently did, too.

"I assure you, we're well adapted to bottled meals," he said. "We will not harm Ms. Heath."

"What do you men do for a living?"

Lynn rolled her eyes. "Triton, you're not my father."

"It's a fair question, ma'am," Ken soothed, and turned to Triton. "David is a web developer. I'm a dance instructor."

Ken watched Triton, waiting for the crack that didn't come.

"A dance instructor? Really?" Lynn gushed. "Would you teach me to merengue?"

"Lynn."

"Chill out, Triton. It's only a dance." She turned back to Ken. "Well?"

"It'll be my honor, ma'am."

With that, Triton was overruled.

Saber knew how to reach the beach house, so I rode with Ken and David. We covered the few miles in minutes, and since I didn't have a driveway, I directed Ken to pull onto the grass instead of parking behind Saber on the blacktopped road. This way the car would be closer to the house, near the flagstone walkway. Couldn't hurt for a quick entrance or exit, though I hoped neither would be necessary.

When I opened the door with pride, Saber's reaction didn't disappoint. He gaped at the changes as soon as he walked inside. The crisp white paint on the wood plank walls and the same treatment on the door casings and baseboards provided a high contrast with the oak floors and exposed beams I'd cleaned, sanded, and restained in a dark finish. The large ceiling fan with its directional lights moved air efficiently throughout the thousand square feet or so. And for being mishmash garage sale finds, the furnishings completed the cozy look of the place.

"You did all this in the few weeks I was gone?"

"I told you it wasn't a ratty shack anymore."

"How did you get licensed people to complete the jobs so fast?"

"I asked nicely."

"Hah," Triton said. "I waited on workers for months when I renovated."

"That's because you aren't a pretty woman," Lynn shot back, then turned to me as she dropped her duffel bag beside one of the two rather ugly wicker chairs I had yet to spray paint. "It's a great place, Cesca."

"Thanks, let me show you around. Ken, David, I need you to take the tour, too."

While Saber and Triton peeled off to poke around on their own, I pointed out that the daybed in the living area had a trundle bed hidden beneath a striped, ocean-colored coverlet. They'd have to move the oval coffee table out of the way to get to the trundle, but it was there if needed.

Next, I showed Lynn, David, and Ken the bedroom I'd painted a light blue gray color. White iron twin beds sat against the far wall, dressed in plain light blue linens from a bed-in-a-bag ensemble. A dark wood nightstand nestled between the beds, and a dark wood chest of drawers stood on the opposite wall.

"I had storm shutters installed all over the house and I've left them closed, but I haven't been here in the bright day enough to know how much sun will still get in."

"We noticed the shutters from outside, but sunlight won't be a problem. We travel with special sleeping bags. We'll do."

"Oh, okay, then, next room."

The bathroom was also off the living room and was a work in progress since the tub and tile I'd wanted was out of stock. A new toilet and an inexpensive pedestal sink had been installed, though, and I'd scrubbed the shower-bath combination thoroughly. It might not be an HGTV quality bathroom, but it was no longer disgusting.

The kitchen and enclosed back porch rounded out the tour. I'd bought new, apartment-sized stainless steel appliances and had replaced the nasty countertop with one made of butcher block. The cabinets and floors had been sanded, and the wood floors stained dark like those in the rest of house. The cabinets I'd left unfinished until I decided on a paint or stain, but the stainless sink and fixtures were new, and every corner had been cleaned. I even had four place settings of dishes, glasses, and utensils, and a few pots, pans, and cooking spoons on the shelves and in the drawers. Garage sales rock.

The storm shutters blocked the ocean view from the porch, but I opened the back door to point out the crude walkway to the beach.

"What a great place to sleep to the sound of the ocean," Lynn said, eyeing the hammock hanging from the porch beams.

"Knock yourself out, if Ken and David are cool with it."

Ken shrugged. "I don't object as long as Ms. Heath understands that we'll need to check on her through the night. No matter where she sleeps."

"Just don't laugh if I snore."

"Word of a Marine, ma'am."

"Okay, then, I just have a few more things to go over."

I led them back to the living room where Triton and Saber sat in the wicker chairs. Saber handed me the list I'd prepared, and I turned on a side-table lamp. Lynn plopped onto the daybed near Triton.

"First, I'll get a small TV if you need one, but I don't have cable hooked up, so the reception might be rotten."

"Don't bother," David said. He and Ken stood facing the door. "If I can get a strong wireless signal, we can watch television on my computer."

"Great." I unfolded my list and handed it to Ken. "Here's the information I thought you'd need. The guy watching Lynn during the day is Vic. He'll be expecting her from before daybreak to after sunset. And don't freak if he stands at the door with a shotgun."

Ken chuckled. "Not a problem."

"Don't take him lightly," Saber warned. "Vic hates vampires and has a history of going off half-cocked. If he gives you any grief, I need to know."

"Will do, Saber."

"Also, here's a sketch of the guy you need to watch out for. Starrack."

David stiffened as soon as he heard the name, and snatched the likeness from Saber. One glance, and he swore under his breath then shoved the sketch at Ken.

I laid a hand on David's arm. "You know Starrack, don't you?"

"Yeah, I know him," David spat. "I built a website for the scary piece of shit."

TWENTY

"Shifter Magic?" Saber rose from the chair, eyes alight. "Is that the website you designed?"

The blond vampire looked pole-axed. "That's the one, but how'd you come across it?"

"I told them about the site," Lynn chimed in. "I was led to meet Triton through a message posted in the forum."

"Ken, you know Starrack, too, don't you? You're clenching your jaw like you want to chew him up."

"More like spit him out, Princess, but yes, I know him. All of us in the Atlanta nest saw Starrack in March when he invaded Vlad's nest."

Saber's cop face crashed into place. "We need to know everything. Now."

Triton rose from the chair. "Since this could take a while, I should call that other party we were supposed to meet tonight. Tell them we won't make it. Lynn, you want to keep me company?"

She might be young, but she wasn't slow on the uptake. She

sprang from the daybed and took Triton's hand. "Oh, sure. See you all later."

"All right, take a seat," Saber said, pointing to the wicker chairs.

The vamps sat stiffly, and I settled on the daybed opposite them. Saber stood for the interview, though I don't think Ken and David were intimidated. Their faces reflected anger, confusion, and a disturbing dose of fear.

"Starrack visited the Atlanta nest," Saber said. "Start our briefing there."

"First," Ken said, "you need to know that some of this is second-hand intel."

"Understood."

Ken continued. "Starrack showed up shortly after we all awoke one evening. It was late February, before the time change. Some of the nestmates were still dressing for their jobs, but most of us were with Vlad to witness his nightly ritual feeding."

"On a human?" I gasped.

"On his favorite female vampire child, Gail. He was big on tradition."

"Go on."

"The concise version is that Vlad ordered two vampires to toss the wizard out." Ken paused and visibly swallowed. "Starrack retaliated. He decapitated Vlad's bodyguard."

The bald statement psychically launched me into Ken's head to see the details in his memory.

The room felt dank, and I put it underground. Uncovered oil-burning sconces broke the darkness here and there, but they cast insignificant light in such a large room. A hulking-huge vampire taller than Tower shielded Vlad, and Starrack stood twenty feet away. He threw off the vampires holding either arm, his eyes cold, calculating. Then the wizard pointed, mumbled words I didn't catch, and a gray beam rimmed in red shot from his right index finger. He flicked his wrist at the bodyguard, and the thinnest of red lines appeared at the male's neck. Starrack flipped his hand sideways, and the male's head toppled to his shoulder then to the stone floor. Blood droplets hit Vlad's face.

I gagged as the vision closed.

"You invaded my thoughts," Ken accused.

"I did, and I'm sorry I didn't ask your permission. It was purely spontaneous."

"Was that," Saber asked, "the only time you saw Starrack?"

Ken eyed me warily.

"I promise I won't pop into your head again."

"It was my sole time to see the wizard, but he returned. This information came from Hank, the vampire who guarded Vlad that night. The rest of us were sent away."

"Fair enough," Saber said. "What did Hank report?"

"Vlad and Starrack argued, and the wizard took a black globelike thing from his overcoat pocket. A few minutes later, Vlad struggled to stand. He gasped for breath, and his skin color darkened."

"Hold it. A black globe, not a big blob?" I looked at Saber. "Could the globe have been the Void in a contained form?"

"Hell, anything is possible. Continue, Ken."

He did so, though his expression remained puzzled. "Hank said that when Vlad broke down and agreed to do whatever the wizard wanted, including loan out certain resources, Starrack put the globe away and Vlad immediately began to recover."

"I was one of those resources," David added. "Starrack contacted me a few days later about the website. He raised hell that it took a month to complete, but he didn't zap me."

"Count your blessings he didn't."

"Princess, what is the Void?" Ken asked.

Saber gave me a go-ahead nod and I sighed.

"This will sound extra weird, but it's a thought form Starrack created. It's an entity in its own right, I suppose, but it's also the disease that's infecting vampires. The difference is that you've seen it as a globe and we haven't. We see it as an oily black ground fog."

Ken frowned. "We thought Starrack made Vlad sick with a spell."

"A spell could be part of the package, but it's likely he sicced the Void on Vlad. Did Starrack tap other vampires from the nest to do things for him?"

"He took Hank and Gail away with him one night in April," David supplied, "but we don't know what he wanted from them. A week after they left, two bodies were dumped at the nest entrance for the human day guards to find."

"Hank and Gail."

"Vlad identified them from their clothing," Ken said. "The bodies themselves were too blackened and shriveled to recognize."

I caught Saber's grim gaze before he spun to pace as he recapped. "So Starrack used David's skills but killed three other of Vlad's vampires. Why spare you?"

David spread his hands. "No idea. Once the wizard stopped e-mailing complaints and updates about the website in late May, I feared I would be next on his hit list."

"Maybe," I said, "Starrack was holding David in reserve for another website project."

"Makes as much sense as anything this guy has done." Saber eyed the vampires. "Did you two know about the extortion payments Vlad was making to an offshore account?"

We'd tumbled onto the extortion scheme a few weeks ago when Jo-Jo tipped us that the Daytona Beach nest was making payoffs to Vlad. Later we'd learned the large nest masters were paying an unknown entity, the money going into a secret account that had since been closed.

"We heard about the extortion in August, after the VPA took Vlad away and confiscated the books," Ken answered. "Vlad's accountant, Charlie, filled us in about the protection money scheme, but he said the payments had been going on for years."

"Years?" I echoed. "They didn't start with Starrack's visit?"

"No, Princess Cesca," David said. "Charlie told us the amount increased after Starrack had been in the nest, but he didn't know who was receiving the money. When Vlad was taken, Charlie closed the old account and reopened another one to protect what was left in the nest coffers."

"Damn smart. Was this a vampire accountant or human?" Saber asked.

"A vampire, but Charlie worked with a human to move the account. The VPA allowed him to split those remaining assets among those of us still living there. We got a nice portion."

I peered at Saber. "You knew Candy authorized the distribution of nest funds?"

He shrugged. "It was the fair thing to do. Every office involved in dismantling nests is offering the same deal."

"Like a severance package."

"We have to pay taxes on our cuts, but the money has helped us move on," David confirmed, "not to mention take this extended vacation."

"Which we appreciate you interrupting for us," I said with a smile. "David, did you bring a laptop with you?"

"I did. Why?"

"We need access to the list of Shifter Magic users. Can you trace a user name to a real one?"

"I can trace to an IP address and possibly find the location of the computer used, but it's hacking. And websites have privacy-protection rules."

Saber snorted. "Screw legalities. I authorize you to do the trace."

"We'll get our gear."

The guys deposited rolled sleeping bags and green Marine Corps

duffel bags in the living room. Then Ken put four six-packs of artificial blood in the fridge while David began setting up his laptop
on the coffee table. I prayed he'd be able to get a wireless Internet
connection.

"All right, I have a wireless signal to piggyback, but it may be
slow. When the server comes up, what's the user name you want me
to search?"

"Magicman1463," I said.

He zipped and clicked the mouse, then typed so rapidly, his fingers blurred. Screen after screen flashed up, and I wondered if new
computers and accessories came in special vampire-speed models.

"Here you go. The user's computer is off, but the address listed
for the last transmission is an apartment complex here in town."
David tapped more keys. "And the winner is Vince Winter."

"Vince Winter?" I gave Saber a blank look. "Who's that?"

"A dead end," he said grimly. "He's one of the thugs found
dumped at Triton's place yesterday."

"Detective Balch shared the names of the victims?"

"What victims?" Ken asked.

Saber held up a hand. "He phoned me this afternoon, but only
told me the identities of the two men with criminal records. I'm sorry,
Cesca, but there are no fingerprints on file for the others. They're still
John and Jane Does."

While Saber filled Ken and David in on the murders, I slumped
on the daybed, deep in thought.

On the surface, it might seem a coincidence of humongous pro-
portions that David had built the Shifter Magic website. To me, it was
synchronicity, just as much as Lynn finding Triton. Okay, the magicman clue didn't get us closer to nailing Starrack, but it did link him
to the murder victim. Call me skeptical, but I had a hard time pictur-
ing career criminal Vince Winter playing an online shifter game.

On the upside, I'd now seen Starrack through Ken's memories. I knew how he moved, the cold energy he exuded. How that knowl-edge might help us was uncertain, but any scrap of information was a bonus.

Triton stuck his head out. "Hey, how's it going?"

"We're wrapping up," Saber answered.

"Good. I think Lynn would like to shower and hit the sack."

Ken stood. "Would she feel more comfortable if we went outside until she's finished?"

"No, I would not," Lynn yelled from behind the door.

"That's okay, Lynn," I called. "We're leaving anyway. Call us if you need anything."

"I'm cool. Go fight evil."

Triton ducked back in the bedroom, I imagined for a farewell kiss. The rest of us trooped out the front door to give them an extra measure of privacy.

"Other than Starrack," Ken said, "should we be on the lookout for trouble from any particular quarter?"

"Just be alert to anything that doesn't look or feel right."

"Or smell right. In the form we've seen, the Void stinks like a tar pit, and someone infected may have rancid breath." I glanced at Saber, whose breath had never been off. "Though rank breath isn't a consistent symptom."

The vampires squared their shoulders.

"We're battle ready, ma'am," David said. "We won't let you down."

"Thanks, and ooh-rah to that."

Considering he was leaving his new love behind with vampires, Tri-ton's mood was surprisingly upbeat as we drove him home. Saber filled him in on what Ken and David had revealed, and Triton made thoughtful comments instead of cracks.

"You're good with Ken and David watching over Lynn?"

"I have to admit, they're okay. I'm not happy about this Gorman character, but Lynn's all over her case study idea."

I looked over my shoulder where Triton sat between the seats. "I like her, Triton. She's good for you."

"Meaning she stands up to me?"

"You wouldn't want a doormat."

"You're right, I wouldn't. I just wish Lia would get that information about Lynn's origins."

"Well, remind her, dummy. If she has answers, she'll tell you. If she hasn't discovered anything, you're no worse off than you are now."

"Pushy, pushy."

"Practical. By the way, what did our illustrious wizard have to say?"

"He's amping up the wards on the beach property and Gorman's place, and he expects us to train after your party tomorrow."

"We'll be there," Saber said as he braked at the 312 stoplight. "Listen, there's something you both need to know. Lynn wanted to swing through downtown today, and we stopped at a liquor store."

"Let me guess," I said. "The manager recognized Starrack from the sketch."

"More than that. He remembers their brief conversation. There's a sign advertising the Greek Festival outside the store, and Starrack asked about it."

My heart stuttered. "That doesn't mean he'll go."

"No, but it confirms he knows about the event and that he's interested."

From his seat behind me, Triton gently squeezed my shoulder. No words, just sympathetic thoughts. Saber accelerated through the green light, and I let a storm of emotion roll through me. What I'd feared from the moment Lynn mentioned the Greek festival looked like more than an academic exercise. I hated Starrack for the evil he'd already committed. I hated him for the future evil he'd commit. I hated him even more for the worry and inconvenience his evil was causing me.

Stupid, I know, but that's how I felt.

Well, the big bad jerk's days were numbered now, because we didn't intend to lose this battle.

Triton cleared his throat and broke the silence. "Hey, Saber, is there anything I can do to help your investigation?"

"Matter of fact, you can cold-call some liquor stores and ask them if they're short any ouzo. I'd like to find out how wide spread or localized Starrack's stealing is, and when it started. I'd like to know if there's a pattern. "

"What happened at the Palatka store today?" I asked, and drew a quick glance from Saber. "Did they have security footage of Starrack?"

"The images were too fuzzy to be useful, but the clerk recognized him from the sketch."

"That's something," I said. "What I can't understand is why Starrack would let himself be remembered at all. Couldn't he wipe the clerks' memories?"

"Probably, but I'll bet he didn't imagine we'd tumble to him having a liquor store connection. He visited the Palatka and St. Augustine stores before we went after him the other night."

"And," Triton added, "the guy is arrogant as hell, according to Lia. I would be, too, if I'd been getting away with stealing for centuries."

Saber parked on the concrete pad behind Triton's store and turned off the engine. "I got more news from Balch, too."

I turned in my seat. "The autopsies?"

"Since the cases looked like the work of a serial killer, a second ME came in to help. The preliminary reports on all four victims state that their hearts stopped beating."

I frowned. "All four had heart attacks?"

"Not exactly. Balch was told that their hearts stopped as if some-one had turned off a circuit breaker."

If that was the case, maybe the homeless girl hadn't suffered, but that's not what I'd seen in her staring eyes. I'd seen horror.

"Did Balch say anything about the press? He told me they'd go nuts over the murders, but I never saw a single reporter, and you *know* Gorman would've ragged me about it if he'd heard."

"The official story is that the two criminals turned on and killed each other, and that the homeless couple died of pneumonia."

"Which makes them unrelated incidents," Triton said.

"That's right," Saber confirmed. "No serial killer, no sensational story, just tragic deaths in the case of the homeless pair."

"Did you tell Balch about Starrack?"

"In the spirit of quid pro quo, yeah. I told him Starrack is our suspect and showed him the drawing."

"Bet he wanted to issue a BOLO right away."

"He did, and I explained why a be on the lookout bulletin would be a mistake. He wasn't happy, but he backed off."

"I'm just glad we're off Balch's suspect list," Triton said. "Get me the names of liquor stores to call, and I'll get on it."

As he opened the car door, I sensed someone hovering in the shadows on the sidewalk behind us. Adrenaline rushing through my veins, I unbuckled my seat belt, and jumped out of the car in a flash.

"Cesca, what the—"

"Hello, Princess," a distinct male voice called.

"Is everything quite all right, dear?" a female voice asked.

Imelda and Clarence Clarke stepped into the street, and I slumped against the SUV.

"We're fine, thank you," I answered as they hustled closer.

I moved to meet them at the tail of the SUV, Triton and Saber joining me.

"We're terribly sorry if we startled you children, but you sat in the car such a long time, we became concerned."

"Are you out for your evening walk?" Saber asked the question lightly, but I heard the undertone of caution.

Melda waved a hand. "Oh, yes. We've taken to coming by every night since this poor young man was attacked."

"Want to do our part to help the Princess, don't you know," Clarence added. "Any friend of hers and all that. That's a lovely sundress, by the by, Princess. Isn't it, Melda? Puts me in mind of one you wore to a dance many years ago. Yours was white, though, with sunflowers."

I elbowed Triton. *Thank them for checking on you.*

"What? Oh, yes, I appreciate you watching out for me. Very kind."

"Pish posh, it's nothing," Melda said. "I just hope your business is concluded swiftly."

I blinked. "Our business, Mrs. Clarke?"

"Why yes, dear. We'll never get our bed and breakfast off the ground if vampires fear coming to Florida."

Clarence nodded solemnly. "We're rooting for you and Mr. Saber; we'll look forward to your visit whenever you have the time to call on us. Come along, now, Melda. We want to look at that new batch of listings in Deland."

Saber, Triton, and I exchanged bemused glances.

"Those two are a trip," Triton said softly, "but I'm glad Lynn's not staying with them."

"Because you'd be more tempted to go see her?"

"No, because she'd be doing another case study. An extended one."

With Melda and Clarence on the job, Triton's property was likely safe, but we went inside his apartment anyway, just to be sure nothing waited in ambush. When all was clear, Saber and I headed home at last.

Snowball launched herself into Saber's arms the moment we entered the cottage, and this time the object of her affection fed and watered her.

I set the alarms then headed to the bedroom. My sundress came off, my St. Augustine lighthouse sleep shirt went on, and I padded back to the living room. Snowball batted a catnip-filled toy around the bamboo floor, while Saber had parked himself on the sofa to watch college football scores and highlights on ESPN. His eyes might've been glued to the TV, but he patted the cushion when I neared.

"I'm catching the scores to unwind."

"Did the Gators and 'Noles win their games?" I asked as I sat beside him and propped my feet on the coffee table.

"Gators won big, 'Noles won in a squeaker over the 'Canes."

"Did your alma mater win, too?"

He grinned, gave me the Hook 'Em Horns sign, and linked his fingers through mine. The sportscaster ran down another list of stats before Saber canted his head at me.

"What?"

"Are you reading my thoughts?"

"No, your nervous energy. Are you worried about the chances of Starrack showing up at the Greek festival of Friday night?"

"Yes, but that's nearly a week away so I'm putting that worry on the back burner. Right now I just want to know if everything is ready for the couples shower tomorrow."

"Tents, tables, and chairs were delivered on time and set up, and Lynn helped me slice onions and tomatoes for the burgers."

"Considering she has hair to kill for, Lynn's growing on me."

With a flash of his sexy grin, Saber turned to face me. "Honey, when a man runs his hands through straight hair, there is no surprise, no intrigue. But when I do this—"

The pulses in my neck thundered and my mouth went dry as he

tips into the thick strands at my temples.

"This is my idea of riding the waves and shooting the curls." He brushed his lips over mine. "Every last lock of your hair is a sensual adventure."

I gulped and whispered, "You feel like surfing about now?"

He answered with a long, deep kiss, and when we finally slept, it was with a lock of my hair wound around Saber's wrist.

My honey's comment about my waves and curls notwithstanding, I flatironed and gooped my hair as straight as possible for the barbeque on Sunday. Guests meeting a vampire hostess was one thing. Meeting one with scary hair was another. I was taking no chances with the success of this party.

The event soon proved a finger-lickin' success. The weather cooperated with even a hint of fall in the air. Saber cooked the meats and veggies to perfection on the new grill he'd bought as his own housewarming gift. And though the guests were Neil's friends and colleagues, they and their spouses were open and friendly with Saber and me, and with each other.

Most of the women gathered under the tents to talk and eat with Maggie. Most of the men ate in the house to watch the Jacksonville Jaguars football game. Most of the gifts, when they were opened at halftime, were hardware store gift cards, so Maggie and Neil didn't have an ordeal loading their haul.

Saber and I cleaned up the mess quickly, sorted the recycling from the trash, and in no time we were ready to change from our party clothes to our training uniforms of shorts and T-shirts.

Triton arrived at Cosmil's place on our heels, and low and behold, Pandora sat at the base of the porch steps in her panther form.

I'd missed the mysterious feline so much, I had the wild impulse to throw my arms around her neck.

Do not embrace me. And do not enter the cabin.

I stopped in my tracks, causing Saber and Triton to stumble into my back. Great. Days, maybe even hours away from fighting the Void, and we were doing the Stooges.

"Any special reason," I said to Pandora, "we're supposed to stay outside?"

Old wizard and the woman are spell casting. She lowered her head to the grass, and nosed first one object then another toward me.

The amulets.

"What's Pandora doing with the amulets?"

"She's playing bocce ball, Triton," I snarked. "Give her a chance to tell me what's up."

"Testy."

"Do you two ever not snip at each other?" Saber casually asked as he picked up the disks.

He curled his fingers around them for a moment then switched the medallions from one hand to the other before holding them out for Triton and me to take.

Most astute, Saber.

"Thanks, Pandora."

I gaped at him. "You heard her?"

Saber grinned. Pandora chuffed.

Come. You must practice healing.

The panther prowled off to the ceremonial area of the circle.

"What'd she say?" Triton asked impatiently.

"That there's magick afoot inside and we're off to practice healing. You didn't hear her, but Saber did? What's up with that?"

"Sue me, I'm preoccupied."

We followed Pandora to the far side of the circle where she stopped and raised a paw over a brown rabbit laying on its side.

"Oh, poor thing," I said, leaning over the animal. "What happened?"

The rabbit was poisoned. Heal it. I must move away to lessen its fear.

"Wait. Does this work like it did on the trees?"

Draw on all your powers. With that bit of nonexplanation, she loped back to the shanty.

"Okay, gentlemen, in case you missed that, Pandora says the rabbit has been poisoned, and we're to use all our powers to heal it. Ready?"

We knelt around the animal that was no bigger than Snowball, Triton on my right, Saber across from us. The spring of cool energy at the base of my spine that had been dormant now stirred like a slow whirlpool, then bubbled through me in rhythm with the warm pulse from the amulet in my left hand. I caught the rabbit's gaze and sent calming thoughts as Triton and I moved in unison to lightly touch the poor panting body. Saber let his hands hover over ours, and I mentally heard our healing intent blend into a soft song.

This time when the rays beamed from the medallions, the light shone as a golden candle glow rather than a white laser. The rabbit laid still under our ministrations, and its breathing eased. Then it extended its limbs in a waking-from-a-nap stretch, and the halo of light from the amulets snapped off. The rabbit got to its paws and scampered into the brush.

"Well done," Cosmil said from behind me.

I startled, lost my balance, landed on my butt.

"You two and Pandora need to wear bells," I complained as I looked to see his lips quirking.

Behind Cosmil, Lia laughed, and I caught a strong undercurrent of cautious elation.

"Bells would have distracted you from your task," Cosmil said. "Come now. No time to sit down on the job. We have much to do and more to plan."

"Tell me those smelly liquor bottles helped you and Lia find Starrack's hideout," I said as Saber extended a hand to help me up.

"Alas, no. Starrack seems to have erased himself and the Void from the ethers, perhaps because you came too close to catching them. But we have learned something helpful through another avenue of investigation."

"Come on, Cos, out with it."

"As you say, Triton." Cosmil inclined his head toward Lia. "It is your discovery. You do the honors."

I took a psychic peek at Lia's thoughts, but they were locked tight. I had the strong premonition that this would be a classic good news, bad news, worse news situation.

"We believe," she said slowly enough to draw out the suspense, "that we've found the spell Starrack used to make the Void."

TWENTY-ONE

"Hold it," I said, hand up in the classic stop signal. "I thought the Void was a thought form."

"It is," Lia said, "but because Starrack was never terribly patient, we're fairly certain he relied on a manifestation spell to speed up the process of creating the Void."

Saber stepped forward. "If a spell made the Void, does that mean you can unmake it with another spell?"

"Unlikely," she answered. "This particular spell calls for the use of blood, Starrack's and perhaps someone else's. There is no way to undo the spell without using the same bloodline."

"However," Cosmil chimed in, "in the course of our research, we spoke with a faerie in the Council records department who put us in touch with an investigator. That led us back to Lia's contact in the nymph community."

I barely kept from gnashing my teeth. "Cosmil, with all due respect, would you spit it out before I get a raging headache?"

He frowned and huffed, but answered me.

"Several nymphs came forward to report they had cavorted with Starrack last September. At the time, he hinted to them that he had a big scheme starting. Then he disappeared."

"A year ago?" Excitement zinged through me, and I grasped Saber's arm. "Isn't that close to when Ray said Rico started getting nutso in Miami?"

"I think you're right. And he threatened Vlad in late February." Saber turned to Cosmil. "What else did you learn?"

"Nothing from the nymphs, but having an idea when the Void was created enabled us to track its probable life cycle patterns."

"This thing has a life cycle?" Triton demanded.

"It is a living organism." Cosmil gave him the disappointed-teacher eye. "To continue, we compared the Void to other documented thought forms created with the same or a similar magical boost."

"That comparison helped us predict when the Void should next be in transition and, therefore, be at its weakest point," Lia added.

"Which is when, for pity's sake?"

"We've confirmed it will be during the Greek festival weekend."

"And the hits just keep on coming," I groaned.

Lia cocked her head. "What does that mean?"

"Saber talked to a liquor-store guy who said Starrack asked questions about the Greek festival and expressed interest in going."

"I see. Then perhaps it's just as well that we've estimated the Void will be most vulnerable on Friday the eleventh."

"When will it be back to speed?" Saber asked.

"It gains full strength the day after the full moon on the fourteenth. That's when it will transition again."

"Transition into what?" Triton asked.

"Possibly an unstoppable force, which is why you each must train with renewed diligence. Saber, you made an excellent point about learning what to expect in a fight with Starrack."

"The problem is," Lia put in, "that we can only recall a few times

Starrack fought head-on against a foe, and that was more than a hundred years ago when the three of us studied together. And since we were the foes, it was not life or death. Starrack may have held back."

"Understood," Saber said, "but can you show us what Starrack did then? What he might do?"

"Yes," Cosmil said, standing tall, "and we will begin now."

He motioned the guys to follow him, and I would've joined them, but Lia took my arm.

"You're worried for the safety of your friends, yes?"

"Duh, Lia, I'm terrified. I almost told Maggie we needed to change plans, but she's over forty, getting married for the first and only time. I want every facet of this wedding to be perfect for her and Neil."

"Cesca, we have warded and spelled homes, neighborhoods, and nearly everyone you regularly see. I truly believe your friends will be safe. Remember, Starrack may not attend the festival."

"Yeah, but I'm not counting on getting that lucky."

She looked up at the night sky then at me. "Very well, there is one more level of protection I might invoke."

"What is it?"

"Would your friends and their guests carry a charmed object to the festival? For instance, a drachma?"

"Greek coinage? Sure, I can invent some reason for them to keep a drachma in their pockets or purses. But I'll need sixteen of them to cover the bridal party and their spouses and dates. And I'll need them by Thursday night. The rehearsal is at six, and I need to be with Maggie before that, so I won't have time to come pick them up."

"I'll see to it, but you must stress that the coins must be on their persons. Otherwise, I won't be able to promise the protection charge will work."

"Got it."

"Good. Now, have you attempted to fly since you came into your power on Friday?"

"For heaven's sake, Lia, flying isn't exactly a normal neighbor-hood activity for me."

"Point taken. Very well, then, call upon your power as you did in the healing and practice. Height and distance. Go."

"Shouldn't I be training with the guys?"

"We'll let Cosmil work with them alone first."

"But, Lia—"

"Go."

I scowled and turned my back on her. The cool, whirling sensation of energy had receded after the healing but erupted like a geyser as soon as I touched it with a thought. The three steps, lift, fly method of take-off Jo-Jo the Jester had taught me became three steps, lift, zoom. I nearly cracked my skull on the branch of one of those ancient oaks at the edge of Cosmil's circle before I veered away.

Then I began to get the hang of flying, and I let my worries fall away. I flew far, all the way to the ocean where I took a left and headed north. I flew high, over my beach house where I was tempted to dip down to check on Lynn, David, and Ken, but restrained the impulse. At one of the tallest condos on the beach and Dondanville Road, a trailer and cell phone–antenna installations stood atop the building. How a trailer got on the roof of the condos baffled me, but I dismissed the thought as I cleared them with room to spare.

En route back to the shanty, I noticed my vertigo wasn't as severe as it had been. To test myself more, I practiced soaring at different heights, cutting around electrical poles, and weaving through power lines. A couple of miles from the compound, I gradually reduced my speed and altitude, and landed in the circle where everyone was gathered without stumbling a bit.

Saber crossed to catch me in his arms the second I touched down. "God, Cesca, you've been gone over thirty minutes. I was worried."

"Sorry, but if I fly too fast, my face gets splattered with bugs."

He gave my ponytail a teasing tug as Lia stepped closer.

"Where did you go?" she barked in her drill-sergeant tone.

"I flew to the coast. Wow, that sounds jet-setting, doesn't it? Then I followed the beach to Dondanville and looped back here."

"How high were you able to fly?"

"Roughly twelve stories."

"Good, good. That'll do for tonight. Now let's all of us go inside to practice hiding and revealing your thoughts."

All of us turned out to include Pandora, and we gathered around Cosmil's coffee table. Lia's method of teaching the thought-shielding exercise reminded me of the children's gossip game. The difference was, instead of whispering phrases or sentences to each other, we started with single words.

We took five turns each, and reading the words projected to me was a piece of wedding cake. I was five for five when Saber, Triton, and Pandora had their turns, four for five when Lia and Cosmil projected their thoughts. None of the team had trouble revealing to one person—or feline—at a time while shielding from the rest of us.

Except for me. Revealing my words to only one player at a time proved to be more difficult than wrestling a gator. I used the submerge-my-thoughts-in-water technique Lia had suggested, but every time I let my word of the moment come to the imaginary surface of the water, everyone read it.

"Focus, Cesca," Lia admonished yet again.

"I am," I snapped. "I need to tweak my technique."

And then it hit me.

"Lia, the point of this is to communicate during our confrontation with Starrack, correct?"

"Yes, though shielding has other applications."

"I'm sure it does, but it's about our intent to broadcast to each other."

She tilted her head at me. "Yes. Yes, it is."

"Okay, let me try this again."

I pictured my word submerged in murky depths this time, and willed the water to clear only for the person to whom I sent the thought.

"Tube," Saber said.

I grinned. "That's it. My turn again."

I repeated the exercise, clearing the waters for random players to read my random words, sometimes clearing for the same person back-to-back. And, except for leaking word-thoughts to Pandora, the new method worked.

"Let's go for phrases now," I suggested, riding the high of success.

"Let's not," Triton countered. "I'm beat."

Cosmil shook his head, but a smile played at his mouth. "You are missing Lynn, are you not? Would you like to peek in on her?"

"Peek in how?" I asked.

"In modern technological terms, I believe it would be called video feed."

"Via crystal ball," Lia added.

"This I have to see."

"I don't want you to see too much, Saber." Triton glanced at his watch. "What if we catch her in the shower?"

Cosmil patted Triton's shoulder. "I will connect the call, so to speak, and you may look at the image alone first. If she is occupied, we will wait."

The wizard set his crystal ball on the stainless steel island, did his conjuring, and rejoined Lia on the sofa so Triton would have privacy. After a moment, he motioned Saber and me closer to see the real-time image of Lynn playing Charades with Ken and David, fully clothed, of course. At least, we surmised that was the game from the scraps of paper on the beach house coffee table and Lynn's gestures. David must've guessed the right answer first, for he and Lynn high-fived, and she did a victory dance that made both the vamps laugh.

"She's having a good time," I said. "Everything is fine."

"So long as she doesn't get attached to those two."

"Trade in a hotshot shifter like you? Never." I stepped closer and lowered my voice. "Have you asked Lia about the skinny on Lynn?"

"Not yet."

"What are you waiting for?"

"An opening."

"Children," Cosmil called. "If you are finished viewing, come sit. The crystal will turn itself off."

I pivoted from the counter a step ahead of Triton and Saber. "Lia, did you ever find out about Lynn's—"

"Cesca," Triton warned from my side.

"Origins," I finished and danced away from the punch he aimed at my arm to plop on the sofa.

Saber sat on my left, and Triton squeezed in on my right to annoy me. Cosmil almost rolled his eyes at us but refrained.

"I haven't heard back about Lynn, but I'll inform you when I do. Now, what are your schedules for the week? Cesca, do you have tours?"

"I'm off the ghost-tour schedule unless there's an emergency, but I have things to do for Maggie and Neil."

"Will you be available to train in the evenings?"

"I will."

"Same here," Saber said. "Triton's helping me investigate missing bottles of ouzo at some local liquor stores, but my appointments with the managers should be during the day."

Cosmil lifted a bushy brow. "So Starrack *has* stolen ouzo? You did not mention this."

"I've only met with two store managers, but both recognized Starrack. The Palatka store security video was a bust, so I'm hoping another store will have useful footage."

"Excellent. Lia sketched a good likeness, but seeing an up-to-date photograph of Starrack could be invaluable."

"Unless he disguises himself," Triton put in.

"He's too vain for that," Lia said stoutly. "As I said before, if he makes changes to his appearance, they would be minor."

"I'll get copies of any tapes that show Starrack clearly and bring my computer so we can all view them."

We all turned to Triton who threw his hands up. "Hey, I'm just minding my shop and making calls for Saber."

"Very well, it sounds like each of you will be free to train in the evening. I will expect you here by eight. Time is short, so we must make it count."

We murmured our agreement, and I had crowbarred myself from between Saber and Triton when Lia spoke up.

"Since the chances are higher that Starrack will attend the festival, have you three thought further about how to lure and attack him?"

"All due respect, Lia," Triton began, "but we've been a little busy. And that was before you gave us your news flash tonight."

"He's right," Saber said. "Cesca and I plan to do a walk-through between the field and the parking garage to scout the area."

"Do it tonight," Cosmil commanded.

I narrowed my eyes. "Why?"

"Call it a hunch, Francesca. Please don't question it further."

"We'll go by on the way home," Saber said.

"I'll come, too," Triton chimed in. "The more of us with firsthand knowledge of the layout, the better, especially when we get to the down-and-dirty planning stage."

I cringed, and Triton took my hand. "Sorry, Cesca, but we can't dance around the subject anymore."

I sighed and nodded. "Let's go scout."

Triton followed us to town in his truck, and since it was well after ten o'clock on Sunday night, we parked in a restaurant lot on West Castillo Drive, right across the street from the four-acre special-

events area. A vision flashed in my mind's eye, one of Maggie and
Neil and the wedding party on the field, but I willed it away. Locked
down my emotions. I had to scout with dispassionate eyes.

Situated due west of the parking garage, the rectangular space
that stretched four football fields in length was dark now. So was the
large children's playground adjacent to the field on the southeast
corner, and tennis courts in the southwest. The playground's wooden
fence connected with the chain-link fencing that surrounded the entire field and tennis courts.

I knew from having attended the Greek festival last year that
large, portable lights would be set up around the perimeter, and large
tents would house the food and beverage service. More tents would
provide shelter for the bandstand, the dance floor, and the diners.
The spaces up and down the rest of the area would be packed with
rows of individual vendors selling everything from art to novelty
items. Greek related or not.

To the east, across the sidewalk and a two-lane street, sat the
more-or-less-square parking garage rising four levels high. All but
the top level provided shelter from the weather. Triton, Saber, and I
crossed to the west entrance, walking right through the traffic lanes.
Large, square, regularly spaced lights were bright enough to easily
see, even with human eyes. Not many cars were parked in the garage
tonight, and I led my troop of two to the right.

"As I recall, there are staircases in each corner," I said as I opened
the southwest stairwell door, "and a fifth set of stairs over by the east
elevators."

"Is this the closest set?" Saber asked as we started to climb.

"If we don't want to dodge traffic coming in and out of the garage, yes."

Florescent fixtures lit the stairwells, making them darker than the
garage itself, but the light was perfectly adequate.

"I haven't been to a festival since I got home," Triton commented as we trotted past the second-level landing. "Is the garage usually full to the top level during big events?"

"I've heard it is for the Fourth of July fireworks on the bay, but I don't know about other times. I suppose we could park up here and block the level off."

"We'd get towed," Saber said flatly.

"Not if we staged your SUV and Triton's F-250 to look like one of them had a dead battery."

"Let's see the layout up there first," Saber said.

We pulled open the fourth-level door and my spirits sank. The space was enormous, much bigger than it looked in my dream. Pole lights bathed what seemed like acres of parking lot, and except for the small elevator hallways on the west side, there was nowhere to take cover. No shadows to blend into. Bottom line, we'd be exposed as soon as we hit the roof.

Then again, so would Starrack and his oily blob sidekick.

"Lots of room to maneuver up here," Saber observed as we neared the traffic ramp, "and the perimeter walls are high enough to conceal us, but containment could be a problem."

"Way to understate," Triton joked. "It doesn't look like blocking this ramp will work, either. There are parking spaces on both sides, and spare room for two cars to pass."

"But if we block the middle of the ramp," I countered, "only a mini-car or a motorcycle would fit through the space that's left."

Triton gave me a doubtful look. "I don't know, Cesca."

Hands on his hips, Saber surveyed the vast expanse of concrete and pole lights. "On thing is sure. Whatever battle plan we come up with, it better be killer."

Monday I was awake by eleven in the morning again. Yes, I had gone to sleep long before dawn had broken, but still. It seemed that the alarm incident of Friday had altered my sleep patterns, and I had no idea how long the trend would last.

Of course, being up, showered, and functional so early in the day did afford me the opportunity to see Saber before he left.

I sat in the kitchen watching him take the last bites of a bologna sandwich. I didn't get the attraction of bologna, but then I wasn't a food aficionado. Except when it came to fig bars, or the texture and taste of gelato.

Snowball, however, loved the lunch meat, yet she wasn't camped at Saber's feet.

"Where's the cat?"

"Hoarding her bologna under the couch. I fed her the kibble, emptied and refilled her litter box, and I'll take out the trash when I leave."

"I'll say it again, you are the man."

He grinned and chewed.

"So what else has my super guy done this morning?"

"Talked with Triton," he said around a swallow. "He got two more liquor store hits, so I'm on my way to see the managers. I'll get an update from Triton while I'm out. If more stores report missing bottles of ouzo, I'll track down the details."

"And if Starrack has hit other stores, we'll have a better idea of how long he's been in the area, too, although I still wonder why he hasn't come at us with everything he's got."

"A full-frontal assault?"

I raised a brow. "Did the war movie we watched last night get into your dreams, too?"

"Yeah. Maybe Starrack is waiting for the Void to do the transition thing Cosmil mentioned."

"Wait, that would make perfect sense," I said excitedly. "And if that's what he's waiting for, and the transition is supposed to happen after the weekend, it buys us more time."

"Unless we're wrong and Starrack is biding his time for another reason." My honey laid his hand over mine. "I know you're worried about putting Maggie and Neil in the line of fire, but if we can flush Starrack out of hiding before their big day, at least we won't worry that he'll crash the wedding."

"Oh, geez, I don't want to think about that scene. You know," I added as he rose to rinse his plate, "there really needs to be Bad Guy Stress Syndrome."

"Yeah? How would that work?" Saber asked, putting his plate and a knife in the dishwasher.

"You know. The bad guy would get an adrenaline rush, then *ack, argh*—" I clutched my chest. "He'd fall over dead. Save the good guys the muss and fuss."

Saber shook his head. "And here Triton doesn't appreciate the tyrant side of you."

He pulled me to my feet for a long kiss. "I may be gone most of the afternoon, but I'll be back before we're due at Cosmil's."

Snowball peeped from under the sofa and meowed as Saber closed the front door. I sighed. I really could get used to this cohabitation thing. Here or at Saber's place. Let's face it, the way my afterlife had gone for the last seven months, Maggie and Neil would certainly be safer if I moved. They'd have no trouble renting the cottage to a nice, quiet Flagler college student.

As long as I had daylight to burn, I was determined to knock one task after another off my maid of honor list. And since both DennyK and John lived out of town, I pulled double duty seeing to the best man and groomsmen chores.

Maggie's wedding dress had hung in her closet since August, so I ticked that item off my list. The tuxes were ready for pick up on Friday, along with the extra-fancy cuff links. The bridesmaid dresses, sans bustles, were also ready and waiting. I phoned the caterer, the florist, and Daphne, diva of wedding cakes, and all was a go. The rental company would deliver and set up the tents, tables, and chairs Saturday morning by noon, and the florist would work her magic inside and out at two. Since my fridge was nearly always more empty than full, the caterer and Daphne would use my kitchen as well as Maggie's.

After putting calls in to the pastor to remind him of the rehearsal plans and the wedding party to be sure everyone knew when to be where, I left messages for Maggie and Neil confirming the week's wedding details had been checked. In Neil's message, I also asked about the parking arrangements and the musicians. I'd sent the business that was letting us use its parking lot a letter a month ago, following up for Neil. We should be good to go on that front, but I needed to know if Neil was paying the valets in advance, or if that was something I'd need to do the day of the wedding. Neil might not want my help with the details he was supposed to take care of, but it didn't hurt to drop a reminder.

Of course, I'd double- and triple-check the details before Friday, but that was my job. I also needed to get both the essential and emergency wedding-kit supplies gathered, boxed in little plastic bins, and labeled. Since Maggie would dress for the wedding upstairs in her bedroom, Neil downstairs in the den, most of the supplies were already in the house. But I'd make up the boxes anyway to save us from searching for needed items at the last minute.

My maid of honor duties for the day completed, I sat at the kitchen table to make a new, completely different plan of attack.

Yep, much as I didn't want to do battle on Friday night, I had to face the strong possibility I'd be doing exactly that. In which case, I needed to move from basic training to war games. I needed to be as prepared as possible to do more for the team than suck Void energy.

Really, it was too bad we couldn't just shoot Starrack.

Or could we?

TWENTY-TWO

❦

"A magical bomb?"

Dumbfounded, Cosmil looked from me to Lia, then at Saber and Triton. He even cast a glance at Pandora lounging in panther form at the front door.

Yes, I'd managed to bring Saber and Triton on board with my mini battle plan. I'd also made a stop at the special events field and parking garage en route to Cosmil's to snap photos from every angle I thought we might need. I'd even flown to get aerial shots.

That's why at eight o'clock Triton, Saber, and I had rolled into the parking area by Cosmil's shack, ready to present a united front.

Though I hadn't expected the question to strike Cosmil mute.

"Yeah, a magical bomb," I repeated. "Like the kind that hit the COA compound. Would that kill Starrack?"

Saber turned to Lia. "You implied that Starrack is cocky. Believes he's unbeatable in a fight with us. With his ego, would he think to ward himself from that kind of attack?"

Her brow furrowed in thought. "I honestly don't know."

"It doesn't have to be a big bomb with a lot of flash," Triton put in. "Just enough bang to do the job."

"We'd try shooting him with a regular pistol, but that will make too much noise and draw attention."

Lia snorted at me. "I should think so."

"Any chance Starrack would use a mundane weapon on us?"

"Like an Uzi?" Her eyes twinkled. "No. He would consider that primitive and beneath him."

"Then we're going to need that bomb."

Cosmil shook his head. "Lia and I do not use our magick to attack others, Francesca. We use it only for defense."

"Technically, Cosmil, you wouldn't be the ones attacking. We would. The best defense is a good offense, and we're gonna need every weapon at our disposal."

"Francesca, you have feared that embracing your powers would corrupt your soul. I believe you are beginning to understand that will not come to pass, but if we use our magick to kill, it may well kill our magick."

"Killing hasn't put a crimp in Starrack's," I groused.

"It still may," Lia said. "Besides, if you kill Starrack before you have some control over the Void, it's likely to run amok without its maker. The ownerless thought form we have locked in the Council compound hasn't yet died, and it's been there three years."

"No problem. I'll be draining the Void's energy as soon as I find enough of it to suck."

"Still, using our power to kill is out of the question," Cosmil declared.

"Then how about making a couple of bombs that will distract Starrack long enough to give us an advantage?"

"A diversionary tactic?"

"With a punch of shock value."

"That we could do. What else is on your mind, Francesca?"

"Did you get Legrand's tissue sample from France?"

"This morning," Cosmil confirmed. "The sample does carry the Void smell, but has not added sufficient potency to our spell to over-come whatever cloaking Starrack is doing. Not yet. Be assured we will not give up."

"Then it's even more critical that I train with Saber and Triton. I know my primary role is to suck bad guy energy, but I have to be ready for the spells Starrack might throw at us in case I need to take up the slack. Fireballs, laser fingers, freeze zaps. Whatever he has up his sleeve."

Lia raised a brow. "You're resigned that the confrontation may take place on Friday?"

"I know when not to fight the tide."

"Very well," Cosmil said. "You will train together."

"We also," Triton put in, "need to know if you and Lia will be with us. Will you physically help out with counter spells?"

Cosmil nodded slowly. "We had planned to be present for the confrontation but out of sight."

I snorted. "Then you better count on a be-invisible spell because there isn't much cover on the roof of the parking garage. I have pho-tos you need to see, and Saber got security video of Starrack."

"You did?" Triton asked.

"Thanks to your phone calls. Two of the four stores that had missing ouzo also had video. The clips are fairly clear, so they'll help ID Starrack when the time comes."

Saber set up his laptop and inserted a DVD. Though I'd already seen the footage, I crowded behind Triton and Lia for another look at what the sketch hadn't shown us. Starrack appeared to be shorter and huskier than Cosmil, but the shape of the chin, cheekbones, and eyes bore out the family resemblance. At one point in the first clip, he looked straight into a low-mounted camera he didn't seem to know was there. In the footage, his eye color showed up as more of a flat, rainy-day gray than Cosmil's brighter blue gray eyes. Starrack's gunmetal gray hair was also different, cut in a shorter style than Lia had depicted.

In each piece of video, Starrack moved with supreme arrogance, whether he wore casual jeans and a polo shirt, or dressier slacks and a button up shirt. His clothing was the only detail of his appearance that changed from store to store, so perhaps he wasn't into disguises.

"Tracking his thefts, Starrack has hit liquor stores from Daytona Beach and Palm Coast to Palatka and St. Augustine. The incidents have been happening for about two weeks are usually on Monday, Wednesday, and Friday." He paused to look at Cosmil and Lia. "Does this pattern mean anything to you, other than he's run out of booze?"

Cosmil shook his head. "It means nothing that I can think of, but it does set him up to strike again on Friday."

"It also proves Starrack was in town when I shifted," Triton said.

"He had to work fast to hire those thugs who beat up Triton."

Lia shook her head. "Starrack could've easily attracted shady characters merely by offering a large sum of money to the criminals."

"Cesca, show them your photos now," Saber said as he ejected the DVD.

I fished my camera with its combo charger and download cord from my workout shorts pocket, and plugged in. When the photos flashed up on the computer screen, I saw they had turned out better than I'd feared they might. My dinky digital rocked.

I pointed out the elevator and stairwell towers, the traffic ramp, and the four-foot safety walls blocking the ramp. With a few clicks of the mouse, I also pulled up a professional aerial shot from the Internet for comparison before clicking back to the pictures I'd taken.

"By Friday night, the light on this level might be brighter because we'll be nearer to full-moon time. Barring cloud cover."

"I see what you mean about the lack of places to hide," Lia said. "What about concealing ourselves in the stairwell?"

"The door does pull inward, but your view of the entire lot would be restricted. Of course, you'd be able to hide in the truck," I added with a gimlet eye at Triton, "if someone would agree to stage a dead-battery hook up."

Triton shook his head. "Cesca, the safety walls are too high for them to observe and react."

"They could stay in your truck until the action starts," I said, pointing at the screen below where the ramp opened into the top-most lot, "then take cover behind the wall."

"If we do set up a roadblock, we should stage it farther down the ramp." Triton slashed a finger across the spot he had in mind. "Less chance of a stray driver stumbling into the battle."

"You're right. That's a much better place. Do you want to be the jumpee or the jumper?"

"I didn't say I'd do it."

But I could tell he was changing his mind, so I let it go for the moment, closed out the computer screens, and removed my camera cord.

We dove into the new training regimen with a vengeance, first identifying each other by essence in a version of blind man's bluff. Next we practiced hiding and revealing our thoughts, projecting both to individuals and to the whole group.

Our final drill of the night was the one I'd anticipated, and the ex-ercise played like dodge ball. Cosmil and Lia began by slow-pitching spheres of energy and gradually zinging fastballs. We practiced leap-ing away from them, and with each flying jump I took, I felt bursts in my cool well of power.

"Watch their eyes," Saber said when we took a break to huddle on the far side of Cosmil's enchanted circle. "It's like in football. If the quarterback looks at his receiver, the defense knows right where to go. Our wizard and sorceress may be going easy on us, but right now they're not looking us off."

"Should we tell them?"

"Hell, no. I'm enjoying winning against magical forces."

While we can. That was left unsaid, but I heard Saber loud and clear in my head. From the grim smile Triton gave me, he'd heard, too.

Tuesday morning saw me up at the crack of eleven o'clock again. My dreams had given me an idea on organizing some of the wedding supplies beyond those I'd put in clear boxes, so I slathered on the super sunscreen to make a run with Saber to Dollar Tree and Target. I bought two hanging shoe storage units with clear plastic pockets for easy viewing, small clear plastic boxes, and white labels. I also stocked up at Dollar Tree on men's and women's toiletries, and plastic zipper bags. I even found the treat that Lia had wanted when she got off the plane, and bought two boxes of chocolate, graham cracker, and marshmallow goodness.

I already had both serious and funny wedding cards for the happy couple, so Saber made his selection while I bought a sewing kit that included thread in nearly every color known to dye lots. Of course, I had spools of thread that matched Maggie's gown and our bridesmaid dresses, but it didn't hurt to have extras for the guys and for those in the bridal party who weren't walking down the aisle.

I spent the rest of the afternoon grouping supplies into categories, stashing them in zip bags, and making labels. Tomorrow I'd get with Maggie to collect those things from the house that needed to be at hand, and to go over the seating chart a final time.

Saber spent his time printing multiple copies of the photos I'd taken, and more copies of the daytime aerial shots of the parking-garage roof we'd found on the Internet. That night at Cosmil's the subject would be strategy.

We again gathered around Cosmil's coffee table, Saber distributing the printouts, me handing out pencils and highlighters. Pandora was present and listening, and I knew she'd contribute if she had anything to say. I also gave Lia her boxes of MoonPies, which she put on the counter for later.

"Let's take it from the top," Saber began. "I'll be with Cesca at the rehearsal. It starts at six, and we should be parked and on the festival grounds by seven fifteen."

"Right. According to the Internet, it will be full dark by seven thirty."

Triton cleared his throat. "A newspaper article mentioned the Nisiotes Dance Troupe will be doing demonstrations."

I blinked at the left-field comment. "So?"

"I've been thinking," he responded. "To lure Starrack to the garage, do we need to stand out in the crowd?"

I read his next thought. "You want us to horn in on the dancers?"

"Yeah. Make a spectacle like we did when we scandalized my mother."

"It could work," Saber said.

"You think?"

He shrugged. "If it feels right at the time, go for it."

"What do you want us to do?" Lia asked from her place beside Cosmil on the sofa.

"Can you set up your tracking-spell stuff in Triton's truck?"

"Of course. We will take care of the security camera on the roof and in the stairwells, too, if you like."

I looked at Lia. "Can you take care of the cameras with magick? Not knock them out, or someone is sure to check on them."

"You want them to show the normal, empty spaces?"

"That'll do," Saber confirmed.

"I'll see to it."

"Then I'll pick you up at six," Triton said, then eyed me. "I've decided to go along with your dead-battery scheme. Should I park on the roof first thing?"

I beamed. "That would be great. We'll drive up, and we can play with how far apart to park so we take up the maximum space. And if Cos and Lia wait in your truck afterward, it won't look like either of the trucks are abandoned."

"Lia," Saber said, "you told us last night that the Void won't die on its own. I know I've seen the Void in places I haven't seen Starrack. The question is, will the wizard show up at the festival with or without his pet?"

"What you likely saw was the residue of the Void, Saber. The trails of the slug, as it were."

"Trail of the sludge in this case," I muttered.

"However, it is my opinion that Starrack keeps the Void close by so it may do his bidding."

"Good, that helps." He took a deep breath. "We're at the part of the attack plan where we wing it. First, if you sense or spot Starrack or evidence of the Void, communicate their locations immediately."

"Cesca and I will dance when we know Starrack is nearby, whether other dancers are on the floor or not."

Saber nodded. "I'll slip off to the garage while you two hook our fish."

"I'll start siphoning their energy in sips as soon as I sense them, and then we'll reel them in and up to the roof."

"How do you propose to attack Starrack once you get him there?" Cosmil asked.

"With everything we've got. Triton can do his dolphin-call thing, Cesca will suck energy, and if you'll supply me with some of those diversionary bombs, I'll keep him busy defending himself."

"I will make enough for each of you to have some." Cosmil

looked at the aerial shots of the roof. "You must stay spread out and keep moving so you will be harder to hit with magick."

"We could run a weave formation like in basketball," I offered. "Work our way toward Starrack so we can whip the amulets on him."

Triton gave me an incredulous look. "Basketball?"

"Hey, I had to have PE credits beyond surfing to get my GED."

Saber turned a snort into a cough. "Cesca's right about advancing on Starrack so you two can take him down. We'll practice that tonight."

"So, let me review this," Triton said, ticking points on his fingers. "We get Starrack to notice us, if he's there. We lead him to the parking roof. We run basketball plays to dodge his magick, advance on him in the process, and then hit him with the amulets."

"You forgot the part where we blast him with our unique skills and the magical bombs," I said, "but, yeah. That's the plan."

"I hope to hell this works."

Training was intense, sweaty, and rewarding. Just as the night before, my pool of power swirled and bubbled and flowed through every muscle, making me stronger with each exercise.

First, we practiced telepathy. Next, Saber and I taught Triton the weave formation, with Pandora taking the role of Starrack.

"Just run in a figure-eight pattern as you move toward Pandora," I told him more than once.

Bless his heart, basketball was clearly not Triton's sport. I could only hope that Starrack wasn't fast and that the Void was, indeed, a slug, because Pandora clearly ran rings around us.

After a break, we played dodge the energy balls again with Cosmil alone pitching hard and fast, and slinging cross throws he hadn't tossed the night before. He landed harmless hits, but I was pleased to realize that we evaded well over half of the bolts he threw. Maybe that's because we caught on to his tell—he twitched his shoulders in the direction he threw, just before he let 'er rip.

"Watch Starrack for his tells," Saber said when we called a halt. "He has to have at least one. Everyone does."

Our final workout of the night was a spectator sport for Cosmil, Lia, and Saber. They sat on the porch steps while Triton and I danced to music he'd downloaded to a CD. As the lively song beat from the speakers in Triton's truck and he took my hand, the years rolled away. I saw us as we'd been the last time we'd danced together.

There had been a party, a wedding, as I recalled, and we'd been sixteen. Old enough to know better, but mischievous enough not to care if we made a small scene. The people of the Quarter would be forgiving. They'd witnessed our escapades since our childhoods and still expected us to marry.

We danced then as we did now, on the grass under the stars. Fellow dancers, dressed in their best homespun clothes, took shape in my mind's eye, all of us in a line but moving in a large circle as we moved through the patterns of the dance. Then Triton squeezed my hand, and we broke from the "line" to execute our own steps. He dipped and leaped and slapped his feet, showing off for me, the maid he was impressing. I skip-stepped toward him then away, twirled, and pretended to drop a handkerchief. And then he caught my waist to swing me in a circle. The big no-no move that had put Triton's mother in a fit for weeks.

In the last stanza, we rejoined the "line," and the dance came to a breathless close. Triton caught me in his arms and twirled me around, chanting, "We still got it."

On the porch, Lia applauded, Cosmil nodded his approval, and Saber grinned. Thankfully with not one sign of jealousy.

"That ought to get the attention you want."

"Let's just hope it gets Starrack to fall into our trap."

As the five of us talked over plans for the next nights' training, Saber and I both checked our cell phones. He tensed a split second before I did.

"I had a call from David at ten thirty," he said.

"Mine came from Ken at eleven. Damn, I forgot about the magical dead zone."

"God, I hope Lynn's okay," Triton moaned even as I hit the call-back button, then put my cell on speaker.

"Cesca, did you get our messages?" David said.

"We didn't bother to play the messages. Is everything okay?"

"Shipshape, but Lynn has some scoop she thinks you should know. Ken will see if she's still awake."

Triton relaxed his stance as we heard knocking on a door and Ken's murmuring voice. Saber and I stayed alert and wary until Lynn's voice floated over the airwaves.

"Cesca, hi. I hope the guys' calls didn't alarm you."

"It's okay, Lynn. What's up? Is Gorman behaving?"

"Other than scaring the pizza-delivery guy half to death, he's being his interesting self."

"Oh, please don't tell me he answered the door with a shotgun in hand."

"The less you know, the better," she said on a laugh. "Hey, I talked Gorman into letting me use his computer to keep up with my classes, and well, I kind of poked around in his files. Want to know what I found?"

"I'm still reeling that Gorman has a computer, much less files."

"Strange, but true. I copied some names I want to run by you."

"Shoot."

"Patrizio and Maria Marinelli, Giuseppe and Trella Marinelli."

My heartbeat seized, and my breath stopped cold at hearing the names of my father and mother, my oldest brother and his wife. I stared at the phone in my hand, not seeing anything but the bitter-sweet past. Not able to voice what I wanted to ask.

Triton crowded next to me. "What the hell is Cesca's stalker doing with the names of her family?"

"Uh, did I do the wrong thing? I'm sorry."

Saber put his arm around me, and I swallowed.

"It's just a shock, Lynn," I croaked out. I cleared my throat. "What is Gorman doing with those names, though? Can you tell by the name of the file?"

"I have a good idea, but you aren't going to like it."

"Better to know than to wonder, Lynn," Saber put in.

"Okay, then. The file name is 'bitch vampire,' and the documents in it trace genealogy. Cesca, from what I could see, Gorman thinks you're his aunt, ten generations back and a couple of times removed."

TWENTY-THREE

"I've heard the adage that you can't choose your family, but Gorman? My gene pool spawned pond scum."

"Ten generations and removed, Cesca," Saber said as we drove to the cottage. "It's not that bad."

"Not that bad? Saber, you despise the guy. You nearly stroked out when I suggested he guard Lynn."

"Yes, but it could be worse. He could want to off you for your money."

"Honey, please. Stop trying to make me feel better."

Wisely, he shut it and drove.

I thought about my past run-ins with Gorman and his extreme loathing of me in a new light. I knew my mother had felt the shame of my Turning, but had she fostered such a deep hatred of me in the family? So deep that it had endured for ten generations? Pardon the expression, but talk about overkill.

Well, I'd told Gorman before, and I'd tell him again. Three words. Get. Over. It.

Snowball met Saber with rapturous meows, scarfed down the can of food he opened for her, and dogged his every move until he stripped to get in the shower with me. Then she tackled the T-shirt out of his hand and rolled in it as if it were high-grade catnip.

Had she experienced another ghostly encounter in the cottage, or was she just starved for Saber's attention? She certainly wasn't cowering in her carrier as she had when Isabella had popped in. Then again, maybe she hadn't been cowering. Maybe she'd just been sulking.

I forgot Snowball's antics when Saber joined me in the shower, lathering my shoulders and back with pear-coconut shower gel. After that, I pretty much forgot even my name for the next hour.

Once Saber slept, I got up to keep a promise I'd made to him. I made a phone call.

Jo-Jo answered his cell on the third ring.

"Good evening, Most Beauteous Princess," he said. "Have you called to take me up on my offer to entertain at the wedding reception?"

I laughed softly as I sat at the kitchen table. "No, you'll be a rank and file guest, Jo-Jo. Donita will be with you, right?"

Donita had been the main squeeze of another vampire until August. Jo-Jo had hired her as his personal assistant to help her get back on her feet, and I had a feeling they might be mixing business with pleasure.

"She will, and the film crew for *The Court Jester* remake will hit town a few weeks after the wedding. The advance people are out there now. Have you met them?"

"No, but I've been a little busy."

"Of course, Your Royalness is the maid of honor. Big job."

"Yes, but that isn't my biggest problem right now. Why didn't you tell me everything that went on in Vlad's nest?"

"Like what?" he asked cautiously.

"Like mention that a wizard killed three of Vlad's vampires."

"You know what they say, oh, Forgiving One. What happens in the nest—"

"Stays in the nest. That's horse hockey, Jo-Jo."

"Not entirely. You didn't ask me for details of my nest life. You only pinned me down about the protection money Vlad and other head vamps were paying to that offshore account. And I didn't know much about that." He paused. "You mentioned the wizard. Have you run into him?"

"Not yet. We're hunting him and something he created."

"Then the rumors are true."

"What rumors?" I tensed, fearing that David or Ken had been telling tales, even though my instincts denied they would betray us.

He sighed. "The vampire bloodvine has it that most of the Florida vamps are sick and that you're tracking what's infecting them."

"How do you know about the vamps in Florida?"

"They don't call, they don't text, and their friends are worried. I'm not keen about coming back to town for this movie if I'm likely to get sick."

"You probably won't. Not if we can help it."

"Princess, what did you really call about?"

I took a deep breath and took the plunge. "I need to know how to Turn someone."

"Saber?" Jo-Jo asked anxiously. "Is he mortally injured?"

"No, no. Not yet. I mean, maybe not at all, but he's begged me to Turn him if there's no other option."

"And you don't know how?"

"I never saw the process, and the other vampires I know well enough to ask either aren't available right now or are too young to have Turned anyone."

"I hate to break this to you, but I've never Turned a human, either."

"Jo-Jo, come on," I cajoled, brushing my still-damp hair out of my face. "You've been around since the Middle Ages."

"Can you see me being responsible for another vampire? I promise you, Your Royalness, I've never Turned a soul, and I can't tell you what I don't know. Maybe you can find instructions on the Internet. Every other piece of information under the moon and stars is there."

He had a point, several of them. But trust Saber's successful Turning to an Internet step-by-step? I wasn't that desperate.

"Jo-Jo, do you know someone who could help me?"

"I could ask around, but I'm not exactly best buds with any vamps."

"Ask soon, will you? I need an answer in the next two days."

"Nothing like performing under pressure. Okay, I'll see what I can do, but no promises, Princess."

We disconnected, and I laid my head in my arms with a soft moan. Could I count on Jo-Jo coming through? No. Not that he'd blow me off. He might truly not know a source to ask. I'd already considered broaching the subject with David and Ken, but I doubted they had any expertise in the subject. One, they were relatively young. Two, they'd experienced only nest life. Vlad wouldn't have allowed his nestlings to go around Turning people. I sure couldn't imagine the Clarkes Turning anyone. Not with dentures, for heaven's sake.

In the end, I looked on the Internet. Lo and behold, there were fifty hits that actually looked viable. The problem was that, similar as the instructions were, I doubted their accuracy. Why? Because every site carried a litany of disclaimers and side effects that rivaled the medicines advertised on TV.

I didn't crawl into bed filled with confidence, but I had to trust that my instincts and my heart would lead me if worse came to worst.

Wednesday. Middle of the workweek. Hump Day. Three days from the wedding. Two days from the rehearsal.

Two days from destiny.

Okay, I was being a bit dramatic but not by much.

I'd awakened at ten thirty, dressed, and played with Snowball while Saber ate his cereal.

"We need to clean out the fridge or take some of your food to your place on Friday."

"The caterer still plans to use your kitchen?"

"And Daphne will store the cake here."

"Then we need to take Snowball home, too. You need any help with your maid duties? I'm at loose ends today."

"You could help me make calls and do the laundry. With all the training and late hours, our workout clothes have piled up."

"Do you want to clean the house while we're at it? Have it nice for all the people who'll be in here Saturday?"

"We might as well. Just in case we don't, uh, get back to it."

He rose to rinse his bowl and spoon, then pulled me from the chair. "Come on. No point in dwelling on what might happen or when. Let's get our chores done, and leave time for a little afternoon loving."

"I meet with Maggie at four after the housecleaning crew is gone."

"I'm flexible."

"Don't I know it."

He slapped my butt, and I danced out of reach.

"Ah-ah. Business, then pleasure."

We divided my list. I called the caterer, the florist, and Daphne again. Saber took the tasks of calling Neil to check on the music and parking arrangements, and then calling the rental company. With each of us on our phones, it sounded like a telemarketing call center, but we got the job done.

Saber dusted because he could reach the high spots easier. I started a wash load of delicates and drove Snowball crazy with the vacuum. Then Saber scrubbed the kitchen and half bath while I cleaned the master bath. Both of us tag teamed the mound of laundry until every item was hung, folded, and put away. If we went down in flames on Friday, at least the cottage would be in pristine shape.

Maggie met me at the back door at four on the dot and led me to the dining room where cutouts representing chairs at round tables sat on a piece of foam board covered with green outdoor carpet. Her covered cobblestone patio was indicated with one-inch tiles, a cutout bar and bandstand stood nearby, and balsa wood showed where the portable dance floor would be. Another area of mini tiles and another cutout at the back of the property stood for my patio and tiki bar that would serve as the secondary drink station.

I arched a brow at her. "Geez, Maggie, is this a seating chart or a design-school project?"

She grinned. "All right, so I went a little overboard. I might be a wee bit freaked about the number of RSVPs we got for the reception."

"Did you find the Lister's response?"

"Selma brought it over Sunday."

"Okay, let's see what you've done."

We pored over the seating arrangements she and Neil had worked up, but I had little to contribute. They'd done an excellent job seating the wedding party in proximity to the bandstand for quick access when it was time to make our speeches. Maggie's dad, Neil's parents, and Neil's few other relatives were positioned just right, too. Seating Hugh Lister near anyone he wouldn't offend was a challenge, but Neil had suggested they put Hugh near the dance floor. The rationale was that the band would drown out Hugh's cursing. I sure didn't have a better suggestion, so except for a very few tweaks, we left the chart as it was.

Next we moved on to my list of things to gather so they'd be at hand.

"I think I have everything, including those purse-sized packages of tissue, but do you have a regular box handy?"

She did, and we ticked our way through the rest of the list until she balked at one item.

"I am not wearing panty hose, Cesca. No woman with two brain cells to rub together wears panty hose in St. Augustine."

"Unless it's for work or a formal event."

"Well, this is *my* version of a formal event, and I won't wear them, so just cross that item off your list."

"But what about Sherry? What if she or Jessica or one of the other girls gets a run?"

"Sherry can bring her own back-up pair, and I *know* Jessica's not going to wear hose. She's due to deliver those babies in a week."

"Maggie, the wedding list specifies having several pair on hand in various sizes. Why not have them, just in case."

"You're obsessive-compulsive about this list, aren't you?"

"Just being a good maid of honor."

"All right, but I will kill you if you mention panty hose again."

"My lips are sealed."

She flashed a grin then leaned back in her chair, looking toward the closed door I knew lead to Neil's office. "Cesca, has Neil told you what he has planned for the music?"

"No, and he won't even tell Saber. They talked this morning."

"He wouldn't do anything crazy, right?"

"And risk upsetting you? Hell, no."

"He's upsetting me by not telling me what he has planned."

"Then hit him with that. And meantime, make sure you have a

place cleared for a harpist. I told him that's what you'd want, and I'll bet that's what you'll get."

"If that's true, why is he being so stubborn about sharing?"

"It's his way of surprising you," I soothed, and realized with a flash of psychic insight that I wasn't entirely lying. "You know about your ring and the honeymoon destination. And since you're not having the traditional rehearsal dinner, taking care of the music is his special contribution to the wedding."

"I suppose."

"Maggie, everyone is on board, everyone will be on schedule, and the wedding will be perfect—including Neil's music arrangements. Trust me."

"Hmm. Does that mean you've caught the bad-guy wizard?"

"Not yet, but we're closing in. Oh, and I had an idea for the rehearsal. A sort of party favor."

"What do you have in mind?"

"Each guest gets a drachma to take to the Greek festival," I said quickly, making up the rules fast. "At the end of the night, those who still have the coin on them get a chance to win a gift certificate to a restaurant. A chain, so the winner can use the gift card anywhere."

"Does everyone get to keep the drachma?"

"Yes, or they can give them to you and Neil for good luck, but you'll have your own coins. You just won't be in the drawing."

Her green eyes narrowed. "Is this a Greek thing? Giving drachmas for good luck."

Damned if I knew, but I nodded. "It used to be, back in the day. I already have the coins taken care of, but we need to decide on a restaurant that will suit anyone who wins."

After a short debate on the merits of various restaurants, I was out the back door, headed to the peace of my cottage and the arms of my love.

* * *

Triton and I started Wednesday evening's training by dancing again, just to be sure we had the steps and timing down.

"Whatever song is played, we'll do one complete circle in the line before we break off. When I squeeze your hand and move, you follow, okay?"

"Got it, but what do we do if Starrack attacks people in the crowd? For that matter, what if he uses powers beyond throwing energy balls?"

"We have spoken of that," Cosmil said, "and he may use some illusion or even disappear when you close in on him. However, it is our opinion that he expects the Void to do the fighting, and, in fact, feels invincible with the Void at his side."

"But," Lia added, "we'll be there to counter illusions and to keep him visible."

Saber nodded. "Whatever happens, just remember our goals are simple. Drain the Void's energy, get Starrack down, and hit them both with the amulets. Any more questions?"

"Just one," I said. "I need the chant that activates the banish setting on my amulet."

Cosmil rose and went to the massive kitchen island, waved his hands, and a small piece of paper appeared. He handed it to me, and I scanned the two lines he'd written phonetically. I pronounced the syllables with Cosmil providing corrections. Though the words sounded like the Hawaiian I'd heard on *Magnum, P.I.*, I had no clue what language I spoke.

"What does this mean?" I asked when I'd muttered the phrase twice.

"The short, loose translation is, 'Light, vanquish the Darkness.'"

"That's it?"

"Magick is not necessarily mumbo-jumbo, Francesca," Cosmil said with a twinkle in his eyes.

"Does it work if I say the same thing in English? I mean, if I forget these words in the heat of the moment."

"It is best to speak the language of the amulet, but I suppose the vernacular would suffice. The disk responds to intent, after all."

"No fears on that score. My intent will be loud and clear."

TWENTY-FOUR

A phone call at ten thirty Thursday morning sent Saber and me into a new flurry of activity.

Neil's sister Jessica had gone into labor at six that morning. His parents, who also lived in Orlando, would still make the wedding, but Jessica's hubby, John, obviously would not. Under the circumstances, Saber couldn't say no when Neil asked him to move from usher to groomsman.

I phoned the formal wear shop about the change of plans, and they had a tux they thought would fit Saber, but he had to get there pronto in case it needed alterations.

He took off, and I finished filling the hanging shoe-storage units and plastic boxes with the items from my list, carefully labeling each box and zipper bag. When I took the containers to Maggie's to stash them in the respective rooms where they'd be needed, Neil was there waiting on the lawn-maintenance crew. I updated them both.

"Saber called. He has a tux, and it just needs one pant hem repaired."

"He wasn't offended that Neil asked him to fill in?"

I waved a hand. "Not at all. How is Jessica's labor coming along?"

"John nearly fainted in the birthing room, but Neil's mom said the babies should be born anytime. Neil and I are just tidying here and there, making sure there are tissue boxes in every room and extra toilet paper in each bathroom—"

"Packing for the honeymoon?"

Neil rolled his eyes. "She's packed and repacked a dozen times in the last two weeks."

"Well, you two relax and wait for the baby news. If Saber doesn't bring all three tuxes home with him today, we'll pick them up tomorrow when we get the bridesmaid dresses."

Saber didn't bring the tuxes home, so they stayed on my Friday list. At two in the afternoon, with the roar of the lawn crew mowing, edging, and hedge trimming, we decided to load up Snowball and everything else we needed to take to Saber's place and get that errand done. We also took our now-fresh workout clothes in case we went straight to Cosmil's later.

Once at Saber's house, we decided to make it shine. We dusted, vacuumed, and changed the linens on the guest bed. Not that Lia would be using the room, but a freshening couldn't hurt.

"Are you out of nervous energy yet?" he asked when we took a break to sit on the sofa with glasses of sweet tea. "If you aren't, we can go clean Triton's apartment."

"Nah, I did that with Lia. Once was enough. I don't think those thugs put his socks under the sofa."

Snowball dashed out of Saber's office where he kept her combination cat condo, scratching post, and gym. She looked at us, and then took a flying leap to sit on a wide-ledged windowsill. Yes, the cat was beyond happy to be home, and she did something I hadn't heard her do at my place. She gazed out the window at the oak tree and chirped at the birds.

Sudden tears clogged my throat. What if I never heard that innocent sound again? What if we didn't get to come home to Snowball after tomorrow night? Come home to each other?

"Honey?"

I looked up into Saber's cobalt eyes, and everything I wanted to say spilled through my mind. My jumble of fears and hopes, and the love I felt for him clashed with the grim reality that we might have twenty-some hours left together.

"Saber, hold me."

"Come here."

I put my glass on the coffee table and crawled into his arms. He cradled me the way he had one night shortly after we'd met. The night we'd watched a *Monk* marathon on DVD. The same night he'd first kissed me.

"Listen to me." His deep voice and steady heartbeat soothed my trembling. "We have a six to two advantage against Starrack and the Void, and we have more firepower. Magical and mundane."

I tilted my head to see him through my sheen of tears. "You're taking the Glock, aren't you?"

"Hell, yes. If Starrack shows up, we end this tomorrow night, period. Triton reunites with Lynn, Maggie and Neil have their happily ever after, and we take that vacation."

He paused to carefully thread his hands in my hair. "I'm serious, Princesca. No matter what happens, we'll be together. Got that?"

"I do."

He kissed me then. A long, slow kiss of exquisite tenderness. I ran my hands under his polo shirt, molding each muscle, adoring the texture and tone of his body. My own body caught fire as he returned my exploration. With each piece of clothing we peeled away, each gentle touch, the heat mounted and power flashed like lightning between us.

The smell and taste of his skin, the feel of his hands, every caress intoxicated me until I barely remembered to breathe. And when he settled over me, when he slid inside me, our powers flared so brightly, an aura of light burst around us.

"See?" he whispered, the aurora shimmering as he moved in me. "This is us, love. This is what we create together."

I cupped his face in my palms. "And we always will. I love you, Deke."

We napped late in the afternoon, even me, and it was gloriously lazy. I'd forgotten how good a siesta could be.

At seven thirty, we were back at Cosmil's shanty, and Triton was already there. None of us mentioned it, but we were all eager to have the battle behind us. Even Cosmil and Lia looked weary.

Tonight we were staging a dress rehearsal, so we ran through the plan from beginning to end. After Triton and I danced, Cosmil took the role of Starrack, and Pandora played the Void. I began sipping their energies, and we dodged everything Cosmil threw at us, drawing nearer as we pressed our attack. Finally Pandora played dead. That was the signal to jump Cosmil and hit him with the amulets—the real ones. We even recited the activation code, though it didn't faze Cosmil. Good to know that there wasn't any darkness in him to banish.

When we tried to give the amulets back to Cosmil for safekeeping, he refused them.

"I have spelled them both to be invisible," he said. "Starrack will not know you have them."

Lia gathered us in the shack before we called it a night.

"Here are the protection charms," she said as she passed out brightly colored cloth pouches tied closed with twine. "I made one for each of us. Sleep with them tonight so they will bond to you, then keep them in a pocket all day. And, Cesca, here are the drachmas. The spell will last six hours."

"Thanks, Lia. Saber and I may need to put our pouches and drachmas in the same pocket. Will that be a problem?"

"One won't cancel the effectiveness of the other, if that's what you mean."

"That's exactly what I needed to know."

"What about the magical bombs?" Saber asked.

Lia produced a small cardboard tray of twenty marble-sized white balls.

She picked balls from the tray and handed them to me. "You and Triton take five of these, and Saber will get ten."

"How do we detonate them?" Saber asked as he held out his hand for his allotment.

"The directions are simple," Lia said. "Throw and go. When the magick strikes anything at all, visible or invisible, it will explode."

"They won't explode in our pockets, though, right? I mean, we could get jostled in the crowd or bump into a table."

"Not to worry. The throwing motion is the activator."

"Please do remember that Pandora will be invisible," Cosmil cautioned with a fond glance at the panther. "We don't want to lose her."

Cosmil and Lia passed along a few more pieces of advice, but none of us acknowledged that this might be our last night together. Since I didn't want to be the one to get maudlin, I said good-bye and headed for Saber's SUV ahead of the guys.

Pandora padded along with me. *Snowball is safe?*

"She's at Saber's house. You're awfully fond of her, considering she's a regular cat and you're not."

What, I cannot have a friend?

I did a double take at her half-snarky, half-wistful tone. "Sure you can. In fact, if something happens, can you get Snowball out of Saber's house?"

Do not worry. Nothing will happen if you stay in your power.

ALWAYS THE VAMPIRE   317

With that, Pandora wheeled away. Triton and Saber's footsteps crunched on the gravel behind me.

"I need a favor," Triton said firmly. "I need to see Lynn tonight."

"That's cool. I should check in with Ken and David anyway."

"You're not going to fight me on this?"

"Not at all. Let's go."

Yes, I had an ulterior motive, and I broached it as soon as Triton was closeted with Lynn in the bedroom.

"Guys, if you don't hear from us by about midnight tomorrow, take Lynn home, and get out of town."

Ken looked from me to Saber. "Tomorrow is the showdown?"

"We believe so," Saber said. "We appreciate what you've done."

"We could do more," David offered. "One of us is plenty to guard Lynn."

"No," I said. "It sounds inane to say this to combat Marines, but we've trained over a week for this."

"And it's a Special Forces op," Ken said with a smile. "Understood. We'll stand by and be ready to move out."

"Thanks. We'll say good-bye to Lynn, and you can kick Triton out in an hour, okay?"

"Will do. Princess, Saber, it's been an honor."

"We'll look forward to meeting again," David added. "Semper Fi."

Always Faithful. I thought about the Marine Corps motto as Saber and I faithfully ran through our Friday errands.

I'd called Maggie before we left the cottage and learned that Jessica delivered twin girls to be named Addison and Emmerson, or Addie and Emmie. Neil's parents would miss the rehearsal but would be in St. Augustine by noon on Saturday for the wedding. I breathed a sigh of relief because Neil's parents would be yet two fewer people traipsing to the Greek festival.

Maggie didn't have any last-minute items to pick up, so Saber and I got the tuxes, dresses, and a restaurant gift card for my drachma "game." I almost bought another six-pack of Starbloods but decided against it. In spite of waking early for the last week, I'd kept to my nutrition schedule of having just one Starbloods between two and three o'clock each afternoon. When we'd moved the bulk of my supply to Saber's yesterday, I'd kept three bottles in my fridge. I'd downed one on the sly Friday morning, hiding the bottle so I wouldn't worry Saber. I'd have a second shot a few hours before the rehearsal to get an extra boost of energy for the long night ahead.

The third bottle I'd drink tomorrow before the wedding. Good Lord willing and the creek don't rise, as Jag Queen Millie would say.

By five, Saber and I were dressed for the evening. He wore black slacks and a dark blue shirt that made his cobalt eyes more intense. I chose the same red blouse I'd worn to meet Triton weeks ago, but I paired it with black capri-length cargo pants and rubber-soled loafers. Not typical rehearsal clothing—or battle duds—but the outfit was loose enough to fight in, and I could kick off my shoes if needed. Most important, the protection pouches, the mini-grenades, and the amulet fit in the zippered pants pockets.

At five fifteen, we were in Maggie's spacious parlor where the wedding ceremony would be held. Maggie would descend her grand, curved staircase, join her dad there, and proceed to the podium that would be at the opposite end of the room, near the dining room double doors. I got a bit misty imagining the picture she would make, but then the doorbell rang, and Saber and I kept busy admitting rehearsal guests into the house and chatting.

The rehearsal itself was brief and went perfectly. Even DennyK, who I'd heard was a wild man, behaved himself. When the minister took his leave, I passed out the drachmas, explained the drawing, and we headed out for the festival. Maggie didn't blink that Saber wanted to take his car. She didn't even fuss when I gave her the drachma game prize and asked her to give the gift card to the winner. Maybe because I lied through my fangs and told her Saber was a bit under the weather.

The western horizon blazed with reds bleeding into purples when Saber and I reached the topmost ramp of the parking garage where Triton waited. He assured us that Lia had worked her magick on the security cameras, so we quickly arranged the trucks, hoods up, and connected jumper cables to Saber's SUV. As I'd thought, a small car might squeeze by our staging, but the driver would have to be desperate or extremely well insured to brave the tight space.

I went to Triton's truck, to the open passenger window, and smiled at Lia. "Any sign of Starrack? Is he still cloaking himself?"

"Surprisingly, we had a faint ping fifteen minutes ago. Not near here, but he'll come. I can feel it."

So could I, so I didn't argue. Lia gave us the thumbs-up from the cab, and Cosmil muttered what sounded like a blessing. With that, Saber, Triton, and I descended the northwest stairway.

On the festival field, Saber peeled off as planned to patrol the right side of the main tent. He'd glance into the vendor booths, proceed to the food tents at the west end of the grounds, then circle to meet Triton and me as we came up the left side.

I thought as we first began the stroll down our side of the tent that the double row of vendor booths wasn't spaced as widely apart as those I'd seen on the right side. The aisle between the rows seemed more jammed, the shoppers moving clumsily. And then I caught eau de Void, that distinctive hot-oil odor that clogged the back of my throat.

I instantly began sipping its energy, but damn it all. If the Void was nearby, Starrack couldn't be far away.

The Void. It's here, I thought at Triton and Saber, Cosmil and Lia.

We don't see Starrack in the spell, Lia responded. *He must be dampening his presence.*

Triton grabbed my hand. *Is it by the tennis courts or closer?*

Closer. Saber, you have anything?

I'm circling your way. If you aren't in the dance tent, get there. I saw people in costumes gathering on the south side near the bandstand.

My nerves more taut with each step, my well of power stirring at the base of my spine, I waded with Triton through the throng to the large tent. We wove our way around the poles and supporting cables, and the six-foot tables filled with diners. I didn't see any of the wedding party and hoped they were in the long lines at the food tents. Anywhere removed from the Void.

We're east of the bandstand. I sent the message to Saber just as a man announced that the members of the Nisiotes Greek Dance Troupe would be out to teach a dance to anyone who wanted to learn.

Saber, it's nearly showtime.

I heard. No visual on the Void, but our man is at the beverage booth.

Stealing ouzo? Triton sent the thought.

Taste testing.

I craned my neck, found Starrack, and reached for his energy, siphoning just a bit and hoping he wouldn't notice. His life force didn't taste like hot asphalt and didn't burn my throat. No, his aura tasted as bitter and dry as cold ashes, and froze my heart.

My chest clenched. My breathing grew ragged. But only for a moment until the well of cool power shot up my spine. I drew one deep, clean breath, then another. Just in time, too, for six men and six women dancers in blue and white costumes emerged from one side of the stage, recorded music blared through speakers, and Triton grabbed my hand.

We're going on, Saber, Triton thought to both of us. *Keep us posted.*

Triton and I joined the lively dance at the end of the long line, falling right into step. I was glad we'd practiced, though, because it was a strain to drain energy from two sources, listen for Saber's intel, and stay in rhythm.

No Void sighting yet, but our target is coming your way.

Triton caught my eye, squeezed my hand twice, and we danced to the middle of the circle. The dance troupe members looked surprised, but the learners seemed to think our breakout was normal. Maybe the "oompahs" being yelled from the audience helped sell us, but Triton put on the performance of a lifetime. He executed his small leaps and foot slaps with flair, and I dipped and twirled, all the while keeping in step. The spins were a bitch to do and still look for Starrack. Faces of the dancers and the crowd zipped by with dizzying speed, but I didn't see Maggie or Neil or anyone else in the wedding party, and that was reassuring.

Southwest edge of the audience. He's made you.

Triton signaled to rejoin the line, which mercifully stopped a few stanzas of music later.

Exit the north side of the tent. I'll work my way to the garage.

Cosmil and Lia?

Know I'm coming. It's time to rock.

One of the men in the dance troupe moved to intercept us, but I captured his gaze and gave him the suggestion that nothing out of the ordinary had occurred. He relaxed, and we slipped out of the tent to take off for the parking garage at a pace that was slower than I'd like but not brisk enough to raise suspicions that we were fleeing a crime scene.

Ironic, since we were on the way to create one.

As we hustled toward the exit, I kept pulling the Void's and Starrack's energy. The Void's was more filling, but then the oil-slick taste was more noticeable.

Saber, we're near the gate. Where are you?

Silence.

Saber?

More silence. My fear flared so fast, I grabbed Triton's arm and stumbled to a stop at the open fence gate.

"Wait, Triton. Saber's not answering. Do you see him?"

Triton stepped in front of me and scanned the area. "No Saber, but evil wizard is following. Halfway down the vendor aisle."

I peered around him, spotted Starrack, and took a big sip of energy. A sip so big, I would've had brain freeze had I been sucking on a milk shake. No brain freeze, but something far worse, far more confusing hit me. The energy I took in didn't taste like ash. It felt hollow, like I was sucking a shell. As if Starrack were there, but no one was home.

Shit, the Starrack chasing us was a damn decoy. An illusion.

Saber, please answer. I listened to dead air. *Lia, Cosmil, Pandora, is anyone there?*

I heard the faintest of whispers, but it wasn't Saber's voice.

"Did he answer?" Triton asked, still looking over the crowd.

"No, and neither did the rest of the crew." I clutched Triton's wrist, dread crashing in waves. "God, could Starrack have snatched them all?"

"You track Saber, I'll track the others. Wherever Starrack has gone, we'll meet up there." Triton laid a hand on my shoulder and squeezed. "Now focus. Where's Saber?"

I closed my eyes and sent my senses in all directions searching for Saber. His laughter. His touch. His love. Two seconds passed. Five. Then I felt it. That core of his essence.

"The fort. Starrack's taken Saber to the Castillo."

"They're on the grounds?"

"No, inside. In the courtyard. But Saber's energy is barely there."

"Then go save him, *tyranoulitsa.* I'll join you as soon as I can."

I wheeled and dashed across the street, running at vampire speed through the west entrance of the parking garage, and dead on through the pedestrian entrance on the east side. Then I flew, straight up and fast. Screw bugs in my face. Screw being spotted. Only Saber mattered.

I flew over the Huguenot Cemetery, over Castillo Drive, over the Green. At the San Pablo Bastion on the northeast corner of the fort, I banked a hard right to skim along the inner wall of the terreplein, the gun-deck. My vampire vision sharpened as I searched the inky darkness of the courtyard more than thirty feet below. The near-full moon had risen close to three hours ago, but it's pale light barely breached the Castillo parapets, and Saber's energy signature weakened by the moment.

There. Movement in the shadows. Two figures in the center of the courtyard. One standing, one prone. The urge to dive-bomb Starrack was strong, but caution won out. I zipped down the long, wide stairs, touching down at the south edge of the courtyard, and willed my vampire vision to adjust to the gloom.

In seconds, it did, and I faced Starrack from no more than twenty feet away. He said nothing, but his expression was one of pure, evil glee as he gestured to the body on the ground.

It took my brain a stuttering second to make sense of what I was seeing, and then I staggered in horror, a low, anguished wail rising from the gash in my soul.

Saber lay wrapped in a black chain from neck to ankles, his eyes closed, his arms pinned to his sides, barely breathing. And as I watched, each link of the chain writhed and shot out tiny, skin piercing thorns.

Dear God. The black chain and the Void were one and the same, and it was eating Saber alive.

TWENTY-FIVE

Power burst up my spine as a river of rage, and only the pulsing amulet in my left pocket kept me from rushing Starrack and tearing him apart. He would die, but we had to kill him right.

"You sick son of a bitch."

I hadn't spoken loudly, but my words echoed off the courtyard walls.

The wizard clicked his tongue. "What coarse language coming from such a proper little vampire princess. If you wanted your pet human safe, you should not have left him alone."

Do not let him bait you, Francesca, Cosmil said in my head. *Take the energy of your enemies. Distract Starrack.*

Hearing Cosmil's voice steadied me, and cold, controlled power flooded my limbs. I took slow steps toward Starrack, sucking his aura and the Void chaining Saber with every tread.

"Why are you doing this? What do you want?" I demanded.

"Fortune, fame, and the amulets. Not necessarily in that order."

"Why the amulets?" I asked, buying time.

"Did I not mention the fortune and fame? Certain parties will make me a god when I deliver them."

"These parties want to destroy darkness? That's what the amulets do, or didn't you know? You'll be first on the hit list."

Starrack shook his head. "The amulets respond to intent. One could rule the world if one desired."

"It won't be you," I said as I moved closer and drew more energy from both Starrack and the Void chain. "You die tonight, bastard. The walls of the fort will muffle your death cries, and I will dance in your blood."

Starrack laughed. "Such fierce talk when you're all alone, and I wield the weapon created to destroy you."

I snorted. "Looks to me like the Void is busy, Starrack. You're on your own, unless you want to call it off Saber."

"The Void? Is that what you named it?" He clapped his hands once, and a black sphere appeared in his open palms. "Did you hear, my friend? You are the Void."

Oh, shit. The Void had two forms simultaneously? I mentally sent the images to Cosmil, then I sucked energy harder. I sucked at Starrack's aura until my tongue was coated with his bitter essence. I sucked at the Void chain until my throat burned, and the globe rippled in response.

"I see my pet is eager to meet you." He tossed the sphere lightly in the air and caught it again. "Shall I release him now? Show you his full power?"

He took a taunting pause, as if he'd challenged me to play ball. Oh, we'd play all right. I'd play in his entrails given half a chance.

I risked a peek at black chain. Were the links thinning? The thorns retracting? I took another long pull of the chain form's energy. When I did, the ball form of the Void squirmed in Starrack's hand.

The wizard looked approving. "Yes, it is time to finish this. I do want to return to my ouzo. Void, my pet, meet the Princess Vampire."

Starrack threw the globe at me and intoned a spell. I dove out of the way just as the wriggling black glob transformed into a seven-foot black blob. I started to unzip my right pocket for a magical marble bomb, but the blob came after me, moving faster than I had dreamed possible.

I jump-flew to escape the attack, leading the blobby Void away from Saber. My fountain of power coursed through me even as I opened my super-Hoover suction to continuously draw energy from both forms of the Void.

"Lovely acrobatics," Starrack called. "Too bad they will make no difference in the end. Attack."

The Void obeyed, mindlessly charging. Again, I dodged contact, and when I landed near the old, covered well, I thought I saw human-shaped shimmers above on the gun-deck. Had my backup arrived? I didn't have time to look closer because the blob moved.

This time I unzipped a pocket just enough to grab a magical grenade. I zinged it at the Void's mass then flew clear. The Void's hulking body absorbed the blow as effortlessly as the coquina walls of the fort had absorbed English cannon balls, but its etheric skin crinkled. I focused on the subtle cracks and sucked the Void's essence while it stood still.

"Now, now, is that fair?" Starrack asked. "I believe I detect my long-lost but not lamented brother on that piece of magick. Is he cowering in that hovel in the woods, leaving you to sacrifice your life?"

"Is that why you made the Void? To show up Cosmil? You're a little old for sibling rivalry."

"You will not rile me with words, but such faerie fireworks will anger my friend. Shall I demonstrate?"

Starrack waved a hand, the Void moved, and so did I. I jump-flew out of reach like a fanged ninja, and I also realized that the Void was active only when it had the wizard's attention.

"Starrack, we can do this all night," I said, forcing my voice to sound bored instead of breathless, "or you can surrender."

He chuckled, his attention on me. Sure enough, the Void remained rooted in place. I sent that thought to Triton, Cosmil, and Lia wherever they were, and prayed they got the message.

"Oh, no, pitiful little princess. I've waited a long time for this encounter. In fact, I believe I'll invite others to the party."

He lifted his gaze skyward, and opened his hands to the heavens, and for a second I feared he'd detected Cosmil, Triton, and Lia. Then he spoke.

"I command you, vampire spirits, come."

Wisps like dark clouds gathered. A moment later, the wisps congealed into recognizable apparitions, and I realized Isabella's warning was coming true. King Normand's ghost appeared, then another nestling whose name I didn't recall. More followed until they flew above the courtyard like a swarm of mutant mosquitoes.

Cesca, what's happening? Triton asked in my head. *I was on my way down.*

My knees nearly buckled in relief to know Triton was nearby and ready to move in.

Ghosts, I answered. *Ignore them, and hold your position until you have an opening.*

"Recognize these shades, vampire?" Starrack taunted. "They are angry that you survived when they did not."

"They aren't mad at me, dumb ass," I snapped at Starrack. "They're pissed at you. Aren't you, Normand?" I called to the largest apparition. "You were king. Powerful, important, feared."

Normand's spirit dipped to hover in front of me as if he listened. The other ghosts streaked through the air in aimless agitation.

I took a deep breath, and another deep draw on enemy energy, and looked directly into Normand's ghost-eerie eyes.

"You know you're being manipulated by a mere wizard, don't you, my king? You didn't stand for such treatment when you ruled, and you won't stand for it now."

Normand turned on Starrack and growled.

"She lies. Attack her."

"You see, my king. The wizard is giving you orders. He commanded that you come, and now he demands more. He's using you."

Normand's ghost eyed Starrack then emitted a roar that shook the fort's coquina foundation. I fell back a shocked step as Normand dove at Starrack. The other vampire ghosts hesitated a beat before they swarmed, too.

"Attack, attack," Starrack yelled as he ducked, stumbled back and away from Saber, and batted at the ghosts.

Just then, my reinforcements rode in. I didn't see Triton or Lia or Cosmil, but magical bombs suddenly exploded in the courtyard. Two in quick succession. Two more. Three after that? I lost count, but the number didn't matter. The Void wavered, its etheric skin fracturing like baked desert soil.

With Starrack's attention off his creation, I acted. I whirled first to Saber. Yes, the Void chain links had thinned to the size of fishing line. I pulled energy until a black stream ran from the links into my body, until not a smidge of the Void was left on Saber. Then I spun to the blob Void, and psychically sucked energy from its fissures. I sucked until my mouth and nose and lungs were on fire, and then I gorged on yet more of its aura until the blobby mass shrank from towering to toddler size to a shiny wet spot on the grass. I mentally lapped up the last drop.

"No," Starrack cried.

I whirled to see the ghosts drive the wizard to the turf, then sprinted to Saber where he lay on his back, and fell to my knees at his side. His skin had darkened and wrinkled, and I fought tears as I checked the pulse in his neck.

In that moment of searching Saber for signs of life and finding it, in that split second of murmuring comfort and encouragement to him, in that nanosecond of losing track of the enemy, Starrack struck.

On his feet again, he sliced the blade of his hand through the air, and my chest burned from shoulder to breast. He slashed his hand again, and a second searing sliced at my neck.

"Come back, my pet. Attack the blood," Starrack screamed, lifting his hand for a third pass at me.

He didn't get the chance. Another bomb dropped from the gundeck, and so did my reinforcements.

As if in a movie, Triton hit Starrack square in his back. The ghosts scattered, Starrack went down face-first, and Pandora materialized in full panther form. In one leap, she clamped her massive jaws around the back of Starrack's neck, puncturing his skin and pinning him with her weight. Rivulets of blood ran down Starrack's neck, and fat drops dripped on the grass.

Cosmil and Lia materialized, he muttering words, she making magical signs. Suddenly, Starrack was spread eagle, his arms and legs shackled to the ground with iron bands. Pandora never wavered in her hold on Starrack's neck.

While Cosmil stood over his brother, Lia and Triton rushed to me.

"Let me see your wounds," Lia said kneeling by my side and peeling back my ruined blouse. I looked down as if from a great distance, the smell of blood beginning to make me gag.

"Your gashes are deep, but not mortal. Can you perform the banishing?"

I gulped bile. "Not until we heal Saber."

"Look at him, Cesca. He's already healing."

I swallowed again and steeled myself, but Lia was right. Even as I watched, Saber's skin tone lightened slightly, and the deep age crags in his face began to smooth.

I gazed up at Lia. "We finish healing him once Starrack is gone?"

"Of course."

"Then help me up."

Triton leaped to take my elbow, one arm around my waist.

"You kicked ass," he whispered.

"So did you, but you're not bloody."

"Hey, at least you wore a red blouse. The blood blends."

I took a lurching step and grinned at him. "Yeah, and I bought it at Walmart. Easy to replace."

"Triton, Cesca," Lia scolded. "Make haste."

"Coming, Lia."

"Lia?" Starrack echoed. "Lia, my love, is that you? Let me up."

"If you believe in a power higher than yourself," she said as she stalked toward him, "you will beg forgiveness before you are banished."

"By the little vampire and the dolphin? Not likely. She will be dead in a matter of minutes. My minion was made to kill vampires. Even now, it is devouring her from the inside out."

"Shut up, Starrack," I snapped, "or I swear I'll kick you into next year and back before I kill you."

"You know the truth, vampire. You know you are dying with each breath. My Void is a black cancer, eating every cell. And when my pet has completed its task, it will find other victims. The Void cannot be destroyed."

"Lia, Cosmil, can you put a muzzle on this piece of crap? Oh, and flip him over while you're at it?"

"Delighted," Lia said.

Cosmil gave his brother's prone form a long look before he sighed and straightened his shoulders. "Pandora, stand down."

The panther moved but sat on alert. I unzipped my left pocket and palmed my amulet as Lia and Cosmil made flipping motions with their hands. Starrack's rigid body levitated three feet, rotated face-up, and thudded back to the packed ground.

The amulet pulsed with warmth, and my skin glowed with Mu symbols. I nodded at Triton. He knelt at Starrack's right, and I knelt on his left. Then I did something I would never have imagined. I saw Starrack's blood in the grass and rubbed my flattened right palm into the congealing pool, smearing the blood from my inner wrist to my fingertips.

"Lia," I said softly, "do you remember the spell you found. The one Starrack used to make the Void?"

"I remember. Why?"

I held up my hand. "Because I believe we have not only the blood-line, but the very blood to unmake the spell. Don't we, Starrack?"

I looked into the wizard's white face and knew that whatever instinct I'd followed, it was right.

"Ready?" Triton asked.

"One more thing." I stared into the cold gray eyes now dilated with fright. "However much this hurts, it isn't enough."

I slammed my amulet on Starrack's chest, Triton hit him on the right, and we chanted the banishing in unison. We chanted the phrase over and over, the rhythm of the foreign words feeling familiar now, weaving power with each repetition.

Bright beams burst from both crystals. Rays shot out in a supernova, piercing the night, boring into Starrack's bucking body. I thought of the murdered homeless couple, even the murdered thugs. I thought of the vampires driven to madness and death, and of those still infected. I fed on the far-flung misery the illness had caused and channeled justice for all of them into the amulet.

Starrack's body suddenly dissolved, leaving only his clothing on the ground, and the light drew back into the crystals so fast, I had spots dancing in my vision.

"Well done," Cosmil said quietly.

"Agreed," a new voice said behind me, "though she is nothing like you reported to the Council, Cosmil."

Triton and I whirled toward the fort's sally port at the south wall to confront the new threat. A man who appeared to be in his twenties strolled toward us, dark hair flowing to the collar of a white shirt. Long, lean, and mean, my senses screamed.

"Legrand?" Lia said as if she mistrusted her eyes. "But you're dead."

"Well, yes. I am a vampire, Lia." His tone mocked, but the Frenchman said the words mildly, with no discernable accent and no particular rancor. "It was very convenient to have Cosmil come looking for me in the Veil, by the way."

"You attacked me?" Cosmil probed, moving a step closer to me.

My muscles trembled with tension, and the gash on my chest still bled sluggishly, but power coiled, too. I prepared to strike at any provocation.

Legrand stopped thirty feet from us. "No, it was Starrack's pet that attacked you. I only provided a body for you to discover, and a duplicate ring, of course. Although I did set the bomb in the Council headquarters. No loss. We needed to redecorate."

"And your ring?" Cosmil asked the question of Legrand, even as he spoke in my head.

Release the amulet to me.

Cosmil's fingers brushed mine, and I didn't question the request but let the disk roll out of my palm into his.

"My ring is right here." Legrand held up his hand, wiggled his fingers, and the carats-huge ruby ring, the one that looked exactly like Normand's, flashed fire in the moonlight.

I looked into his head and sucked a harsh breath. "You were behind Starrack all the time. Why?"

"Although one cannot have enough money, my motive is as always. Power."

"You ran the protection money scheme," I accused. "You bled your own kind."

"You sound so righteous," he said on a chuckle. "In truth, the oldest vampires have paid me for decades to represent their interests with the Council. Sadly, the stateside vampires balked when my price increased. Then last July I acquired Normand's ring, and you were resurrected in August. With both rings, I doubled my power and saw the opportunity to put a new plan in motion."

"You sicced Starrack and the Void on the reluctant vampires. They acted as your enforcers."

He sketched a bow. "Indeed, and the scheme worked, but you were a threat to my continued success."

"How could I be a threat?" I scoffed. "I didn't know about the scam until a few months ago."

"But the old vampires knew about you. They knew the legends, even though I had destroyed every written record." Now his voice betrayed an edge of anger. "The virgin vampire princess who would come into all of Normand's powers and add her own? No, I couldn't have another of Normand's royal line alive to challenge me."

"I'm no challenge."

"Because you want to live your pathetic little normal life? How long would it have been before you wanted more? Wanted to rule vampiredom?"

"That's your ambition talking, not mine."

"No, you would challenge me sooner or later, just as I challenged Normand. I would rather eliminate that threat now."

He shifted his weight, just a subtle tell, but enough that when he rushed me, I met him headlong. We grappled four feet above the courtyard until I landed a knee thrust to his groin. Legrand grunted, faltered, fell into a crouch. I touched down, gripped his head with both my hands, and brought him to his feet. Then, following another instinct, I held his brown eyes with my gaze and breathed the Void at Legrand.

He laughed, not even bothering to break my hold. "You think to slay me with rancid breath?"

"That's a bonus."

He clucked his tongue. "Foolish wench. My blood helped create Starrack's creature. It will not attack me."

"Guess again."

Quick as a striking snake, I raked my nails down his cheeks, then slapped my hands on the welling blood and squeezed his head harder.

"The blood that made the Void will unmake it, but not before it destroys you. Lia," I called, "say the spell."

"Don't waste your time, fair Lia," Legrand yelled.

"Do it. Oh, and Normand, if you're hanging around, you're welcome to join me."

Legrand smirked, then his cold eyes widened as he stared over my shoulder. He twisted away, but Normand's apparition tripped Legrand. He stumbled, and I recaptured him in a flash of fang.

With Normand at his back, I clamped Legrand's head in my hands once more and captured his gaze. I hadn't believed that one vampire could enthrall another one, but I gave Legrand my idea of the death glare and he froze. Then, with a push of power willing the Void to invade a new body, I exhaled in a long, slow breath. Black fog spewed from my mouth in shiny ribbons that wound around Legrand's head. His eyes widened first in disbelief and then in horror as the ribbons twisted around his neck and shoulders. His body stiffened and spasmed with seizures, but I held fast and exhaled the Void again and again until the vampire's white skin began to blacken and shrivel and turn rubbery in my hands.

Normand's ghost misted away as high, horrible shrieks came from what had been Legrand's mouth, and his legs buckled. I held on, rode him to the ground, and flung my consciousness to every infected vampire that might yet carry a molecule of the Void. I felt the blackness flow from Ray and Tower and all the rest, even from vampires whose names I didn't know, but whose energy I touched. I drew every last vestige of the evil Legrand had helped to make and sent it into his decomposing body.

I felt no remorse, no compassion as I watched the writhing figure, and for a heartbeat that worried me. Then Triton stood at my right shoulder, the amulets in his open hands. Our gazes locked in complete accord.

I took the disk, and together we knelt to banish what was left of Legrand and the Void.

"Third invocation for healing," Cosmil said as Triton and I knelt over Saber minutes later.

High damn time, I thought without filtering who heard me. Since Triton patted my hand, I guessed he did hear, but his sympathetic expression told me he understood.

Saber lay still as a corpse, but his color had improved, and both his body and face appeared less shrunken. That had to be a good sign, right?

"Ready?" Cosmil asked softly.

We gently placed the amulets as Cosmil directed, first over Saber's heart, and then over his ribs to treat his lungs. The brilliant light cast an aura around his head and torso, smaller pinpoints dancing along his arms and legs in rope beams, just like the ones that had encircled the ailing palm tree. Where the Void chain links had pierced Saber's skin, the twinkles of light absorbed into his skin.

I don't know if Saber's vampire or werewolf blood boosted the amulet healing, but he regained consciousness far faster than I'd dared hope.

"Cesca?" he asked, struggling to sit.

Tears suddenly streamed down my cheeks, and it was all I could do not to hug the stuffing out of him. "Be still, honey," I said instead. "You're in rough shape."

"I missed the fight?"

"Not the one for your life," Triton said. "Damn, you are one tough SOB. I'm glad I didn't have to battle you for Cesca."

Saber's lips quirked. "So is somebody going to tell me what happened?"

TWENTY-SIX

Bells didn't chime on Maggie's wedding day, but they might as well have.

The perfect fall day was mild and cloudless. Every delivery and setup I'd scheduled was made precisely on time. Neil's parents arrived at high noon. Maggie, Sherry, and I were dressed and ready for the photographer at four thirty. I wore a Victorian-style dress of rich burgundy, and Sherry wore the same dress in a deep rose color.

Best of all, Saber and I were alive and well. Okay, in my case, underdead, but we were healthy and together.

And—ta-da!—even my hair cooperated. With a little help from a smoother Maggie had found, I flatironed my hair until it was straight enough to be manageable but just wavy enough to have bounce.

The other guests attending the ceremony showed up promptly, and so did Neil's harpist. She played so beautifully, I got teary as a radiant Maggie joined Neil at the podium in the parlor.

With the reception winding down, candles in white Victorian-birdcage lanterns on the tables bathed the backyard in romance, and the light of the nearly full moon added to the ambiance. The toasts and speeches had been given, and the cake had been cut. Neil had engaged a string quartet to play classical music during the first forty-five minutes of the reception and had swept Maggie to the floor for their first dance as a married couple. They'd had the traditional exchange of dances with their parents, too, before a second band took over. This band played more popular music, especially from the years Neil and Maggie had been dating.

The bride and groom circulated among their guests, and Neil even shook hands with Jo-Jo. A while later, I caught Maggie's high sign that it was nearly time to toss the garter and bouquet. I mouthed "fifteen minutes." She nodded.

Saber tapped me on the shoulder, and my breath caught as I turned to him. He looked so handsome in his tux, so sinfully hot. I sent yet another silent prayer of thanks that he'd not only survived, but was also completely healed.

"Hey," he whispered in my ear, "we have visitors."

I raised a brow, and he jerked his head toward my tiki bar. Among the guests near the secondary beverage station, there stood Lia and Cosmil, Triton and Lynn. All four wore clothing dressy enough to blend into the crowd—the guys in dark slacks and white button-up shirts, Lynn in a sundress, and Lia in a linen pants suit—but they hung back, off at the corner of my cottage.

Each of them looked well enough. In fact, Lynn's expression was downright giddy. Still, I couldn't help a twinge of worry as Saber and I worked our way across the yard through the milling guests. The memories were just too fresh.

When Saber could stand more or less on his own last night, Cosmil and Lia had transported us through the Veil to the shack and to Cosmil's sacred circle. I didn't remember the details of my own treatment, and I suspected an anesthesia spell accounted for that. I did recall my part in treating first Saber, then Triton, just to be certain every last smidgen of the Void was eradicated from their bodies. Both physically and metaphysically.

After the healings were completed, Cosmil had done his wizardly wellness scan before he transported us through the Veil again, back to our trucks at the parking garage. From there, Triton had raced to pick up Lynn at the beach house. I'd driven Saber to his home where we'd collapsed in his bed, quietly holding each other until sleep finally came.

I didn't know for certain what had happened to Legrand's ring, but I hoped Cosmil had locked the sucker up tight until he could return it to the COA.

"Is everything okay?" I asked when we reached the foursome.

"Everything is wonderful," Lynn said as she threw her arms around me, then withdrew, still grinning hard enough to strain her cheek muscles. "I know you all didn't trust me at first, but if things hadn't happened as they did, I'd never know about my mermaid family."

I blinked. "You're a mermaid descendant?"

Triton put an arm around Lynn's shoulder. "Lia got the scoop from the merfolk on the Council just today."

"That's right," Lynn bubbled. "I guess I shouldn't be so excited because the whole story involves inbreeding and a gene mutation in the royal mer line, but between having met Triton and getting this news, I feel like I really belong."

"Your mer relatives kept the human adoption from going through, didn't they?" Saber said.

"They did," Cosmil confirmed.

Now my grin was as wide as Lynn's. "This is wonderful, Lynn. Will you meet your other family soon?"

She nodded. "I think so, but there are a lot of details to work out. Lia's helping with those, but for now, I just wanted to thank you both."

Lynn embraced me again and gave Saber a shy hug, too. Then she took Triton's arm to drift toward the bar. They did make a striking couple, but I had to wonder if the two dolphin shifters would produce more dolphin shifters, merfolk, or plain humans. I shook my head. Time would tell.

Cosmil cleared his throat, and I gazed expectantly at him and Lia. "What's up?"

Lia straightened and smiled. "Francesca, Princess of the House of Normand, the Council of Ancients formally invites you to become our new vampire representative."

"They what?" Saber and I blurted together, then exchanged a shocked glance.

"Without Legrand," Cosmil explained, "vampires of various camps are jockeying for the empty position, but each vampire has his or her own agenda."

Lia nodded. "The Council believes you will be a strong yet impartial presence. Just what we need as we regroup."

I shook my head. "Tell the COA thanks but no thanks. Suggest Ken or David. Heck, suggest Jo-Jo," I added, waving my hand at his lean form on the dance platform.

Lia took a long look at the comic soon-to-be actor but shook her head. "The members will not accept anyone but you."

"Then tell them to suspend the position until they find another vampire," I said firmly.

"You won't consider filling the seat?"

I twined my fingers in Saber's and smiled up at him. "Nope, Saber and I are due for some downtime."

"Perhaps you will think on it," Cosmil said, "but we will leave you now, Francesca. Your friend Maggie wants your attention."

I turned to see Maggie wave at me as she and Neil approached the microphone on the bandstand. Damn, we were going to miss the tosses if we didn't hustle.

With a few words each, Maggie and Neil thanked their guests for taking the time to share in their wedding celebration and invited the bachelors to come forward. Saber and a few others gamely gathered on the dance floor, and good-natured hoots and whistles filled the air as Maggie lifted the hem of her wedding dress so Neil could remove one of the two garters she wore.

Ham that he could be, Neil bowed to Maggie before he waved the garter for all to see. Then he slingshot the bit of lace and ribbon dead center at Saber's chest. DennyK made a dive for it, but Saber snatched the garter, his hand moving in a blur.

I blinked. My stinker sweetie had used his enhanced speed to nab the prize, had he?

The single women gathered next for a shot at catching the bouquet, and not one of them hung back like the guys had. Nope, these females elbowed for space like they were shopping at the last sale before Christmas. Maggie waved the nosegay specially made for this tradition, turned, and let it fly over her shoulder. I used a little vampire leap and caught the bouquet two handed.

The women melted away, and the bandleader announced the last song.

Saber sauntered toward me, twirling the garter on his finger. The blue garter that seemed weighted with something gold and sparkly.

"You know what tradition says about catching the garter and the bouquet, don't you?"

I swallowed at the intense heat in his eyes. "That the catchees will be the next to marry?"

"Uh-huh."

"It's just a whimsical piece of folklore."

"Unless the parties involved want it to be something more."

He took me in his arms then, and the pulse in my throat beat so fast, I felt dizzy. He lowered his head, his lips hovering over mine.

"Princesca. Still want to take that island vacation with me?"

I brightened. "Sure. When do you want to leave?"

"As soon as you answer a question."

"W-what is it?"

He dangled the garter before my face, the garter that was slip-knotted through a diamond ring.

"Will you take the trip with this on your finger?"